CW00765739

ADJACENT

The Disappearance of Brooklyn Nicholson

KAY EMBEE

ADJACENT

Copyright © 2024 Kay Embee

All rights reserved. No part of this book may be reproduced, copied, distributed, or adapted in any form or by any means, including photocopying, recording, or other electronic or mechanical methods, without the prior written permission of the publisher, except in the case of brief quotations embodied in critical reviews and certain other noncommercial uses permitted by copyright law. For permission requests, contact the author at kayembeepublishing@outlook.com.

ISBN: 978-1-0685495-1-9

DEDICATION

To my parents, for their endless support and love, even throughout my weird and questionable stages of life.

To M.C., for listening to me rambling on about this story—and *nothing* else—for the past 2 months straight.

To my housemates at Cardiff Met who read this book with me every night (instead of working on their dissertations).

To the state of Washington, and the town of Merthyr Tydfil.

And to 14-year-old me, who never had any other career in mind besides being a best-selling author.

Here's to making it.

ADJACENT

THE DISAPPEARANCE OF BROOKLYN NICHOLSON

ADJACENT

Shadows fall, but the truth's adjacent
In the echoes of a silence, so complacent.

— UNREST STAND

ADJACENT

2 DAYS AFTER THE DISAPPEARANCE OF BROOKLYN NICHOLSON

LUCY | 11:58 AM

Brooklyn Francesca Nicholson was born on August 26th, 1979. She'd just turned 15.

She had these large, dark eyes, and dark hair down to her mid-back, typically styled into two neat braids. With a face full of freckles and a small build, she looked a lot younger than she really was. But she was pretty. Real pretty. Her natural beauty radiated through each photograph, becoming more and more prominent as she got older.

All in all, though, not much really stood out about her. I mean, there wasn't anything about her appearance that made her any easier to find. Nothing worth noting.

She was a good kid too—at least, from what we'd been told. Brooklyn had maintained straight A's since elementary school and had an impressive 4.3 GPA. As a sophomore, she was on track to graduate a full two years early, aiming to finish high school the following year. Alongside her academic achievements, she juggled a packed schedule: advanced violin and piano lessons, ballet, and cheerleading. She was the youngest student ever to make the varsity cheer squad at St. Mary of the Assumption Academy. And despite all this, she still managed to work part-time at a local restaurant on weekends.

She'd never been in trouble before, but she had been grounded the night she went missing, despite her mother not liking to use the word "grounded". According to her mother, the punishment was only meant to last one night.

Her mother had gone out for drinks with her colleagues that night, celebrating 30 years on the job. Brooklyn's father had stayed home with his daughter. Her mother worked as a receptionist at the general hospital, while her father was a regional operations manager for a corporate logistics firm. They had other kids, besides Brooklyn, but we didn't know much about them yet either. According to the mother, Brooklyn's father had fallen asleep watching TV, and she was gone by the time he'd woken up.

At first, they figured the same as us; she was staying with a friend, rebelling against her parents for laying down the law for once. Perhaps she figured the rules didn't apply to her. According to the mother, however, this would be out of character for Brooklyn. She never lied. She never tried to cheat them out of anything.

Brooklyn was a good kid. The best.

When they found out she wasn't home, Brooklyn's parents mutually decided that it would be best to wait a couple of hours before calling us. As it turns out, Brooklyn's siblings weren't as sensible as her growing up, which led to her parents reporting their children missing on numerous occasions. But the kids would return home safe and sound every time. So, even though they considered Brooklyn to be a saint compared to her siblings—and her mother could *not* push this point across enough—neither of them wanted to waste our time.

So, they waited.

They waited for two days.

When she didn't show up, they called us. The news got to Lieutenant Thurman first, and he then assigned the case to me and Anderson. He swiftly briefed us, giving us the family's address and sending us on our way. I didn't realize until we were leaving the lieutenant's office that Brooklyn's family had reported her missing the night before, just over 12 hours before we were officially briefed. It didn't take a genius to figure out that Thurman, and everyone else, had assumed that this was just another runaway teen scenario, which was why there was no real urgency to get the ball rolling. This was a low-priority case.

It also explained why, out of a team of 47 officers, they decided to send me.

"You calling shotgun?"

After briefly scoping my surroundings to make sure no one else was around, I stuck my middle finger up at Anderson, who jingled the car keys toward me in retaliation. The lieutenant had given the keys to him directly, which hadn't come as a surprise to either of us. I'd been with the MVPD for almost a year and a half, and I still hadn't gotten to drive one of the cars yet. I'd barely even gotten to leave the office. Anderson had been around a lot longer than me, so, naturally, he got the keys, and I got shotgun.

It didn't bother me too much, though, jumping into the passenger seat for the hundredth time. As close as we had gotten over the past year or so, Anderson wasn't much of a talker, and I had long gotten used to our comfortable silences. By cutting out the small talk, and letting him drive, I got to spend the whole journey envisioning what was going to happen next.

And that's exactly what I did.

As we left the station and made our way up toward the nicer part of Mirrenville, a hundred thousand thoughts ran through my head at once. Neither of us had seen so much as a photograph of the family, aside from Brooklyn, and I knew better than to judge anyone before hearing them out, but… well, I already had a weird gut feeling about the dad. He'd convinced the mother not to call us right away. And, sure, that made sense when I remembered that they had other kids that used to run away, and they didn't want to waste our time, blah blah blah, but why wasn't he even a little bit concerned? If Brooklyn was such a "good kid", wouldn't she have left a note?

Despite not having any kids of my own, I figured that I, personally, would've gotten a little worried if my near-perfect child who had never run away before had suddenly, you know... run away.

Another thing that struck me as unusual was that the Nicholsons lived in a nice neighborhood. One of the nicest neighborhoods in town, in fact; mainly occupied by doctors, lawyers, accountants, and their devoted wives and families. We rarely ever got called over there. Most of the kids who lived in those houses were sent off to private schools across the country, so it caught my interest pretty early that all four of the Nicholson children had attended—or were still attending—our local schools. Another thing: neither Mr. nor Mrs. Nicholson was a doctor, lawyer, accountant, or anything of the sort. How could a regional operations manager and receptionist afford to raise their children in one of the nicest houses, in one of the nicest neighborhoods in Mirrenville? Maybe the grandparents had money. Or, maybe something more sinister was going on beneath the wealthy family facade...

I shook my head ever so slightly as if I could eject the ridiculous thoughts by rattling my brain a little.

I was fully aware that we were about to pull up into their driveway, only for their "missing" kid to show up a few hours later, rendering this whole thing a waste of everyone's time. This wasn't my first rodeo. I hadn't even *had* many rodeos, but I'd seen enough runaway teenagers over the months to dampen the very idea that this could turn out to be something a little more interesting. There was no point in speculating what could've happened because we would find out what had really happened very, very soon. We weren't lucky enough to experience any other outcome.

I shook my head again, realizing how awful that sounded. Of *course* the best-case scenario was that the kid came home, safe and sound.

That being said, would it kill anyone to make this one—

4

just this one—a little more interesting?

I swear to God, birds started chirping the second we drove past the first few houses. I could've even sworn the sun shone a little brighter as we made our way further in. We were only 20 minutes or so from the station but somehow it felt as if we'd been transported to a separate realm in time and space.

All the houses were so white and pristine, with rose bushes and flags offering pops of red, white, and blue. Every lawn was freshly mown, and each sidewalk was completely clear, aside from the joggers, the dog walkers, and the mothers with their strollers. It felt safe, but it didn't feel comforting. It all just looked a little too bright. Too clean.

"...*this is it...*"

We pulled up outside one of the houses. It didn't stand out against the others at first glance, but the closer we got, I started picking at the smaller details. A slight crack at the top of the front gate. The rusted bike tucked away at the side of the porch. A scratched-up food bowl that'd been knocked over and had landed upside down at the bottom of the steps.

"You ready?" I heard Anderson ask, and I nodded silently. We opened and shut our doors in unison and began making our way toward the house.

Judging by the lack of barking as Anderson pushed open the creaky gate, I figured the bowl belonged to a cat. We made our way up the steps, and Anderson rasped his knuckles against the door three times as I quickly fixed the loose strands of hair that had draped past my eyes during the car ride, and it wasn't long before keys were being jangled on the other side of the door, unlocking from the inside. I quickly straightened up, clearing my throat.

Showtime.

The door opened, and a lady peeked her head around the door. She didn't fully open it, so we could only see her face. I knew immediately, based on the descriptions we'd received, that this was the mom.

She stood at around 5'7", maybe, and held the same slim physique as her daughter. In fact, it was clear that Brooklyn had inherited many of her physical attributes from her mother—same eyes, same nose, same slender face shape. The only major difference was their hair color; from what I could see of this lady through the narrow gap in the door, her hair was more of a reddish brown. And her skin was a lot lighter in comparison to her daughter's olive complexion. Light freckles speckled her face.

She'd started to examine me back, scanning the two of us with her eyes. Up and down. Her disappointed expression was enough to tell me that Brooklyn hadn't come home yet.

"Mrs. Nicholson?" Anderson said, and she opened the door up a little more. "I'm Officer David Anderson. This is Officer Lucy Hardie."

"Have you found her?"

"I'm afraid not. May we come in?"

An overpowering scent of lavender hit me the second I stepped inside, and the house itself didn't surprise me at all. It was perfect in every sense of the word. The hallway wasn't overly spacious, making it feel all cozy and homely, and it was completely spotless, right down to the staircase in front of me; not a pair of shoes or a pile of laundry in sight. No clutter. Not a single speck of dust. I refused to believe anyone lived in this house, let alone a family of six.

A small crucifix hung on the wall beside one of the doorways, reminding me that the Nicholsons were a family of strong faith—or, at least, Mrs. Nicholson was. Anderson and I had been briefed about her active participation in the church community. I'd noticed the rosary beads clutched tightly in her hands ever since we'd entered the house. She twisted them nervously, continuously; her fingers moving over the smooth, cool beads.

"You have a beautiful family, ma'am," I heard Anderson saying behind me. I span toward him, noticing the family portrait that he was referring to. It was a large painting of the four children.

I recognized the youngest daughter—with her braids and her big brown eyes—sitting next to another girl who looked a similar age, if not a little older. The older girl had her mother's red hair, but that was where the similarities ended. An older boy stood behind them, holding a baby. Well, a toddler. A little boy.

"Thank you," Mrs. Nicholson said with a smile, moving between us so that she could place her finger on the face of the girl with the braids. "That's Brooke."

"I thought so."

"And that's Allie." She slid her finger across to the girl sitting next to Brooklyn, before moving it again to the teenage boy behind them. "And that's Michael. He's holding Cam."

"How old is the painting?"

"We had it painted just before Mickey's nineteenth birthday, so… nine years ago? Ten?"

The eldest child—Michael, or Mickey—had to be almost 30. He was older than me, and Brooklyn was only 15. If she was five or six years old in this painting, that would mean there was a decent-sized age gap between her and the baby too. I figured she and her sister had to be close in age, but otherwise, there seemed to be pretty large gaps between the children.

"…you know that monster was released Friday, right?" I heard Mrs. Nicholson saying behind me, scoffing a little. "Well, of *course* you know… it's all I've thought about, wondering if—"

"Don't you worry about him," Anderson interrupted as I continued to study the painting. "We're on it. Are your other children home right now?"

She sighed. "Cam's at school, and Mick moved out a while back, but… well, Allie's here. She's upstairs."

"Is she still in school?"

"She graduated this year," she replied, folding her arms. "She was looking at colleges, but, uh… well, I'm not really sure what happened there. But she's picking up more shifts at the little Italian downtown. Both of my girls work there. Cucina di Mama?"

"I don't think I've been—"

"It's great," I blurted out, a little too enthusiastically, stumbling over Anderson's words. "Their focaccia is *incredible*… it tastes like real Italian."

"My husband says the same," Mrs. Nicholson smiled slightly, even if it seemed a little forced. "He's Italian. Well, his *mother* was Italian."

"I lived in Lombardy for a while when I was a kid. Me and my mom traveled around a lot."

"Ah."

I'd never heard a less enthusiastic "*ah*" in my life. But who could blame her? She had a thousand and one questions in her brain at that moment, and not one of them had anything to do with my childhood.

We were all on the same page. I had a lot of questions I wanted to ask her too.

"So," Anderson said finally, recapturing Mrs. Nicholson's attention. "Your other daughter's upstairs right now? Allie?"

"Oh, yeah, she's just up in her room..."

I turned back to the painting while they continued their conversation without me. I'd seen so many photographs of Brooklyn that morning, but the other kids were completely new to me. The other daughter looked so much like her mother—far more than Brooklyn did—yet, at the same time, she looked so different. They had the same hair and the same glasses, but the more I looked at her, the more I could pick out: the thick strands of frizzy hair bursting out from her pigtails; the small orange stain on the left shoulder of her cream dress; the ever-so-slight smirk on her face. She wasn't quite as picture-perfect as her sister, who had not a single hair out of place.

"...do you want to come and take a seat?"

An overwhelming sense of nostalgia hit me as we followed her into the living room. Everything, from the décor to the scent, reminded me of my grandma's house when I was a kid. It felt peaceful. Comfortable. I sank down onto the couch, immediately feeling at home. A slender black-and-white cat slipped silently into the room behind us, confirming my prior suspicions. The cat paused in the doorway, its sharp amber eyes fixed on me and Anderson. It circled the armchair slowly before sitting down, tail curled neatly around its paws.

The sudden sound of metal clattering in the next room brought me back to the present. Anderson's eyes followed mine as we both heard something moving around, just behind the wall. "Mrs. Nicholson—"

"It's Liz," she interrupted, shaking her head with a forced smile. "Well, it... it's Elizabeth, but call me Liz. Everyone calls me Liz."

"*Liz*... if it's possible, we'd like to speak to you *and* your husband," Anderson commented, lowering himself down onto the couch. "Is he around?"

"Of course! Just take a seat, and I'll be back…" She walked back over to the door, before quickly turning back toward us. "Would either of you like a drink? Coffee? Water?"

We both shook our heads appreciatively, and she left the room.

There was complete silence as we sat on the couch, waiting for her to come back. I couldn't decipher Anderson's thoughts just by scanning his face—it was a blank canvas, just as it always was whenever we were alone together. He wasn't a bad guy or anything. He wasn't even a particularly serious kind of guy; he was actually pretty funny at times. He was just kind of dry, I guess. Especially when he was on the job. Like I said, I'd gotten used to our shared silences, so I just took the moment to inspect the room as much as I could.

There were more pictures of the children on the mantlepiece behind us, and hardly any of them seemed to have been taken recently. I tried to picture what the other three children would look like now; Allie and Michael were adults, and the youngest kid—Cam—would've been 10 or 11. He was just a baby in most of the photographs.

Interestingly, there *were* a handful of recent photos of Brooke. There was one of her doing ballet and another of her holding a trophy. The trophy itself was displayed in a cabinet just across the room, along with some other awards. Some of them had Brooke's name on them. The others had another name on them, but I could barely read it from that distance. I could just about make out the letter *'F'*.

"…*honey*?!"

There was a loud bang from the room next door, followed by mumbling and heavy footsteps. The cat flinched at the sound, its ears flattening against its head. Honestly, at this point, I was expecting the father to walk in wearing a hockey mask, carrying a bloody knife.

When Liz finally re-entered the room with a normal-looking human being following her, I was somewhat surprised. She walked in first before stepping to the side, making way for him to make his introduction. No hockey mask. No knife. But he did look a lot worse-for-wear than his wife. He looked just like what you'd expect the parent of a missing child to look like; hair all disheveled, sticking up in all directions, and he was wearing this grimy, torn-up bathrobe. Suddenly, I felt bad for him. Liz was presenting herself well, with her perfect hair and nice clothes, but this guy was clearly going through something. There was something so familiar about him, and I couldn't quite put my finger on it.

"They've only just got here," Liz smiled, linking arms with him, and leading him over to us. "Let's sit…"

The closer they got, the less I wanted to look at his face. He looked too sad, and I didn't want to make the guy feel worse by being weird and staring at him. He sat in the armchair opposite us, and Liz sat on the arm, still holding onto him. He just stared at the floor, almost ignoring us. Liz must've pinched him or something because he finally looked up. He looked at Anderson first, and then at me. We made full-on eye contact. His eyes widened ever so slightly just mere seconds before I could work out why.

My heart dropped.

"Mr. Nicholson," I heard Anderson saying whilst I struggled to break eye contact with the man I now recognized. "I'm Officer Anderson. This is Officer Hardie."

His blank expression very slowly melted into one of terror. Or maybe I just imagined it. I'm not sure. In my eyes, he looked terrified. My entire body had hardened up. Oxygen was being vacuumed up from my lungs and out through my nose and mouth, like I was a balloon that'd just been jabbed with a knife. At first, I thought maybe I had gotten it wrong. Maybe he just looked like him. I tried to tell myself that for the first second or so, but his defeated expression was abruptly disproving that theory. But maybe I was seeing things. Maybe I was overthinking it.

His eyes very slowly moved from mine to Anderson's, and he very slowly held his hand out toward him. It occurred to me that, maybe, he wasn't moving very slowly, and that it was, in fact, my vision that was becoming distorted. The whole fucking room was churning around like a carousel. The next thing I heard made everything stop.

He licked his lips slightly, taking Anderson's hand into his own. "Frank."

Their hands shook in slow motion.

At that moment I thought there was no way he would ever turn to me and do the same. Surely he wasn't that stupid. But I was wrong. His whole body, along with his extended arm, started swiveling toward me, and I wanted to scream. It took all my strength to extend my hand, reach out, and hold his in mine. Sweat glided between our palms, and I wasn't sure who it even belonged to. Our wrists limply rotated together.

"Wait a second..." Anderson interrupted, laughing a little. "I thought I knew you from somewhere... you're the guy from that band, right?"

Everything started to move at normal speed again. Only just. I pulled my hand back, bending my fingers into a fist. Gliding my fingertips against the sweat on my palm. If there had been any doubt before, it had been diminished with Anderson's awkward chuckling.

This was all, somehow, very much real.

"Uh... yeah," Frank laughed back, but it sounded like he was underwater. A slight buzz filled my ears.

"You're Frankie Flash?"

"Yes, sir. I-I mean... well, I mean, that *was* me. Before."

My brain glitched and scrambled to come up with an excuse that would make the most sense if I were to throw up all over their red and brown floral rug at that exact instant. I had to come up with something fast. I wasn't sure what was going to happen next, and I couldn't rule out vomiting. If anything, at that point, it felt like a certainty.

"I used to listen to you guys all the time! What was that song..." Anderson, entirely uncharacteristically, began humming a somewhat familiar tune, trying to find the words: "...*duh duh-duh-duh... duh-duh... SO complacent*—"

"*Echoes of a Silence*," Frank interrupted with an awkward laugh, clearly wanting to get whatever this was over with. "Yeah... that was the big one."

Something hard dug into my ribs. It took a second to recognize that it was Anderson's elbow. "He was in this band, and they were huge in my day," he laughed as I nodded emotionlessly. "This was before you were even *born*. Hey, what were you called again?"

"Unrest Stand." I hadn't even realized that those words had left my mouth at first. I could've sworn someone else had said it. Once again, it felt like time was slowing down. His eyes were burning into my face.

Anderson made a *hmm* sound, breaking through the silence enough for me to calm myself down. Just a little. "You've heard of them?" he asked. I nodded stiffly.

"My dad was a fan."

I don't think anyone noticed. Maybe I was just better at covering it up than I gave myself credit for.

With that, Anderson leaned forward, and I suddenly remembered why we were even here. That realization alone shook me further. I had spent all morning wondering who Brooklyn Nicholson's dad was. All the theories. All the assumptions.

Fuck.

"So, we're here to find out everything we need to know about your daughter," Anderson continued, and in the corner of my eye, I saw Frank straighten up. He moved so quickly that I flinched.

"Have you found anything?"

"Not yet. That's why we're here," Anderson replied soberly, and I watched as Liz's arm tightened around her husband's. "We need as much information as possible about the last time that you saw Brooklyn. We need to know what she was wearing. Where she'd been. Where she might've been going."

The odds of this ever happening had been so slim. Not impossible, sure, but very unlikely. I never could've imagined myself sitting opposite him, in his own living room. I was in *his* house. I was looking for *his* missing daughter.

The black-and-white cat, now curled up at Frank's feet, seemed to fix its gaze on me at this point. Its golden eyes didn't waver, almost like it knew something. I felt a strange sensation, as if the cat could sense the tension I was holding back, could read the questions I wasn't asking. It watched me with an eerie calm, like it was waiting for me to say what I hadn't yet said, or acknowledge the unspoken thoughts swirling in my head.

Looking back, I *should've* said something. I should've screamed it at the top of my fucking lungs. The opportunity was *right* there, *right* in front of me, and I knew, too, that this would've been my final opportunity. This was my only chance to do something. Anything.

But I didn't.

"Frank, Liz... first things first. We need to know exactly when you first discovered that Brooklyn had gone missing."

ADJACENT

THE DAY OF THE DISAPPEARANCE OF
BROOKLYN NICHOLSON

LIZ | 8:52 AM

I'd caught a glimpse of the time while sliding my shoes back on, preparing to jump out of the cab, pleasantly surprised at how quickly I'd gotten home. I'd lost count of how many cuts and blisters I'd gained the night before, and at this point, the agony that accompanied them seemed to merge into one singular pain that covered the entire surface area of my feet. Even putting my shoes back on felt like I was dipping my toes into a bathtub of razors.

The thought of making the brief 20-feet walk from the car to the front door made my eyes water. At the same time, I couldn't wait to get back to the comfort of my own home.

Every second I was closer to collapsing on my couch and shutting my eyes, but the seconds weren't passing fast enough.

As I handed two notes to the driver, I spotted myself in the rearview mirror. I didn't look too sloppy, all things considered. I'd made the smart decision to wipe off all my makeup the night before, and I'd brushed out my hair before bed, ready to tie it back up before I left. I just wished I'd taken some spare clothes with me.

It wasn't as if I did this every weekend, so I couldn't blame myself for being unprepared. I could barely remember the last time I'd gone on a night out on the town, let alone staying out for the night. I'd been so sure that I was going to hate it, and it wasn't even as if I'd had a choice—it'd all been planned for me, so I couldn't exactly turn it down. The original plan that I'd formed before leaving the house the evening before was that I would stay out for a drink or two before heading back to the hotel when everyone else was distracted. By the time I'd had a drink or two, however, I didn't want to leave. I was having fun... and well, it'd been a long time since I'd last had fun. Real fun, I mean.

"Fun" that didn't involve fingerpainting or Play-Doh.

I took my change from the driver and slowly lifted myself out of the car, limping toward the front gate as he took off. The street was completely silent. The thought of anyone peeking out their windows and watching me hobble onto my porch was enough to motivate me to speed up toward the door. As I scrambled through my purse for my keys, I noticed the door was already open. At any other time, that would've angered me—how long had it been left open? *Who* left it open?! Thankfully, for whoever had left it open, I was in too much pain to care. I stuck a pin in it for later.

I kicked my heels off the second I shut the door behind me, wincing in pain as I dragged myself into the living room. The pain was so strong that I didn't even hear the snoring until I saw Frank in the armchair, mouth wide open. His snoring kept me up most nights, and I wasn't being dramatic; he sounded like a broken lawnmower. At first, it was so loud that I didn't even stop to think about why he had fallen asleep downstairs.

He never did that. Ever. No matter how tired he got, he'd always drag himself up the stairs, into our bed. Sleep was something that my husband took very seriously.

My heart began to swell when I pictured him waiting for me to come home, falling asleep in the process.

I mean, I couldn't understand *why* he would stay awake for me to come home. I told him that we'd booked a hotel. Maybe he forgot. Or maybe he just didn't listen to me in the first place. The latter was more likely. Still... the thought of him trying to stay awake for me made me smile. I would've never expected that from him. I genuinely couldn't remember the last time I felt so happy to just look at him, even with his mouth wide open, gulping the air so forcefully that the whole chair shook. I even looked past the trail of drool on his chin.

As I slumped back onto the couch, I thought about letting him sleep a little longer. I made it around 20 seconds before my thoughts started working into overdrive. Was Brooke okay? Had he called to check on Cam? Had Allie come home yet?

I leaned forward and shook him by the shoulder.

"Honey?"

It took a couple more shakes for him to start stirring, moving his head from side to side before eventually—slowly—peeking out from his left eye. When he caught a glimpse of me, both eyes began to open. "You're back?"

"Just got in."

"Mmm..." He rubbed his eyes, slowly taking in his surroundings. He seemed confused when he realized where he was.

"How was your night?" I asked as he pulled himself up straighter, stretching his arms behind his head. He mumbled something inaudible at first.

"*Mmm*... yeah. Quiet."

"You didn't have to wait up, you know. I told you I was staying out for the night—"

"Huh? Oh, no... no, I must've just fallen asleep watching TV." Ah.

"How was your night?" he asked, finally taking it upon himself to actively take part in the conversation. I thought about shrugging it off. "*It was okay*". That would've been a good enough answer for him, and he wouldn't have questioned me further.

"It was great," I smiled slightly, sitting back on the couch. "It was so nice to just... *relax*, you know? To be *me*. I never have nights like that anymore."

"Glad you had fun, honey."

I waited out the silence for a brief moment, waiting for him to follow up that statement with a question. *"What did you get up to?"*. *"Where did you end up?"*. *"How are you feeling now?"*. Anything along those lines. When the silence continued, the pressure inside my head expanded with each *tick* from the clock. I decided to give him the benefit of the doubt. He'd just woken up.

"You know," the words came from my mouth before I'd even realized I'd thought them; *"we* could go out sometime."

He actually looked up. He looked me dead in the eye, and I detected a hint of confusion. Well, maybe more than a hint. In fact, I don't think he tried to hide it at all.

"Huh?"

One word. He could only give me one word, and it wasn't even a real word. It was a *"huh"*.

"You know, like a date night," I explained, desperately trying to ignore the frustration building inside me. "Food. Drinks. Something like that."

"Are you asking me out?"

If the slight smirk curling in the corner of his mouth hadn't given it away, I would've likely assumed that he was genuinely serious. It caught me off guard. I was barely expecting a response, yet I received a joke—not just a reply, but a *humorous* reply. We didn't have a whole lot of banter these days, so the interaction felt almost alien, but I decided to force a laugh and go with it.

"Come on, Frank... it's not like the kids are babies anymore. Allie can babysit, and we can just go get something to eat. See a movie, maybe. Nothing too expensive, but, well... it's been a while, right?" A "while" was the understatement of the century.

To my surprise, he nodded almost immediately. "Sounds good."

"When's the last time we went on a date, huh?" I pressed on, eager to keep the conversation going for just a little longer. "A *real* one."

"I don't know."

"Before Cam was born?"

"Probably."

We nodded in agreement before slipping back into silence. I tried not to let myself get too disheartened; I mean, at least we'd agreed on a date. It'd been almost a decade since the last one, so this was some sort of progress.

I pulled myself up from the couch, shaking it off. "Coffee?"

"*Sure*," I heard him saying as I slid into my pair of slippers and made my way toward the door.

"Is Brooke up yet?"

"*I haven't heard her.*"

"Did Allie come back?"

"*Not sure.*"

Father of the year.

With that, I started climbing the stairs, dragging myself up the banister with both hands. I had visions of finally sitting down with my coffee—*finally* relaxing—just for the girls to come downstairs and ask for their own. And, well, they weren't going to ask their father to make it for them. They never did.

As I got to the top of the staircase, I considered taking a left and heading straight into my room. Collapsing onto my bed. Sleeping for the rest of the day.

I took a right instead, making my way toward the girls' room.

The door was shut, so I figured at least one of them was in there. I had a feeling Allie hadn't come home yet, and that was probably a good thing. If I'd opened the door to the two of them, life would've been a lot harder for me. Brooke would've told Allie that I'd yelled at her, and then *Allie* would yell at *me* the second I opened the door, and I just couldn't deal with that. My head was throbbing enough already. Dealing with them one-on-one was far easier.

It still didn't feel real—the fight with Brooke.

I'd had countless screaming matches with Allie over the years, and Mickey before her. Even Cam had spoken back to me at times, but *Brooke*? She was my angel. I'd never had to raise my voice at her, even when she was a little kid.

And she'd *never* raised her voice at me. Flashbacks of her words, the tone of her voice, and even her face came flooding back to me, and it made me feel nauseous. Maybe Frank was right;

maybe I had pushed her too far.

But was I really wrong to want the best for her?

She had her dance practice on Monday, a piano lesson on Wednesday, and her cheer competition on Thursday. On top of that, she was prepping for an important music exam next week and had two major tests to study for over the weekend. She couldn't afford to slack off, not if she wanted to graduate early. We'd talked about this before, and she seemed to understand. She was the one who'd dragged me and her father to colleges all summer. I told her it would be hard work, but she knew that. And she wanted it. I was simply reminding her of what she was working toward.

Maybe one night with her friends would've been okay. Maybe I'd made the wrong call.

We had to talk about it, that was for sure.

I lightly rasped my knuckles against the door, looking up at the bedroom door signs hanging above my head; both had faded a yellowish color over time, and the glitter had almost completely worn away. The first sign read "Brooklyn's room" with a drawing of Cinderella, and the second read "Alex's room" with Snow White. They didn't have "Allie's room" at the store, or even "Alexandra's room", so we just had to choose the closest name. We'd got them in Disneyland, long before Cam was born. It was the only vacation we'd ever had with just the girls.

The ache in my chest got a little stronger each time I looked at those door signs, realizing how quickly time had passed. Brooke was 15. Allie was *18*. It'd been a long time since they'd wanted to be Disney princesses.

I knocked on the door again, swallowing hard.

"Girls? It's me."

No answer. I waited a moment, wondering whether to come back later. If it was just Brooke in there, maybe she didn't want to see me. Allie would've yelled something by now, something about waking her up. Brooke would've just stayed silent.

After debating the right thing to do for a brief moment, I decided to push the door open and find out for myself.

I pressed it open, peering inside when something darted for

my ankles. A startled gasp escaped my mouth as Misty darted out of the room the moment the door cracked, his black-and-white fur blending into the dim hallway as he bolted past my feet. I stepped back for a second, watching him scurry off before focusing again on the room.

The curtains were shut, and the lights were off, yet I could still vaguely make out the clutter covering the furthest side of the room. For as long as I could remember, the girls' room seemed to have an invisible divide directly down the middle, and it was so blatantly clear—just from a single glance—which side belonged to which sister. Allie's side was furthest from the door, and her half of the floor was always completely covered in piles of clothes and trash; a complete fire hazard. Posters were peeling off the wall, half ripped, including the signed Unrest Stand poster above her bed. I never understood why she treasured a poster signed by her father and her uncles so much, but it had remained above her bed for the best part of a decade anyhow. I didn't recognize half of the other bands in the posters. I wasn't even sure if Frank knew who they were.

Where the invisible line had been drawn in the ground, the dirty clothes and cluttered trash stopped. The floor on the side of the room closest to the door was completely clear, and the walls were pretty empty in comparison. Instead of hanging up posters, Brooke draped medals and framed certificates of each of her competitions and achievements on her wall, along with a handful of photographs. Everything was neatly tucked away; no crumpled-up t-shirts or crunched-up Pepsi cans to be seen. Brooke had always kept her side of the room immaculate and had done so since she was a little girl. I often felt bad for her, having to share a room with her sister. I knew her pain, having shared a room with Vic when I was her age. But my sister had been a clean freak in comparison to Allie.

Stepping over endless piles of dirty laundry, I finally managed to pull the curtains open, allowing some natural light into the room. The mess looked worse than ever. I began picking up empty packets of candy, dirty socks, and scattered postage stamps in an attempt to clear a pathway, and I noticed along the way that Allie's bed was empty. It hadn't been made, either. None of this surprised me. My eyes wandered over to Brooke's bed, which *had* been made, but was also empty. *This* did surprise me.

I stood there for a moment, glancing at the empty bed. Trying to work out if she was under the covers or something. She wasn't. The bed had been made so neatly that it would've been impossible not to notice her under the sheets.

My eyes eventually latched onto their bathroom door, which had been left slightly ajar. I dropped the trash and clothes onto Allie's bed, making my way over to see if she was hiding in there instead.

"Brooke?"

Upon discovering the bathroom was empty at first glance, I yanked the shower curtain back, once again revealing nothing. No one was there.

"*Brooke*?"

After scanning both rooms one last time, I walked out, leaving the door open. I started checking every other room upstairs: my room, Cam's room, all the en-suites, plus the main bathroom. All were empty. I made my way back down the stairs, picking up speed with each step. Checked the kitchen. Checked the backyard. At this point, my walk had progressed into a light jog. The pain in my feet had become virtually non-existent.

"*I thought you were making coffee*," I could've sworn I heard Frank mumble as I moved past him, checking every inch of the living room before opening the door that led into the garage. Empty. As I switched directions and placed my hand on the doorknob to Frank's office, I heard him speak again: "*Hey—*"

I heard a sharp screech behind me, followed by a "*shit*" from my husband. It wasn't the first time he'd stood on the cat, and it wouldn't be the last.

I pushed my way inside, almost twisting the handle clean off the door. I knew, deep down, that neither of the girls would be in there, but I knew I couldn't rest until I'd checked every single hiding spot in the house. My eyes quickly scanned the tiny room, even checking underneath his desk. She wasn't there either.

If she wasn't there, then that meant she wasn't here.

"*Liz—*"

My head lightly tapped against the door as I instinctively pulled away from Frank's hand, which had lightly touched my shoulder. He was behind me now. Or, rather, in front of me, since I'd spun around the second he tried to touch me. The words came spilling out before I could fully process the situation: "They're not here."

Frank watched me with a blank expression. No reaction. "What do you mean?"

"What do you mean, *"What do I mean"*?!" I repeated, starting to get angry. "They're not here!"

"The girls?"

"*Yes*, the girls! They're not in their room, they're not in *any* room—"

"Allie went to that party. She's probably not back yet."

He should've known that I wasn't talking about Allie. Allie wasn't home most Saturday mornings; that wasn't the issue, and he knew it.

"Where's *Brooke*?" I asked, finally asking the question that I really wanted answered. His eyebrows knotted together, confused, and I had to wonder if he was sleepwalking. There was no way someone could really be this stupid.

"I don't know—"

"Well, you should know, Frank," I interrupted, hearing my own voice getting louder with each spoken word; "because she's *grounded*. She's supposed to be *here*."

"Maybe she went to grab some milk."

"Without telling you?"

"I was asleep! Maybe she left a note—"

Before he'd even finished his sentence, I was pushing past him.

I began examining the coffee table, the mantlepiece, *every* single surface I could find in the room. When I didn't find a note, I ran to the kitchen. Frank followed.

"Liz, calm down—"

"*Don't* tell me to calm down," I said through gritted teeth, grabbing every piece of paper I could find on the kitchen counters. None of them were notes. Not a single one was written in Brooke's handwriting.

"Jesus, just relax, alright? She's probably just—"

23

"It's nine in the morning, and she's *grounded*," I interrupted, turning to face him. "The front door was open... she must've not shut it properly when she left! And *stop* using the Lord's name in vain—"

"Now, hold on—"

"Well, it wasn't *you*! You always check the door is locked, *every* night," I started shouting, "and Allie wouldn't have just... just *shown up* for five minutes before walking back out, and *not shutting the door*! *Brooke* did this! For the *love* of *Mary... why didn't she leave a note*?!"

I scrambled my fingers across every surface in the kitchen, trying to find anything that would make this make sense. She wouldn't have just taken off without telling us. No matter how mad she was at me, she never would have just left. Not without leaving a note.

My heart rate began picking up speed as it hit me that something wasn't right. "Look..." I felt Frank's hand on my shoulder once more. "I'm sure she's just—"

"One night."

"What?"

"One night I left you with the kids."

"Liz—"

"*One* night I left you in charge," I said through fleeting gasps. "*One night* I went out and did something for myself, and left *you* in charge... for the first night in *years*... and *one of the kids is missing*—"

"She is not *missing*—"

"*THEN, WHERE IS SHE*?!"

"I don't know! She's just *not here*," Frank shouted back before quickly shaking his head, trying to maintain his composure. "Look... you grounded Brooke, and now she's gone out *anyway* to prove a point. How many times has Allie done that?"

"We're not talking about Allie."

"It's the same thing—"

"No, it is *not* the same thing," I yelled, struggling to even comprehend how he couldn't understand what I was saying. "*Brooke* wouldn't do this! She knows we'd worry about her! Good *Lord*, Frank, how hard is it to look after a *teenager* for

ONE NIGHT?!"

"Okay, you know what? Whatever." He turned around, leaving the kitchen. "I'm not doing this…"

I stood there for a moment, trying to compose myself. Trying to think clearly enough to figure out what to do next. Maybe he was right. Maybe I was overreacting. Sure, if this was Allie, I wouldn't be worried—that went without saying. In fact, amongst all the panic, I'd forgotten that Allie was, also, technically missing. The difference was that Allie had done this *hundreds* of times, whereas Brooke had never done anything like this. Brooke was the responsible one. If she was going to "prove a point", she would have at least left a note. She knew that, if she didn't, we would call the police.

With that fleeting thought, I picked up the landline. "I'm calling the cops."

"*What*?!"

Frank came back into the room just as I dialed the final '1'. I couldn't even look at him, but I could sense him staring at me. I knew he was looking at me like I was nuts.

"I'm not going through this again," I said shakily, gripping the phone. "I'm *not* going through this again, Frank, not after—"

"You're not calling the cops."

"Well, what do *you* suggest we do?! Just sit around and wait for her to come back?!"

"*Yes*!" He laughed suddenly, approaching me. "How many times do we have to go through this? If we call the cops now, she'll show up an hour later. We haven't even asked around yet… what about your sister? Vic was taking her to one of her music things—"

"That was last week."

"What about Hayden? I mean, that's almost definitely where she is. The whole point of you grounding her was so that *she couldn't go to Hayden's*."

I paused.

"You really think she'd…" I stopped, narrowing my eyes. "You really think she'd just… rebel like that?"

"She's fifteen, Liz."

"But she *listens* to me! She's never done anything that would make me not trust her," I exclaimed, becoming more conflicted by

25

the second. "I don't know… I-I genuinely don't think she'd do that. Something feels off… something's not right, Frank, I'm telling you…"

He came over, gently prizing the phone out of my hand. It was only then that I realized how much I was trembling. He took my hands in his, squeezing them. "Like you said, this *isn't* like her," he said calmly. "But there's always a first time for everything, right? She'd never even been grounded before last night!"

"Exactly—"

"*Yes*, exactly," he repeated, laughing again. "Maybe she's trying to prove a point. *My* guess is she's trying to show you that you can't control her, so she's hiding at Hayden's for a little while. She might've even snuck out last night. I fell asleep, so I wouldn't have noticed—"

"And what if she's not hiding at Hayden's?" I interrupted, staring back at him. "What if I'm right, and something *is* wrong?"

"Then we call the cops."

"When?! At what point am I "*allowed*" to be worried?" I asked angrily, making quotation marks with my fingers. He groaned loudly.

"Why are you getting so worked up over this?"

"You *know* why."

Suddenly, he was silent. I pulled away from him, folding my arms tightly. Digging my nails into my arms. Part of me regretted even saying those three words—I should've known it would strike a nerve. Another part of me wished I'd said it sooner.

Just as I'd expected him to turn around and leave the room again, he did the opposite. He put his arms around me, pulling me in. Hugging me so tight I couldn't breathe. I froze up at first, not used to the feeling. His embrace felt completely foreign to me, and that realization made me feel even worse.

"…we'll call Hayden," I heard him say as he pulled me closer. "*We'll call around the family, and if she's not there, we just give her space. If Hayden says she hasn't seen her, we'll assume she's lying for Brooke until we hear otherwise.*"

"And how long do you suggest *waiting*?" My voice

dripped with sarcasm. He just held me tighter, letting it slide.

"*Give her a couple of hours. She'll come home before then.*"

I scoffed loudly, even though I knew he was making sense.

He finally pulled away from me, smirking a little while tucking a strand of hair behind my ear. "Like you said: she's not Allie, and she's *not* Mick," he reminded me. "She's just out there somewhere. You're going to feel stupid when she gets home later. I promise."

I really wanted to believe him, so much so that I somehow managed, at that moment, to convince myself that he was right.

She was, without a doubt, hiding in Hayden's bedroom, waiting for me to start looking for her. She wanted to prove a point—she wasn't a kid anymore, and I was *never* to treat her like one *ever* again. *She* was in control. Maybe it had taken her a little longer to get to that rebellious stage compared to her siblings, but in hindsight, it made perfect sense that she would do something like this. And the worst part was that Brooke was smart enough to *know*—for *certain*—that this kind of stunt would work. She knew I'd panic.

That's why she didn't leave a note.

Within less than a minute of thinking it over, I'd convinced myself that I had been wrong the whole time. She was going to come home at some point. Frank was right, and everything was going to be okay.

She'd be home soon.

ADJACENT

2 DAYS AFTER THE DISAPPEARANCE OF
BROOKLYN NICHOLSON

HAYDEN | 12:08 PM

"I heard Fitz Bird cheated on Melissa MacKenzie on Friday."

"Nuh-uh," I shook my head, rummaging through my rucksack. "Didn't happen. I would've known about it."

I jammed my arm fully inside, digging through the hundreds of crumpled-up pieces of paper that had all somehow meshed at the bottom of the bag. Two weeks' worth of assignments, and not a single one had seen the light of day since the moment I'd been given them.

Finally, I felt something hard and round, and something sharp dug into my palm. *Bingo*.

"I heard a couple of seniors talking about it on my way to chem," I heard one of the girls across the table say as I pulled the mystery Blow Pop out from the darkness, examining the color. There were a couple rolling around in there, and I just so happened to have selected the red one. Cherry flavor. "Melissa MacKenzie walked in on him. Everyone's talking about it."

As I ran my fingertips across the wrapper, trying to find the crease to rip it open, I glanced over at the Meteorite table.

An untrained eye scanning the table from a distance would only be able to vaguely decipher the obscure blur of blonde hair and green pom poms, but I knew exactly where to find Melissa MacKenzie.

Despite the whole squad having the same hairstyle, same makeup, and same clothes, she happened to have a glow about her that made her stand out from the others. Some would call it a radiance of beauty. I saw it more as a subtle gleam of evil— a warning signal to avoid all contact, or else risk having your soul sucked away in some form or another.

I watched her dipping a spoon into a yogurt, swirling it around, barely acknowledging anything else around her. Weird. Usually, I would hear her grating, excessively deafening laugh a mile away, like she wanted the whole world to know that her life was way better than theirs at every given moment. She was quiet today. Seemed pretty out of it.

Maybe she really had caught Fitz dicking down some preppie. I couldn't even remember seeing her at the party.

When I turned my attention back to my own table, it shook me a little, noticing how many people were gathering around. Five minutes ago, there was only six or seven of us, but now a small crowd had begun to form in a circle, surrounding us. Well, surrounding me.

Word had got out about Friday night, and now everyone in our year wanted to ask me about it. I'd been the topic of all conversations. I was on the tip of everyone's tongues.

I was the sophomore who got into Fitz Bird's party.

"...I heard them say that she caught him in bed with some other gir*l*." The conversation continued across the table. "You know... *doing it*."

My eyes rolled back into my skull. "Fitz Bird did not have *sex* with another girl," I interrupted, putting full emphasis on the word that the others were still too scared to say out loud.

"You really think he'd risk it at his own party? With so many people around?"

"How many people were there?"

"A couple hundred," I shrugged, sticking the freshly unwrapped Blow Pop into my mouth. "Maybe a thousand."

"Did you drink alcohol?"

"Duh."

Amongst the whispers and chatter surrounding me, I heard a slight chortle from across the table. It was only at this point that I spotted the World's Biggest Buzzkill sitting directly across from me, sucking on a gel pen while flicking through the world's thickest textbook. Rhea Darlow was a sleeping pill incarnate; even just looking at her made me want to snooze.

I was about to ask her what was so funny when Sarah Fredson poked me in the shoulder. "Didn't you hook up with Donnie Booker?"

The whole crowd fell silent. All eyes were back on me. My eyebrows knit together as I tried to figure out why she would even say that, or where she would've heard it. Everyone watched me with sparkling, wonder-filled eyes. Well, everyone except Diarrhea Darlow, who was now glaring at me as if I'd pissed on her homework.

"Who said that?" I asked, turning to Sarah Fredson with the straightest facial expression I could muster up.

"Someone said it in the girls' room."

Here's the thing: Mirrenville was a small town, which meant that there were certain names that everyone recognized. There were popular kids in every year, but everyone—at both St. Mary's *and* M. High—knew who the Eezys were.

The name had been around for years, long before I even made it to middle school. By the time I got to high school the "Eezys" had grown into a bigger group, and it had completely switched up since last year's seniors had graduated. But the original Eezys were Donnie Booker, Fitz Bird, Freddie Kowalski, and Patrick Hurley: 'E', 'E', 'Z', and 'Y' were the last letters of their names— Donnie, Freddie, Fitz, Hurley.

Joaquin Garcia and Mandy Melfi joined later. And I guess Allie counted too, at one point.

As the years passed more and more people wanted to join in

and call themselves "Eezys". But everyone knew who the originals were.

Donnie, Hurley, and Mandy went to our school while Fitz, Freddie, and Joaquin went to M. High, but everyone at both schools knew who all of them were. They weren't *popular* in the way that the Meteorites were, but everyone knew that they were the ones who really ran the school. Or, at least, they would've if they cared enough. If they were cool with you, you were untouchable, and that was all that mattered.

And, obviously, *I* was cool with them. And that's how I got in Fitz's party.

And that's how I knew Donnie.

"I don't know who's spreading that shit around," I shrugged a little, fully aware that my smirk was now giving the game away. "But I'm not the kind of girl to put my business out there, so—"

"Since when?"

I stared directly across the table, kinda amazed that she'd actually spoken up. It wasn't like Diarrhea to feel confident enough to talk in front of a crowd, although judging by how red her face had become, I was pretty certain that she was already regretting it.

Unfortunately for her, it was too late to back down now. I straightened up, turning my body fully toward her.

"Did you say something?" I asked, loud enough that everyone around us could hear. She stared back, her face getting darker by the second. "Hmm... *weird*... I could've sworn you said something—"

"You said you don't put your business out there," she said quietly, her voice shaking ever so slightly. "So I said, "*Since when?*", because, you know... that's all you ever do."

Muffled laughs echoed throughout the crowd, but I didn't react to it. I just kept staring her right in the eye, knowing that she'd crack sooner or later. In a way, I almost felt proud that she'd managed to get a jab in... well, if you could even call that a "jab".

"If you're that bored of the conversation, why are you sat with us?" I asked, smiling as I took a lick of my pop. "Wait a minute... who said you *could* sit with us, anyway? No one here is your friend, Rhea. Look around. Brooke's not here."

Her face suddenly fell, but I'm not sure if anyone else noticed the pain in her expression except me. The conversation had already changed. Mumbles and whispers buzzed around the circle.

"*Where is Brooke?*"

"*She wasn't in class this morning—*"

I should've known better. One mention of her name, and the crowd went wild.

"*She never takes a sick day—*"

"*Has anyone seen her?*"

"She's probably got some music thing going on," I interjected, laughing slightly. "You know, whatever nerdy shit she's got going on this week."

"*Did she go to the party?*"

"Of course she didn't," I heard Rhea piping up again, and my eyes rolled so far back that I lost consciousness for a split second. "She's not stupid. She's got three exams this week, and the competition with the Meteorites—"

"Sounds like you know her whole schedule," I chuckled, and her face flushed a deep pink.

"What, because I actually listen to what she tells me about her life?"

"She's not your friend, Rhea."

"I-I'm more of her friend than—"

"Back to the *topic*," I sang, spinning around in my chair to face the rest of the crowd. "I don't know what you heard about what happened on Friday… you know, with me and Donnie Booker… but I'm not confirming. Or denying."

A muffled "*nor*" could be heard from Rhea's direction but, at this point, I decided she wasn't worth acknowledging. She was dragging the mood down, and everyone knew it. This was probably why the conversation began to turn in a different direction, as suddenly I heard one of the girls ask: "*So, did Brooke go to Fitz's party?*"

"*She never misses school,*" someone else added. "*She had an award last year for not missing a single day of school since, like, first grade—*"

"*She's never even used a sick note—*"

"What am I, her mother?" I said through gritted teeth, trying to keep it cool in front of everyone. "I don't know where she is."

"*Did she go to the party?*"

"No," I snapped suddenly, exasperated by the overload of questions. "And, you know, how would *I* know anyway?!"

"*Because she's your best friend?*"

She wasn't.

She hadn't been for a long time, and it kinda pissed me off that no one had worked that one out.

"Does Brooke even go to parties?" Sarah Fredson asked, nudging me a little before taking a bite of her PB&J. I shrugged, giving my Blow Pop another lick.

"Sometimes."

"*I heard she had one over the summer,*" someone directly behind me added to the conversation. "*I heard the Eezys were there.*"

"*Fitz Bird was there. And Donnie Booker.*"

"That's not true—" I began to argue, but Rhea decided to answer at the same time. Her skin had reset to its usual shade of porcelain, so clearly her confidence bar had filled back up enough for her to rejoin the conversation.

"Obviously last year's seniors were going to go to a party if Brooke had one," was her answer. "Her *sister* was a senior. They were *her* friends, not Brooke's."

"*Ah,* but Allie wasn't there," I pointed out with a smile, jabbing my pop toward her. "Brooke had a free house."

"Even if Allie wasn't there, they still know Brooke through her. And *you* knew them through Brooke—"

"Actually, Brooke knew them through *me,*" I corrected her, trying to cover up my rapidly increasing frustration. "Most people don't even know they're sisters, *idiot.* Can we please move on? She's not even here. It's a dead topic already."

"So, did you…" Someone started speaking across the table, before hesitating. "Did you… *do it?* At the party?"

Everyone was listening now.

All were leaning in, dead silent, waiting for me to speak. I sat still for a moment, sucking on my pop. Looking around at all their faces. It was entertaining to say the least—I mean, more than half of them hadn't even kissed a boy yet. Most of them didn't even know what sex was. Not really.

"Like I said," I said finally, swirling the pop around inside my mouth, pushing it against the inside of my cheek; "I'm not going to get into it, because it's really no one's business, but—"

"When is *anything* you do no one else's business?"

Jesus fucking Christ.

It was as if she couldn't help herself. This was honestly the most I'd heard Rhea speak in my entire life, and it was the *one* time that Brooke wasn't around. No one else at the table even knew who she was. *I* only knew who she was through Brooke. Part of me wondered what Brooke would've said if she was there. Whatever. It didn't matter. I stared directly into Rhea's eyes, sucking on the pop as the table remained absolutely silent. As I pulled it out of my mouth, creating a satisfying *pop*, I pointed it back at her silently. Her face darkened again.

"You ever held hands with a boy, Rhea?"

"It's "really no one's business"," she replied without missing a beat, staring right back at me. Her words dripped with sarcasm, but she stumbled ever so slightly over the first two words, rendering her whole facade futile.

I leaned back a little, continuing to stare her down. "You've never sucked a cock before, that's for sure."

Sniggers rippled through the crowd.

A lot of the faces surrounding me fell, as if the words I'd said out loud had deeply offended them, while the remaining faces lit up with excitement. Rhea was part of the former crowd. Her eyes began to flicker away from mine, but I pressed on. My mouth was moving before I even knew what was coming.

"You know, boys might actually be interested in you too if you just… I don't know…" I gestured toward her again; "got rid of the bowl cut. And the glasses. You seriously remind me of my nana, and she died, like, five years ago."

More muffled laughter. She was seriously struggling to maintain eye contact at this point, but she wasn't giving up just yet, despite her skin deepening to the same shade as my pop. If I didn't already despise her, I would've almost felt proud of her for actually attempting to keep the *tough guy* act up, even if it wasn't fooling anyone.

"I-I don't care—"

"*Oh*, you don't care?"

"You think everyone thinks you're cool just because you give it up to boys at parties," she replied angrily, causing a couple of *oohs* to flow around the table. "No one thinks you're cool. They think you're dumb."

"Mm-hm."

"And I'm proud of who I am. At least I'm not disappointing God... *or* my mom..."

The whole table burst out laughing.

I winced internally, almost feeling bad for her. *Jesus*. She'd basically handed me the next ten insults on a silver platter, but at this point, I wasn't even sure if I needed to use them. She'd just committed social suicide in front of everyone.

"Oh, my God..." I shook my head slightly, trying to hold back my laughter. Rhea was pissed now, glaring at everyone around her. The laughter was spreading, making me realize that there were a *lot* more people surrounding us than I'd first thought.

"Thessalonians 4:3," she continued, raising her voice above the overly stimulated crowd. ""For this is the will of God, your sanctification: that you abstain from sexual immorality—""

"Oh, cry me a fucking river, Rhea—"

"My mother would never, *ever* forgive me if I were anything like you."

"Well, *yeah*," I chuckled again, pulling a face. "My mom wouldn't either. You're not supposed to sit them down and tell them about every time you've gotten laid."

"And God? You think *He's* not watching you?"

"Why don't you stop blaming God and your mother for you being such a fucking virgin?"

More *oohs* and muffled giggles surrounded us, but they were a little quieter this time. Again, I think the word "virgin" had caught a lot of people off guard. It seriously amused me that the word was supposedly this huge insult, yet the majority of the people sitting at that table were one.

I guess the reason my words hit even harder, in that instance, was that everyone there knew that Rhea was going to be one the longest.

For whatever reason, this seemed to be her final straw, as she quickly stuffed all her things into her bag and stood up. Before she stormed away, she looked me in the eye one last time: "I'll pray for you."

The crowd erupted as she left. Someone even threw a half-eaten apple in her direction; sticky juice and sodden fruit stuck to her blazer as she made her escape. I chortled at the sight, crunching straight through the final layers of my pop.

As I dragged the gum from the stick with my teeth, someone to the left of me poked me in the arm. "*...so, you really don't know where Brooke is*?"

My face automatically scrunched up the second I heard her name, yet again. It seriously bugged me how everything had to be about her—every second of every day—even when she wasn't in the room. I was about to tell this girl, for the final fucking time, that I didn't know, and I didn't care, when I heard another grating voice in the distance:

"*MISS BUTLER*!"

My eyes rolled back so far into my head that I became temporarily blind. Unfortunately, my sight came back just in time to catch Sister Bennett towering over me, leaning so close to my face that I could smell her rancid breath. For a split second, I thought she was going to try to kiss me. It wouldn't have surprised me. She was so obsessed with me, it would've made sense that she had a thing for me.

"Up," she hissed. "*Now.*"

Whispers and gasps surrounded us as I threw my rucksack over my shoulder, leaving everything else at the table. I figured this wouldn't take long. It never did. Bennett just liked the sound of her own voice, even if no one else did.

I followed her to the side of the cafeteria, where no one else was around to hear us. She glared down at me, and I looked up at her with a smile. "Yes?"

"What did we talk about last week?"

"Uh…" I peered over at the table where all the girls were. They were all watching us carefully, trying to read our lips. I figured I'd have to speak a lot louder if I wanted them to hear us.

I didn't get the chance, though, since Bennett decided to answer her own question: "Last Friday, we spoke about our dress code. And, I believe, we spoke about it the week before. And the week before that."

"Really?"

"Do you remember what we spoke about specifically?"

"Um…" I turned my head slightly, catching a glimpse of the girls at the table. "That I got hotter over the summer?"

Muffled giggles set off from the direction of the table as if I had my very own live audience.

"Don't act the clown, Butler," Bennett replied in a warning tone, her eyes narrowing into tiny, snake-like slits. "You were told to dye your hair back to its natural color."

"This *is* my natural color."

In my defense, I'd figured that the color would've washed out by now. I'd read that Kurt Cobain had put Kool-Aid in his hair when they played *Saturday Night Live*, so I tried it. And it worked.

It wasn't as if it was even as bright as it was when I first dyed it at the start of the summer—it was neon red when I first tried it, after bleaching my hair, but I'd put dark brown dye over the top since then. Sure, maybe I'd topped it up a little before the party on Friday, but it'd barely made a difference. I'd only used half a pack.

"I'm a redhead, Sister," I insisted, slipping my hands into my pockets. "I can't help it. Besides, do you have any idea how much bullying I have endured throughout my school life, having red hair? Do you have any idea of the *injustice* I have suffered?"

"Cherry red is not a natural hair color," Sister Bennett muttered. "You look like one of those punks on MTV."

"Thank you, Sister."

More laughter from the sidelines.

"Are you going to tell me that you were also born with that bull ring in your nose?" she asked sarcastically, jabbing her finger toward my nostril. I flinched backward.

"Bulls have rings in the middle of their septum, Sister. Mine's on my left nostril—"

"*Stop* wisecracking."

"Like I told you last week, it takes around four months to heal. If I take it out, it's gonna close up! So, you know, if it's okay with you—"

"As it stands, *no*, it is *not* okay with me." Her voice rose with every word, sharp as a ruler. "You have been informed, time and time again, that you are representing this school while you wear this uniform. Every time you leave the house looking like *this*, you are letting St. Mary of the Assumption Academy down."

"But how come Olivia Preston gets to wear all those earrings? Huh?" I argued, trying to keep my cool as she leaned in even closer. "I actually believe that this could be a form of prejudice… you know, because I—"

"You need to watch what you're saying, Miss Butler," Sister Bennett hissed, her voice dropping to a harsh whisper only I could hear. "Those accusations may sway other members of staff, but they do *not* work with me."

She leaned in even closer, so close that our noses almost touched. God, her breath *stunk*. It was as if something was rotting away deep inside her throat. On closer inspection, she had a hell of a lot of wrinkles too. Hundreds of them.

I'd heard a rumor that she'd been teaching here for almost 90 years. I believed it.

"…I am *sick* of you," she said so quietly that no one else could hear. "And if it were up to me, you'd be on your way to another school as we speak. Unfortunately, that's not up to me."

"Right."

"I think we should talk to the principal." She straightened up, not breaking eye contact. "The three of us should talk about your hair and your nose, along with your lack of completed homework over the past month. I'm sure he'll also be curious as to why Rhea Darlow just ran from your table in tears—"

"Oh, Rhea Darlow's a *bitch*."

Shit.

Even I knew not to curse in front of a Sister, and in my defense, I genuinely had not realized that the word had left my mouth. Her eyes completely glazed over, and a lump formed in my throat. Holy shit. I watched as her mouth twitched, waiting for the explosion.

"Come with me," she said finally, in a low, quiet tone that somehow scared me more than anything. I swallowed hard, trying to shrug it off.

"But I haven't finished my lunch—"

"Am I not making myself clear?"

I spun back toward the table before she'd even finished her sentence. She really was a scary-ass bitch. She didn't faze me too much, though—she was all bark and no bite. And, besides, she loved me really. Like, seriously, she was in love with me. The way I dressed distracted her, and if anyone else noticed, she'd lose her job. *That* was why she cared so much.

When I got back to the table, I'd expected a little more of a reaction. For whatever reason, they'd all stopped paying attention—half the crowd had cleared off, and everyone left at the table was now talking amongst themselves. The subject had switched back to that guy that had been released from prison. That teacher. Someone had even sat down in my seat, pushing all my shit to the side.

Whatever. Their loss.

Part of me felt proud; this was my fourth time being sent to the principal's office this term, and we'd only been back a couple weeks. I considered that an achievement.

Not the Brooklyn Nicholson kind of achievement, but one, nonetheless.

THE DAY OF THE DISAPPEARANCE OF
BROOKLYN NICHOLSON

FITZ | 3:24 PM

I jammed my thumb so hard and so fast it started cramping up. A dull ache ran through my right hand, slowing me down. My teeth scraped against each other as I watched my character fall to the ground again and again.

"...*yo, where are my keys?*"

My bar was almost completely red, while Freddie's remained green, as it always did. I wasn't sure why I thought this time would be any different.

"No, no, no," I muttered as I repeatedly jabbed the button. "No, no, no, no, no, *no*—"

"—*where are my fucking keys*?!"

Red text flashed across the screen: *Finish Him.*

I threw the remote onto the table, groaning. Freddie laughed manically as his guy ripped mine's head and spine from their body, blood spraying everywhere. "Nice try, Bird," he said as I jumped up from the couch, running my hands through my hair. "You know, I'd just give up if I were you—"

"Fuck you."

"Stop!" Mandy suddenly yelled, re-alerting me to her existence. I'd forgotten her and Hurley were still here, sitting atop each other on the armchair on the other side of the room. I turned toward them, watching as Donnie stuck his hands inside the chair, wedging both arms underneath their asses.

They both jumped up, and Hurley pushed Donnie backwards. "What the *hell*, dude!"

Donnie ignored him, continuing to rummage through the armchair. Hurley slumped down onto the couch next to Freddie while Mandy just stood there with tightly folded arms, glaring at Donnie as he threw pillows across the room. "Fuckin' *perv*—"

"Do you have to yell?" I interrupted, covering my eyes with both hands. "Better question: you guys going home at any point today?"

The lights in the room were burning into my brain, and the yelling was about to make my head explode. Beads of sweat dripped past my forehead. All I wanted was to go back to bed. *All* I wanted was for everyone to fucking *leave*.

The party was over already, but, as usual, these guys were outstaying their welcome. I couldn't understand how I was the only one with the worst hangover known to man.

"...can't go 'til I find my keys..." I heard Donnie moaning. "...did someone move my car last night?!"

"Nichy was driving last night," Freddie said, barely turning his head as he clicked through the home screen, selecting a new character.

"Why would she move my car?"

"Uh, why was Allie driving at *all*?!" Mandy interjected, sounding pissed. "She was *wasted*—"

With that, Scruff started barking as loud as he could, merging with Donnie and Mandy's yelling.

My eyes shot open, and every light in the room merged into one, blinding me. The game started up again, seemingly at full volume. The sound bounced off every wall in the room. Scruff bumbled over to the door, his thick, shaggy coat bouncing with each step.

My eyes slowly adjusted to the light, and I finally figured out what had caught his attention. Through the window, I noticed a figure standing in the garage.

For years, I'd hated the window on the wall that separated the small living room from the garage for this very reason—I'd be chilling on my own, playing a game or watching TV, just to be scared shitless by an unknown figure watching me from the other side of the window. It was even creepier at night, especially since the walls of the garage were soundproofed, so I couldn't even hear if a car pulled in. It caught me off guard, every single time.

It took a second for my eyes to fully adapt to the light, making it harder for me to recognize the dark figure in the garage. Oddly, I recognized the white Mercedes-Benz behind them before I recognized the person who had parked it.

"What's she doing here?" Hurley asked suddenly, following my gaze. Mandy responded with a dull guffaw.

"You're in *trouble*..."

If Hurley hadn't been there, I probably would've told her to shut up. Freddie started laughing, and my mind raced back to the night before. Most of it was a blur, but the one thing I *could* remember was the exact reason why my girlfriend was now standing in my garage, glaring so deeply into my face that it burned.

Yeah... I was in trouble.

"...*you gonna let her in*?"

I hadn't even noticed Joaquin wandering over to the garage door, kneeling next to Scruff to calm him down. He reached up toward the door handle before shooting me a questioning look. I nodded slightly, silently giving him permission. He nodded back, twisting the handle.

Aside from the pained grunts and the background music blaring from the TV, the room fell silent as the door opened. I just stood there for a moment, watching her. Unsure of what to say.

"Hey, Melissa." Mandy was the first to break the silence. The guys followed her lead, each mumbling some form of greeting.

Mel nodded silently, barely faking a smile. She didn't say a word back. She wasn't even paying attention to Scruff, who was pawing at her shoes. He used to jump all over her, but his legs had gotten too bad over the past few months, so this was now his only way of getting her attention.

Still, she barely even acknowledged him. That was how I knew my day was about to go from bad to *so* much worse.

"Come on, boy..." Joaquin sat down on the floor, struggling to pull Scruff—all 80 pounds of him—onto his lap. He barely fought back but continued to whine at Mel. It was as if she couldn't even hear him. She just kept staring directly at me, and I figured I had to do something. Quickly. I also knew there was no way we could have this conversation in front of the guys.

I forced myself to walk over to her, putting a hand on her shoulder. She immediately tugged away from me coldly.

"Come on..." I nodded toward the garage, and the two of us walked outside. As we left, I felt Mandy and Joaquin's gazes follow us. The others hadn't even noticed us leave; Donnie was still ripping the armchair apart, and Freddie and Hurley had started a new game. Based on the last thing I heard before shutting the door, Freddie was already winning.

As the door shut, everything fell silent—the beauty of having a soundproofed garage. This was when I first saw her face properly. Her eyes were all red and puffy, and her cheeks were wet.

I tried to pull her in without thinking. "Hey, what's wrong?"

She immediately shoved me away, stepping backward. "I came for my stuff," she sniffed coldly, rubbing a tear away from her cheek. For some reason, I figured the best course of action was to pretend that I had no idea what she was talking about.

"Your stuff? What do you—"

"Oh, *fuck you*, Fitz."

"What?!"

"Don't you dare act like you don't know what this is about—"

"I have no idea what you're talking about!"

In all honesty, this wasn't our first rodeo.

44

It'd been a couple of months since the last time we'd had this conversation, and it sucked every time.

The only difference this time around was I was violently hungover, and I wasn't sure I had the patience or the willpower to make it through to the other side.

"I *saw* you," she spat, confirming what I had already suspected. *Shit.* This was already going to be way harder than last time.

"Babe, listen—"

"*You* said I had *nothing* to worry about!"

"I-I wasn't lying…" I rubbed my forehead, trying so hard to ignore the throbbing sensation inside my skull. "Look, you've got nothing to worry about, alright? It was nothing—"

"*You fucked her!*"

I paused, thinking about it for a second. Trying to remember.

"No…" I shook my head slowly, recalling exactly what had happened. Frame-by-frame. "No, I definitely didn't—"

"I *knew* you liked her! This *whole time!*"

"Are you kidding me right now?!" I forced myself to laugh, instantly regretting it as the shaking movement rattled my already sensitive brain against my skull. "Mel, I don't know what you've heard, or what you think you saw, but… I-I was *wasted*—"

"So, you *fucked* her?!"

"I didn't *fuck* anyone!"

I genuinely didn't.

I mean, I could understand why she might've assumed that I had, based on what she saw, but I was telling the truth here. Hand on heart.

"You know…" She paused, hesitating before looking me dead in the eye. "You know, I actually thought you were different. I thought I could trust you."

"Oh, baby, come *on*…" I tried to hold her hands, but they kept sliding out of my grip. Honestly, I had no idea what I was supposed to say at this point. I didn't have it in me to fight.

I just wanted to sleep.

"Mel, I was *wasted*…" I repeated, and she scoffed loudly. "And, I… I-I didn't know what I was doing… I… you know, I actually think maybe for a second, I thought she was *you*, and—"

"*That*'s your excuse? Are you *kidding* me?!" she started

yelling. "Even if you were the most *fucked up* you'd ever been, how the *hell* could you mix us up?!"

She had a point.

I wasn't even sure why I said it.

"...she had the same..." I actually had no idea how I was going to end that sentence. I was fully aware that I was going to hear the end of that sentence at the same time as she did. "...*hair*..."

My head spun 90 degrees.

I groaned loudly as lights flashed like stars around me, cupping my hand over my cheek. The sound of the slap seemed to occur a long time after I felt it, kind of like how you see lightning a couple of seconds before you hear the thunder.

"*Fuck you,*" she was screaming. "*FUCK YOU!*"

"Okay, okay—"

"Get my stuff together and I'll get it later," she began to sob, turning from me. "I don't have time for this... I've got to go—"

"Just wait—"

"If I'm not home in an hour my mom's going to freak, and I've got to get to the police station before—"

"Why are you going to the police station?"

"Oh, don't pretend to care *now*—"

"No, wait, Mel," I tried to grab her arm again, but she continued to slap me away. "What happened? Are you alright?"

She folded her arms awkwardly, and her face softened a little. Tears were still dripping down her cheeks, but something had changed. Her eyes flickered toward the house.

"Because... no, don't worry about it," she interrupted herself, shaking her head. "I just... I saw something last night. Whatever."

"What, *here*?"

"How many were there?"

I paused, confused for a second. Trying to figure out what we were talking about.

"What?"

"How many times?"

Oh.

"Look… Mel—"

"I know about Tammy," she interrupted before I could say anything else. "And Heather… and Michelle Taylor—"

"Babe—"

"And obviously that… that *slut* last night, and I bet it wasn't your first time with *her*—"

"Baby, baby, *please*…" Even I wasn't sure why I was still trying at this point. "There was no one else, alright? It was just… just…"

"*Just* them."

"Aw, come on. You know what I mean."

"I sure do," she laughed angrily, pulling her car keys out from her pocket. She started walking back to the car when the words came pouring from my mouth.

I don't even know why I started begging. It was clear at this point that she was done with the whole situation, and you know what? I wasn't even mad about it.

If I was being completely honest, I didn't even care that this was happening. I just wanted it to be over.

"Mel, come on…" I shouted after her, groaning a little. "Mel, I… I *love* you…"

She stopped in her tracks, staring at me. I could tell by her face that she didn't believe it any more than I did.

"You love me?" she repeated, completely deadpan.

I nodded silently, unable to say it again; mainly because I was so drained—both physically and mentally—but also because I didn't mean it.

Don't get me wrong, I liked her a lot. And, you know, I liked being with her. We had fun together. And every single time something happened with someone else, I made *damn* sure she never found out about them because I respected her that much.

I mean… how the hell did she find out about Michelle *Taylor*?

"Fitz… I want you to know that I do love you…" Her eyes started filling up again. "But I know you don't love me. I know you don't, so don't make me look even more of an idiot by lying to me. Please just have the decency, right now, to tell me the truth."

I looked down at my shoes.

"I…" I stopped, clearing my throat. "I… look, I—"

"*Forget it.*"

She stormed over to her car, jumping into the front seat. Slamming the door shut.

It was at this point that I noticed Mandy's head peering through the window, watching the whole thing go down. I tried to subtly shoo her away, glaring at her, but she was glaring right back at me. She was shaking her head disapprovingly, like she was my mother or something. I wished Mandy could just drop shit like this and let it go, like the guys did. I already knew she was going to lecture me the second I walked back through the door.

I didn't get it. It wasn't as if I'd ever fucked *her* over. Mandy was the only girl I'd never cheated on. Sure, we were only, what, in ninth grade at the time, but... still. I was good to Mandy.

She was mouthing something through the glass: "*Stop her*", I figured.

I turned back toward Mel, but it was too late. She was already backing out into the driveway.

In all honesty, I wasn't torn up about it. Maybe it was the hangover talking, but in a way, this felt like a good thing. A clean slate. If we were being real about it, this had been a long time coming, and things were only going to get harder when she went off to college. Mandy and Hurley were barely making the whole long-distance thing work, and they were the best couple I knew. She'd only been gone a month, and she'd already come back to see him.

Once Mel had disappeared into the distance, I made my way back into the small living room. Freddie and Joaquin were playing a new game, and Hurley was back in the armchair. Donnie was gone. Mandy was shaking with anger.

"You're an idiot," she hissed, pushing past me to get to Hurley. She sat on his lap, and he absent-mindedly put his arms around her as he focused on the TV. Freddie was destroying Joaquin—obviously. I just stood there for a moment, watching Freddie's guy rip Joaquin's head off.

Without turning his head, Freddie asked the question that he already knew the answer to: "So, who was the lucky lady, huh?"

Mandy took off her shoe and threw it at his head, narrowly missing. He burst out laughing, taking the controller out of Joaquin's hands before turning around to offer it to me with a subtle wink. I snatched it from him, kneeling to stroke Scruff who was gently tugging at the hem of my jeans. He slowly rolled onto his back, happy to finally get some attention.

It was kinda sad, in a way. He was going to miss her way more than I was.

ADJACENT

2 DAYS AFTER THE DISAPPEARANCE OF
BROOKLYN NICHOLSON

ALLIE | 12:13 PM

I was *so* not in the mood to see two cops sitting on my couch first thing in the morning. All I wanted was to make a cup of coffee and sit on the couch for five minutes for a switch-up of scenery before heading back to bed, but even that wasn't an option anymore.

There were two of them: one guy, one girl. They sat on the small couch, and Dad was sat on the armchair while Mom stood behind him.

Usually, when cops came around, it had something to do with me. But I hadn't done anything... had I? I thought back to everything I had done over the past few days, but none of it had been worth being questioned over. There was the party—

obviously—but I couldn't remember anything notable happening.

Not that I could remember much.

A cold sweat broke out for the hundredth time since the morning before, and I began to shiver. As I crossed my arms, hugging myself to provide some form of warmth to my freezing cold body, I wanted nothing more than to return to my bed. There was just one issue: how could I be sure that someone wasn't going to run up to my room to wake me back up if I tried to go back to sleep? The thought of being woken back up made me feel sick, especially after how long it had taken me to find the strength to come downstairs in the first place. This was the mother of all hangovers.

"...*wait a second...*" The guy cop laughed suddenly, interrupting whatever Dad had just said. "*I thought I knew you from somewhere... you're the guy from that band, right?*"

Even rolling my eyes made the ache in my skull intensify.

I shut my eyes for a moment, covering them with my palms. Every light in the hallway seemed to be getting brighter, forming into stars. The pain was unbearable. I'd already taken five or six blue pills since I'd woken up, but even Tylenol wasn't doing shit. I just couldn't pinpoint how or why this was happening to me.

Did I take something at the party? I couldn't remember.

I couldn't remember *anything*.

I'd thought about calling one of the guys to find out what had happened, but at the same time, I didn't want to speak to anyone. The shame and anxiety were enough to convince me to isolate myself from the world a little longer, but the aches and the cold sweats seemed to be getting increasingly worse with time, so being sociable in any form was simply not an option. Not to mention the itching. I'd almost ripped my skin off from scratching so hard.

All I wanted to do was crawl back upstairs, curl up in bed, and die.

"*...we're here to find out everything we need to know about your daughter...*"

I'd zoned out of the conversation when they'd started talking about the band, but this single sentence brought me back into the room. Or, well, outside of the room.

Shit. Maybe I *had* done something.

A flicker of worry shot across Dad's face, and for the first time since I'd been watching them, I noticed that Mom seemed a little scared too. "Have you found anything?" Dad asked, and the guy cop shook his head.

"We need as much information as possible about the last time that you saw Brooklyn. We need to know what she was wearing… where she'd been—"

They were here for *Brooke*?

"…we need to know *exactly* when you first discovered that Brooklyn had gone missing—"

As I pressed my back against the wall, trying to remain invisible in the dimly lit hallway, I heard the faintest creak. The door was widening. A black shadow slinked past my legs, and I felt the soft brush of fur against my ankle. *Misty*. Before I could react, the furry bastard had nudged the door completely open, widening the gap just enough to reveal my hiding spot. The door creaked louder this time, drawing everyone's attention to the doorway.

I glared at the cat as he moved around my ankles, just to turn back into the living room. As he lay back down, he stared right back at me, his yellow eyes gleaming with satisfaction.

God, I hated that scruffy little shit.

"Allie?"

My heart pounded in my chest as all eyes turned in my direction. My eyes immediately met my mother's.

"Come in here, quick…" She came speed walking up to the door, swinging it wide open and firmly gripping my arm before I'd even had a chance to process anything.

She grabbed onto me so tight that she almost cut off the poor circulation that was already attempting to trickle through my veins, but she did it in a way that appeared non-conspicuous in front of the cops; something I remembered her doing many times when she took me to the supermarket as a kid. It fucking hurt, but no one else could see it. She was a pro.

"This is our other daughter, Allie," Mom kindly introduced me as she nonchalantly dragged me over to the big couch, pulling me down with her. "Allie, this is… I'm sorry—"

"Officer Anderson," the guy cop finished her sentence, gesturing to himself before nodding toward the girl cop. "Officer Hardie."

"S'up."

I had never noticed how bright the overhead light was until that moment—it shone directly into my eyeballs, making the pain inside my head so much worse. Beads of sweat slid down my forehead, soaking into my eyebrows. It made my face start to itch.

"They're here about Brooke," I heard Dad saying at the side of me, and I pulled a face as I stiffly wiped the sweat away with my sleeve, rubbing a little harder to scratch the itch.

"What did she do?"

"She's missing."

Looking back, I probably could have given a more concerned reaction, especially since the news itself really did surprise me. I half-remembered the guy cop saying that she'd gone missing just a few seconds earlier, but I'd barely processed it.

"Do you remember what she was wearing Friday?"

"She went missing *Friday*?" I started counting back, trying to work out what that even meant. I wasn't even sure what day today was. All I knew was I got home Saturday morning. Everything else was a blur, and I had no idea what was going on anymore.

How the hell would *I* know what Brooke wore on Friday? I was at the party. She was at school.

"Was she not wearing her uniform?" I offered, barely able to get the whole question out. My mouth was so friggin' dry. My eyes felt kinda dry too. Everything seemed to be drying up.

"She was still in her uniform when I left the house," Mom added before turning to Dad. "You were the last one to see her. Did she change?"

The girl cop hadn't said a word since she'd gotten here—or, at least, since I'd been listening to the conversation—but all of a sudden, she couldn't take her eyes off me. She kept staring right at me like I had something written across my forehead and she was trying to decipher it. Maybe I looked worse than I thought.

"When was the last time you saw her?" Guy Cop asked Dad, who looked confused already. I could almost hear the cogs meshing inside his head, desperately trying to form a single thought. You know, I was impressed that he'd even noticed that she'd gone missing. Dad didn't pay a lot of attention to his surroundings. Half the time, he called *me* "Brooke".

"Uh... around six, maybe."

"Six in the afternoon?" Girl Cop asked suddenly, breaking her silence. She was *really* pretty. Too pretty to be a cop, you know? Maybe that was what caught Dad off guard. He suddenly started stumbling over his words a little after she spoke. I could've sworn I felt Mom stiffen up a little at the side of me.

"Yeah... y-yeah, I'd say that's about right," he nodded. "She had some food, and then she went up to her room—"

"And that's the last time you saw her?"

"Yes."

"You didn't check on her?"

"No."

"Why not?"

"Because she's fifteen." His tone got a little deeper, becoming seemingly irritated at this back-and-forth interrogation. "I just let her go and do her own thing, and, well, I just stayed downstairs. I was here if she needed me."

"And you fell asleep down here, right?" Guy Cop asked, gesturing toward the couch that Mom and I were sitting on. "On the couch?"

"On this chair. Yeah."

"Do you remember locking the door that night? Your wife mentioned that the front door was left unlocked when she got home Saturday morning," he went on, and I absent-mindedly nodded in agreement, despite this being the first time that I'd heard of it. "And that you make a habit of making sure that everything is locked before going to sleep."

"Yeah... I mean, I think I did," Dad answered, not sounding 100% certain. "I usually do."

"This could be a key factor in your daughter's disappearance."

Something shifted in the air, and reality finally hit.

Were they saying that they thought she'd been taken? Or that she'd run away?

Brooke had never run away before, but I couldn't imagine someone breaking into the house and just... *taking* her. I mean, sure, she was little, but she wasn't that little. Plus, Dad was a light sleeper, so he would've definitely heard something like that happening, especially if he'd slept downstairs.

Trust me—I'd know. I'd spent half my life trying to sneak out at night, and I'd had, maybe, a 75% success rate. Brooke wouldn't have stood a chance. Or a mystery abductor.

It suddenly occurred to me that there was *no way* I'd slept longer than a day. Mom wouldn't have let me spend the whole weekend in bed. It was either Sunday, or possibly Monday... why were they calling the *police*? Brooke would stay out for weeks at a time, especially if she was staying at Hayden's.

"You sure she's not with Hayden?" I asked, speaking the thought out loud before I'd had a chance to dwell on it. Mom scoffed as if I'd just asked the stupidest fucking question she'd ever heard.

"No, we've checked," she replied, slightly irritated. "Of course we've checked. Hayden hasn't seen her."

"Who's Hayden?" Guy Cop asked, and I began spelling her name out as he jotted it into his notepad: *H-A-Y-D-E-N, Butler*. "She's a friend of Brooke's?"

"Her best friend since preschool," Mom interrupted before I could say anything, leaning in as if she was sharing a secret: "She's, you know... well, her *mother's* from around here, and her youngest daughter looks just like her, but... Hayden, her oldest... she's, you know... she's *colored*. But she's a really lovely girl!"

Guy Cop's jaw tightened just a bit, the professionalism on his face faltering for a moment. A knot twisted in my stomach as I cringed inwardly.

"*Biracial*, Liz," Dad said quickly, cutting in before I could. His laugh was forced, and his eyes flicked to Guy Cop—who's black, by the way—clearly trying to smooth things over. "Hayden's biracial."

Mom's head snapped toward Dad, visibly confused. "That's what I said!"

Guy Cop managed to smooth over his initial reaction with

a mask of calm professionalism. Girl Cop, on the other hand, looked just as awkward as I felt.

And, of course, Mom was oblivious. She took the heavy silence as permission to just plow ahead. "Well, I called Hayden's mother on Saturday, and neither of them had seen her."

"And you *believe* them?"

Without even turning, I could feel Mom's glare burning into me. She knew I was right, but that didn't matter. "Why wouldn't I?" she asked in a semi-cold tone, her voice brimming with that familiar defensiveness.

The answer was simple: Hayden was a compulsive liar, and her mom was a borderline-functioning alcoholic.

Neither of them could be taken seriously.

"And where were you Friday night, Allie?" Girl Cop asked suddenly, switching up the subject matter. I turned to her, somewhat relieved that I didn't have to talk about Hayden Butler any longer, though this new question was hardly any better.

My mind scrambled for the right way to answer, piecing together fragments of a night I could barely remember. "Yeah, uh…" I shook my head slightly, scratching the itch on my arm. "I went to a party."

"A party?"

"It was my friend's birthday," I added slowly, carefully rubbing my eyes in a futile attempt to soothe the thumping headache. "And he's just got this new place… kinda… so a couple of us went around."

"Was this Fitzgerald Bird's grandson's party?"

I paused, staring back at him. Either he was a really good guesser, or something was up.

"Uh… yeah?" I nodded, forcing a smile. "How—"

"We were called there Friday night," Guy Cop explained, shooting a knowing look to both my parents. "There were a *lot* of noise complaints. It makes sense now, knowing that the grandson has moved in."

"I think it's just ridiculous," Mom laughed, leaning forward in her seat. "Leaving a house *that* size to an 18-year-old? He's barely out of high school. I thought Mr. Bird had a little more sense… I thought he would've left it to his son, but I guess—"

"Fitz lived with his grandpa until he died," I interrupted,

surprised at how defensive I became for a second. "He was the only one that looked out for him."

"Still, Al, what's a kid like him going to do with a *mansion*? Would *you* know what to do with a mansion?"

"Hang on," Guy Cop chuckled, shaking his head. "The *grandson's* called Fitzgerald too? The same as his father, *and* his grandfather?"

And we *never* let him forget it.

He would've had better luck being shipped off to whatever private school his parents wanted him to go to by the time we'd finished with him. Even shortening his name to "Fitz" didn't stop us from calling him by his full legal name every so often.

Fitzgerald Everett Bird III.

I mean, come *on*.

"Did Brooke go to the party?"

I started laughing again, abruptly coming to a halt when a stabbing pain shot through the center of my brain. Everything went white for a moment. Like lightning.

"Brooke doesn't do that whole... scene," Mom answered when I couldn't, giving—roughly—the same answer that I would have. "She's a good kid. And Allie would've seen her there, surely."

Both cops turned to stare at me. Girl Cop's expression switched up as she looked at me again, giving that weird look that I'd caught her throwing my way a few minutes previously. A look of concern, maybe? Worry?

I could feel myself getting worse and worse as more time passed, so it made sense that I looked like shit too.

"*Did* you see Brooke?" Guy Cop asked, pressing his pen to his notepad. I shook my head silently, shakily reaching up to wipe my forehead. "You sure?"

"I-I can't remember anything."

I could've sworn I'd heard Dad mumbling something like "*Is she okay?*", but I could've just imagined it.

Everything just felt all woozy all of a sudden. *I* felt all woozy. Mom definitely said something under her breath, but her tone sounded a lot less concerned. I ignored it. There was no point saying anything back, and even if I'd wanted to, I was running dangerously low on energy.

"Were you drinking? At the party?" one of the cops asked. At this point, all sounds were blurring into one, so I wasn't even sure which one of them had spoken.

It took all my strength to shake my head again. "I didn't..." I stopped, taking a deep breath. "I don't remember."

"I've always done all that I can to keep my kids safe," Mom started saying, nudging me playfully. "*And* to make sure that they abide by the law... I've never had any issues with Brooke, or even much with Mickey, but *this* one? She can be difficult—"

"I didn't drink, Mom," I interrupted, becoming more and more breathless with each spoken word.

"—we've always tried to keep them on the right path—*both* of us—but there's only so much you can do as a parent—"

"I *didn't drink*!"

At least, I wasn't *supposed* to drink.

I mean, that was why I took the car.

The plan was to show up early, catch up with the guys, and leave before things got too crazy. One of the last things I could actually remember was Joaquin trying to pass me a drink, but I said no. I had a beer, but that was it. One beer. Maybe two, but definitely no more than that.

"I was driving," I said finally, suddenly realizing that I was full-on dragging my nails up and down my forearm, scratching vigorously. "I was meant to drive home, but I don't remember... *anything*... after an hour of being there, or whatever. I woke up in my car the next morning, and I've felt like microwaved shit ever since—"

"Language—"

"*Ugh*, are you even listening to me?" I groaned, turning to look at Mom properly for the first time since I sat down. Her eyes actually widened a little when she saw my face. "Maybe I *did* see Brooke... I mean, I-I seriously doubt it, but who knows? I have no idea what happened at that f-freaking party..."

Mom put her hand over my forehead. Her skin felt ice cold. It felt good. I leaned into her until she pulled her hand back, wiping it dry on her blouse. "Good Lord, Al, you've got a *fever*—"

"What's the last thing you remember from the party?" It was Girl Cop talking this time. It was, what, the second sentence I'd heard her speak since I'd sat down?

"How am I supposed to remember not remembering anything?" I responded dryly. Mom dug her elbow into my side—once again, subtle enough that no one else noticed, but hard enough that I winced. My sleeve brushed against my forearm, reactivating the itchiness just as I'd managed to forget about it.

"What's the last thing you do remember?"

"Uh… I don't know…" I pinched my sleeve and began rubbing it against the red bumps on my arm. "It was dark out, but I don't know what time. I just… I can't remember *anything…*"

I'd blacked out *hundreds* of times in the past.

There had been so many nights when I'd drank too much, getting so wasted that I couldn't remember a thing from the night before.

This was different.

"Do you think there's *any* possibility your sister could've been at the party?" Girl Cop's eyes had completely lit up at this point. It was as if she was actually getting excited at the idea.

"I mean… maybe?" I said between vigorous scratches, completely exasperated. "Hayden could've dragged her along to it, but I don't see why they *would've* come—"

"I think we need to take you in for a test."

Guy Cop turned to look at her, clearly confused. Maybe just as confused as the rest of us. Mom straightened up, staring at Girl Cop. "What kind of test?"

"A drug test."

Mom completely stiffened up, and a cold chill fell over me. Why the fuck would she say that? *Jesus*. I mean, *yeah*, I'd been wondering if I'd taken something at the party too, but did she seriously have to rat me out to my parents?

"Okay, so, there's been a couple of recent cases in Seattle with girls being hospitalized due to their drinks being spiked with benzodiazepines," Girl Cop started to explain, slowing down when she noticed the confusion on our faces. "The side effects include memory loss, nausea, dizzy spells, cold sweats, *and* some people experience itchiness for a couple days following consumption—"

I paused, mid-scratch.

I suddenly became aware that she was watching my hands. Watching me scratch myself. Fireworks flashed through her pupils, like she was having this *Eureka* moment.

"I'm sorry," Dad spoke for the first time in what felt like forever. "Benzo-di-*what*?"

"Benzodiazepines," she repeated. "Uh... tranquilizers. The one in Seattle is kinda similar to Rohypnol, except it's a lot stronger and lasts a little longer... you know, the date rape drug?"

I froze.

"If Brooklyn *was* at the party, there's a chance someone might've slipped it in her drink too," she rambled on, her eyes widening with each word that flew from her lips. "There's that forest behind Fitzgerald Bird's house, right? Behind the church? It's possible that she could've blacked out and... well, gotten lost. Maybe she's still there."

"You think..." Mom took a deep breath, shakily running her fingers over her rosary beads. "You think... Brooke... was *date raped*?"

You could hear the absolute horror in her voice.

She was devastated, just at the possibility that this could've happened to Brooke, yet here *I* was, sweating like a fucking pig and ripping my skin off, completely unaware of what had happened to *me* on Friday night. A small laugh slipped out, and I quickly covered it up with a cough.

In the corner of my eye, I noticed Misty had curled into a tight, anxious ball. It was like even he could sense that something was up, like he had been following the conversation the whole time. Even the damn cat, who usually strutted around like he owned the fucking place, seemed all wound up because something might've happened to *Brooke*.

Just like Mom, who was practically falling apart at the idea of something bad happening to her youngest daughter.

Who gave a shit about the older one, right?

"Well, we can't assume anything about Brooke," Girl Cop corrected her, not taking her eyes off me. "But I think Allie might be suffering from the aftereffects of Ziapodine. If Brooke was at the party, there's a chance the same thing could've happened to her."

She just looked *so* proud of herself.

She sat there with this odd smile on her face, looking up at Guy Cop for approval, like a puppy waiting for a treat. He actually seemed pretty impressed, too. I half-expected him to pull a doggy bone from his pocket and start ruffling her hair.

"Normally these kinds of benzos stay in your system for, at most, 48 hours, but Ziapodine is known to stick around for a little longer. Sometimes up to a week," she explained while Guy Cop jotted something down in his notes. "If it's in your system, it'll come up on a test. We need to get you tested right away. Is that okay with you?"

"Wait, does this mean someone tried to…" I laughed slightly, too nervous to get the words out. "Someone at the *party*…"

Who the fuck would've spiked my drink?

I mean, there were a *lot* of people at the party. I didn't know half of them. A lot of them were kids from our year at school— a lot of people coming back from college for the weekend, just for the party—and I only remembered hanging out with my usual group: Freddie, Donnie, Mandy, Hurley, Joaquin, and obviously Fitz.

I'd only had one drink, and I was with the guys the *whole* time, and I knew none of them would've done it.

My stomach turned ever so slightly when I looked down at my clothes, the same clothes that I'd woken up in Saturday morning: a huge black sweater and men's shorts. Only at that moment did I question why I was wearing someone else's clothes.

But no matter how fucked up I had gotten, there was no *way* I would've forgotten seeing my sister there.

Seeing her at a party would've sobered me up immediately. And, besides, she hated that sort of stuff. Parties, I mean. The only way I could've seen Brooke coming to Fitz's was if Hayden had dragged her along, but I couldn't get why Hayden would've even shown up to begin with. She didn't know my people.

Reality began to sink in. If I had gone missing for a couple of days, no one would've given it a second thought. Hell, I used to do it every other week… but this was *Brooke*. She didn't *do* shit like this.

Where the hell *was* she?

HAYDEN | 1:31 PM

I slammed the door shut behind me, barely blocking out the screaming.

"...*HAAAAY-DEEEEN*..."

I shoved everything off the top of my bed: gum wrappers, Pepsi cans, an empty box of relaxer, all tumbling to the floor with a hollow thud. Old magazines and homework followed, scattering across the carpet as I cleared space.

With a heavy groan, I jumped onto the bed, sinking into the worn-out mattress, and grabbed the clicker. The TV flickered to life, buzzing softly as music videos blared through the screen.

I turned the volume up as high as it would go. Mom was passed out on the couch, and I knew nothing would wake her.

"...*HAAAAY-DEEEEN*..."

Not that it mattered that I was home early.

Last I'd heard Principal Myers was calling Mom to come get me, and there was no chance of that ever happening, so I cut out the middle man and made my way home. What were they going to do—suspend me for doing what they wanted me to do anyway? Send me home for *going* home? The school was a fucking joke. There was more of a chance of Michael Jackson giving me a ride home than Mom.

And based on the drool on her chin, plus the two empty bottles half-rolled under the couch, she'd been out of it for hours.

"...*HAAAAY-DEEEEN*..."

Mom didn't hear me come home, but Harleigh did.

She must've climbed out of her crib again. I couldn't get why she couldn't start some baby-care-thing until she started Pre-K. At least she wouldn't be bored in the house all day if she was with someone else. Not that she was my problem; I wasn't getting paid for babysitting duties.

And, besides, I wasn't even supposed to be home yet.

Not my problem.

Harleigh wasn't quite tall enough to reach my door handle yet, and I was making the most of this while I still could. There was nothing I could do to stop her from banging her tiny fists against the door, but at least I could keep her locked out for now.

I continued jabbing the volume button until her voice was almost completely drowned out by Green Day's new video. I must've seen it around a thousand times already.

They'd played Seattle a week or so ago, and the thought of them being so close drove a knife through my heart. I should've *been* there.

It was so fucking unfair.

"*...HAAAAAAAAY—*"

Even with the volume on max, I could still hear her crying.

I threw myself backward onto my bed, grabbing a pillow. Pulling it so tightly over my face that I couldn't breathe. For whatever reason, I started screaming. It didn't make a sound. No one could hear me, not even myself.

I just kept screaming.

Between breaths, an idea popped into my head: I could shave my head. I could just shave it all off, like Sinead O'Connor. They couldn't keep me out of school if I had no hair.

I mean, what could they even say about that?

Nothing.

For all they knew, I could've had cancer, or that disease that makes your hair go all gray and fall out.

They couldn't say anything if I just shaved it all off.

BANG-BANG-BANG.

Every thought in my head came to a complete halt with every scream. every time I stopped, I started pictured myself without hair. Would I look good? Would I look *better*?

I could just cut it all off and no one would be able to stop me. No one would know.

BANG-BANG—

I loosened my grip on the pillow, grabbing my hair in fistfuls. Tangling my fingers until they were locked onto my scalp. Strands stretched like spaghetti, snapping off in tufts as I pulled. I wondered how hard I would have to pull for it all to come out.

It took me a second to notice that everything was getting quieter.

The whole world got less loud, and I wondered if this was it. The music had finally deafened me. Or maybe the screaming into a pillow had popped my eardrums. Weirdly, the thought comforted me. How peaceful would the world be if I couldn't hear anything?

The TV started crackling.

I paused, slowly removing the pillow from my face. As I sat up, I realized I wasn't alone. The door was open, and my little sister was sitting at the foot of my bed.

"*Harleigh—*"

"Look! Hayden, *look!*"

I snatched the clicker out of her hands, almost knocking her off the bed. She climbed off herself, running over to the TV and smudging her tiny fingers all over the screen.

"Get *off* the TV—"

"Hayden, *look!*"

I was about to switch back to MTV when something on the screen caught my eye. Some news channel. The same one Mom watched. Harleigh must've memorized the number, or something.

I was about to click away when Harleigh pulled her hands back from the TV, revealing some reporter stood outside some house.

Except I recognized the house.

I stared for a moment, trying to work out where I'd seen it before.

"*...with her sister reportedly being the victim of a date rape scandal, the family are becoming increasingly concerned about the—*"

"*Bwooke!* Bwooke!"

"Yeah, yeah..." I sat up slightly, rubbing my face. Trying to figure out how to get Harleigh out of my room before she started repeating that name over and over and over. She hadn't seen Brooke in a while. She'd learned how to say her name, and now she wouldn't stop saying it. One of the many reasons I wanted to keep her out of my fucking room.

"Bwooke—"

"*Yes*, Brooke," I repeated angrily. "I get it—"

Then I recognized the house on the TV.

Maybe it was hearing her name—over and over—that really made the connection form in my brain. I watched the reporter as she continued to talk outside the house that looked an awful lot like Brooke's.

"*...with new and troubling details emerging, police have shifted their full attention to Brooklyn Nicholson's disappearance, intensifying their investigation...*"

It was at this point that they displayed her photograph. Her school picture.

Shit.

It really was her.

"*...she was last seen at her home in Mirrenville on Friday evening... when her parents woke up the next morning, she was already gone...*"

I slowly leaned forward, reading the headline below the picture. The writing was yellow. *LOCAL TEEN GOES MISSING*.

"*...her family say that it is out-of-character, and, frankly, very concerning that she has just left home without giving any explanation...*"

They were filming right outside her house.

I'd spent half my life walking past that house, and being inside it. I'd spent every Friday night in that house since the third grade.

"*...Brooklyn's father—Frankie Flash—has been living a low-profile life since his days of fame in the 1970s, choosing to settle in Mirrenville to raise his family...*"

You know, I always forgot that Brooke's dad was kind of famous. Or, at least, he used to be.

The headline changed to *FRANKIE FLASH'S DAUGHTER MISSING*, and I could only imagine how hard

Brooke would've cringed if she was watching this. It was kinda lame, you know—calling an old guy something as uncool as "Frankie Flash".

I don't think it had really hit me, at this point, what all of this meant. It wasn't really sinking in.

I instinctively grabbed my walkie-talkie from my bedside table, pushing the red button down. My mouth opened, and I was about to speak into it when it suddenly hit me what was really going on.

Oh, shit.

I knew where she was.

The reporter kept going on and on about how her parents didn't know where she was, and it became so blatantly obvious what was going on. She wasn't *missing*. She just hadn't told her parents where she'd gone. She wouldn't have even told Allie.

Any other time, she probably would've told me... but, well, we weren't friends anymore.

I hadn't felt particularly concerned when I first saw the headline, but now I felt less concerned than ever. I knew exactly where she was, and I knew why she was there. And the thought of her *being* there lit a fire in my chest, making me feel physically nauseous, but not because I was scared for her. It was because I was *mad* at her.

She was the smartest person I'd ever known, yet I had never known someone to be as fucking stupid as she was. I knew exactly where she was—and why she was there—because Brooke was the most predictable fucking person that had ever lived.

She was a fucking *idiot*.

They were showing her parents now. They were standing in the front yard, looking all serious and shit. I mean, I guess they really were worried about this. *They* didn't know where she was.

Their names came up on the screen as they spoke: *Elizabeth Nicholson* and *Frankie Flash*.

So fucking embarrassing.

"*...she went up to her room, and when I woke up the next morning, she was gone,*" Brooke's dad said, causing my eyebrows to instinctively knit together. "*She could've left at some point in the evening. We're not sure.*"

"*Someone slipped drugs into our oldest daughter's drink at a party on Friday,"* Brooke's mom added. *"And we're not sure if it happened to Brooke, too... we don't know what happened..."*

An abrupt laugh burst through my lips.

I mean, come *on.* Allie didn't need another person to slip something into her drink. Slipping Allie drugs would be like slipping vodka into my Mom's coffee—no point. There's already some in there.

One part of this wasn't making any sense, though. I was just mulling it over when I sensed someone standing behind me. Before I even turned to look at them, I knew it wasn't Harleigh; they were too tall. I twisted my whole body toward the door to see three figures standing in my doorway.

I wasn't sure what surprised me more—the two cops standing outside my bedroom, or Mom suddenly being awake.

"They want to talk to you," Mom sniffed, tugging at her robe to cover her chest.

I'd learned early on not to get too comfortable around cops. They'd smile at my mom—even when she was entirely shit-faced, which she usually was—but *me*? They looked at me different.

Like I seriously needed to be reminded that I didn't look like the rest of my family.

It was at that moment that I began subconsciously scanning my surroundings to figure out where Harleigh had gotten to. Maybe she was hiding. Dumb move—if she'd shown herself at that moment, maybe the cops would've swooped her away to a nicer home. She seriously had no idea of the opportunity that she was missing here.

I wished they could've taken me, but something told me I was too old for them to care about at this point.

"Hello, Hayden," the guy cop said, and I folded my arms.

"They were going to send me home anyway."

He watched me, visibly confused. So did the girl cop. I shrugged my shoulders, imagining Sister Bennett calling the cops on me. She *seriously* was obsessed with me.

"There was no point staying," I continued. "They were going to call my Mom to come get me... it wasn't like I was skipping school or anything—"

"We're not here about that."

My eyes wandered back to the TV, back to Brooke's picture. Reality finally dawned on me.

Oh.

"We know you and Brooklyn are close..." The guy cop stepped into my room, causing me to instinctively freeze up. "So we wanted to ask you a couple of questions. Maybe you could help us."

"I don't know where she is."

No one hated Brooke more than me at that moment, and I *knew* how good it would've felt to have tattled there and then.

But I wasn't a snitch. Never had been.

"Just relax, alright? You're not in trouble—"

"I know," I replied, staring right back at him. "Because I didn't do anything."

"No one is saying you did."

We weren't even *friends* anymore.

I hated her guts. And she hated mine. And yet, somehow, here I was, *lying* to the *law* just to keep her out of trouble. She didn't deserve me. She never did.

"We just want to find her and bring her home," the cop said, his face softening a little. "You want that too, right?"

I turned back to the television, watching her parents. Watching her dad. They kept going on about how she might've *run away* on Friday night, and that was the last time that *anyone* saw her. They saw her just after she got home from school, and that was it. Never seen again.

See, that was the part that I didn't get. *That* was the part that confused the shit out of me.

I mean... why were they lying?

ADJACENT

3 DAYS AFTER THE DISAPPEARANCE OF
BROOKLYN NICHOLSON

FRANK | 7:23 AM

"*Why are they just standing there?*" I heard Cam ask as I stood at the window, staring out at the topic of our conversation: three reporters huddled near the curb, their breath visible in the chilly morning air.

They were all wearing these long trench coats, the kind that made them look like they'd come straight off the set of a detective show. One of them was holding a microphone in one hand, occasionally raising it as if ready to pounce on any movement from our front door.

A network logo was emblazoned on the mic. *That* surprised me. All we'd done was speak to the local news the day before. Suddenly, the story was network-worthy.

"Grab a bowl," Liz said suddenly, trying to catch Allie's

attention as she wandered into the room. I was surprised to see her up so early, especially given what she'd been through over the past few days.

"I'm not hungry," Allie muttered, unscrewing the lid from the carton of OJ. She lifted it to her lips and took a long gulp, only for Liz to snatch it from her hands.

"Then grab a *glass*."

It was weird for me, being there in the morning. On a weekday, at least. And what made it feel even stranger was seeing one less person at the table than usual.

As Allie lingered over her little brother's shoulder, swiping a dry piece of toast when Liz wasn't looking, my eyes drifted to the empty chairs around the table; more specifically, to the one Brooke had always claimed as her own. It was the one in the corner, furthest from the door, the place she'd chosen to be as far from the chaos as possible.

As the morning stretched on, it was becoming abundantly clear why she did so.

"How are you feeling?" I asked suddenly, noticing Allie scratching her arm. There was a raw, lumpy patch on her skin from where she'd been clawing at herself. She stopped almost immediately, as if she hadn't realized what she was doing before that moment.

"I'm good," she replied, leaning against the door. "I guess."

"The fever's gone down," Liz said as she placed a hand over Allie's forehead. "Dr. Longden said it should all be out of your system by tomorrow—"

"Stop *touching* me—"

"I just hope you learn from this! You can't just… leave drinks lying around," Liz went on. Allie groaned loudly, moving away from her. "And the fact that you think it's okay to drink at your age is beyond me."

"You should ground me," Allie replied dryly, causing me to tense up. "That usually works, right?"

The tension in the room thickened as Allie's words hung in the air, laced with a bitterness that twisted the knife even deeper. Even Cam froze up, watching his mother and his sister with his mouth wide open, milk dribbling down his chin.

Thankfully, Liz hadn't heard her. Or, at least, she ignored the comment. She continued to rush around the table, picking up plates of food that no one had even gotten the chance to touch yet.

"Mr. Bird would be rolling in his grave if he knew that his property had been turned into some... some *fraternity house*," she continued, her face scrunching in disgust. "Such a beautiful house, too. What was he thinking, leaving it to Fitz?"

"It was his birthday, wasn't it?" I asked, to which Allie nodded. "The kid's allowed to have a birthday party, Liz. And he already lived there. It would've been worse for Bird to kick his grandson out of the house he already lived in, right? It must be hard enough for him already, losing his grandfather."

"But he should *respect* the house," she replied sharply, piling up the empty plates that weren't being used. "And I'm surprised his father is letting him get away with it."

"Why do they call it the "Bird House"?" Cam asked suddenly, grabbing the box of Frosted Flakes to pour himself a second helping. "It doesn't look like a birdhouse. It looks like the White House."

"That's their name, kiddo," I replied, moving closer to ruffle his hair. "It's the *Birds'* house."

"I wish I could go there."

"Well, you're not," Liz said, tugging the cereal box from his hand. "You're going to school. Go get dressed."

He pulled a face, wiping his milk-soaked chin with the back of his hand. His Power Rangers pajamas were a size too big; the cuffs dragged slightly on the floor as he hopped down from his chair. Despite the tension that had filled the room just moments ago, his innocent curiosity and boundless energy brought a brief, welcome distraction.

"Aw, *Mom*, I wasn't *done* yet," Cam protested as Liz began blotting the mess on his shirt with a napkin.

"You'll survive until lunch," Liz replied, her tone softening a little as she folded the cereal box and set it aside. "Hurry up. You can't miss the bus again."

He began stomping out of the room, grumbling about how he wished he could live in a big house like Fitz Bird's instead of going to school. His demeanor quickly switched as he scooped the cat up from under the table, carrying him with him out of the room.

What followed was the sounds of deep hissing and my son's

high-pitched singing: "…*magical Mr. Misty-fee-fee*…"

I watched him go, the sound of his feet thudding against the stairs fading as he disappeared down the hall, dragging the cat along with him. I smiled at the door, shaking my head. "How the hell does he have so much energy in the morning?"

"Well, I've said it for months—we need to switch to something sugar-free," Liz replied, her tone carrying a hint of exasperation. Allie picked up the box, sticking her arm inside.

"But… *theeeey're GREAT!*" She tossed a handful of golden flakes into her mouth, crunching loudly as she leaned against the wall. Despite her best efforts to maintain a rebellious front, I could see a faint glimmer of amusement in her eyes. Liz pushed past her, barely acknowledging our daughter's dumb impersonation.

It suddenly occurred to me that this was the most normal our lives had felt in almost 72 hours.

For the past few days, everything had been consumed by a thick fog of dread and uncertainty. The police, the phone calls, the endless pacing—none of it felt real. But in this small, fleeting moment, with Allie's snark comments and Liz's frustration, there was a flicker of the everyday life that had almost gone forgotten.

"Are you working today?" Liz asked Allie, and she shook her head. "Good. You can help us with posters."

And just like that, we were brought back to the present.

"I've photocopied a bunch of your sister's school pictures," she continued, picking up Cam's now-empty bowl. "And I've put all her details on it… her hair color, eye color, height—"

"You seriously think anyone's going to look at her eye color?" Allie's voice was flat, almost disbelieving. She then glanced over at me, for backup. I subtly shook my head, silently reminding her not to question her mother's motives.

I agreed with her, of course—seriously, who would notice her eye color?—but Liz was on a mission, and there was no point in arguing with her. She was keeping herself busy. It was all any of us could do.

"It's just… *what you do*," Liz said quietly, trying to hold onto some semblance of control, her voice wavering slightly as she moved into the kitchen. "The police said it's important… *every detail matters!*"

As she left the room, Allie's eyes locked on mine. She lowered her voice as she folded her arms. "I still think she's with Hayden."

"Well, she's not," I replied, turning back toward the window. "Your mom went there yesterday. Spoke to her mom."

"They could be hiding her."

A faint siren began playing outside, seemingly getting closer. I moved closer to the window, trying to get a better look. The siren's wail grew louder, piercing through the quiet tension of the morning.

"...*what color eyes does she have, anyway*?"

My gaze followed the road just in time to see a police car speed past the house, its lights flashing. I watched it disappear around the corner just as quickly as it appeared; the screeching of its tires echoing in the stillness of the neighborhood. I barely had a moment to process before another police car followed, and then a third.

"...what's going on?"

Allie's voice broke through my thoughts. I turned to see her standing next to me, her face a mix of confusion and fear. Her presence was almost ghostly, as if she had materialized beside me without me even noticing. A chill ran down my spine as a fourth car sped past down the street. Part of me was relieved that they weren't stopping at our place, but it raised further questions. They were moving quickly.

Allie and I turned to face the kitchen door at the same time, noticing Liz in the doorway. Her eyes locked onto mine, and I knew the same thoughts were running through her mind. She began moving her hand in that familiar pattern—forehead, chest, shoulder to shoulder.

"*Are you seeing this*?!" Cam's voice suddenly bellowed down the stairs. "*This is SO COOL*—"

"I'm going to call the station," Liz said suddenly, turning back into the kitchen. "Maybe they've found something—"

"They'd call us if they'd found something." The words came from my mouth before I could even think about what I was saying. "They'd come straight here. Something else must be going on."

Nothing *ever* happened in Mirrenville.

The most excitement we got was the occasional minor traffic incident or a neighborhood dispute. Seeing multiple police cars racing down the street like this was not just unusual—it was downright startling.

Something bad had happened.

"It's *fine*, honey," I called out, hearing Liz unhooking the phone. "They'd stop at the house if they thought—"

"You think it's something to do with Brooke?" Allie asked suddenly, her eyes widening. I shook my head, keeping cool. Trying my damn hardest to prevent any of them from panicking further.

"They'd come *here* if it was that," I repeated calmly, moving past her to get to the kitchen. "Liz, just put the phone down..."

A fifth car zoomed past the window, and I heard Cam giggling with excitement at the top of the stairs. It suddenly occurred to me that this was the first time he'd ever heard police sirens in real life. Allie, on the other hand, was a stark contrast to her little brother; she was biting her nails, her gaze flickering between me and the window, desperate for some sort of reassurance that I didn't have.

"...hello? Yes?" Liz's voice echoed from the kitchen. "*Yes*, I just wanted to know why half a dozen police cars just came *flying* past my house—"

Outside, the distant sound of sirens continued to fade, and the neighborhood returned to its usual quiet rhythm. I stared out the window, a million and one scenarios running through my head. I told myself there was no point speculating. It wouldn't help anyone.

I knew we'd find out soon enough.

FITZ | 7:34 AM

I probably wouldn't have heard the knocking if Scruff hadn't started whining at the foot of my bed. Looking back, I don't think I was fully conscious. I didn't even know what time it was.

The past few days had all been a blur, and I still hadn't fully recovered from Friday night.

When the second knock came, I continued to ignore it.

When the *third* one came, I became overcome with dread, realizing that I probably had to answer it.

I slowly sat up, stretching my arms out as I dragged myself from my bed and made my way over to the ladder. As I climbed down to the first floor of my room, I tried to remind myself how excited I got when Grandpa first brought up the idea of converting the attic into a "second bedroom". When I was a kid, it was the best thing ever. Now, it just meant it took longer for me to get from one side of the house to the other.

It had only hit me recently—since Grandpa died, and especially since me and Mel broke up—how big the house really was.

When I stayed over as a kid, it somehow seemed smaller, and it wasn't until I got older that I realized that I'd never even entered half of the rooms. Thinking about it, I'd never seen Grandpa going into a lot of the rooms, and we still hadn't gotten around to clearing them out. Dad kept saying he was going to do it at some point, but he never had the time.

I would've thought that he would've been mad about Grandpa leaving the house to me, but he never fought it. Guess he didn't need another property, and I'd basically lived here for the past few years anyway. It was more my home than anyone else's.

The door knocked for the fourth time. It was harder this time.

It was still dark outside, giving me some form of indication that it was, at least, earlier than 9 am. It had to be Mom. She called in sometimes if she was passing on her way to work. Or, if she had food. But she never came this early, not while it was still dark out.

By the time I got to the top of the main staircase, I caught a glimpse of Scruff, pawing at the front door. He'd gotten there before me.

"I got it," I called out as I got closer, kicking on an old pair of sneakers that had been left at the top of the stairs. "I'm *coming*…"

He trailed over to me, slumping down at my feet as I got to the bottom floor. I ruffled him a little, stretching again with a yawn. I could barely make out the outline of a man standing outside the front door, just through the glass.

It wasn't Mom, which threw me a little. There was no way it was one of the guys this early in the morning.

It wasn't Mel, either; the outline was too tall. Besides, I hadn't heard from her since Saturday, and I seriously doubted I'd ever hear from her again. It'd all felt pretty final.

I unlocked the door, pulling it open to reveal two cops staring back at me. A guy and a girl.

"Mr. Bird?"

"Uh… yeah…" I slowly nodded, struggling to take it in. "What's up?"

"We'd like you to come with us to the station."

"I, uh… wait, what?"

A police car was parked up on the driveway, just behind them. For a second, I had to wonder if I was still asleep.

"What's going on?" I repeated, laughing nervously. A million thoughts ran through my head as I tried to figure out why this was happening.

"We'll explain everything once we get you to the station," the guy cop said, and I looked down at Scruff. He was staring back at me, head cocked to the side. Guess he was pretty confused too.

"Right now?" I asked, rubbing my neck. "Am I in trouble?"

"We'd appreciate it if you just co-operated with us, Mr. Bird."

Something felt off.

Don't get me wrong—this wouldn't be my first time getting into the back of a police car. But this was the first time that I had no idea why I would be doing it. The looks on their faces kept throwing me off, too. They had these weird expressions, especially the girl cop.

"Uh… sure." I nodded again, gesturing behind me. "I just need to get changed—"

"No need."

Scruff was whining again, pushing up against my legs. He knew something was up too. "Well, what about my dog? Can I call someone to come get him?"

"You can make personal calls at the station."

They didn't like me. I could see it on both their faces, clear as anything. As my brain became more awake, I started to wonder if this had anything to do with Allie's sister.

"I won't be long," I said as I kneeled down next to Scruff, pulling him in for a hug. "I won't be long, alright? Be good."

With that, I grabbed a jacket and shut the front door behind me, locking it up behind us. I couldn't remember if Mom was working or not. Someone had to feed Scruff, and I wasn't sure how long this was going to take.

The girl cop opened the back door of the car for me to get inside, and I couldn't shake the feeling that something bad had happened.

It had to be something to do with the party.

It *had* to be.

No one said a word while we were in the car. They didn't even switch the radio on.

I looked out the window, trying to think rationally about the whole thing. Trying to work out what the hell was going on here. I groaned quietly as I realized that I was going to have to explain this to my parents. Dad wasn't going to take it well. He never did.

The station was only a 20-minute ride from my place, but for some reason, they took the long way around town.

I noticed pretty quickly that we were moving toward St. Mary's. We were going to pass Mel's house. *Great*. The last thing I needed was for her to see me riding past her place in a cop car. I still didn't know what time it was. Maybe she was in school already.

As we got closer to the school, we passed another police car. Then, another. There were a couple of them, all heading in the same direction.

As we got past the school—toward Mel's street—I noticed them all parked up. They'd all pulled up right at the end of the street, near her house. The sirens got louder as we got closer.

Then I noticed the yellow tape.

It was wrapped around the front lawn of the house on the end. Cops were swarming the place, guarding the house.

Mel's house.

"What's going on?" I asked, not realizing how loud my voice was at first. The pieces hadn't fit together yet. A pit of dread pooled in my stomach as the sirens got louder and louder, but my question was left unanswered. No one said a word. It was as if I hadn't even said anything.

A bunch of people were gathered around outside the house, trying to get closer. Some of them were crying. Cops were turning them away, clearing the area. That was when I spotted Tanya—

Mel's mom. She was outside the house, behind all the tape, hugging some guy… Mel's dad. Jesus. She was *hugging* Mel's dad.

Mel said they'd split up when she was a kid, and they hated each other. This was the first time I'd ever seen them together. And they were *hugging*.

No… no, they weren't hugging.

He was holding her. She was crying. Sobbing.

Mel wasn't with them.

"What the *fuck* is going on?!" I started shouting, grabbing the seat in front of me. The guy cop spun around, glaring at me.

"You stay quiet—"

"WHAT THE FUCK IS GOING ON?!"

Tanya was barely standing. Mel's dad was holding her up, and… and he was crying too. I'd never seen him cry before. He just wasn't that kind of guy. He never cried.

"JUST TELL ME WHAT'S GO—"

The words trailed from my mouth as I saw guys in white coats leaving the house. They had masks on. They were carrying something.

I couldn't see it. I couldn't see what they were doing.

I just kept scanning the crowd, trying to find her. It didn't make sense. *It didn't make sense.*

We turned around the corner, leaving the house behind. It started to get quieter, and I could hear my heartbeat in my ears. Complete panic set in. Hysteria. I couldn't think. I couldn't process anything.

I heard Tanya MacKenzie one last time.

I could've sworn I heard her scream.

4 DAYS AFTER THE DISAPPEARANCE OF BROOKLYN NICHOLSON

ALLIE | 3:14 PM

Any other day, my little brother would've attempted to swing so high that he'd fly over the top bar, making a perfect loop. He'd gotten close a couple times. Every time he'd beat his own personal record, getting just a little bit closer each time. It was impressive, honestly.

Today, he'd barely even gotten himself off the ground. He just kept kicking himself up a little, barely moving.

It felt different, it just being the two of us.

Every Wednesday I'd pick him and Brooke up from school, and we'd drive by the playground for an hour. Mick used to do it with me and Brooke when we were little kids, and when I got my license, I took over the responsibility. We did it every week without fail. It was our thing.

"*...where do you think Brooke is?*"

I dug my heels into the soil beneath me, slowing myself down to a halt. Of all the things to come out of his mouth, I had not expected that question. He'd barely said anything since we'd gotten there, and it was one hell of an opener.

"I mean…" He kicked a rock from beneath him, watching it skim across the field ahead of us. "Do you really think she ran away?"

"I don't know, Cam."

I didn't want to make a big deal out of it, but he hadn't even so much as mentioned Brooke since everything had happened.

He wouldn't talk about her at all, no matter how many times Mom tried to make out that "*everything was fine*" and "*we should still talk about her*". He'd either change the subject or go real quiet whenever she was mentioned. I figured he was just as scared as the rest of us, if not more so. I mean, he was just a kid.

The thing was, I didn't want to talk about her either.

"I don't think she did," he went on, continuing to kick the grass beneath his feet. "She was happy. She didn't want to run away."

"We don't know how she was feeling," I replied, unsure of how I was supposed to safely navigate this conversation with a 10-year-old.

"Did she say anything to you? About not being happy?"

We hadn't said a whole lot to each other that week. I couldn't even remember our last conversation.

"She was stressed about school, and everything," I thought back, trying to remember the details. "But, you know… that's the way it's always been. She's always got stuff going on."

"Her big competition was this week," he added, kicking himself a little higher. "With the cheerleaders."

"Yeah."

"Do you think they'll still do it, now that cheerleader's dead?"

That caught me off guard.

Maybe it was how casual he sounded, or the fact that it just hadn't sunk in yet. And how the hell did *he* know about Melissa MacKenzie? He'd been in school all day. It was all over the news, sure, but it'd only been a couple hours since her name had been officially released.

The one thing that had amazed me over these past few days—

more than anything else—was how quickly news could spread.

"Was she friends with Brooke?" he asked, and a laugh slipped out. I quickly shook my head, trying to rein it back in. It felt inappropriate, given everything that had happened.

"No," I replied, trying to keep a poker face. "They weren't."

"Why not?"

Because Melissa MacKenzie was a fucking asshole.

"Because Melissa MacKenzie was cheer captain, and she put a lot of pressure on Brooke," I said instead. "She... well, she singled her out all the time. Yelled at her a lot."

"How do you know?"

I thought back, remembering how many times I'd walked into our room to find Brooke hiding under her covers, bawling her eyes out.

I thought about each time she'd refused to say a word on the ride home because she was scared of what I would do if she'd told me too much.

I'd told her so many times that *I'd* deal with Melissa. Hell, I would've made damn sure that she never said a bad word against my sister ever again. Brooke wouldn't let me get involved, and it tore me apart every time I had to watch that smug bitch walk past my car after school, biting my tongue until it bled.

And I knew damn well that if I hadn't held myself back, not only would Brooke have gotten mad at me, but it would've caused shit between me and Fitz too. I'd have to reason with myself every single time, in my head, convincing myself that it wasn't worth it.

Don't get me wrong—no one deserves to die, especially not in the way that she did. It was so scary what had happened to her. And Fitz was my best friend; I felt so bad for him, *and* her family. The whole situation was so fucked up.

But, my *God* she was a bitch.

"Al?"

"Hm?" I cleared my throat, dragging myself back to the present moment. Reminding myself of what I could and couldn't say in front of my baby brother. "I don't know... we talked about it sometimes."

I just couldn't shake the weird, heavy feeling inside my chest whenever I remembered that the two people we were talking about—two people that I once saw on a daily basis—were gone.

One of them was never coming back.

"Maybe Brooke killed Melissa."

My head snapped toward him. "That's *not* funny, Cam—"

"I'm not kidding! Maybe… maybe Brooke got sick of Melissa pushing her around, so she finally did something about it," he started rambling, a glint of excitement glazing over his eyes. "And *that's* why she ran away!"

His reaction was nothing new to me. I'd seen it on so many people's faces over the past 48 hours, whenever Brooke or Melissa were mentioned—whenever someone had come up with some sort of theory of what had happened. They just thought it was all so *exciting*. One big *mystery*. Everyone wanted to know who killed Melissa MacKenzie, and in which room, with what weapon.

My best friend's girlfriend had been brutally murdered in her own home, and my little sister had been missing for four days. I just couldn't find the excitement in either scenario.

And I didn't even care when I first found out. About Brooke going missing, I mean. I used to run away all the time, and when *I* left, I was usually gone for a lot longer than four days. And Brooke had all these *recitals* and *tournaments* and *school shit* coming up, and Mom was on her back, so it made sense that she needed to get away for a day or two. Whatever. I got it.

I did *not* give a shit until I heard about Melissa.

They were on the same cheer squad. Same school. Similar ages. I mean, what were the odds, right?

It'd been four days, and there had been no word from anyone. Not a *single person* had any information that helped us. In a town this small, it just seemed impossible that someone like my sister could go missing. Everyone knew her… or, at least, everyone knew *us*. Everyone knew my family.

It'd been less than six hours since I'd found out what happened to Melissa, and since then, it was all I could think about.

"Just…" I shook my head. "*Jesus*… don't say shit like that."

He stayed quiet, fidgeting with the flimsy bracelet around his wrist. I hadn't seen it in a while, and I hadn't noticed that he'd started wearing his again. I hadn't seen mine in a while. Brooke had made one for the four of us when she was a little kid; they all had a bead on them with the first initial of our names.

Cam's was yellow. I think mine was purple.

Birds were chirping in the trees above us, and I almost felt peaceful for a moment. I closed my eyes. Cam kept swinging beside me, and I just waited, already dreading what was going to come out of his mouth next.

"...*Al?*"

"Yeah?"

"*If I knew something about Brooke, but it could get someone in trouble, should I still say something?*"

My eyelids sprung open. "What?"

"I was just—"

"Do you know something?"

"*No,*" he scoffed, sounding just a little too defensive. "I was just... I don't know—"

"Cam," I stared right at him, but he was avoiding eye contact. "If you know *anything*, and you think you should say something, you tell me. Do you hear me?" He stayed quiet. I shoved him hard, almost knocking him off the swing. "Do you *hear* me?!"

"*Yes!*"

"I'm *so* serious right now. She could be in *serious* trouble, so if you know *anything*—"

"I was *kidding!*" He blew a raspberry, turning his head. "Like she *ever* talked to *me* about that kind of stuff... she never told me *anything*—"

I stopped listening when I noticed someone was watching us.

It was so strange; I wasn't even sure why—or how—I noticed them. They weren't even doing anything out of the ordinary. It was just some guy wearing a dark green hooded sweatshirt... or, I suppose it could've been a girl. I couldn't see their face, and I couldn't work out how tall they were from that distance.

They were standing just across the road, lingering in the entrance to the alleyway next to the Turtin bar. They weren't doing anything weird, per se.

But they *were* watching us.

My initial instinct was to stare back. I knew, through personal experience, that staring back usually made the other person feel awkward enough to look away. There were a lot of creeps around Mirrenville, but half of them would give up a staring contest once they'd realized they'd been caught.

But this person didn't.

"Who is that?" I heard Cam asking, and some sort of maternal instinct kicked in. I shook it off, turning back to face him.

"I don't know."

"They're wearing your sweatshirt."

At first, I wasn't sure what he was talking about.

I had no idea why he would even think that, but suddenly, it clicked. The green sweatshirt. It looked just like the ones the guys wore in school: Hurley, Donnie, and the rest of the guys. The *Eezy's*... God, even just thinking of that word made me throw up in my mouth a little. I *hated* that everyone called us that. It just sounded so lame. I couldn't even remember who came up with it. Thinking back, it was probably Freddie.

As I looked back over at the mystery stalker, it became clear to me that it *was* an Eezy sweatshirt—not just a school one.

Ours had everyone's names written on it in black marker, faded to purple. We all had one, even though they were technically made for St. Mary's students only; we'd entirely defaced ours, though, with black marker. Mine was stuffed somewhere in the back of my wardrobe, and I hadn't seen the others wear theirs since graduation.

Upon this realization, I automatically lifted my arm to wave at them. I wondered if I'd be able to recognize who it was based on their response. It *had* to be one of the guys.

Before I could figure it out, they began moving backward, retreating inside the alleyway.

That was when I knew something was wrong.

"...*is it one of your friends?*"

No one ever went inside that alleyway.

No one from around here *ever* went through there. It was just one of those unwritten rules. The alleyway was pitch black inside, and it stretched on for miles. The thought of someone walking inside made me freeze up in fear, knowing that none of my friends would've done that. None of them would dare.

As they disappeared from my line of sight, it hit me that something was seriously wrong.

I had no idea who this person was.

"...*maybe it's the killer*..."

I rotated back toward Cam with a heavy force. Rage and terror rose up inside me simultaneously, ready to burst out. "Stop it—"

"I'm just *saying*! And the only reason you're getting so freaked out is because you know I could be right!"

I stood up from the swing, staring back toward the alleyway. They were gone. Or, at least, they were out of my sight. The idea of them standing in the darkness, watching us from within, made me want to throw up. I could not pinpoint why this made me feel so uneasy, but my whole body was freezing over.

"It's time to go."

"Why?"

I didn't answer him.

Instead, I grabbed his wrist and pulled him up off the swing.

"Al, *stop*—" He tried to tug away from me, but my grip was unbreakable. I dragged him through the gate, toward my car. I just couldn't shake the feeling that something sketchy was going on. There was no doubt in my mind that we were being watched, even if I couldn't see them anymore.

When we got to my car, I finally looked down at him. He looked pretty unsettled. I quickly unlocked the car, trying to calm myself down. I spun back toward the empty alleyway, seeing no one. Not even a shadow.

Maybe I'd overreacted.

"Hey... it's just some weirdo," I said finally, squeezing his hand. "Probably some drunk guy from the bar."

"Well, why were they wearing your sweater?" he asked, and the coldness returned, even if just for a second. A lump formed in my throat.

"They weren't," I said, not entirely sure why I was lying to him. Maybe I was trying to convince myself that was the truth. "It's fine, alright? We're fine. Don't worry."

"Why would I be worried?"

Such a smart-ass.

"Just... get in the car," I opened the door, ushering him inside. "We're going home."

"*Jeez*...whatever..."

LUCY | 10:55 PM

"*...all units, be advised, we have a report of a 187 on Pine Street...*"

A few words over the radio. Easy to miss.

If I'd been in another car, with anyone but Anderson, we might have missed it. Neither of us had said a word on the ride back to the station, so the call rang clear into both our ears.

"*...proceed with caution and await further instructions...*"

With a muffled groan, Anderson began reversing out of the parking lot, taking us back onto the road which now appeared warped and blurred.

My heart was beating so fucking fast. It's crazy to think that less than a week ago, a call like this would have been so unexpected we wouldn't have believed it. Now, not only was it expected, but we'd been silently anticipating it for our entire shift.

I wondered who it was.

The whole ride there, I thought about each of the faces that I knew. Freddie Kowalski. Fitzgerald Bird. Allie Nicholson's profile flashed through my brain and I almost threw up all over the dashboard. It *couldn't* be her. It wouldn't be fair.

It occurred to me—of course—that this wasn't going to be fair on *whoever's* family it had happened to. All I could do, at that moment, was pray that Frank and Liz Nicholson hadn't lost another daughter.

"*...the victim is described as male, 18 years old ...*"

A sigh of relief escaped my mouth, my lungs collapsing internally. Thank God. Thank *God*.

"*...EMS is en route...*"

Anderson seized the radio so forcefully that it made me flinch. He held it to his mouth, steering the car with one hand, and he hesitated for a moment. I stared at the road ahead, somehow already knowing the words that were about to leave his mouth.

"Dispatch, confirming the 187 at Pine Street," I heard him say. "Any information on whether Donnie Booker is on the scene?"

He shouldn't have asked that.

I'm not entirely sure why he did.

"*Negative, Officer.*"

We had just located Donnie Booker's car deep in the woods, about five miles out from Fitz Bird's place.

Donnie hadn't reported it missing himself, but we'd received word that someone else had. Some guy walking his dog in the area had reported a burning smell, leading us to the burnt-out vehicle. It was a total loss—hardly making sense at that point—but conclusions were already being drawn. Donnie Booker knew Melissa MacKenzie, and he knew Allie, which potentially connected him to Brooke.

Despite finding nothing salvageable in the car, with everything being reduced to ash, it was safe to say that we were all silently presuming the same scenario.

I really, really hoped we were wrong.

"It's got to be one of them," I heard Anderson mutter, allowing me to return to the present. I nodded in silence, agreeing.

Part of me wanted to talk about it out loud. I wanted to ask him who he thought it was. The victim, I mean. If it wasn't Donnie Booker, that could only strengthen our current theory.

The streets lit up red and blue as we pulled onto Pine Street, guiding us through the darkness. I barely got to collect my thoughts before we were jumping out of the car, tunneling our way through the crowd. Anderson led the way, moving everyone out of his path. I tried to keep up.

Most people weren't moving, and I couldn't see past them. There were so many of them—the whole street had made an appearance, trying to figure out what had happened. We were just far away enough at this point that we couldn't see what was going on for ourselves, so those around us really had no idea what was going on. They just knew that it was something bad.

I wasn't sure if I felt better or worse, knowing in advance.

"*MOVE!*" Anderson yelled as he squeezed his way through, clearing the way like a bulldozer through loose gravel. I caught glimpses of mothers holding babies, standing back while their kids ran wild, standing on tiptoes for a better view of what was going on. It shook me, how invested they were getting.

They could hear the sirens. They *knew* what had happened to Melissa MacKenzie less than 24 hours prior.

They should've known better.

The closer we got, the quieter it got. Everyone toward the back of the crowd was talking, laughing, speculating—figuring out what was happening. Those at the front of the crowd could see what had happened, and they knew better than to speak. They stood in silence, allowing us to pass through.

I caught a glimpse of two officers winding yellow tape around the front of the yard. Anderson walked straight up to them, pulling out his badge. I reached for mine. My fingers were so sweaty that the metal almost slipped from my grasp.

The one officer nodded slightly, taking a step back. "Go ahead." We ducked under the tape, entering the yard.

I couldn't see any ambulances, leading me to believe that we were some of the first on the scene. I'd never seen anything like this, and I was fighting so hard not to let it show. But the truth was, I was terrified. I wasn't there when they found Melissa MacKenzie.

This was going to be my first time.

"...*just over there*," one of the officers said to Anderson as I attempted to snap out of my gaze. "*Friends of the deceased are still with him. They've got to get out of here.*"

"Has he been identified?"

There was a group of them, loosely scattered in one small area toward the back of the yard: three on the ground, two standing. Four boys and a girl.

I recognized all of them.

Freddie Kaminski was standing against the fence, holding himself up, and a boy I half recognized was staggering around just across from him, vomit spraying from his mouth. On the ground, Fitzgerald Bird was cradling a girl whose face I'd definitely seen before. The fourth boy was lying across her lap, soaked in blood. His own blood. Fitzgerald was holding the girl, and she was holding the body.

Everyone was screaming, but I couldn't hear it. We were inside a vacuum where everything and nothing was happening all at once. It all stood still. The boy's name appeared in whispers around us.

Patrick Hurley. I knew him. His mother taught at the high school. He looked just like her.

He was 18 years old.

I'd honestly believed, up until this point, that I would never see anything as traumatizing as the photographs taken at Melissa MacKenzie's crime scene. It hadn't occurred to me that, seeing it up close, would be so much worse.

Based on the blood seeping through his shirt, the stab wounds were in the same areas of the abdomen as Melissa MacKenzie's. The blood pooled onto the shredded fabric covering his stomach. He was entirely saturated in blood from head to toe. So was his girlfriend.

So was Fitzgerald Bird.

"*...come on, Mand...*" I could hear him saying to her, his voice breaking; "*...he's gone...*"

He was trying to stroke her face, or her hair, but his hands were shaking so much he was practically smacking her. She was sobbing so loud that it was clear she couldn't hear him. He was trying to ease her away. She wasn't letting go.

"We need to get them out of here," Anderson said quietly, and I nodded. That was all I could do.

Even if I'd known what words to say at that moment, I was not physically capable of speaking them out loud.

"*It happened here,*" another officer said. "*They heard it happen, and they came out.*"

"Did they see who did it?"

The officer must've shaken his head, because Anderson let out a grunt. I just couldn't peel my eyes away from them. Even when Fitzgerald Bird looked up—locking eyes with me—I couldn't look away.

"His girlfriend and his friend, on the same day?" Anderson muttered as I continued to stare at him, unable to break away. "What are the odds of that?"

"And *that's* his ex-girlfriend," one of the officers replied, his voice barely rising above the screaming. "The girl... and she's the deceased's *current* girlfriend."

I slowly turned my head toward Anderson and the other officer, desperately blinking away the tears. My head shook on its own as I tried so fucking hard to hold myself together. I couldn't understand how they were so calm. So casual.

"Both victims were part of the same friendship group," I

finally spoke, trembling with each word. "They went to the same school—"

"The same school as Brooklyn Nicholson."

My gaze briefly returned to Freddie. He'd barely paid attention to us up until this point, but now, he was staring right at me. For a fraction of a second, we locked eyes. His had completely glazed over.

"I want to talk to him again," Anderson said, and I had to assume that he was still talking about Fitzgerald Bird. He'd been onto him ever since the party, and now, two murders later, his suspicions were locked in place. Even finding Donnie Booker's car hadn't completely swayed him.

"We need to talk to *all* of them—"

"I know. But I don't trust him, Hardie."

It was so hard, at that moment, to see Fitzgerald Bird as anything but a broken, traumatized kid.

I couldn't even begin to imagine how it would've felt to lose a girlfriend *and* a friend in this way. I scanned each of their faces, trying to conceive the grief they must've felt… and the *fear*. There was no doubt in my mind that they would have each been wondering—*fearing*—who was going to be next.

I think we all shared that exact thought.

6 DAYS AFTER THE DISAPPEARANCE OF
BROOKLYN NICHOLSON

LIZ | 5:37 PM

"I don't understand why they can't just call you."

"They want to see me in person to go through some stuff," Frank replied, grabbing his coat. "It's just to make sure that everything is dealt with while I'm gone. It's fine."

"It's Friday evening, Frank," I muttered, folding my arms. "What could they possibly need you to do this close to the weekend?"

I hadn't even called into work during the first few days after Brooke went missing. The thought hadn't even crossed my mind. When I finally called, they were completely understanding and told me to take as much time off as I needed, no questions asked.

I couldn't understand why Frank's work couldn't extend to him the same courtesy.

"I won't be long," he said, barely even looking me in the eye as he made his way to the front door. "I promise."

"Hm."

I turned back to the dishes as he wandered away, staring at the running tap. It took me a moment to realize that my mind had wandered elsewhere. The sink had almost filled to the brim, spilling over the side. I quickly turned the water off, getting angry with myself.

It just kept happening. The daydreaming. I wasn't even thinking about anything in particular; it was as if my thoughts just escaped me, rendering me numb.

That was the part that confused me. The numbness.

It had been almost a week since I'd last seen my daughter, and despite the initial horror that I felt upon first discovering that she had disappeared, an odd emptiness had taken its place over time.

When the water stopped running, I heard voices coming from the front door. One of them was Frank's, and once I'd worked out that the other voice wasn't Brooke, I immediately lost interest. I dried my hands, taking a moment to notice Misty perched silently on the windowsill, watching everything with his usual indifference. He was just there, as he always was: part of the background, like a piece of furniture.

I wasn't one to read too much into a cat's mood, but there was no denying the change in his demeanor over the past week. He used to be a little more active, more curious, usually following Brooke from room to room. Now, he just sat there, his once-bright eyes clouded over. Even he was lost without her.

My attention wandered back to the voices at the front door, and I wondered if it was Malcolm. He'd been over a lot over the past few days, checking up on us. It was nice, I suppose; he lived almost three hours away, so it was a long drive just to see us. He thought a lot of Brooke, though. He thought a lot of all of us, and we thought a lot of him. He was the closest thing Frank had to a brother.

It wasn't him at the door, though. It was a girl's voice.

My next assumption was that it was Vic. I hadn't seen my youngest sister in almost a month, and no one could get hold of her. It wasn't unusual for her to disappear now and then, but I thought she would at least answer my calls. She was close to Brooke—she was close to *all* of us—but she'd never been the most reliable person.

None of this stopped me from picturing my sister's face at the front door, and the disappointment that filled up my chest when it wasn't her was all too familiar.

"...she said white lilies are her favorite," said the tiny figure standing in my doorway, barely making eye contact with Frank. "And I found these at the store."

"Well, thank you... uh—"

"Rhea Darlow," I interrupted, getting close enough to recognize her face. She looked up at me, smiling sheepishly.

"Hi, Mrs. Nicholson."

Misty slinked past me, brushing past my legs. Rhea's eyes widened as he edged toward her, and she took a step back, clutching the bouquet like a lifeline. Misty, for his part, didn't seem to care. He just sat there, examining Rhea as he figured out whether or not she was worth his attention. Rhea's gaze flicked nervously from Misty to Frank as he swiftly scooped her up, defusing the situation.

"Don't worry, he doesn't bite..." he said with a chuckle, practically tossing him back into the house like a football. "...*too* hard."

I laughed awkwardly, wishing he could just act like a normal human being for five seconds. "Frank, this is Brooke's competition," I quickly interjected, lightly squeezing his shoulder as I moved closer. "She's graduating St. Mary's next year too."

"I-I wouldn't say there's much competition going on," she replied quietly, still nervously eyeing Misty. He continued to linger in the doorway, staring right back at her. "Brooke's practically a genius. I'm just trying to keep up with her."

Brooke and Rhea had been competing for the top spot in school for years—always neck and neck. Rhea was a hard worker, and if anyone could give Brooke a run for her money, it was her.

I was just glad that they weren't letting the rivalry get in the way of their friendship; Brooke seemed to admire Rhea, and based on her actions that day—bringing us flowers—it appeared that the feeling was mutual. It warmed my heart.

Frank handed me the bouquet of white lilies before kissing me on the forehead, swiftly making his way past Rhea. "Well, it was nice to meet you," he said, putting a hand on her shoulder before making his way to his car without saying another word. The shock of seeing Brooke's friend at the door almost made me forget that Frank was in a rush to get away.

I shook my head slightly and forced a wide smile at Rhea, who was watching him drive into the distance. "Thank you so much," I waved the bouquet slightly, "for these. This is really thoughtful of you."

She shrugged slightly, avoiding eye contact and fiddling with the hem of her shirt. Her face was getting redder and redder by the second. I'd only met her a handful of times, but this was the most we'd ever spoken to each other. She was always so quiet. So shy. The complete opposite of Hayden.

"Would you like to come inside?" I asked, and she quickly shook her head. "Are you sure? I can make some hot tea, or I can get you a glass of water—"

"Sorry, Mrs. Nicholson, but... i-is Allie here?"

"Allie?"

If Allie *was* home, I certainly wouldn't have known.

We'd barely seen her over the past few days, not since we found out what happened to Patrick Hurley. She had completely shut herself away from us. Frank had tried talking to her, but even he couldn't get through to her.

I wasn't even sure how close she was to this Patrick Hurley. I recognized the name, but I wasn't sure if I'd ever met him.

I understood that it had to be a shock, especially after what had happened to Tanya MacKenzie's daughter, but the last thing I needed was to worry about Allie on top of everything else. I was already fighting to keep it together for Cam and Frank, and I had to be ready for Brooke when she came home.

Allie wasn't like me in many ways, but she had my strength, and my mother's. Us Crowe women had a knack for keeping it together in the most difficult situations, and I knew she was capable of it—deep, deep down. She just needed some time to adjust.

I only wished I could take some time to adjust too... but, well, *someone* had to keep it together for our family.

"I just wanted to talk to her," Rhea said quietly, her face almost completely hidden behind her scarf. "About... stuff."

"What kind of stuff, sweetie? Anything I can help with?"

Her eyes widened, and I heard footsteps coming from the top of the stairs. I almost couldn't believe it. I turned my head, catching Allie making her way down the stairs for the first time in over 48 hours.

She looked awful. I mean, really awful. The knotted hair and ragged PJs told me what I'd already guessed: she'd been in bed the whole time. Each step creaked as she moved.

"She's *alive*!" I laughed slightly, ignoring the evil look she immediately shot my way. "Come say hi, Al."

"I can't find my sweater."

I shot her a look, trying to subtly indicate that we had company. She barely noticed, as usual. "Al—"

"The easy one, with the writing…" She slowed to a stop when she got to the bottom of the stairs, staring directly at Rhea. "Who are you?"

I wanted to hit her.

"Hi," Rhea barely whispered. "Uh… I'm Rhea. Rhea Darlow. I'm… I'm friends with Brooke."

Allie didn't say a word, and I couldn't stand the silence that followed. I quickly waved the bouquet in front of her, smiling so wide that I thought my face would crack. "Rhea brought flowers! Isn't that thoughtful?"

More silence.

I would've whacked the flowers across her head if we hadn't had company. She really had never looked worse: black eyes, pale skin, and her hair a tangled mess.

She seriously needed to get it together.

Her and Frank were exactly the same—did either of them think that *I* wanted to get up in the mornings? Did they think *I* didn't wish I could just… just take a day or two off to let myself *rot* in bed?

For the first few days, after Brooke went missing, I understood that Allie was going to feel unwell. She had been spiked. The police said it would take a day or two for the drugs to exit her system, but it had been almost a week at this point, and she was still spending her days decomposing in her bed, moving around the house like a zombie.

She had to get it together. We *all* had to get it together.

"What did you want to tell Allie, Rhea?" I asked suddenly,

breaking the silence yet again. Rhea shook her head slightly, looking straight toward my eldest daughter.

"It's… it's nothing, really—"

"Oh, come on Rhea, you've come all this way!"

Her eyes kept anxiously darting between Allie and the ground beneath us. At this point, the silence was killing me. If someone wasn't going to speak in the next few seconds, I thought I would just crumble to the ground. I just couldn't stand it.

To my surprise, it was Allie who spoke first.

"Did you see her the day she went missing?" It came out as a croak, barely legible. Rhea nodded a little, and it suddenly hit me that that should've been a question that *I* asked her.

That should've been the first thing I asked her when I saw her at the door.

"She was in school…" She paused again, her face flushing red. The way she ended her sentence—or, rather, paused her sentence—made me realize that she was about to say something important. Something that she should've been telling me, not just Allie. "I… well… I'm not sure if you know, or not, where she went *after* school."

At first, I wasn't entirely sure what she was talking about. She worded it so oddly. Every word was a struggle for this girl, and while I was empathetic to her nerves, I was starting to become impatient.

"Do *you* know?" I asked, just as Allie was opening her mouth. "I mean… of course, she came home after school, but we're not sure where she went after coming home, or when she left—"

"She went to the party. At the Bird House."

Allie shifted quickly in the corner of my eye, causing me to flinch. I wasn't entirely sure what she did—maybe she stood up a little straighter, or stepped forward. Her reaction was very quick and sudden. It almost distracted me from what Rhea had said.

"She was at the party?" Allie repeated, and Rhea nodded. "*What*… how do you—"

"I'm not entirely certain," she interrupted, her cheeks deepening to a dark shade of red. "But I-I'm, maybe, ninety-nine percent sure. I'm almost positive."

"What makes you say that, Rhea?" I asked, but before she could answer, Allie jumped in:

"She was with Hayden."

She didn't ask it as a question. She didn't even say it in an inquisitive tone. The words came out as if she were stating a fact, and as Rhea nodded, it confirmed her confidence.

"She told me the Friday before that Hayden wanted to go to a party," Rhea continued, looking directly at Allie now. "But... but she didn't want to go. She told me. And then, on the day she went missing, Hayden said that *she* went, but she started acting all... all *weird* when we all asked her if Brooke was with her."

"Hayden said that Brooke didn't go with her," I corrected her, disappointment filling me up as I realized this was a dead end. "She told the police—"

"Hayden's a liar," Allie interrupted in a dull tone, and a small laugh left Rhea's mouth. The two gave each other a knowing look, and I suddenly felt that I wasn't in on the joke. I knew Allie had never been Hayden's biggest fan, but it surprised me that Rhea felt the same way.

"Yeah... I don't believe her," Rhea added, crossing her arms. "She wouldn't have gone without Brooke. She said that the guys they usually hung out with were going to be there, so I figured that Brooke would've gone eventually, even if she didn't want to—"

"What guys?" Allie asked.

I was still trying to catch up, mentally. The image of Brooke being at a high school party seemed so foreign. She wasn't the type of girl to go to parties. She wasn't *Allie*.

"The seniors from last year."

"What seniors?"

"Mandy Melfi, Donnie Booker..." Rhea began listing off some other names that I vaguely recognized, and I felt Allie taking a step forward. "...you know... the Eezy's."

I turned to my daughter, wondering if she had any idea what on earth she was talking about. The easy *what's*?

Allie was smiling, indicating that she, somehow, had understood whatever phrase Rhea had just said out loud. But it wasn't a genuine smile. She appeared to be confused. Frustrated, even. "Brooke didn't hang out with those guys."

"She hung out with them all the time at school."

"No..." A laugh slipped out as Allie tried to find her words. "No, she doesn't know them. They're *my* friends."

99

Rhea's face darkened to a shade that I had never seen a person's skin become before. Her eyes darted to me, and then back to Allie. She began picking at her fingernails, creating this awful *snapping* sound that seemed to go on forever.

"Um… okay… Mrs. Nicholson, is it okay if I-I just talk to Allie for a moment?" she asked quietly. "Please?"

Something told me that I needed to hear what she said next.

"You can tell us both, sweetie," I said with a smile.

"Mom—"

"I'm not going anywhere." The words escaped my mouth a little harsher than intended, but something on Rhea's face told me that she was about to say something important. Something that was going to change everything. I felt it in my gut. "What is it, Rhea?"

She paused, inhaling deeply. Holding her breath. Allie had stepped forward so far that she was practically pushing me backward, leaning into Rhea's face. She could sense it too. Rhea stared directly at her fingers, ripping away at the skin around her nails.

Finally, she took another deep breath, nodding a little, as if she was reassuring herself. "…she didn't want anyone to know… sh-she—"

"Spit it out."

"*Al.*" I dug my elbow into her side, but she barely budged. She was practically breathing directly into Rhea's face, so close that their noses almost touched. The poor girl was on the verge of hyperventilation.

"…it's… it's Donnie Booker."

Misty, who had slumped into a ball at my feet during this conversation, suddenly arched his back and let out a low, menacing hiss. It was a sound I had never heard him make before. It was a remarkable coincidence, almost as if he had some instinctive reaction to the name we were discussing. And clearly, he wasn't fond of it.

I'd heard this name a couple of times over the past few days. Donnie Booker. Again, it was just another name that I associated with Allie. One of her friends from school, I figured. Allie had so many boy friends that I often mixed them up.

Something must've clicked in Allie's head because she

completely tensed up at the mention of his name. "What about him?" she asked slowly.

Rhea finally looked up. Barely. "*Stuff*... happened... between him and Hayden. At the party."

It took a second to understand what she was getting at. It wasn't processing. What *stuff*? What did that mean? Did they have a fight or something?

"I don't know what you're talking about," Allie answered before I could. Maybe I was imagining it, but I could've sworn I sensed a warning tone in her voice. Cold anger. Not that Allie had many other ways of communicating, but it felt odd that she would use this tone with Rhea Darlow.

"It's j-just—"

"What do you mean, "stuff"?" I asked, genuinely confused. "Who is Donnie Booker? Isn't he your friend, Al?"

"Brooke doesn't know any of my friends," Allie added, completely ignoring all three of my questions. "And neither does Hayden. She doesn't know Donnie, or Fitz, or any of those guys—"

"She knew Donnie."

Allie scoffed, shaking her head. I couldn't have felt more out of the loop if I'd tried. It was as if they were talking to each other in their own language, but neither of them wanted to clue me in.

"*Who* is Donnie?" I asked for the second time, but neither of them looked at me. They continued to look straight at each other as if I wasn't even there.

"There were other parties," Rhea added, becoming a little more confident with her words. "They went to them all the time over the summer. Brooke and Hayden. They had one here at one point, just before school started back—"

"There was a party *here*?" I repeated, turning to glare at Allie. "You threw a party *here*?"

"No, Brooke did," Rhea corrected me, but that didn't make any sense. She must've confused my daughters. Brooke would never have thrown a party at our house. Not without telling us.

I continued to watch Allie, who was becoming more and more squeamish as time passed. I couldn't fully work out if she was angry, or confused, or maybe both.

Either way, I had no idea what was going on, and *I* was

becoming angry and confused as the conversation continued.

"So, did Brooke know this Donnie Booker or not?" I asked, only to be met with an immediate "*yes*" from Rhea and a sharp, cold "*no*" from Allie. My brain scrambled to put a face to the name. Was he the kid with the big curly hair? The brown boy whose mother worked at the hair salon on the square? I could not, for the life of me, figure out who we were talking about.

"I just wanted you to know because I think it's important," Rhea replied, once again speaking directly to my daughter. "And I don't think Hayden's going to tell the truth about what really happened that night."

"Sounds like Hayden," Allie muttered, and the same old urge to defend Hayden Butler arose in my throat, just like it did every time Allie had something bad to say about her. She'd never liked her, even when Brooke and Hayden were little kids.

Sure, Hayden's family was a little rough around the edges— and her mother could be more than a handful—but Hayden herself had always been sweet to me.

I just could not comprehend why Allie hated her so much.

"Maybe you should talk to her," Rhea suggested, and Allie laughed again. "Maybe she'll tell you what really happened."

"And how do *you* know what really happened?" Allie asked in a cynical tone. "Did *Hayden* tell you all this?"

"She told all of us at lunch, the day Brooke went missing. She told us about Donnie, and… well… whenever one of us brought up Brooke, she got all weird. I figured something happened with Donnie. Maybe there was a fight after Brooke found out—"

"Okay, can someone *please* tell me what this Donnie boy has to do with *any* of this?!" I asked for the third and final time, becoming exasperated. "Who *is* he?!"

"He's no one."

With those final words, Allie spun around and began making her way back up the stairs. I turned to watch her in total disbelief. As she walked away, I heard four more words: "*Thanks for coming, Rhea.*"

I turned back to Rhea, but she had already made her way up the path, toward the front gate. She'd escaped before even saying goodbye.

I stood still at the door for a moment, trying to process what had just happened. As I struggled to make sense of it all, my gaze fell back on Misty. He had gotten up from his spot and was now pacing back and forth with noticeable agitation. He occasionally shot annoyed glances toward the door, as if the very mention of this mystery boy's name had entirely disturbed his peace.

There were a million-and-one new questions in my mind, but one kept floating back to the forefront each time:

Who on *earth* was Donnie Booker?

LUCY | 5:59 PM

Coffee shops felt more like home to me than anywhere else.

Their warm, inviting atmospheres made it easier to adjust to the damp, misty air of Mirrenville, which was so different from what I had grown used to. Growing up, we'd always stayed in warmer places because my mom couldn't stand the cold, but I'd always found comfort in the colder climate. There was something so soothing about stretching my fingers around a steaming cup of coffee while rain tapped away against the windows. Coffee shops, more so than anywhere else, softened the unfamiliarity of my new surroundings.

Volta Coffee—the little place on the edge of the town square—had very quickly become my new favorite place since moving to Mirrenville. It was my third most-visited place, closely following the station and my apartment.

I usually sat toward the front; just close enough to the counter that I wouldn't have to move too far to grab another drink, and just close enough to the heater that I could keep warm, but not *too* warm. My usual seat was a little round table in the corner, directly adjacent to the big wooden clock, so I could check the time without really having to move my head. Tonight, some couple got there before me, and almost every other seat had been taken, so I had to find a place toward the back.

It wasn't a bad seat, by any means; I could still see everything from this table. I could see every person that entered the room, but I was just far enough away that no one could see me.

No one would notice us sitting together.

If he even showed up, at least.

A Nirvana song began playing through the speakers as the clock struck six, and I tried to remember the last time that I had gone a whole day without hearing any of their songs. It wasn't unusual to hear them on repeat anywhere in the world these days, let alone just a couple miles out from Seattle. I genuinely couldn't recall the last time I'd gone 24 hours without hearing one of their songs.

I continued to sip my coffee, telling myself I'd wait just ten more minutes. No longer than that.

I turned to face the window as I waited, catching a glimpse of a Christmas store that was already opening up across the road. It lit up the whole street. I watched as one of the workers dragged a Christmas tree across the store floor, stumbling and cursing as his foot caught on something just beneath the branches.

I rolled my eyes, quickly turning back to the more appropriate autumnal scene inside the shop. It was September, for Christ's sake.

A chill suddenly swept through the room, causing me to instinctively tighten my hands around my coffee cup.

The front door had swung fully open, and there he was, dripping wet from the rain outside. He immediately began scanning the room, looking for me. My whole body shook, and I wondered if it was because he was holding the door open, letting all the cold in, or if I really was as terrified as I had tried to convince myself I wasn't.

It took him a moment to spot me across the room. We locked eyes, and my heart dropped. He began making his way over, and I clasped my hands around my coffee to keep them warm. Huh… still shaking.

Maybe I was terrified after all.

The one thing that never failed to surprise me was that no one ever recognized him. Or maybe they did recognize him, but they just didn't care enough to stop him. Unrest Stand was *huge* when I was a kid, and I never would have thought, back then, that

Frankie Flash could ever walk into a coffee shop without getting swarmed by fans.

They'd mentioned the band a couple of times on the news, when they talked about Brooke, but that was about as much publicity as they were getting nowadays. He wasn't a rock star anymore. He was just some guy.

As he got closer, I was reminded of how different he looked recently. He'd seemingly aged ten years within the past week alone. His face was all drawn, and the subtle, white specks that once lightly peppered his hair and beard had multiplied.

He finally managed to push his way through the room, pulling out a chair and sitting opposite me in silence. As he tugged off his coat and draped it over the back of his chair, it hit me that I had been preparing for this moment for what felt like a lifetime, yet I still felt intimidated by him.

All the hours spent overthinking had done nothing to prepare me for this moment.

"You're late." I practically forced the words to exit my mouth, desperate to break the silence sooner rather than later. Frank looked up at the clock at the side of us.

"I had to come up with something," he replied, not even attempting to make eye contact. "She didn't want me to leave."

A tinge of guilt lit through my stomach like wildfire.

"You cut your hair."

No shit, I almost said out loud.

I suppose I just really didn't want this to start on a bad note, especially considering that it was almost definitely going to end on one. I just nodded, lightly running my fingers over the freshly shaved hair on the back of my neck. "I'd wanted to cut it all off for a while."

"I remember."

It had been one of the first conversations we'd ever had.

It was a conversation that I had been having with someone else, and he jumped in, stating his opinion on a matter that had nothing to do with him. I'd said I wanted to cut my hair off—all 26 inches. I wanted it short and spiky, like Winona Ryder.

He told me I'd regret it.

Little did either of us know that, of all the things that had happened since that first conversation, cutting all my hair off was the one thing I regretted the least.

"It suits you," he stated, and it took all my strength not to scream. None of this felt natural, or right. It felt like we were reading from a script.

"Are you going to get anything?"

"No, no, I can't stay long." He sat up a little straighter, looking me in the eye for the first time. "So, what's going on? Has something happened?"

I sat back in my chair, trying to come across as nonchalant. Trying to make out that I didn't give a shit that we were here, and we were talking, and that none of it mattered. "I just think we need to talk."

A slight laugh escaped his mouth, but there was no smile on his face. He sounded defeated. Looked it, too. I guessed he had been looking forward to having this conversation just as much as I had.

"Okay," he said finally, looking over both shoulders before continuing in a lower voice. "Why are you doing this?"

I paused for a moment, observing him. "What do you mean?"

"I just... I thought there was a rule, you know... that you can't be involved in cases that involve people you know."

"I don't know your daughter. I didn't even know she existed."

The bitterness slipped out before I even got a chance to stop it. I couldn't even bring myself to watch his reaction. *Cool it*, I told myself. *This is not how we want this conversation to go.*

"And, well, I'm assuming no one knows I know you," I added, looking up. He shook his head slightly, barely lifting his head.

"Course not."

"I figured."

"I was going to..." He paused, shifting in his chair. "I was *meant* to. The day after."

"You were going to tell her?"

"I wanted to do it before anyone else did."

"Why didn't you?"

"Our daughter went missing," Frank answered, his tone becoming cold and monotone. "It wasn't the right time."

I hadn't expected to feel anger.

Until he arrived, all I felt was anxiety and uncertainty about what would happen. But now, here I was, filled with anger toward this man I once thought I could *never* feel angry toward. He wanted me to feel sorry for him, but I couldn't.

I just... I *couldn't.*

"I don't expect you to understand, but we're going through the unimaginable right now," he went on, shaking his head. "This is something that you could *never* understand, and I hope you never do—"

"She still deserves to know."

"Luce—"

"Don't call me that."

"What, your name?"

He had a point, but that didn't change anything. All week he'd only referred to me as Officer Hardie, and for some reason, that had made everything a little easier.

"Is that seriously what this is about?" Another laugh came out as he stared at me. "Is that why you asked to meet me here?"

"Would you rather we carried on like nothing was wrong?"

"Yes!"

I had to physically bite my tongue to stop whatever was about to come out of my mouth next.

The strange thing was, I genuinely expected him to understand why I was doing this. I genuinely thought he felt the same way. Looking back, of *course* he would've preferred to have kept it swept under the rug. I wasn't sure what I had expected from him at this point.

Finally, I brought myself to look at him—to *really* look at him. Someone that I thought I knew so well. Better than anyone. That was the hardest pill to swallow of all: the realization that I truly had no idea who this man really was.

"It was a year, Frank. *Over* a year"

A sharp exhale escaped his mouth as he pinched the bridge of his nose, wiping his fingers across his face. He didn't say anything at first. I was about to continue but he eventually placed both hands on the table, straightening up. Opening his mouth. "We hadn't been getting along so well, alright?" he said finally. "I... you know, I even *told* you that—"

"Don't you dare—"

"Things were bad long before Brooke went missing, and I... I didn't know who I was anymore. I needed something to... to *change*."

"What if *Liz* needed something to change?"

He lowered his head again. My heart was thumping so hard against my chest as I tried so hard to keep it all under control, set up to immediately fail.

"How would you have felt about that? Tell me, Frank," I pressed on. "Seriously. How would *you* have felt if you found out that *all* the times your wife had stayed out overnight, all the times she said she was working late, or going to the *bar*—"

"Stop—"

"—she was actually staying at some *shitty motel* with someone *half her age*, while *you* stayed at home taking care of your three kids? *Three* kids!"

"You don't understand—"

"*Don't I*?!"

Just like that, staying calm was no longer an option.

The floodgates opened and *everything* came pouring out, and I forgot why I even wanted to see him in the first place. God, I didn't even want to *look* at him.

And he had the goddamn fucking nerve to glare at me like *I* had done something wrong. Like *he* hadn't been the one to start all this.

"Alright, maybe I don't understand how *you* feel, but you know what?" I hissed, leaning closer to him. "I know *exactly* how your *wife* feels! You… you *fucking asshole*…"

I had to reel it in. I knew I had to. No one had turned their heads just yet, but they would if we kept this up. I had to get it together, for my sake. Not his.

Fuck him.

"…I'm sorry."

He didn't mean it. Of course he fucking didn't.

But then I reminded myself that it didn't even matter. That wasn't why we were here.

I took a deep, *deep* breath, reminding myself why we were doing this. We didn't need to go through all this shit again. It was just laughable that I'd honestly figured I could get through this, sitting across from him, without wanting to slap him. But there were bigger things at stake. This wasn't about that.

"Don't apologize to me," I muttered, counting backward from

ten inside my own head. "It's not me you need to apologize to."

"I know. I promise you, I was going to tell her. I just can't do it right now... not with all this going on. It'd break her. It'd break the family."

From the second I saw him walk into the living room on the first day of the investigation, all I thought about was Liz Nicholson.

Before the case, she was this nameless entity that I never thought I'd ever actually meet. And I never *wanted* to meet her. But I had to sit across from her as she smiled at me, thanking me for helping her family... God, I *hated* that she liked me. It made everything so much fucking harder.

But *he* could live in the same house as her. He shared a bed with her. He could look her dead in the eye—*each and every passing day*—without saying a single word.

"What happens when she finds out you weren't home that night?" I reminded him, and he covered his face with his hands. "What happens if the police find out first?"

"You can't let that happen—"

"*Really*?!" A smile stretched across my face so fucking wide that every muscle ached. "So, you're happy for me to risk my job for you too? You want us *both* to lose everything?!"

"No, no, *you* put yourself in that situation when you took on the case," he fought back, shakily pointing a finger at me. "You could've told them from the beginning. I told them I stayed home that night, and you didn't say a *word*. What happens when they find out that *you* lied to them?"

I gritted my teeth, barely believing that we were even in this situation.

He was right. For the first time in this whole situation, he was right, but he wasn't saying anything that I hadn't already gone through in my head a thousand times over. I couldn't get into this with him. That wasn't why we were here.

"My worst-case scenario is that I lose my job," I replied coldly, eyes locked on the finger that was still pointed in my face. "*Your* worst-case scenario is that they assume you had something to do with all this."

"If it gets out, I'll explain myself. I am *not* putting my *wife* through this while our *daughter* is missing. Not if I can help it."

"She's going to find out—"

"She is at *breaking point*, alright?!" His voice cracked, despite the sheer anger on his face. "I just… I *need* Brooke to come home first, and then I… I'll tell her everything, alright? Like I wanted to, *that* morning. Like I *intended* to do. I just… I *can't do it yet*. I *can't*."

The worst part was that I could understand exactly what he was saying.

She didn't deserve any of this.

Frank was a shitty fucking person, sure, but she wasn't. He didn't *want* to hurt her… or maybe he just didn't want to hurt his family. This would tear them apart. He may have been a shitty husband, but hell, he was a father too.

I still had trouble wrapping my head around that part.

"If they find out you lied, and it doesn't come from you… *or* me…" I paused, trying to work out how to say it. "If you get caught, you're going to lose a lot more than your family. They're going to assume the worst."

"I've got an alibi," he replied coldly, despite breaking down ever so slowly. "I was with you."

"I wasn't with you the whole night."

"Wait…" he scoffed slightly, giving me a weird look. "Do *you* think I had something to do with this? With… with—"

"I don't know anything about you, Frank."

He stared right at me with the most horrified expression. The truth was, I *didn't* know what happened that night after I left. I had no idea what he did, or where he went. And I truly felt, examining him across that table, that I had no idea who he was.

He was a married man. He had four kids—an entire *family*. What else didn't I know about him?

Before either of us could fully grasp what the situation had become, it had become an interrogation. My fingers almost stretched out to touch the non-existent tape recorder on the table, making sure that it was on.

For a second, I forgot why I hadn't told Anderson, or Thurman, or any of the others. Despite everything, Frank *was* a suspect in this case, and by all means, he deserved to be treated as one.

He completely turned his head from me, covering his face again. It felt like forever had passed before he finally spoke again.

"I was out of the house for *four hours*. I was back at the house before midnight. You think I'm not wondering—*every fucking second*—about whether or not she was *there*? Or if she'd already *gone*? You think I don't wish with *everything* in my *fucking body* that I *hadn't* left her that night?!"

His voice began to waver. I looked away.

"She was *in her room...*" he continued, his voice getting louder with each spoken word. "And I... I *told* her I'd be home by midnight. I told her I'd be home, and she didn't say *anything*. There was nothing to *say*! Maybe I should've checked in on her when I got home, but... *Jesus*... she's *fifteen*! She's not some... some *little kid* that I have to check up on... *she* said she was staying home... I trusted her, and maybe I shouldn't have but I've *always* been able to *trust* her... *she's the good one...*"

His shoulders started shaking, and my heart began racing faster and faster. Jesus. It was unsettling, seeing him like this. He'd just always seemed like such a strong, "together" type of person, and now he was falling apart right in front of my eyes.

It scared the shit out of me.

"*I can't lose them, Luce...*" I could barely hear him. "*...Liz, Allie, Cam... they're all I've got... I'll lose them, and I... I can't—*"

"Frank—"

His head suddenly snapped up, as if something inside him had switched on. He stared at me with these huge, teary eyes, and something about his expression scared me. "Do you know anything?"

My heart skipped a beat, immediately realizing what he meant. I decided, at that moment, that my best move was to pretend that I didn't. "What do you mean?"

"I know you're not supposed to say anything..." He could barely get his words out. "But there's got to be something... with all these kids getting... *killed*..." A tear rolled down his cheek.

Five seconds before, I'd wanted to kill him. It suddenly hit me that this was exactly why I shouldn't have gotten involved with the case. I should've said something from the start. *This* was why. Another tear fell and my heart tore itself apart, shred by shred.

"*...and they all went to school with Brooke—*"

"We have no reason to believe that the cases are related," I tried to say as calmly as I could, hiding as much emotion as possible.

"And the car?" he added, his face hardening. "The one you found in the woods? By the Bird House?"

I froze.

"How…" My eyes narrowed as I tried to think straight. "How do you know about—"

"It's a small fucking town. People talk."

"Hey—"

"Someone set a *car* on *fire*. We're supposed to pretend that's not relevant?"

"We don't know that it *is* relevant."

"*Bullshit*," he snapped, causing me to flinch. "You find a burnt-out car in the woods days after my daughter goes missing and I'm supposed to believe those two things aren't connected?!"

"We didn't find anything in the car," I snapped back, regretting it as soon as the words left my mouth. "Forensics found *nothing*—"

"How could they?! If it was as *burnt* as they're saying—"

"Bones don't burn, Frank. Not at that temperature."

My blood flushed cold the second I said that out loud.

His eyes widened. I watched as the blood drained from his face, and I could not understand why I thought that was okay to say to him. In my head, as the words came out, I thought it would be a comfort. It had certainly been a comfort to everyone else on the case.

Yes, everything else in the car had been incinerated to a crisp, but there were certain things that would've remained if… if *someone* had been in the car when it was set alight. There were no signs of human remains. This was a good thing.

I completely understood, however, why those three words were enough to send Frank into complete shock.

"She wasn't in the car, Frank," I quickly added, resisting the urge to grab his hand for comfort. "Look… you want to know the truth? There were a *lot* of people who were expecting to find something in that car. Myself included. But there was *nothing*."

He began to nod slowly, but his eyes remained wide and glassy. It took all my strength to keep myself away from him. I just wanted to hug him. Touch him. Anything.

"And as far as the other cases go," I forced myself to continue, suddenly becoming very aware of my own voice starting to waver, "we have *no* reason to make any real connection with Brooke. Those... *children*... their bodies were left at the scene of the crime. It wouldn't make sense for... you know..."

He continued to nod, and I just hoped that he understood what I was saying. The thought of anyone at the station finding out that I was giving this information away—to Brooklyn Nicholson's father, nonetheless—made me fear for my life, but I couldn't stop myself. I wished I could.

The next sentence that came from his mouth made my stomach drop even further: "Do you know whose car it was?"

There was no way I could tell him that. There was no way that information could get out yet.

"We're working on it," I said semi-truthfully.

He was going to find out for himself very soon. It was a short matter of time before the press found out that we had Donnie Booker in custody, and once that got out, the rest of the story would follow.

As much as I wished I could tell him at that exact moment, he couldn't hear it from me.

"I just don't understand why you're not looking into that teacher," he said suddenly, throwing me off guard. "He was released the *day before* she went missing, and that's not enough for you? He *knew* Brooke—"

"We've questioned him," I cut him off, not wanting to get into it with him. "Multiple times. There's nothing to suggest he had anything to do with this."

Frank's jaw tightened as his fists remained clenched, the knuckles white. "Nothing to suggest?" he repeated, his voice rising. "After what he did?!"

I glanced away, feeling the familiar prickle of frustration. "There's no evidence tying him to Brooke, Frank. And until there is, we can't—"

"*Can't?* Or *won't?*" Frank's voice shook, his anger flaring. "I just... *I don't get it.* What's *really* going on here?!"

I bit back a sigh. "Don't do this."

"What?!"

"I'm just doing my job, Frank," I said in a cold whisper,

sharper than I intended. "Alright? And I am trying my *damn hardest*. I am working day in, day out, barely *eating* or *sleeping* because *all* I'm trying to do is find *your daughter*! So, don't you *dare* tell me how to do *my* job. Trust me, alright—I am doing *all* I fucking can."

The frustration spilled over, and the words hung heavy between us. Frank's face changed in an instant. The anger drained away, replaced by something that almost looked like regret.

His fists slowly unclenched.

"Luce—"

"Don't." The word shot out once again. It truly surprised me, every time, how hearing him saying my name out loud somehow stung more than anything else.

"I'm sorry." His tone was completely different now; gentler, almost ashamed. "I just… I'm sorry."

"Mm-hm."

"You're doing a great job. Seriously. I'm sorry… I just… I can't handle this." The words caught in his throat. "Any of it."

I hadn't even noticed, at this point, that I had done the one thing that I'd tried so hard not to do the whole time we'd been having this conversation: I'd taken his hand in mine. It felt so natural that I hadn't given it any serious thought.

When I realized what I'd done, my whole body tensed up. Just as I was about to pull away, he flipped his hand, taking mine in his.

I tried to tell myself that it was fine. Comfort—that was all it was. I'd done what anyone would've done in that situation. I even found myself squeezing his hand slightly, reassuring him, and he weakly squeezed back.

Then he looked at me.

I'd spent the past five days hating him. Wanting him dead. Somehow, all that negativity dissolved in just one brief moment of eye contact. His hand was still in mine. He held onto me, not letting go, and it was as if nothing had ever happened. He needed me.

Maybe I needed him.

No.

I pulled myself away, and he did the same, as if he had gone through the exact same thought process in real time. I re-wrapped my hands around my coffee cup, wishing it was still hot enough to scald my palms. The coffee was almost stone cold at this point. I couldn't feel a thing.

I made myself look back up at him. For a moment, I watched him, wondering if his thoughts really were the same as mine. He wasn't giving anything away.

I didn't think it would be this hard.

"You need to tell them you weren't in the house the whole night," I said finally. "It's going to end badly for you if you don't."

"No."

"Frank—"

"I've lost my daughter," he interrupted, suddenly extremely cold. "I can't lose anyone else... I'm sorry, I can't. Not yet."

I sat back, letting his words sink in. Weighing up the true reality of the situation. He still had two kids at home, and they'd lost a sister. They could lose their dad too.

Gravity had never felt so heavy as I came to the realization that the greatest year of my life—that the decisions that *I* had made—could tear apart an entire family in just one second.

I couldn't change what had happened. I just wasn't entirely sure which course to take next to save them from any further pain. Every potential decision led everyone involved into a darker place.

I wish I could say that my decision-making process came entirely from a selfless angle, that I was only thinking about the Nicholsons. But the truth was, I couldn't lose my job. I'd worked too fucking hard to get to where I was.

Frank was right; if he told the truth, I'd lose everything too. It was too late to fix it. That decision had been taken from us the second we pretended not to know each other five days previously.

It hit me—or, maybe it simply occurred to me—that we had no other choice. "I need you to promise me something."

He looked up, his face softening again. Tears were streaming down his cheeks. I dug my fingernails into my fingertips behind my coffee cup, rapidly trying to come to a concrete decision before committing to anything.

"What?" he asked, and I swallowed hard. It didn't feel right. But then, none of my options felt right. The opportunity to make the right decision had long passed.

I took a deep breath and forced myself to look him in the eye once more. "Promise me that you don't know where she is."

His face slowly hardened back into a scowl, as if he could not understand why I was questioning this again. But he hadn't answered me the first time. I needed that answer before I could proceed.

"I can give you an alibi up to elevenish that night," I went on, refusing to break eye contact. "But... I don't know, for certain, that you went home after—"

"Are you serious?"

"I *need* your word, Frank."

"I left the motel just after you did," he replied icily. "I got in my car, and I *drove home*... I swear on Allie's life, Cam's life, Mick's life... *Brooke's* ... I swear to *God*, I would never... I-I'd *never*..." He started choking on his words, and I had to resist the urge to take his hand again.

"Okay, okay..." I straightened up, using my last moments to confirm what I was about to do next. "As long as you can promise me that, I... I'll make sure this stays quiet. For now."

His eyes widened. "Shit... Luce... I-I..." He took a deep breath, closing his eyes. "*Thank you*."

"When she comes home, you tell Liz everything. But you leave my name out of it. You understand?"

"Of course. Of *course*. I would *never*—"

"You keep your promise, and I'll keep mine. But don't make me regret this."

"I won't... I-I promise..."

I picked up my ice-cold coffee, forcing myself to swallow the final few drops before placing it back on the table. As it hit the hard surface, I inhaled heavily, wondering how—and *why*—I had managed to drag myself even deeper into this inconceivable nightmare. And all this for a man who had shattered my heart into a thousand pieces.

"*...thank you, Officer...*"

All for a man who had completely torn my life apart.

"Don't mention it."

7 DAYS AFTER THE DISAPPEARANCE OF BROOKLYN NICHOLSON

FITZ | 5:12 PM

I couldn't remember Hurley and Mel ever actually talking to each other. Not directly, at least.

There had been plenty of times when we'd all hung out together, when I'd brought Mel along to the hangouts, but I couldn't recall a single moment when the two of them had ever spoken one-on-one. Maybe they never had. I could vaguely remember Mandy talking to her once or twice, but never Hurley.

Not that it was unusual or anything—it wasn't as if any of us ever really went out of our way to chat to each other's girlfriends. Mandy was the only exception, because, you know... she was one of us.

The way they placed photos of Hurley and Mel together all over the school made it seem like they really knew each other.

There weren't many pictures of them actually together—in the same photo, I mean—but there were hundreds of individual images hung up, side by side, stretching all across the school.

There was one photograph I'd found of the two of them together. Me and Mandy were in it too. I'd never seen it before this moment, but I wished I had. Hurley and Mel were in the middle, and I was at the side with my arm around Mel, and Mandy was riding Hurley's back. They could've cut the photo up, if they'd wanted, to make it look like it was just Hurley and Mel together. It would've made more sense, I figured. There were thousands of pictures of the rest of us, though, all with Hurley. And there were some of me and Mel.

I couldn't believe how many of the photographs I'd never seen before this moment.

"...*hey, that's a good one...*"

I'd been standing in the corridor for so long that I hadn't even noticed anyone approaching me. Everyone else was outside. Freddie had snuck in at some point, and I hadn't even noticed.

He reached an arm out in front of me, plucking a pin out of one of the photographs of all seven of us: me, him, Hurley, Mandy, Donnie, Joaquin, and Allie. He slid it away from the wall, stuffing it into his back pocket.

"I don't think you're supposed to take them, Fred," I commented, barely pulling my eyes away from the wall of photographs long enough to acknowledge him. He chuckled, reaching up to grab another one.

"What are they gonna do? Suspend me?"

This was probably the first time Freddie and Joaquin had even set foot inside St. Mary's High. I hadn't been back in a while, not since Mel's prom last summer. Us three were the only ones who went to M. High, so it felt a little alien walking through the halls of the school that the others went to.

St. Mary's was a lot nicer than Mirrenville High. It was more *deluxe*, you know? It was weird being there and not seeing everyone walking around in their little green blazers and ties.

Freddie put an arm around my shoulder. "How are you doing, bud?" I shrugged loosely, not entirely sure what I was supposed to say.

It wasn't as if I could be completely honest about how I was feeling—it would've felt weird. And awkward. And it wasn't as if he didn't feel whatever I was feeling at that moment, anyway. He was there when Hurley died too. Sure, I'd lost Mel too, but it was all relative. We both knew what it felt like. What was the point in talking about it?

"Come on... there's a surprise for you outside."

He spun me around and began guiding me past all the pine green lockers, toward the back entrance, and I couldn't help but laugh at his line delivery. Here we were, at a high school memorial for my best friend and girlfriend, and he said the word "surprise" as if a stripper was waiting for us on the other side. I couldn't imagine even that would make me feel better.

Before we'd even gotten to the door, I could hear the school band playing some Mariah Carey song. They sounded fucking awful. Voices got louder as we got closer, and I started mentally preparing myself for the same old people approaching me, telling me they were *so sorry* for my losses.

And, I mean, that was the best-case scenario. Some kids had actually come over to ask what it was like, watching Hurley bleed to death. They wanted the *real* details.

There was a reason I'd made my way inside.

I'd only wanted to stay for half an hour, but every time I'd tried to get away, someone managed to find me to bring me back to all the action. This time, it was Freddie.

"I think Mandy's gone..." I heard him saying as we made our way outside. Everything got ten times louder from the moment we stepped outside the door. "...she wasn't looking so good... think it was all getting to her..."

That made me want to leave even more. The one and only upside to coming to this thing was to see Mandy, the only person who really knew what I was going through. The only real difference was that her and Hurley were still together when he died.

Not that anyone knew about me and Mel.

I hadn't been given the chance to tell the truth before the flowers started arriving at the house, and all the sympathy cards. By the time things had cooled down in that sense, it felt like it was too late to actually come out and say that we'd broken up. Everyone just assumed we were still together when she died, and

I didn't have the energy to correct them.

None of the guys had said anything, either, and they were the only ones that knew about us breaking up. It just felt too weird to say anything at this point.

"Is Donnie here yet?" I asked when I finally found the words, trying to speak loud enough that Freddie could hear me above the crowd. He shook his head.

"Nah, man. No one's seen him."

Him and Allie were the only ones that hadn't turned up.

I wasn't too surprised about Allie—I mean, we hadn't really seen her in a couple months, aside from the party. We didn't really see much of her anymore.

It was weird, though, that Donnie hadn't shown face. We hadn't seen him since the party, either, but that wasn't like him. He was closer to Hurley than any of us.

Through the crowds of green hoods and flowers, I finally spotted what Freddie was guiding us toward. Joaquin was standing just under the bleachers, talking to a girl with her back to us. A pang of sadness flooded my chest when I realized that we were walking toward the only other person left in our group. Since Donnie had disappeared off the face of the earth, and Mandy not wanting to be around anymore, it really was just me, Freddie and Joaquin left.

The group just kept getting smaller and smaller, and that hurt more than anything.

Joaquin noticed us approaching him, and he started waving toward us. Someone patted me on the shoulder as we got closer.

"...sorry for your loss, man..."

I wasn't even sure half these people even knew Hurley. They would've known Mel, sure, but they didn't *really* know her. So many people were crying, and it felt like some kind of huge joke that I wasn't a part of. They didn't *know* them. Not really.

"Where'd you go?" Joaquin asked, holding something out to me; a silver flask, barely hidden inside his sleeve. Subtlety had never been his strong suit, but I appreciated the gesture. I took it from his hand, sliding it up my own sleeve before any of the teachers speckled through the crowd took notice.

"Where'd you get this?" I asked with a forced chuckle, unscrewing the lid. Jack Daniels hit my nostrils before I even took a sip. This was such an Allie thing to do—bringing a drink to a memorial.

It certainly wasn't a Joaquin thing to do.

"Nichy brought the goods."

It was only then that I remembered the girl standing at Joaquin's side, now facing me.

It genuinely took me by surprise that I hadn't recognized the knotted tuft of orange curls when she had her back to us. Just like that, the flask made sense. I'd known all along.

For the first time since arriving at the school, I almost felt happy.

"You look like shit," were the first words that came from Al's mouth upon my arrival. I hadn't expected anything less. I laughed genuinely for the first time in four days.

"You don't look so hot, either."

She shrugged, slipping her hands into her pockets. I found myself smiling at her, and it didn't feel forced. Just seeing her made everything feel… not so bad. Maybe it was because I hadn't seen her in so long. It was almost as if things had gone back to normal, her being there with us.

But something about her seemed different. Like something was off. She probably thought the same about me. I figured it hadn't been the easiest week for her, either.

"How are you feeling?" she asked, and it almost felt odd hearing her getting serious for a moment. Not that she was being entirely serious; after all, this was Allie we were talking about. She still said it with a semi-goofy grin, lightly punching me on the shoulder.

I took a sip from the flask, wishing that we could just pretend for a second that everything was good. My throat burned as it slipped down. "Never better," I replied, trying so damn hard to cover up the splutters that accompanied the straight whiskey burning a hole through my esophagus. She smirked, pulling the flask from my hand.

"Yeah." She looked down for a moment, and I already knew what she was going to say next. "I just… I'm really sorry, Fitz. I really am. I mean, you'd been together for a while, you know, and I…"

I nodded quickly, swallowing the hard lump forming in my

throat.

"…and… I-I should've been there, you know… when Hur—"

"I'm sorry too," I interrupted, stopping her before she could say it. "About your sister."

It was funny, you know, because we were exactly the same in this way—we didn't do the "serious stuff". Even when shit hit the fan, we never got into it. I'd crack a joke, and Al… well, she'd pull a flask out.

I pulled my pack of cigarettes out of my pocket, offering one to her. She shook her head and pulled out her own. I held out my lighter as she put one in her mouth, and she leaned forward so I could light it for her. I watched her take a couple of drags, and I wondered how many people had apologized to her too. I just hoped no one was asking her the same questions they were asking me.

"I'm surprised they let you in," I said finally, realizing that this was likely the first time that she'd entered the premises since she was kicked out in seventh grade. She pulled a face, flicking her cigarette.

"Really?" She looked over at a group of teachers standing just a couple feet away from us. "*I'm* not. You seen the people they let teach here?"

I shifted awkwardly, remembering. I'd heard about it on the news—that teacher. He'd been let out of prison after serving, like, half his time. It'd all happened before I'd moved to Mirrenville, but the guys had filled me in.

"Yeah, but… I figured they'd have security out for you, at least," I laughed slightly, trying to fix the sudden switch in the atmosphere. She scoffed, almost cracking a smile.

"Piece of shit school, anyway."

"Go Meteorites."

It stunned me how saying those two words out loud almost knocked the wind out of me.

I hadn't realized what I was saying until it was already out there. Al tensed up too, just enough for me to notice. It was hard enough seeing all the other cheerleaders making their way around the field, every single one of them in tears. Some of them had *MacKenzie 1977-1994* painted onto their jackets. Others just had *Nicholson*.

"Is it true..." Al hesitated, and something told me that I wasn't going to like the second part of her sentence. "Is it true that you were with him that night? Hurley? When..."

God damn it.

I took a deep drag, trying to figure out what I was even supposed to say. I guess it wasn't a total shock that it was on her mind—she was one of us. And she wasn't there. I wasn't entirely sure what was worse: being there and seeing it happen, or finding out about it later. She loved Hurley. I mean, we all did, but... I don't know. They were pretty close. Especially when Mandy wasn't around.

I close my eyes for a second, mad at myself for even thinking about that. It wasn't the time to think about it.

When I finally looked up, she was watching me carefully. I kept waiting for a smile, or a stupid comment, but neither came. She was serious now. Time passed, and the awkwardness only multiplied with each second I remained silent.

Finally, she shook her head, maybe realizing the severity of what she was asking of me. "I'm sorry, I shouldn't—"

"Yeah," I said finally, not entirely sure how I found the strength to speak. "We, uh... we were at his place. Me, Fred, Joaquin... and Mandy. Obviously."

"Mm-hm."

"He died in my arms."

Her face fell, and I wasn't sure why I said it. There was no real reason for me to tell her that, and I certainly didn't want to talk about it. This was the first time I *had* spoken about it, since I'd told the police.

"Mandy was screaming... 'cause, you know, she found him first," I continued, as if the words were flowing without any real participation on my behalf. "And I ran out, and... I don't really remember how it happened but... yeah. There was... there was a lot of blood."

Her face had turned completely white.

Something shifted, and I finally managed to muster up a couple sentences of my own: "Ruined my favorite shirt. You know the white one with the car on it, and the writing? Yeah... straight in the trash." I forced a laugh, pointing a shaky finger up to the sky. "Thanks, Hurl."

She didn't laugh. She didn't even crack a smile. Her entire demeanor had switched, and I felt fucking awful.

"I should've been there." She just kept shaking her head, unable to look at me. I reached out, grabbing her shoulder.

"Hey, come on—"

"I wish I'd been there, with all of you—"

"I wish I hadn't," I said with another forced chuckle, unsure of what I could do at this point to calm her down. Her skin was practically translucent. All clammy and wet.

"I'm sorry—"

"Don't be."

"I miss you." Her voice cracked a little, but she quickly straightened herself up, clearing her throat. Crossing her arms so tightly that they almost snapped across her chest. "All of you. I think about you guys all the time."

"We miss you too."

"And I-I know it's not the same thing," she sniffed, looking away, "but... I mean, we've both lost people, right? And it's all just so... so fucking *weird*... and it's kind of scary, right, knowing that this could... you know... it could happen *again*..."

I kept a straight face, pretending this hadn't been the only thing on my mind nonstop for the past three days.

It seemed pretty clear, at this point, that it *was* going to happen again. Bile rose in my throat as it all came flooding back. Hurley's blood on my shirt. Mel's blood on my hooded jacket I'd let her wear, the one she wore the night she died. Two items of clothing that I could never wear again.

I thought about saying this out loud to Al, making another joke out of it. Something about how I couldn't afford to lose another shirt.

"I don't know what I'd do if it was you, you know?" She laughed suddenly, surprising me. "I-I honestly... I don't know *what* I would do..."

I thought about saying the same back.

It wasn't as if the thought hadn't been bouncing around in my mind for the best part of a week—how it would feel to find out that something had happened to her, too. Instead, I did what I probably should've done at the start of the conversation: I put my arms around her, pulling her in for a tight hug.

She didn't hug me back at first. She fell limp in my arms, barely moving. Eventually, I felt her hands on my back, holding me loosely.

"I love you, kid," I said firmly, squeezing her shoulders. I heard her sniff before pulling away, taking a quick drag from her barely lit cigarette. Then she scoffed.

"Shut up, freak."

It was only at that moment that I remembered Freddie and Joaquin were still there, but they were standing pretty far from us at this point, talking to a group of other people.

It was hard to remember the last time that all of us had been together. *All* of us.

There had been a time when we spent every day together. Me, Al, Fred, and Joaquin would practically run from school the second the bell rang to get to the Turtin, where Donnie, Mandy, and Hurley were already waiting for us.

I wondered if Al and Hurley saw each other at the party. They *must* have. I vaguely remembered a bunch of us standing together in the front yard at one point, but I couldn't fully remember who was there and who wasn't. It was all just a huge fucking blur. We were all out of it... Al, more than anyone.

I took another drag, trying to figure out how to bring it up. "I heard shit went down at the party." She looked up at me with a blank expression.

"What do you mean?"

"Something about you having a bad trip, or... I don't know," I went on, watching as her eyes lit up. She nodded, scoffing a little.

"Oh, yeah. I got spiked."

"Wait, what? It wasn't something you took?"

"I didn't take anything," she replied, seeming a little defensive when she saw my face. "I wasn't even *drinking*, Fitz. I drove, remember? I was meant to drive home that night."

"You think someone put something in your drink, or something?"

"Someone *did* put something in my drink," she corrected me, shrugging again. "But it's all good now. I just felt like shit for a couple days." She paused, flicking her cigarette. "And, you know... they did a bunch of tests, and everything, to make sure that no one... you know..."

"What?"

"I mean, it was a date rape drug," she laughed slightly, seeming a little shaky all of a sudden. "But no one raped me, or anything. They, you know… they tested me for that."

"Oh… shit." I nodded quickly. "That's… great?"

She laughed again, nodding back. "Silver linings, right? Take 'em where you can get 'em."

"So you really don't remember anything?"

She shook her head silently, and my heart started beating so fast that my vision went blurry for a second. Shit.

She really didn't remember anything.

"I was in the house one minute, and the next I'm waking up in my car," she went on, flicking ash onto the ground before looking me in the eye. "What was I like? I mean, when you saw me? Was I acting weird, or anything?"

I thought about the last time I saw her that night.

"You were pretty fucked up," I replied truthfully, deciding against going into any further details.

"Shit, really? How bad?"

"I hadn't seen you like that since that time we all camped out in tenth grade."

She groaned loudly, her whole face scrunching up. A smile crept across her face, though, and up until that point, I really had considered telling her what had happened. Her smile is what convinced me not to. "That's so *bad*…"

"You were pretty fuckin' stoked to see me," I added, and she rolled her eyes. "It was like you were surprised to see me in my own house—"

"Well, I hadn't seen you in forever!"

"Whose fault is that?"

She pulled a face, crossing her arms again. I could tell she was still half-kidding around, but her expression glazed over again, just a little.

I thought about asking her why she'd disappeared over the summer. It was something I'd thought about a lot. She'd been my best friend for over eight years, and this was the first time she'd ever blanked me out like that. I'd thought about it a lot, trying to figure out if I'd done something wrong, or if it had something to do with Mel.

"Hey, can I ask you something?" she asked before I got the chance to say anything. I nodded. "Did you know my sister?"

"Your sister?"

I'd had no idea she'd even had a sister until everything had unfolded over the past week.

I knew she had a brother—maybe even more than one—but she'd never mentioned a sister. She didn't really talk about her family a whole lot, so this wasn't a huge deal. I'd always figured it was because she didn't like talking about her dad... because he used to be famous, or whatever.

"She goes here, right?" I asked, gesturing toward the building behind us, and she nodded. "I kinda recognized her picture on the news, but I figured that's 'cause she was on the team with Mel. I don't think I ever spoke to her."

Al nodded, not replying right away. Her expression was completely blank for a moment, and her mouth twitched as if she was going to say something else. But she didn't.

"*Fitz! Nichy!*" I heard Freddie shouting from across the crowd, waving toward us. "*You hungry?*"

The smell of charred meat wafted into my nostrils, and I couldn't believe they were having a barbeque at a high school memorial. It all felt borderline inappropriate. I hadn't eaten all day, though, and it smelt pretty good, so I turned back to Al with a questioning look. She shook her head, stamping out her cigarette. "I better go."

"Well, we're all heading to my place after this—you coming?" I suggested, and she shook her head again with a sad smile.

"I'm good... maybe next week?"

"We'll hunt you down if you don't." I pulled her in for another hug, and she actually hugged me back this time. She held onto me really tightly, as if she didn't want to let go. We just stood there for a moment, holding each other. I wasn't entirely sure we had ever hugged before that day, which struck me as really strange, considering how long we'd known each other. We just never really did this kind of thing. We'd never had to before.

"*...we probably shouldn't be hugging...*" I heard her say, as if she was reading my mind. "*...people might get the wrong idea, you know... you hugging another girl at your girlfriend's memorial...*"

If anyone else had said that to me, I would've totally taken it the wrong way. If anyone else had brought up Mel in front of me, it would've sent me spiraling, just like it had all day. But for some reason, in that moment, it didn't. Instead, I had to stifle a laugh.

"Can you not be a fucking bitch for five seconds?" I pinched the back of her arm, and she pushed me away from her with a grin, shoving me again for good measure.

Her face softened as she took a step back. "I love you, dude."

She began to walk away, and the next words slipped from my mouth before I could even think about it: "Look after yourself, alright?"

She turned back slightly, nodding with a smile.

I hoped she knew that I meant it, more than anything. It was easy to forget how close we used to be, you know? There was a time when I was closer to her than anyone. I wasn't sure what I would do if I ever lost her. Red images flashed through my mind once more, for the hundredth time that day, and I took a deep breath to compose myself. Telling myself that this had to stop.

Everything was *fine*.

I watched until she was out of sight, and I thought about what she said about Mel. I wondered what she really would've thought if she knew me and Al had that moment at her memorial. It was a clear and cut answer, and one I didn't want to spend too much time thinking about. The truth was, she wouldn't have even wanted me there in the first place.

She died hating me.

ALLIE | 5:21 PM

As I stumbled back down the hallway of my old high school, I took another swig from the flask tucked inside my sleeve, the burn of the whiskey momentarily numbing the ache in my chest. The taste was almost comforting, even if it wasn't doing much to dull my thoughts. That novelty had worn off a long time ago.

The only real comfort I felt was that Fitz seemed to have no idea. Thank *God*.

I knew Joaquin and Freddie wouldn't give a shit, but I'd expected a little judgment from Fitz. I figured he was too wrapped up in his own grief to notice how wasted I really was. Or maybe I was just covering it up better than I'd expected. That would've been impressive if the latter had been true; I'd eaten a single jelly sandwich since Thursday, and my body was now being fueled purely by Jack Daniels and black coffee.

Mom and Dad hadn't noticed. The guys hadn't noticed. I began to wonder if I could keep this up forever without any unwanted intervention.

As I made my way out the front entrance, lightly leaning against the wall to keep myself upright, Fitz's last words to me rang through my brain: "*Look after yourself, alright?*" I wondered if he would remember those words if anything did happen to me.

I knew I certainly would remember them if anything happened to him.

The fresh air hit me like a slap in the face. I squinted against the bright sunlight as I made my way outdoors, wishing the rain would come back. I loved the rain, you know. I know it's cool to hate cold, dark weather, but I found it comforting. No one gave a shit if you stayed indoors when it was raining. No one expected you to be outside, living your life when the fucking heavens opened up.

The abrupt show of sunshine made everything seem too vivid, too real, as if the universe was mocking me in my inebriated state. I took another sip from the flask, my vision blurring slightly as I tried to focus on my surroundings.

And that was when I saw her.

Hayden fucking Butler.

I hadn't seen her in a *long time*, but she looked just as trashy as I'd remembered. And she had red hair now.

I shakily tugged another cigarette out from my pocket, patting myself down for my lighter as I tried to figure out what she was doing. She was talking to someone. Or maybe she was talking to a group of people. There were a lot of people standing around her, so I wasn't totally sure how many of them she was addressing.

The guy in front of her—directly in front of her—was holding a microphone. One of those big microphones that they used on TV. On the news.

Holy shit... she was talking to a fucking *reporter*.

I fumbled with my lighter, my hands shaking as I finally managed to light the cigarette. The first drag did little to calm my nerves. I wasn't even totally sure if I could trust what I was seeing. The world was spinning too fast; everything was too bright and too loud.

The guy was holding a microphone. And Hayden was talking into it. I took a shaky step forward, the world tilting slightly as I moved.

"*...Hay... Hayden...*"

It was so weird—even just seeing someone connected to Brooke felt like a lifeline, even if it was frayed and fragile. It was almost soothing to look at Hayden, even if she was pissing me off. But I couldn't remember the last time I looked at Hayden and didn't feel pissed off.

She was just... *ugh*... she was fucking *annoying*, man.

"*...Haaay-den...*"

Each step I took felt like a monumental effort, my legs heavy and uncooperative, like I was walking on the moon. "*...one large step for mankind...*" I muttered as I pushed forward.

The world around me continued to blur and tilt, the noise of the crowd a dull roar in my ears.

With a deep breath, I prepared to yell one last time: "*...HAYD—*"

Suddenly, the world around me spun at colossal speed.

Everything around me moved in one gigantic blur. I was spinning back in time. Something gripped onto my arm, and I didn't question it at first. Too much was happening for me to question anything.

"*...are you fucking drunk?!*"

The voice entered my left ear. A girl's voice. It was a very familiar voice, but it took me a moment to work it out. It wasn't Hayden. I wasn't even sure what had *happened* to Hayden.

Somehow, I was now walking in the complete opposite direction.

"*...Jesus Christ, Al...*"

"Mandy?!" I laughed, gripping onto her arm. "No *way!*"

She kept pulling me forward, leading me onto the open road. I had no idea where she was taking me, but things were getting pretty exciting. We were going on a girls' trip; just us girls.

The two *Eezy girls.*

"I thought you went *home!*" I started telling her, trying to pull the cigarette into my mouth as we traveled at what felt like an insane speed. "Joaquin said you w-went home—"

"I was looking for *you.*"

"You were looking for *me*?!"

I'm not sure how long we were walking, or what we even talked about on the way, but somehow we ended up crossing the road toward the Turtin. *That* got me excited. The whiskey in the flask was starting to warm up, and I needed something colder.

"Wait... *no...* where are we going?!" I moaned as she pulled me away from the entrance, pushing me forward. "Mandy, *stop...*"

She sighed for what felt like the hundredth time since we'd been walking. "Can you just try and pretend to be normal? For ten more seconds? *Please?*"

Mandy had a keen eye. She'd noticed in, what, *five* minutes what the guys hadn't noticed in, like, an hour. She was pretty smart, you know. That was why she was the only one of us that made it to college. I still wasn't 100% sure why she'd come home so soon. Maybe she missed Hurley already.

Then I remembered that he wasn't here anymore.

Every time I remembered, vomit rose in my throat. Suddenly, I became *very* nauseous.

"Come *on...*"

"I-I saw someone here last week," I slurred as we got closer to the Turtin alleyway, pointing toward the park across the road. "I brought my little brother here, and there was someone standing *right* here... watching us... w-wait, why are we..."

She pulled us inside the alleyway, and I began to sober up immediately.

I started dragging my heels, pulling us backward. "Are you trying to get us *killed*?!"

She didn't stop.

At this point, we were engulfed in complete darkness. Glass

crunched beneath my feet with each step, and I stuck my arms out, trying to find a wall to guide me. Someone grabbed my arms and pinned them down, and I began to scream.

A hand immediately clamped over my mouth, and I remembered that it was Mandy. I'd almost forgotten she was there.

"*Jesus*, dude..." I pulled her hand away, laughing at my own stupidity. "What the hell are we doing here?!"

"How drunk are you?"

"*Eh*... I-I'm sobering up..."

"Shit." She sighed again, letting go of my arm. "Look, I just need you to listen to me, alright? We don't have time."

"Hey... look..." I took a deep breath, remembering again. "I know we haven't seen each other in... in a w-while... but, Mand, I am *so sorry* about Hur—"

"We don't have time for that."

"Oh—"

"I needed to see you before I left."

"You're going back to c-college?"

I couldn't even remember which one she got into. I knew it wasn't too far away—maybe Oregon. It was somewhere in that direction.

She grabbed my arms again, pulling me closer to her.

"Al..." she said so quietly that I would've barely heard her if her voice hadn't echoed off the walls of the alleyway. "*They saw us.*"

My heart stopped as I mistakenly assumed that she was talking about me and Hurley.

For some reason, when she said "us", I assumed she meant me and Hurley, and that *she* had seen us. That wouldn't have made sense, though, because she was in Oregon... or wherever she was. And we'd parked up in some empty field just off the highway.

And, hey—for the record, I felt like shit about it, alright?

Despite what everyone might've thought—including Mandy herself—I *liked* Mandy. I thought her and Hurley were good together. *He* came onto *me*. What was I supposed to do? It didn't mean *anything*—

Bam.

I remembered Hurley was dead again.

I stumbled backward, leaning against the wall behind me. Mandy barely held me up, gripping onto my wrists. "Al, listen to me—"

"Oh my *God*..." I began shaking. "Wait... he's... h-he's really *gone*, isn't he—"

SLAP.

My head jerked to the side, followed by a burning sensation all across my cheek. "Al, I swear to *God*..." Mandy hissed in the darkness, and I suddenly felt *very* sober. "If you don't listen to me, we are *both* going to die. Do you understand?!"

The shaking stopped.

I paused, trying to find her face in the darkness. My eyes were adjusting slightly, so I could vaguely make out the dark blob moving around in front of my face. "...what are you talking about?"

"You know what I'm talking about."

"What—"

"At the party. You were there. We *saw* you."

I paused again, trying to think back.

"*Oh*... yeah, I don't know if you heard, but, uh... my memory was kinda *zapped*," I explained, laughing slightly as I jabbed a finger to the side of my head. "Someone spiked my drink at Fitz's... so, if we're going to talk about the party, I'm gonna have *nooo* idea what the fuck you're talking about—"

"You seriously can't remember anything?"

I shook my head, despite knowing that she couldn't actually see me in the darkness. She must've taken my silence as a "yes", because she just carried on talking.

"Okay... *shit*... I thought you were lying about it," she said, sounding a little defeated. "Because of what happened."

"What happened?"

"Al... if you *do* remember, you can tell me. You can trust me."

It suddenly hit me that something was seriously wrong.

The tone of her voice. The way her grip had loosened around my wrists. She was actually serious. "Okay..." She took a deep breath, letting go of my wrists. "So... we were in the woods that night. Behind Fitz's house."

"We were?"

"Me and Hurley were sat a little further up. We could see you, just below us. You were on the ledge just above the old bench."

I hadn't thought about that bench in a *long* time.

It was this old, white bench in the middle of all these trees in the wooded area behind Fitz's house.

We used to pass it all the time when we walked home from school. It was weird, because the bench itself didn't look like it belonged there—it was all chipped and splintered so you couldn't really sit on it, but otherwise, it looked good as new. It really stood out from its surroundings, and it seemed no one really knew why it was there, or how it got there. It was one of those small town mysteries, you know?

"Melissa was just below you, walking around near the dirt path behind the house," Mandy went on, and it chilled me a little, hearing Melissa's name. "We could see everything because we were so high up."

"Okay—"

"*Just let me talk.*"

I sucked my lips in, signaling that I wasn't going to say another word. Obviously, she couldn't actually *see* my lips, so again, she just had to take my silence as a sign to carry on with her story.

"It was around midnight, and we saw a car coming up the dirt path," she continued, and I listened in silence. "We couldn't see what car it was, or who was in it... but... well, they were dragging something into the car..."

It was at this point that I began to wonder if any of this was actually real. It didn't *feel* real.

"...it looked like a person, Al. A body."

I froze up.

"At first, we figured it was someone passed out from the party, and they were just giving them a ride home, or whatever... but... the way they *looked* at us... they were *staring*. Then they looked at *you*, and then *Melissa...*" Her voice cracked. "They drove away, and then... then, obviously, Melissa died, and then... you know... Hurley... they were *both there*. They saw it happen, and *now... now, they're...*"

She started choking on her words. Couldn't get them out.

"Al... they were killed by the same person."

"I don't understand—"

"And the day before Hurley died, he got a letter."

"A *letter*?"

I heard a rustling, and then she pressed something into my palm. The abrupt contact made me flinch. She twisted my fingers, making me grip around whatever she had just placed in my hand.

"I found it after he died..." she went on, her voice wavering. "And... well... it's a *poem*. It's got all this weird, cryptic shit in it. It's from *them*. And at first, I thought maybe they just wanted to keep him quiet, but... *now*... now, I think they were warning him. They were telling him that they were going to kill him."

"You think the guy with the car killed him?"

"I *know* they did."

None of this was making any sense to me.

"Here's mine, too," she said, pressing something else in my palm. "Keep them safe. *Don't* read them until you get home, and *don't* lose them. You *can't* let them get in the wrong hands."

I stuffed both pieces of paper into my back pocket, making sure they were tucked in securely.

"You need to go home, and you don't say a word about this," she continued, sounding desperate. "*No one* can know that we've seen each other today."

"Alright—"

"I don't know who the killer is, but it's *obviously* someone we know, because *they* know who *we* are... they recognized us that night, and they *know* that *we saw them*... and they *know where we live*. Hurley *and* Melissa were killed in their own homes."

Despite not fully understanding the severity of this situation— partially due to not knowing if it was really happening or not—the tone of her voice scared me to fucking death.

It was really eerie, the way she was saying everything. It was like something from a movie.

"Mand... look, I—"

"Just go home," she interrupted angrily, grabbing my arms again. "*Read the letters*. You're going to get yours soon—"

"Wait, *what*—"

"I don't know what happened to Melissa's, but I'd bet my life that she had one too... I... *I*..." She started sniffling. Then sobbing.

Jesus... she was, like, full-on sobbing.

My heart stopped, unsure what I was supposed to do. I still

couldn't see her, so I wasn't sure how to reach out to her. She was still gripping my arms. It was all getting a little too real. Too weird.

"*...I think I'm going to die tonight,*" she laughed shakily. "*And... and I don't think there's anything I can do to stop it... I-I'm going to try and get out of here, but I-I don't know... I think it's too late—*"

"Mand—"

"*You have our letters. You need to find out what's going on before you get yours... if you don't, we're ALL going to be dead by the end of the week.*"

As I slowly sobered up in real-time, I felt that I was finally getting a better grip on the situation before me—she'd just witnessed her boyfriend die a violent death. She wasn't doing so well. Hurley dying had officially broken her brain.

It was the only way that any of this could make sense.

I tried to reach out to her, but she kept shaking me away. Pushing me back. "*...just... just read the letters, and you'll get it. Please try and work it out. If I die tonight, you'll know what happened.*"

"Why tonight? I mean, how do you know—"

"*Hurley got his letter two days before he died. I got mine two days ago. It makes sense.*"

Not a *single word* that she had just said made sense.

She clumsily grabbed hold of my shoulders, gripping tight onto them. It was becoming harder and harder to breathe. Her jagged breaths were getting louder. "*...find out what's going on, Al... you HAVE to... I've just got this feeling that... that the body in the car...*"

My whole body tensed up when I realized what she was saying.

I didn't need to hear it.

I staggered backward, falling back against the wall. Everything fell silent. Time passed, and suddenly, I couldn't see the dark blob in front of me anymore.

I waved my arms around, trying to feel for her. But she was gone. She'd just... disappeared. She didn't even make a sound.

I'd imagined the whole thing.

I'd *never* drank so much that I'd hallucinated before—hell, I wasn't even sure it was possible—but there was no other way to explain it. Either that, or Mandy was a ghost. Maybe she was dead already.

Ha.

I gripped onto the wall behind me, struggling to keep myself on my feet.

The weirdest part was that Mandy was a *lot* of things, but she wasn't a liar. She never had been. If she really *had* been there with me in the alleyway, I had absolutely no reason not to believe her.

Why the fuck did they have *letters*?

Why didn't Mandy just… *tell the cops*?

Hurley's face popped back into my head, and it was like he was right there. Right in front of me.

Almost instantly, pure acid came rushing up from the depths of my stomach, pouring out of my mouth and nose.

I almost fell onto my knees, barely holding myself up, projectile vomiting all over my white Reeboks. Liquid fire torched my sinuses and throat, and I saw Hurley's face in his car, clear as anything—hunched over me, turning his head to peek through the steamed-up window.

"…*she can't find out about this…*"

Oh my *God.*

Once my stomach had completely emptied, I found the strength to straighten up. Barely.

I managed to place one foot in front of another, sloshing through the slop on the ground. *Guilt.* That's what it was. I felt *guilty.* And I was losing it because… well, because I'd lost a friend. I'd lost *Hurley.* He was dead. Gone forever.

And I was, potentially, the last person he'd ever fucked.

Ah.

I saw Mandy because I felt *guilty.*

As my feet splashed against the floor, I made one last effort to confirm my theory, reaching into my back pocket. I grabbed a handful of crumpled-up paper.

In a second cruel twist of fate, it turned out that my stomach wasn't empty after all.

ADJACENT

8 DAYS AFTER THE DISAPPEARANCE OF BROOKLYN NICHOLSON

FRANK | 5:57 PM

"That'll do it…" Malcolm said with a grunt, dropping the shovel to the ground and rubbing his hands together. "Good as new!"

I stared at the lawn stretching ahead of me, nearly restored to its original shade of green.

Just an hour ago, the whole patch of grass was charred black, burned to a crisp. Even the smell had disappeared. I wasn't entirely sure how Malcolm had done it; hell, I wasn't even sure when he had decided to become an amateur landscaper. I figured being self-employed and having no kids gave him more time for new hobbies.

He had truly transformed the yard. It was as if the fire had never even happened.

"I owe you one," I muttered, nodding in his direction.

He just laughed, taking a sip from his beer. "You don't owe me shit. I only ask one thing of you—don't light any more fires. You're not good at it."

I'd lit thousands of fires in my life.

It seemed easier when I was a kid—I'd just pile some dried-out logs together and flick a match onto them. This time, I had to use an old newspaper to get it going, and once it'd caught, the flames went from 0 to 100 in seconds. The wind must've blown it the wrong way. Even the damn cat almost got burnt to a crisp, moving too close to the flames.

I managed to grab a bucket of pond water before it got too serious, but Liz wasn't happy about the state of the garden. As if a burned patch of grass was the worst thing happening in our lives at that moment.

"I've got an old firepit back home," he went on, following me back inside the house. "You can have it. I got a new one last month."

"Thanks."

"It's nice in the evenings, you know… sitting there with a beer, watching the flames dance. Keeps you warm. Helps you to think about stuff." The last sentence lingered, and I felt him watching me a little longer than usual.

I wasn't even sure what to say. The worst part was knowing that there was so much I could've said to him, and he would've been the best person to have said it to. Malcolm was the closest thing I'd ever had to a brother, and he was the closest thing we had to immediate family, aside from Vic. We'd grown up together.

I knew that I could've told him what was really going on. Maybe I would have if Liz wasn't home to hear it.

"The guys have been on the lookout every night," Malcolm continued, throwing his empty bottle into the trash. "Work's been crazy over the weekend, so I haven't been out as much as I've wanted to, but I'll head back out tonight."

He'd been organizing search parties every night since Brooke went missing. I wasn't even sure who made up these search parties, but from what Malcolm had told me, there were around 20 to 30 of them each night. But I hadn't expected anything less.

Malcolm didn't have a family of his own, and I wasn't sure if he would ever have kids at this point, but he'd spent the past 30 years going above and beyond for mine. He came over as soon as he found out about Brooke, and it was almost a three-hour drive from his place to ours. He'd been over almost every day since; it had been the most we'd seen each other in months. It had come to no surprise, but that didn't mean I didn't appreciate it.

He was a good guy, you know?

"You've already done enough," I replied, shooting him a look. "You know how much we appreciate what you're doing, but you need to take a break, Mal—"

"Are *you* going to take a break? From trying to find her?" he asked, wiping the sweat from his brow with his rolled-up sleeve. "I'm not going to stop until she's home, Frank. I just wish I could do more."

I reached out, silently squeezing his shoulder.

It felt so strange, not knowing what to say to him. I'd become accustomed to repeating the same phrases over and over: "*Thank you so much*", "*We appreciate it*", "*It means so much to us*". Obviously I meant it—every time I said it—but it was all starting to feel monotonous. The same words were being spoken over and over, but nothing was changing. I just wanted to be able to say something different.

When he turned his back to me, grabbing something from the counter, I quietly dropped the charred notebook into the trash, shoving it as deep down as it would go.

Like I said, I could've just explained everything to him there and then. I could've told him that I'd spent the whole night scribbling into that notepad, trying to keep note of what I could say, and what I couldn't say. I'd spent the whole night scribing everything I could remember from mine and Lucy's conversation on Friday. Trying to remember everything that she had said not to do, and not to say.

I made my way through a bottle of Gordon's as I did it; I couldn't find the whiskey, and I'd never been the biggest fan of gin, but I had to make do with what I could find.

But none of it mattered in the end, anyway.

I'd panicked.

I envisioned Liz finding the notes, piecing it all together. I couldn't risk it. I tore out the pages, grabbed some logs and newspaper, and set the whole thing ablaze, setting the garden on fire in the process.

I wondered if it had been a bad omen—setting those words on fire. I'd written Brooke's name a dozen times. Lucy's, too. I'd never believed in witchcraft, or any of that hippie-dippie shit, but ever since I threw that match onto the pile, my thoughts had multiplied. I'd been thinking about Brooke ever since she'd gone missing, but I'd done my best to forget about Lucy. I told myself that I didn't have time to think about her.

Now, I couldn't stop.

Next to Brooke, she was all that occupied my thoughts.

I was genuinely considering just telling Malcolm, there and then. If there was anyone on this earth that I *could* talk to about it, it was him. I was under no illusion that he was going to be on my side; he'd spent the best part of the past three decades reminding me how good I'd gotten it with Liz.

If he'd chosen tails instead of heads that night we flipped a coin to see who would take her out for dinner—the night we played our first big show in Mirrenville, the summer of '63—our lives would've looked pretty different. Maybe *I* would've become the master landscaper, searching for *his* kid.

As I began to imagine what Malcolm's children would've looked like with my wife, she made her way into the kitchen with a stack of envelopes. She barely looked up at either of us at first, but it was as if a switch flipped the moment she remembered that Malcolm was still there. It never failed to amuse me how she could just completely switch personas whenever she realized we weren't alone in the house. She had to put on a show for visitors. She just couldn't help herself.

"Are you sure you don't want anything to eat?" she asked Malcolm, and he shook his head, pulling his keys from his pocket.

"I'm heading to dinner at seven, but I really appreciate it."

"Well, make sure you say goodbye to Cam before you head out."

I made my way back into the living room, slumping down into my armchair, taking the same position that I'd found myself fixed into for the past eight days straight. The evening news was on, and I couldn't remember the last time we'd changed the channel. The anchor's voice droned on about usual politics and weather updates, none of which registered with me.

At least they weren't talking about us, I figured. That made a change.

"*...back to our breaking news in East Mirrenville.*" The anchor's tone shifted, catching my attention at the mention of our town. "*Yet another victim has been found dead in her home...*"

I sat forward, blinking to clear the haze.

"*...Frank?*"

I barely heard my own name being called in the background as I focused on the photograph being displayed on the television. It was another girl, the same age as Allie.

"*...authorities have confirmed that 18-year-old Amanda Melfi is the third teenager to be murdered in Mirrenville in the past week...*"

Amanda Melfi.

The name tugged at my memory. I wondered if it was another one of Allie's friends.

I hoped it wasn't.

"*...the police are urging residents to stay vigilant and report any suspicious activity,*" the reporter continued, and my eyes flickered up to the ceiling, toward Allie in her room. "*There have been unconfirmed reports that a curfew might be imposed in the coming days to protect teenagers and young adults from the ongoing threat—*"

"You should've said goodbye to Malcolm."

I barely heard her.

I barely even noticed her entering the room. It was only as she slammed a pile of envelopes onto my lap that I somewhat broke out of my daze.

As I turned my attention toward her, I saw that she hadn't even so much as glanced toward the television. She wasn't hearing what I was hearing. "I can't open any more envelopes," I heard her saying, her voice buzzing through the sounds coming from the television. "They're all the same. I don't even know who half these people are."

I gazed down at the envelopes on my lap, picking them up one by one. There were hundreds of them. My hands shook slightly as I shuffled through, unable to completely zone out from the news that continued to play in the background.

"…hello?!"

I looked up to find my wife glaring at me. The showman persona had completely dissolved now that Malcolm had left. I shook my head slowly, unsure of what to say next.

I didn't find the words fast enough.

"Your suit," she said coldly. "For tomorrow."

"What about it?" I asked, and her face completely hardened, as if I had just told her to go fuck herself.

"Did you find it?"

I continued flicking through the envelopes, wondering if she found any enjoyment in these conversations. Life would've been so much easier if we'd always had company in the house—someone constantly hanging out in the kitchen, ensuring that Liz stayed in hospitality mode. The second we were left alone together, she turned into a monster.

"It's upstairs," I replied, avoiding eye contact.

"Has it been ironed?"

My eyes flickered back to the television.

They were showing another photograph of the girl now; this was a much older photograph. She must've been around Cam's age in this picture, maybe younger. This particular photograph felt very familiar, and I couldn't pinpoint why.

"Yes," I mumbled, remembering to answer her.

"You need to shower and get ready for tomorrow. We need to look presentable."

Almost every single envelope had the same names written on the front: *Mr. and Mrs Nicholson*, or *Frank and Elizabeth Nicholson*, followed by our address. There were even a handful of *Frankie Flash*'s, and *Mrs. Flash*'s. It took me a couple of shuffles to find one that wasn't addressed to us.

"…my cream dress is hung upstairs," Liz went on, seemingly to herself. "And the coat I wore to your sister's wedding—"

"There's one for Allie here."

"Are you listening to me?!"

I lay the envelopes down, turning to face her properly. I knew I had to think very carefully about what I said next. Getting frustrated was going to get me nowhere. Even raising my voice slightly could tip her completely over the edge.

I took a moment to compose myself, forcing a smile.

"I'm sorry, alright?" I laughed slightly, and her face flushed a deep shade of red. "But I just can't get... *excited* about it like you are—"

"Excited?"

"I don't really care about what we're going to wear, that's all."

"Well, maybe you should." Her eyes burned into my skull. "Because this is our opportunity to officially speak to the press... to the whole *world*... and if you stand up there looking like *that*, they're not going to have a lot of nice things to say about this family."

"I don't care what they say about—"

"Well, *I* do!"

"This isn't about putting on a show, Liz," I began to argue, but she wouldn't let me finish. She never could.

"It's about *putting out a message*!" Her voice got louder as she threw her arms in the air. "It's about showing that we *care*, and that we *want* our daughter to come home—"

"I just don't see how me wearing a suit affects that—"

"Why are they talking about him again?"

Her tone shifted completely, leaving me momentarily confounded by the sudden change. She had turned toward the television now, finally paying attention to what they were saying, but a new photograph had appeared on the screen at this point; a picture of a man who felt disturbingly familiar.

A deep-seated anger churned in my stomach at the sight of his face, and it took me a moment to remember why.

A couple of words and sentences jumped out at me: *St. Mary's High School*; *seven years ago*; *accused*; *imprisoned—*

"Oh, my..." The words left Liz's mouth very softly, barely making a sound. "Mandy Melfi."

The screen had returned to the photograph of the murdered girl, and Liz's demeanor completely changed. This only confirmed that she had to be one of Allie's friends. At that moment, I made the connection between her and the man in the photograph.

Before I could even process what I was doing, the screen went black.

The remote hung limply in my hand, my thumb still hovering over the Off button. A few seconds passed in silence. There was no doubt in my mind that the same thoughts were running through both of our heads. As reality set in, a million further questions were raised.

My eyes flickered toward the kitchen, as if I could see the telephone with x-ray vision. My first instinct was to call Lucy.

I needed to hear it from her.

"We have to tell her." Liz's voice snapped me out of my trance. But she wasn't talking about the same "her" that I was thinking about.

I looked back up at the ceiling, trying to remember the last time I'd seen my eldest daughter for longer than a few seconds.

She barely left her room anymore. She was losing herself completely. Every time we broke another piece of bad news to her, it was like we were losing another piece of her.

These were her *friends*. The kids she'd grown up with. And they were dropping like flies.

I ran my fingers over the envelope with Allie's name written on it, hoping that whatever was inside was something good. She needed a pick-me-up. We were all going through this, but it was affecting her more than any of us. And I had no idea how to fix it.

Liz kept looking at me, and I realized what she meant. She wanted *me* to break the news.

Right.

I gripped the envelope, pulling myself out of my chair, desperately trying to figure out what the hell I was supposed to say to her when I got to her room. Each time something bad happened, it felt like things couldn't possibly get any worse.

I was proven wrong, every time.

The two photographs on the news kept replaying in my head, and I realized that telling Allie about her friend was going to be the easy part.

I began dragging myself up the stairs, each step heavier than the last. As I caught sight of her and her sister's bedroom door, I hesitated, knowing that beyond it lay a conversation that would shatter her world even further. We couldn't keep doing this to her. *I* couldn't keep doing this to her.

I knocked gently, waiting for her familiar, weary response. It was time to face the unimaginable for the fourth time in just over a week. It was strange how the unimaginable was slowly but surely becoming the inevitable.

I could only hope that, somehow, we'd find a way through the darkness together. I was her dad: this was my job. My priority.

I feared that soon, there might not be many pieces left to pick up.

HAYDEN | 6:13 PM

"...early this morning, the third victim was discovered, apparently killed by the so-called "Madman of Mirrenville"..."

My head hung over the trashcan as I threw up.

"...she was found at her parents' home with multiple stab wounds to her abdomen, believed to have been killed in a style almost identical to the previous victims, Melissa MacKenzie and Patrick Hurley..."

Vomit poured from my throat like a waterfall. Crippled by stomach cramps, sweat dripping down my face, I collapsed to my knees, retching until there was nothing left. Wrapping my arms around the trashcan, I tried to hold myself up. They just kept talking about it.

They wouldn't stop.

"...here's what a student from St. Mary's High School—the school that all three victims had attended—had to say when we spoke to her yesterday ..."

My face flashed onto the screen for the hundredth time that day.

They'd been playing the footage over and over, like it was super important or something. I just couldn't understand why they kept coming back to it. Three people were dead, and they were acting as if *I* had something to do with it.

I never even got to say anything about Melissa or Hurley.

They'd never asked me anything about them.

They just wanted to talk about Brooke.

"*...we walked home together after school*," I heard my own voice crackle through the TV; "*and, yeah... I mean, that was it. She didn't come to school on Monday.*"

"*What can you tell us about the party?*"

Everyone just wanted to know *all* about the party.

It'd become this whole fucking conspiracy. They were turning it into this whole horror movie scenario, making out that everyone who had set foot in Fitz Bird's house that night was now cursed. And everyone had just come to their own assumptions that Brooke had been there too.

"*Was Brooklyn with you? At the party?*"

I shakily set the trashcan down on the floor beside my bed, trying to block it all out. A bazillion thoughts flashed through my head, and all I could do was try to make sense of it all.

They were acting like the party was the only connection between Melissa, Hurley, and Mandy, when it was clear to *anyone* who actually knew them what the real connection was: they were the freaking *Eezy's*.

Well, okay, maybe Melissa wasn't, but she was one of their girlfriends—she was basically an Eezy groupie. She hung out with them. *That* was her connection.

I thought about every time that *we* had hung out with them. I wondered if the short amount of time that we'd spent hanging out with them meant that we were on the list... and, I mean, it was becoming pretty clear at this point that there *was* a list.

They'd even said it on the news: this was a fucking *serial killer*.

"*Did you see anything unusual at the party?*"

I wished I'd never even gone to that fucking party.

KNOCK-KNOCK-KNOCK.

My heart raced as I waited a couple of seconds, listening out to hear if Mom would answer the door. Last time I saw her, she was in the backyard. She probably couldn't hear the knocking out there.

I didn't want to be the one to answer the door. A *lot* of people had been murdered on their doorsteps lately.

"...*are you sure she wasn't there?*" the news reporter asked for the billionth time as the door knocked again, harder this time.

I peeked out the window into the backyard; Mom was still in her chair with the radio blasting next to her. She hadn't moved in hours. Even if she were awake, the music was blocking out all sound.

KNOCK.

KNOCK.

KNOCK.

I slowly stepped out of my bedroom, facing the stairs.

The hallway felt longer than usual, the shadows creeping up the walls like they were watching me move. Each step echoed, my heartbeat louder than my footsteps. I reached the top of the stairs and hesitated. Maybe this was a bad idea.

Maybe they really were here for me.

KNOCK-KNOCK-KNOCK-KNOCK-KNOCK—

They kept hammering on the door, even when I got to the bottom of the stairs. The whole door was shaking like they were trying to break it down; a couple more times and they probably would have.

I tried to unlock the door as fast as I could. My hands were shaking so much I couldn't turn the key. It kept jamming in the hole.

The door swung open.

At first, the sight on the other side of the door calmed me down. This wasn't some crazed killer with a machete; it was just Allie Nicholson.

She was just standing there with her clenched fist stretched out toward me, red and raw from pounding against the door. She didn't have a weapon or anything.

I, stupidly, assumed I was safe.

"I-I didn't hear the door—"

"You're a *fucking liar!*" She stepped toward me, forcing her way into the house. My immediate reaction was to shut the door, pushing her back outside. She pushed back. She was stronger than me. *"WHY ARE YOU STILL LYING?!"*

"What—"

CRACK.

My head hit the ground.

I saw the ceiling. It happened so fast. It took me a moment to realize why I was on the floor and how I got there. I stared straight up, unable to move. Sharp pain between my eyes. *Intense* pain.

My face was wet. Something was dripping.

I could taste metal, like coins.

Allie leaned over me. The faint scent of alcohol filled my nose, merging with the metallic taste in my mouth. My eyes couldn't focus. The blurry outline of her body was moving fast.

She grabbed the front of my shirt, pulling me just off the ground. I had no choice but to accept that... well, this was it.

She was going to kill me.

"A-Al—"

My mouth filled with thick liquid. It dripped down the corners of my lips, streaming down the sides of my face.

"SHE WAS WITH YOU—"

THWACK.

My head snapped to the side.

CRUNCH.

Burning. Darkness.

She hit again.

And again.

And again.

"...*I SWEAR... TO GOD...*" she screamed with each blow, *"IF ANYTHING HAPPENED TO HER... ANYTHING..."*

Something dripped down my chin.

"...*I WILL FUCKING KILL Y—*"

Maybe I blacked out. I'm not sure.

The next thing I saw was a smaller, blurry figure standing over me. I kept swallowing the thick liquid pooling in my throat. The punches had stopped. Everything blurred into one. The room swayed from side to side, like a carnival ride.

"*...uh oh...*" A small voice came from the darkness. "*...Hayden boo-boo...*"

My *nose*.

Each inhale stung like shit.

"*...yes... yes, my daughter has been attacked...*"

I barely recognized my own mother's voice in the distance. All I could do was lie there. I couldn't move. I couldn't see. All I could do was feel.

And everything burned.

Everything.

"*...yes, I saw her... Allie Nicholson...*"

I couldn't *breathe*.

"*...Allie Nicholson attacked my daughter...*"

LUCY | 7:01 PM

Anderson entered the room first, barely holding the door open for me to follow. I heard her voice before I saw her face as I turned back around to shut the door behind us: "*Can I go home already?*"

When I finally caught a glimpse of her, I understood what everyone else had been saying.

This wasn't the same Allie Nicholson that we first met at her house a week earlier—her eyes were dark, her hair frazzled, clothes covered in tears and holes. Her skin was bordering transparency.

Above all else, she reeked of booze.

"I'm going to give you some advice, Al." I watched as Anderson pulled a chair up in front of her. I stood in the corner, wondering how he was going to approach this. "And I really think you should take it."

She stared back at him, entirely fearless. Barely flinching.

"While there's an unsolved murder case *and* a missing

person's case ongoing, I really wouldn't suggest calling attention to yourself by attacking a minor. You've got enough eyes on you as it is."

Hayden Butler was going to be fine. A broken nose and a couple of scratches would fix itself in no time.

The person in real danger was Allie, who had been spotted and reported by several members of the public. Based on Hayden's injuries—no matter how superficial they were—Allie had completely lost her shit on her. Photographs had been taken. The press was already all over it.

"All charges have been dropped against you," Anderson went on, sitting back in his chair. "Hayden's mother agrees you need to be given a break... everyone understands you're under a lot of pressure right now, but if you ask me, you *really* need to—"

"She's a liar."

Anderson stared at her, barely breaking his poker face. She stared right back, entirely unintimidated.

This wasn't her first time at the station. I'd looked up her files a couple days before and she was no stranger to this building. Nothing too serious—just a couple of cases of underage drinking, vandalism, petty theft—but enough for her to get flagged up on the system.

"I'm sorry?" Anderson's face hardened, but this didn't discourage her. I wasn't entirely sure that she understood the severity of the situation.

"She was with my sister the night she went missing. She's lied to you. And she's telling reporters, too. She's a *liar*."

"You know..." Anderson hesitated, shaking his head a little. "I think you need to reflect on what happened today. It puts you in a bad light. It puts your *family* in a bad light."

"If they've dropped charges, can't I just go home already?"

Anderson peered over his shoulder, shooting me a look. I moved forward, gripping the documents in my hands. There wasn't a chair for me to take a seat, so I leaned against the desk instead. I cleared my throat, wondering how the hell we were supposed to break the news to her.

"Actually... we were wondering if you could answer a couple of questions for us first," I replied, and her eyes flickered toward me. She looked down at the papers in my hand before locking eyes with mine. Nothing in her expression had changed.

"A couple of points have come up," I continued, glancing away. "We've been talking to Donnie Booker. You know him, right?" Her face fell slightly at the mention of his name. Maybe I wouldn't have noticed the change in her demeanor if I hadn't known the truth.

She immediately began shifting in her seat, breaking eye contact. "What did he do?" she asked, her voice a little shaky.

"He told us about his relationship with Brooke."

Now we had her attention. Her eyes widened, darting between the two of us. Confusion clouded her expression as she stammered a single word: "What?"

"We're aware that the relationship was kept secret—"

"Wait, no, Brooke didn't..." She cut herself off with a laugh. "She doesn't know him. They've never even met."

Anderson looked over at me once more, barely giving me anything. I wasn't sure how much I was giving away, but her reaction had certainly surprised me.

I believed her, too. I believed that she actually had no idea about any of this, based on her reaction alone.

"They were in a relationship for almost three months," Anderson confirmed, to which Allie scoffed loudly. "We've spoken to a number of people who have confirmed it, including Donnie himself—"

"It's not true."

"Allie—"

"It's *not*." Her voice was getting higher and higher with each word, and there was no doubt in my mind that she was being serious. She'd genuinely had no idea about this.

This revelation was only going to make the rest of the conversation even more difficult.

"We assumed that she would have told you," Anderson continued, but Allie just kept shaking her head defiantly. "Donnie told us that only a handful of people knew, and we assumed you were one of them."

"There's *no way* this could've happened without me knowing about it," she continued to laugh, becoming more visibly confused as the seconds passed. "*She* would've told me—*he* would've told me! Who even told you about this?! It's not true!"

From what I'd gathered, despite their differences, the Nicholson sisters had always been close. They shared a bedroom, for Christ's sake. And it certainly didn't make sense that Brooke could've hidden this from Allie, knowing how close she and Donnie were. With that, Anderson took a deep breath, folding his arms across his chest. I knew exactly what was coming, and I wasn't sure that I wanted to be there to see Allie's reaction.

"The reason we're bringing this up," he said finally, clearly stuck for words in his confusion; "is that we found something while searching your room. You and Brooke share a room, correct?"

She nodded silently. Anderson cleared his throat, nodding toward me. Toward the papers in my hands.

I really didn't want to be the one to say it. I *really* didn't want to be the one to break this to her. I pulled out the top sheet on the pile, holding the photocopied document in front of Allie's face. She locked eyes onto it, and I watched as the blood rushed from her face.

"We found this in the trash," I said finally, carefully examining her facial expressions as she stared at the photograph of the pregnancy test. "It was negative, but it had been recently used. Your mother confirmed that the trash bag had only just been replaced, the day before Brooke went missing—"

"Does my mom know?" she asked suddenly, barely moving her eyes from the image. "About... that?"

"Not yet."

"You think it was Brooke's?" Her voice was so quiet that I almost couldn't catch what she had said. Her eyes burned into the document with such an intensity that my hands began to shake. "I mean... if it was negative, why does it matter? What does this even mean?"

"That's why we're asking you."

Here we go, I thought to myself.

Anderson took the paper from my hand, holding it down flat in front of her. I already knew she wasn't going to take this well. She was clearly unstable. Her whole demeanor had switched ever since we'd mentioned Donnie Booker, and I was preparing myself for the explosion that was coming next.

"We know about the pregnancy, Al. *Your* pregnancy."

154

If I didn't know any better, I might've assumed that she had no idea what he was talking about based on her initial response. Maybe she was a better actress than I'd originally thought. Her facial expression had barely shifted. "I don't know what you're talking about—"

"Donnie told us."

An abrupt laugh suddenly shot out, but her face told another story. She was unraveling. "I don't know what *he's* talking about, either—"

"He told us about your relations over the summer."

"*Relations*," she scoffed, shaking her head. Her hands tremored as they danced across her lap, picking away at loose strands on her jeans. It was unsettling, watching as she slowly crumbled with each new piece of information.

"You were sleeping together," Anderson corrected himself, and she blew a raspberry, completely avoiding eye contact at this point. Her face was getting redder and redder, and I wanted to tell Anderson to stop.

But I couldn't.

"Why would he—? I-I... I..." She couldn't even get the words out. "I don't... did *he* tell you that? *Seriously?*"

"Is it true?"

Words were pouring out of her mouth, but she could not string a full sentence together, no matter how hard she was trying. The muscles in her face were distorting into an expression that I couldn't recognize. "...I-I... *once*," she said finally, exasperated. "Literally *one* time."

"While he was with Brooke?"

"That's *not* fucking true," she suddenly snapped, jabbing a finger toward Anderson's face. "I would've *known*—"

"Donnie seemed to think that you had told her."

"*Donnie* didn't even know I was *pregn*—"

She stopped, gasping a little. Swallowing it back. I watched as the cogs seemed to click into place, hardly slotting together.

"Did Brooke know?" The words came from my mouth before I could even think about it.

She couldn't look at me. She wouldn't look at either of us. That was the one thing we couldn't get from Donnie—*how* he had found out that Allie had been pregnant. According to him, she'd hidden it from her.

The only plausible explanation would've been that Allie had told Brooke, and Brooke had told him.

"I-I didn't know..." she began to stammer, her eyebrows knotting together. "I-I don't... I... I *didn't*... what the *f-fuck*—"

The implication here, of course, was that Brooke had broken up with Donnie Booker after finding out that he'd gotten her sister pregnant.

This was enough motive for anyone to run away from home.

"We just need to know if the test in the trash was yours," Anderson said, placing the document face-down on the desk. "If it wasn't, we need to consider the fact that Brooke may have thought that *she* was—"

"It wasn't mine."

"Are you sure?"

"Am *I*..." she repeated breathlessly, laughing like a crazy person. "I... why the *fuck* would it be *mine*?!"

I had been watching her closely ever since we'd entered the room, carefully scanning her body when she wasn't looking. According to Donnie, he hadn't had sex with her since early June, and her stomach was completely flat. If anything, she'd seemed to have lost a significant amount of weight within the eight days that I had known her.

She had a point: why would she take a test if she knew she wasn't pregnant anymore?

"No one is saying this is your fault," Anderson said, but I could barely hear him over Allie's gasps and groans. "We're sorry to bring it up, but we have to consider everything when trying to understand why Brooke may have run away—"

"You *seriously* still think she ran away?!"

There was a brief moment of silence.

I turned to Anderson, who seemed unsure what to say next. It was awful. She was clearly falling apart, right in front of us, and she somehow still couldn't put the pieces together for herself. This information alone had completely changed how we were looking at this investigation—Brooke was 15 years old, and she'd just found out that her boyfriend and her sister had been sleeping together. It seemed clearer than ever that she *had* run away.

Yet neither of us knew how to say this out loud. It didn't feel fair. Despite her anger, it was clear that she was blaming herself.

How couldn't she?

She glanced at me, then back at Anderson. A sudden strength had taken over her demeanor. "It wasn't mine," she said coldly, gesturing toward the paper on the desk. "Is that everything?"

More silence. I had no idea what we were supposed to say next.

"Am I under arrest?"

"What? No," Anderson shook his head, treading carefully. "Of course you're not—"

"I know my rights," she spat, unsteadily prizing herself from her chair. "You can't keep me here. I've told you what I know. I-I want to go home now, alright? I'm not a… a fucking *hostage*, or w-whatever…"

I opened my mouth, but Anderson held his hand up, stopping me. "Thank you for helping us out," he answered quietly. "Of course, you're free to go. We'll call if we have any more questions."

"Have you told my parents?"

My blood ran cold as my thoughts fled back to Frank.

I imagined our next encounter—me having to lie to him for once. I wondered what he'd think if he knew. Liz, too. We hadn't told them yet, and as far as I knew, we had no plans to tell them. Allie was 18. We had no reason to.

She turned to me, and I shook my head silently. I just hoped she could see how sorry I really was.

If she did, she didn't give it away. She barely even reacted.

She stormed past the both of us without looking back, running through the door and slamming it shut behind her. An involuntary gasp left my mouth, and I quickly spun to check if Anderson had heard it. He hadn't.

He had picked the paper back up, taking another look at the copy. He spoke one last time without even looking up to acknowledge me: "She's got one hell of a temper."

ADJACENT

9 DAYS AFTER THE DISAPPEARANCE OF
BROOKLYN NICHOLSON

FRANK | 5:56 PM

When I was just a little older than Allie, I performed in sold-out stadiums every weekend. Night after night, I played in front of tens of thousands of people without a second thought.

It'd been close to 20 years since I'd last stood on a stage, and before this moment, I hadn't really thought about it too much. I'd gone over it in my head, sure, but as far as I knew, there were only going to be a couple of hundred people in this crowd. Easy work. Nothing too crazy.

As I stood on stage for the first time since 1979, my senses were heightened to the point of overload. The room was awash with thousands of flashing lights, and the air buzzed with anxious whispers. There were so many reporters. So many cameras.

"...*Brooklyn has been missing since September seventeenth, and she was last seen in her home at approximately six pm...*"

We were all seated in a row, staring out into the crowd.

The lieutenant had been talking for a while, going over all the details that we already knew. I sat on the left side of the stage with Liz, while Lucy was on the right, sitting at the opposite end of the panel. I barely recognized anyone sitting in the seats between us, and I thought it was odd that Officer Anderson hadn't shown up.

Lucy sat on her own, standing out from the rest of us in her blue uniform; a single pop of color against an otherwise muted ensemble.

As the lieutenant continued to address the audience, I found myself frequently glancing over in her direction. She remained facing forward, barely moving. I felt every movement that Liz made at the side of me, churning everything up even further.

"...in light of recent events, our concern for Brooklyn's safety is more urgent than ever," the lieutenant continued, his voice crackling through the microphone. "We urge anyone who may have seen Brooklyn or has any information regarding her whereabouts to come forward."

He was holding up Brooke's most recent school photo, taken just a week or so before she went missing.

When she'd first brought it home I hadn't really paid much attention to it; Liz had just propped it up on the mantlepiece with all the other pictures. Since then, this image had been plastered over countless posters and newspapers, and I had become closely familiar with each and every detail.

Only recently I had noticed that Brooke had a tiny beauty mark above her lip, just like my mother had.

The lieutenant's voice droned on, but the words began to blur. "...effective immediately, there will be a strict eight pm curfew for all residents under the age of eighteen," he announced, his tone firm. "This is in response to the recent murders of three teenagers in our community. We believe this measure is necessary to ensure the safety of our youth while we continue both investigations."

Murmurs filled the room, a ripple of unease spreading through the crowd as parents whispered to each other, exchanging anxious glances. The reporters in the back jotted down notes, their pens scratching furiously against paper.

"...we want to be absolutely clear that at this time, we have no evidence linking Brooklyn's disappearance to these tragic events," the lieutenant stated steadily, his voice rising above the murmurs. "Our investigations are ongoing, and we are pursuing every possible lead in both cases. However, I understand the fear this community is feeling, and I want to assure you that we are doing everything in our power to find Brooklyn *and* bring those responsible for these heinous crimes to justice—"

They were like vultures—the reporters. Ready to pounce on anything. The knot in my throat tightened as I stared out at them, accidentally making direct eye contact with several of them.

"...the former teacher..." The lieutenant's voice cut back through the noise, but it was distant, like I was underwater. "...worked at the school during the time Brooklyn attended... I know there have been rumors, but..."

I only caught fragments. I couldn't focus.

"...*no evidence... no connection......*" His words floated in and out, my head too full, too loud to grasp what he was saying. "...*no reason to believe...*"

Across the stage, I caught sight of Lucy's profile. Even from a distance, I could see the strain etched into her features, the tightness in her shoulders.

"...*I now want to take a moment to recognize Brooklyn's family...*"

A couple of *woo*'s echoed around the room.

I'd already spotted one or two Unrest Stand shirts in the crowd, and I honestly wasn't sure how I was supposed to feel. A month ago I would've been ecstatic; it'd been a long time since I'd run into a fan. Now, sitting on the stage, surrounded by flashing lights and countless photographs of my youngest daughter, that thrill had been replaced by a gnawing ache.

The cheering felt out of place; a stark reminder of another life. Those were the days when the stage was a sanctuary, a place where I felt invincible. This stage felt like a prison.

The lieutenant was now gesturing toward myself and Liz, indicating that it was almost our time to speak. A knot tightened in my stomach. "I can't imagine a more difficult time for a family," the lieutenant went on, and a mumble made its way through the crowd. "For any *parent*…. my heart, and all our hearts, go out to them…"

Liz tensed up at my side. I automatically slid my hand onto her knee, squeezing lightly. She didn't respond.

"…I will now be handing over to Frank and Elizabeth Nicholson. They will be giving an appeal but will not be answering any questions at this time. Thank you."

The lights began flashing faster and brighter than before as all attention turned to us. All I could think was how lucky we were to be sitting down. I wasn't sure I could do this standing up. All we had to do was speak.

I forced myself to look directly into the crowd, and the room began to spin. There were a *lot* of people. A *lot* of cameras.

The whole fucking world was watching us.

I leaned forward toward the microphone, sensing that Liz wasn't going to speak first—she had become entirely rigid, barely breathing. I cleared my throat slightly, causing a loud feedback screech to pierce the ears of everyone sitting in that room. I nodded to myself, taking a moment to process everything. Allowing myself to breathe.

"Good afternoon, everyone," I began, my voice wavering slightly. "Or, is it good evening? I-I'm not sure what time it is…"

Brief laughter echoed around the room.

I lightly dabbed my forehead with my sleeve, unsure whether to laugh back. I wasn't sure what was deemed appropriate, and Liz had spent the past 48 hours drilling into me that we *had* to act right. I wasn't sure what "acting right" even meant. "We appreciate you all being here today, to help us find our daughter. Brooke."

A thousand words ran through my mind as I tried to figure out what to say next.

I had thought about it—a *lot*—during the build-up to this moment. At that moment, though, it didn't feel right doing all the formalities; the police had already done all that, and I didn't want to repeat what they'd already said. I wanted to keep the crowd's attention.

I took a deep breath, steadying myself.

"She was our third child," I continued, unsure where to look.

"Our youngest daughter. She's fifteen years old and one of the brightest people I know… if not, *the* brightest. I'm still not sure where she got her brains from."

More laughter made its way through the room. Liz moved slightly; I hoped she was laughing too.

"She's always been ahead of the curve. She's graduating high school next year—two years early—so we've spent the past summer driving her across the country to check out colleges. Her heart's set on Julliard, but…" I paused, turning to look at Liz for the first time. "Well, my wife's got her heart set on med school. The thing is, Brooke once cried for a week straight after accidentally stepping on a snail. I'm not sure she'd make the best doctor."

The more the crowd reacted, the easier it became. The less I really thought about what I was saying.

"But we both know she's destined for great things, no matter what she decides to do in the end. She is *incredibly* musical… she gets that from me," I said with a faint smile, ignoring the further *woo*'s sounding from all corners of the room. "She plays the piano and the violin, though singing… well, that's not her strong suit. Never has been. But that never stops her from trying, and that's what I love about her, you know? She's determined. Ambitious. I know I'm her dad, and I'm *incredibly* biased, but I swear to you— whatever Brooke decides to do with her life, she's gonna do it."

I glanced back at Liz, who was frozen into place, pain etched on her face. I thought long and hard about what I was going to say next.

"She has a brother and a sister at home." My voice cracked, the weight of the situation coming down hard on me. "And they miss her more than anything. We *all* do. We… well, we don't know what we're doing without her."

The lump in my throat was expanding rapidly, and a laugh escaped my mouth as I tried to keep it together. *Jesus.*

I wasn't sure if I'd ever cried on stage before.

"…*Brooke*…" I stopped myself, fighting so fucking hard to keep my voice from trembling. "Brooke, if you can hear this—"

A blur of blue to my right moved in a way that caught my attention. I knew I couldn't look at her; the whole world was watching. I shook my head ever so slightly, pushing her out of my mind. The brief distraction was welcomed, in any case.

"...if you're safe, and you're hearing this, or... or you're watching it... I-I don't know... if you're hearing me right now, please just... please come home. If something's wrong, we can work through it. We're not mad, alright? We just... *we love you...* and we need you to come home now, okay?"

Liz's hand squeezed mine.

"If you're... if you're *not* safe," I pushed on, quickly wiping my cheek, "and something *has* happened... just know that we are not going to stop until you're home. You *will* come home. I promise."

It occurred to me that I wasn't entirely sure who I was making that promise to. Brooke. Liz. Myself.

All I knew was that I meant it.

Liz's hand landed on my shoulder, and I wanted to push her away. She was making it worse. Tears slipped through my shut eyelids, and the more I tried to keep still, the more I shook. Feedback echoed throughout the building, and suddenly I could hear Liz's shaky breaths through every speaker in the room.

Cameras snapped ahead of us, and I saw red at the thought of me being plastered over some paper the next day, every headline reading *Frankie Flash Cries like a Fucking Baby*.

I angrily wiped the tears away, scratching my face with the sleeve of my coat. Liz still hadn't said anything yet. I eventually managed to return her favor, squeezing her hand under the table. She kept taking deep, steady breaths, in and out. Everyone stood at a standstill, waiting for her to speak.

Her mouth opened.

A scream came out.

I sat completely frozen, staring. Liz's eyes met mine; they were so wide that the whites were completely exposed. Her mouth was still open. She still hadn't made a sound.

It wasn't her scream.

The room erupted.

Lucy was the first to jump up. My head snapped toward her as she shot up from her seat, staring into the crowd with huge eyes. I followed her gaze, watching as the crowd exploded into chaos. People were shouting, pushing, moving away from the center of the commotion. As the crowd parted I saw a figure standing in the middle, stumbling through the throng. They were screaming. They were covered in blood.

I blinked, struggling to process what I was seeing. My mind raced, and a cold dread settled over me.

But I couldn't move yet.

The figure was getting closer. The crowd parted around them. Liz recognized them before I did. The first word that came from her mouth was a name.

Our daughter's name.

Before I could fully process the situation I'd jumped from the stage, adrenaline propelling me forward. The chaos around me blurred as I made my way through the crowd, blood pounding in my ears. Liz was screaming now. Bloodcurdling screams encircled me.

As I got closer, I saw her clearly—disheveled, covered in blood, eyes wide with terror.

She collapsed to the floor.

No one was moving. I shoved through, pushing anyone in my way to the ground.

"*MOVE*," Lucy yelled at the side of me.

I caught a glimpse of her shoving through the crowd beside me, moving faster than I could. She was going to get to her first. My heart raced, desperation clawing at me as I finally broke through the crowd, my eyes locked on the last place where I'd seen her.

"*…it's happening again…*" someone sobbed not too far from me, their voice breaking through the commotion; "*…they did it again…*"

"*…the fourth victim…*"

I lunged forward before freezing in horror.

"*…they   killed   her…*"

HAYDEN | 6:03 PM

Something was happening in the city hall. Something big.

I slowed my bike, dragging one foot along the ground as I tried to make sense of the chaos. People were screaming in there... like, really screaming. The doors were all shut so I couldn't see what was going on, but it sounded bad. It was like someone was getting murdered in there.

There were no police cars or anything near the building, which made the whole thing seem even weirder. It was as if something had only just happened, and I'd just happened to have ridden past as it was unfolding.

My eyes flickered over to the phone box just across the road. Was *I* supposed to call the police? What was I even supposed to do?

And it wasn't even as if anyone else was around—the streets were completely dead. My mind started racing, imagining all the scenarios that could've been unfolding inside that building. What if there was a fire? I couldn't see any smoke. Maybe they were cheering... but it didn't sound like cheers. It sounded like screaming.

And I mean *scary* screaming. Like someone was dying.

My heart pounded in my chest as I weighed my options, the screams getting louder with each passing second. The police station was only a couple of minutes away—it would've been faster to ride over there and tell them in person. Maybe they were already on their way over. There was no *way* the people living nearby couldn't hear what was going on. It was like something from a freaking horror movie.

I was just about to start pedaling again, despite not really knowing where I was headed, when one of the doors swung open. A guy stepped out.

At least, I think it was a guy.

He was pretty tall, and he had a St. Mary's sweatshirt on with the hood up, so I couldn't see his face. He was moving fast. Real fast. The way he was rushing made me freeze up completely. I couldn't pinpoint why the sight of him made me so uncomfortable. The hood slipped down a little, and I caught just a tiny glimpse of his face.

Before I could fully process what—or, well, *who*—I was looking at, my whole body filled with rage.

"...Donnie?"

Shouting his name created a dull ache throughout my sinuses, rattling through the cuts inside my nose. His head snapped up, and his eyes locked onto me. For a moment, his face was completely blank, and we just stared at each other. My mind flashed back to the last time I saw him, and a knot tightened inside my belly. Anger flooded my senses.

His eyes widened, and I really hoped that he was remembering what happened at the party.

Brooke's face flashed through my mind. I could feel my face contorting into a glare, my eyes burning deep into his face. At that point, I wasn't even scared. I wasn't thinking about the whole logistics of the situation—you know, *why* he was running away from a building filled with screaming people. I just knew I hated him. I hated him more than anything.

Before I could say anything else, he bolted.

He was moving so fast, sprinting past me and away from the city hall. Sirens started blaring in the distance, getting louder and closer, and blue lights began flashing everywhere.

I couldn't take my eyes off Donnie; he was disappearing down the streets behind me, fast. Two police cars came racing around the corner and screeched to a halt outside the city hall. Four officers jumped out before I even had a chance to process what was happening, or what *had* happened. They practically kicked the doors down and rushed inside.

I slowly turned back to where I'd last seen Donnie, but he was long gone. My grip on the handlebars of my bike tightened, and I wondered what would happen if I tried to chase him. I wondered what would've happened if I'd caught him.

The screams inside were getting louder. I heard someone shouting in a deep voice, creating further commotion. My blood ran cold as Brooke's face flashed through my mind one more time.

LUCY | 9:21 PM

I shoved the door open with all my strength, bursting into the office. Anderson was sitting at his desk, barely reacting to my entrance. I held onto the door handle, catching my breath, struggling to mask my frustration.

"Where *were* you?!"

He didn't answer me.

I wasn't sure if he even heard me; he was shuffling papers on his desk, not even acknowledging my presence. I moved into the room, shutting the door behind me. My hands were still shaking. I hadn't had a moment to process anything that had just happened, and seeing Anderson sit so casually at his desk made me want to explode.

"Allie Nicholson's in hospital."

He finally looked up. He barely reacted.

"She was *stabbed*," I stammered, pushing through the anger. "She just... she showed up at the conference, just... *covered* in blood—"

"Is she going to be okay?"

I was practically gasping for breath, inhaling vast gulps of air. I took a moment to compose myself, appalled by his lack of interest in what I was saying. He was so calm. Too calm.

"She's fine," I replied shakily, leaning against my desk for support. "Surface wounds. She got away before they could—"

I couldn't finish that sentence.

"Good."

"*Good*?" I repeated, suddenly realizing that this was the first time that I'd ever so much as raised my voice at him. "Where the hell *were* you?! We had to evacuate a room of two hundred people who thought their *lives* were in danger! They thought—*we* thought that Allie was *dead*! They're *traumatized*!"

He finished whatever he was doing at his desk, wiping his hands before finally looking up at me. I felt like I was going insane. He just watched me in silence, giving no reaction, as if I wasn't having some sort of meltdown right in front of him.

"Did she see who it was?" he asked finally, and I shook my head, wiping the sweat from my brow.

"No... no, but Donnie Booker's back in custody. They caught him running away from the building."

"Good," he replied, picking something up from his desk and pulling himself up from his chair. "That saves us some time."

"What's that?"

He lifted it up, giving it a small wave. A videotape.

I'd only ever seen Anderson smile maybe twice in the whole time I'd known him, and while he wasn't exactly smiling now, he looked fairly satisfied.

"This," he said, holding the tape toward me, "is our game-changer."

He made his way over to the portable television in the corner of the room, wheeling it closer to me. I watched him in silence, trying to calm myself down with deep, steady breaths. Everything was catching up to me all at once. I clenched my fist tightly, still feeling the dampness from Frank's shoulder from when I'd attempted to prise him away from his unconscious daughter.

Liz Nicholson's voice thanking me at the hospital echoed in my mind, over and over. "...*you have no idea how grateful we are...*"

I quickly swallowed the bile that had risen in my throat, pooling in my mouth as I remembered everything she said.

"...*you've done so much for us...*"

I hated Frank more than ever.

He'd hung back, too scared to come near us—as if the idea of me talking alone with his wife was more than he could handle. As if I wasn't just as terrified as he was. The only difference was that I had no way to escape the situation. I had to stand there and take it. I had to listen to her *thanking* me, telling me how much she *appreciated* me... I couldn't even bring myself to look at him, peering over her shoulder like a scared little schoolboy.

I hated him.

I *hated* him.

"You ready?" Anderson asked, breaking me out of my thoughts. I looked up through hazy eyes, barely catching a glimpse of what was playing on the screen. It was all too fuzzy.

There was a date in the corner of the screen: *09/05/1994.*

"What the hell is this?" I muttered, unable to mask my irritation. It had been a long day, and I wasn't in the mood for any more surprises.

"Labor Day," he replied, standing next to the television. "Got an anonymous call earlier. Some girl. She said we needed to take a look at some footage from behind the Turtin bar, on the other side of the alleyway. Gave the exact date, time, location... and then hung up. Couldn't trace it." He moved his finger to the television, hovering over the Play button. "Ready?"

I nodded in silence, utterly defeated. None of this was sticking to my brain, and I was ready to get whatever this was over with so I could get home. I hadn't eaten in 12 hours. I was fucking exhausted.

He pressed the button and the footage began to play.

It was so grainy that I could barely make out what I was looking at. I squinted at the screen, barely recognizing the entrance of the dimly lit alley, partially obscured by overflowing dumpsters and scattered debris. Two figures appeared onscreen, emerging from the opposite direction: a boy and a girl. The boy was tall and bald, dressed in dark clothes, and I could've sworn I recognized him.

When I got a good look at the girl, it all came together. I could've recognized those braids anywhere.

"Is that—"

Up until this point I'd only seen Brooke Nicholson in photographs.

There was something so surreal about seeing her moving around, brought to life before my very eyes. Suddenly, she was more than just a picture.

It was only then that I realized who the second figure was. Dread settled in the pit of my stomach as I watched two of the most prominent figures in our case leaning against a wall, speaking to each other, completely unaware of how different their lives would be just a couple of weeks later.

Brooke Nicholson and Donnie Booker, in the flesh.

What surprised me the most, based on what I'd seen so far, was how skinny Brooke was. Despite the graininess of the footage, it was clear that her clothes were sagging from her, barely fitting her tiny frame. Donnie was wearing dark jeans and a hefty leather jacket. They were both stood against the wall, facing the back end of the alley opposite the station, directly behind the Turtin bar. They were talking about something, but I couldn't hear a word.

"You couldn't get audio?" I asked Anderson, and he just shook his head. I turned back to the screen, struggling to gauge exactly what was going on as the television crackled through the silence in the room. Brooke seemed tense. Awkward. Donnie's arms were crossed, but he was staring directly at her while she was looking away.

She seemed uneasy, but he looked pretty comfortable.

Suddenly, she pulled away from the wall, flailing her arms around. She had turned her back to the camera, but it was pretty clear that she was yelling at him. Her shoulders bobbed up and down as she threw her arms out toward him. He barely reacted.

I wondered if they were talking about Allie.

Donnie's body swayed a little as if he was laughing at her. I couldn't get a clear view of either of their faces, so it was difficult to determine their exact expressions. Brooke launched forward, shoving him back into the wall. Jesus... she was small, but she was strong. She knocked him back, but he kept attempting to move toward her. It looked like he was trying to put his arms around her but to no avail. It seemed like a friendly approach: maybe he was trying to calm her down.

But she wasn't giving in. She pushed him again before taking a step back. Neither of them moved again for a couple of seconds. I would've given anything to have heard just a brief moment of their conversation.

Then, something switched.

I leaned closer to the screen, straining my eyes to get a better look at Donnie's face. He wasn't moving anymore. Whatever Brooke had just said, it had struck a nerve, and his posture had completely stiffened, his faint swaying abruptly coming to a halt. The tension in the air was palpable, clearly visible through the grainy footage. Brooke continued to stand her ground, her body language still defiant, but now there was a hint of hesitation. She shrunk in his shadow, only ever so slightly.

Donnie's arms slowly uncrossed, and he took a deliberate step forward—his movements were controlled, but there was a menacing undercurrent. Brooke didn't back down, but she no longer seemed as sure of herself. The dynamic had shifted entirely.

I felt myself leaning closer to the screen as I tried to decode the situation. Something had changed. Something had been said.

Donnie said something, his lips moving with precise, sharp enunciation. Brooke flinched, the impact of his words visible even from this distance. She shook her head, responding with equal intensity, but her gestures were more erratic now, less confident. She folded her arms as she became smaller and smaller.

Donnie's hand shot out, grabbing her wrist.

"What is this?" The words cracked as they left my lips. My mouth had completely dried up as a sense of uneasiness made its way through my body, flooding my veins. Anderson's silence angered me more than anything.

I just wished he could've warned me about what was about to happen.

Brooke had tried to pull away, but his grip was ironclad. He yanked her closer, his face inches from hers, their confrontation escalating rapidly. The aggression in his stance contrasted sharply with his earlier casual demeanor, and in return, Brooke was now trying to escape him. She wasn't mad anymore.

She was scared.

He slowly spun her around so that she was facing the camera, and his back was to us. His hand was still wrapped around her wrist as he moved in so close that she was backed against the wall. Her head twitched as she, seemingly, searched for an escape. But there wasn't one.

He grabbed her other wrist and pushed his body against hers, pinning her to the wall.

She tried to pull away. He moved his face so close to hers that she couldn't look away.

He tugged her dress up, sliding his hands underneath.

I thought about Frank.

I thought about how he would feel, watching this. How he would feel if he knew *I* was watching this.

Donnie spun her around, pushing her against the wall. In the corner of my eye, I saw Anderson's head drop. As I slowly covered my mouth with my hand, Donnie covered Brooke's with his.

He hitched up her dress.

"I've seen enough." I stood up, turning away from the screen.

For the first time since the tape started playing, I was grateful there wasn't any audio. But Anderson didn't switch off the tape; it continued to play behind me, crackling as the tape ran.

"You think *I* wanted to see it?" I heard him saying, and my stomach dropped. "This is the reality of the job, Hardie."

I turned back to the TV, slowly moving my eyes back to the screen. I immediately wished I hadn't. My heart cracked into a million pieces as I forced my gaze to remain locked onto the footage.

"How long does it go on for?" I asked quietly, blinking hard to prevent my glossy eyes from giving me away.

"Not much longer."

It felt like hours.

I thought about how much longer it must've felt for her.

Frank's face flashed through my memory. Liz's, too. It was better for me to watch it than them—after all, I didn't know Brooke. Not really. Whatever I was feeling in that moment, I felt it for a stranger.

It came to an end after what seemed like an eternity. The screen had distorted through my eyes, all becoming one big blur. My eyes were filling up faster than I'd anticipated. Anderson finally wandered back over to the television, pausing it as Donnie staggered away, moving off-screen. Brooke was on the floor.

"Well, there we have it," I heard Anderson say. I could've sworn I heard a smile in his voice. "We've got him."

I couldn't even look at him.

"What are you talking about?" I asked quietly, unable to break my gaze from the floor beneath his desk.

"He's not getting out this time."

"This was almost two weeks before she went missing. This doesn't mean… this doesn't…" I paused, my eyebrows knotting together. Trying to figure out—in real time—what any of this meant. "Why didn't she tell anyone? Why didn't she report this?"

Anderson shrugged with such disinterest that I wanted to

scream at him. He was so completely unaffected by what we had just witnessed. It made me feel as if there was something wrong with me.

"Doesn't matter," he replied, entirely emotionless. "We've got enough to keep him in custody, and we can charge him with assault, at the very least. Now we've got time to make him talk."

I continued to stare at the floor, struggling to process what had just happened. She was still there, on the screen, crumpled on the floor against the wall. I didn't want to see it anymore, but the image had burned itself into my brain.

I knew I was going to be seeing that image long after he'd switched off the television.

"This was almost two weeks ago," I repeated, unable to look up. "This doesn't necessarily mean he's responsible for her disappearance."

"We've got him on sexual assault and evidence of a troubling pattern. It's not just the footage, Hardie; it's the *context*. We've been looking for a solid lead, and this is it!"

"I just don't understand why she wouldn't report this."

I barely glanced up, catching him shrugging again. His disinterest was palpable. "You'd be surprised. Maybe she was scared. Thought no one would believe her."

A solid wave of frustration and helplessness washed over me.

On the one hand, everything seemed so clear-cut; after all, Donnie had connections with each of the murder victims, and we'd found his car burned out in the woods. Now, knowing what he'd done, it seemed more certain than ever that he must be involved in Brooke's disappearance, if *nothing* else.

But it just didn't feel right.

I couldn't put my finger on it, but something felt off. "There's got to be more to this," I whispered, barely noticing that I'd said those words out loud. Anderson laughed without humor.

"There's always more," he said flatly, as if I'd just told him that water was wet. "But we deal with what we have. We have enough to keep him in custody. We'll build the case from there."

I wanted to argue—to push back—but the weight of what I'd just seen made it so hard to find the words. I glanced back at the screen. She just looked so vulnerable. Defeated. It lit a fire in my belly as I imagined a small fragment of what she had gone through in the weeks leading to her disappearance.

"Alright," I said, finally looking up at him properly. Finally finding the strength to look him in the eye. "What do we do now?"

A smile flickered across his face. It wasn't genuine happiness, but there was a brief glimmer of excitement in his eyes as they locked onto mine. I wished I could share his enthusiasm. Instead, I felt a wave of nausea. Disgust. Complete and utter heartbreak.

But he was right: this was the step forward that we'd been waiting for. This was what we needed to push the case ahead. And maybe, just maybe, Donnie Booker really was the key to unraveling it all.

As Anderson began outlining the next steps, I fought hard to steady my racing thoughts. This was far from over, and despite the unsettling weight of the footage, I knew I had to move on from this somehow. I couldn't dwell on it. I *couldn't* let it get to me.

I just wished I could stop thinking about Frank.

ADJACENT

10 DAYS AFTER THE DISAPPEARANCE OF
BROOKLYN NICHOLSON

LIZ | 7:14 AM

The front door slammed into the wall as I shoved it open, flying into the hallway with a speed that surprised even me. My heart was pounding in my chest, not just from the rush to get home, but from the overwhelming need to see my son.

I hadn't seen him in almost 24 hours, and the thought of him waking up without me there—it'd gnawed at me all night.

"Cam?!" I called out, my voice echoing through the house. I could hear the sound of the TV coming from the living room, but there was no immediate response to my call. I was about to call out again when a figure came around the corner, peeking through the kitchen door.

"He's getting dressed."

Relief flooded my senses as I recognized Malcolm in the

doorway. As he spoke, I heard footsteps above me, creaking through the ceiling. I sighed loudly, clutching my chest. "Has he had breakfast?" I asked breathlessly, to which Malcolm nodded without skipping a beat.

"I made bacon," he replied, waving the spatula in his hand. "There's plenty left. Want some?"

He was wearing a shirt and tie, which confused me for a moment. Then I remembered that he'd come straight from work the night before. He hadn't had time to change his clothes. The guilt tightened in my chest. He'd done more than I could have asked of him, as he always did.

The sudden change in my expression must've caught him off guard because he quickly began tripping over his words: "Should I have not used the bacon? I wasn't thinking—"

"*No*, no…" I cut him off, catching my breath. "Thank you so much. Seriously. We cannot thank you enough—"

"*Don't* thank me." He came over, putting a hand on my shoulder. "Like I said: I'm here. Any time."

His sudden touch snapped me out of my daze. I began grounding back to reality, looking around the hallway. He'd cleaned up. All the laundry that I'd left on the staircase the day before was gone, and the shoes had been tidied up on the shelf. He'd done too much, but I hadn't expected anything less from him. This was Malcolm we were talking about.

"We don't deserve you," I mumbled, absent-mindedly following him into the kitchen. The scent of crispy bacon filled the air, flooding my nostrils. Malcolm began pouring coffee into my favorite mug, and I wondered how he knew.

"I didn't think you'd be back so early," he replied, passing it over to me. "I told you I'd take care of it."

"I know, I know… I just…" I took a sip, shutting my eyes for a moment. "I couldn't stop thinking about Cam. I didn't want him to worry, with everything going on…"

I wasn't even sure what he knew. Cam. I couldn't remember if I'd told him, or if Frank had told him, or if he'd seen it on the news regardless. Malcolm could've told him.

Part of me wished, more than anything, that I could've shielded him from all that had happened, but he wasn't a little kid anymore; he was ten. He was old enough to find out the truth for himself, no matter how hard we tried to cover it up.

"So, how is she?" Malcolm asked as he poured a bag of dry kibble into Misty's bowl. I shook my head slightly, staring straight ahead.

"She's... shaken up," I managed to say, my voice barely above a whisper. "Physically, she's okay. The wounds weren't deep, thank *goodness*, but..."

I trailed off, unable to find the right words. How could I talk about it? She was alive, yes, but she almost wasn't. No matter how hard I tried, I couldn't get the image out of my head. The blood. The crowd closing in around her.

It didn't feel real. None of it.

"They're discharging her later," I added, attempting to shove it all to the back of my mind. "I'm so sorry for keeping you here—"

"Stop apologizing."

"Frank's there with her now," I continued, trying to focus on the practical aspects rather than the overwhelming emotions. "It's just—I just wanted to make sure everything is okay here before I head back. I needed to see Cam. I have to see him."

Malcolm gave me a reassuring smile, though it didn't quite reach his eyes. "He's fine. He's a tough kid."

"Does he know?"

He nodded awkwardly, leaning back against the counter. "He was asking questions, and I didn't want to lie to him. But he's fine! He's just worried about his sister."

"He's sensitive," I said, my voice trailing off as I absorbed Malcolm's words. "He's had a lot to process lately, and he... he feels things a lot, you know? And this is a lot for him."

"It's a lot for *all* of you," he replied, still forcing a smile despite everything. "We're going to get through it though, right? All of us."

The sincerity in Malcolm's voice was both comforting and unsettling. His eyes met mine, holding a gaze that was just a touch too lingering. I should've been grateful for that moment; a fleeting moment of calmness before I had to inevitably return to the chaos that our lives had become. It didn't feel right, pausing time to have a coffee with an old friend. There wasn't enough time. There was too much to be done.

"How's Frank?" Malcolm asked suddenly, breaking the silence with a question that seemed both out of place and necessary. I blinked, momentarily caught off guard by the shift in topic.

"He's fine," I replied, trying to sound more certain than I felt. "He, uh... he did great yesterday. At the press conference."

"Yeah?"

"Yeah."

"Good," Malcolm said, his voice carrying a hint of relief. He shifted slightly, as if searching for the right words. "Take it easy on him. He's finding it hard, you know?"

"Yeah, well, we all are."

He nodded. We stood in silence for a moment; a shared understanding that went beyond the immediate situation. I scanned his face—something I did so often, whenever I got the chance to see him up close—noticing the lines that had deepened over the years. The memories of how he looked when we first met were still so vivid in my mind, and it never failed to catch me off guard whenever I reminded myself of how long ago that had been.

In that moment of quiet, the familiarity of his presence was both comforting and poignant. I wanted to hold on to it, to capture the brief sense of calm before returning to the chaos of the present.

The silence was quickly broken by the sound of thudding footsteps. Within seconds—as if he could move with super speed—my youngest child was in the doorway. His eyes lit up the second he saw me.

I held my arms open, welcoming him in as he jumped on top of me, almost knocking me off my feet. "*Mommy*!" His small arms wrapped around my neck, squeezing tightly. I laughed softly, feeling the familiar rush of love and relief.

"*Oh*, my *baby*..." I squeezed him tight before pulling back, noticing the stains on the front of his shirt. "Oh, Cam, you couldn't find something clean? Really?"

"Where's Allie?"

I opened my mouth, but the words initially got caught in my throat. My eyes instinctively moved to Malcolm; for a moment, I mistook him for Frank. Thankfully, he took over, just as I would've expected my husband to: "She's still in hospital, champ."

"*But* she'll be home later," I added, brushing Cam's hair from his eyes. "The doctors just need to make sure she's well enough to come home."

"Is she hurt?" he asked, his face falling slightly. My heart sank.

"She's got a couple of bruises, but she'll be fine," I reassured him, tucking his shirt into his pants. "Don't worry, okay?"

"She's just like her brother," Malcolm said, moving closer to poke Cam in the belly. He giggled quietly. "*Brave... and strong!*"

Cam put his arms in the air, tensing his "muscles". Malcolm mirrored him, tensing his own. Then he gave Cam a hearty pat on the back, nudging him toward the doorway.

"Come on; let's get moving! We've got..." Malcolm looked up at the clock behind my head; "*six* minutes! Go, go, *go!*"

I quickly ran over to kiss Cam on top of his head before he ran back out of the room, scrambling back up the stairs. I sighed slightly, giving Malcolm an exhausted smile. "Where would we be without Uncle Malcolm?" I asked, my voice tinged with genuine gratitude. He shrugged nonchalantly, though his eyes softened just a tad.

"Completely and entirely lost," he replied jokingly before squeezing my shoulder again. "I'm always here, alright? Don't ever forget that."

"How could I?"

Malcolm's smile lingered, but he quickly shifted gears, looking down at his watch. "Alright, Uncle Malcolm's temporary school bus leaves in t-minus *five* minutes... you want to take the leftovers for Frank? Allie?" he asked, gesturing toward the bacon. I shook my head, still smiling. "Then get out of here. Go!"

He began guiding me toward the hallway with a light-hearted urgency. I sighed, experiencing an equal mixture of appreciation and relief. "Thank you so mu—"

"Less talking," he interrupted, playfully nudging me forward. "Send Allie my love... oh, and I ordered takeout last night. There's plenty left in the fridge, so don't worry about cooking later, alright?"

I lingered at the front door for a moment, my hand hovering over the handle. I stared at him, pondering the depth of his generosity.

There was a warmth and ease in Malcolm's presence that I so

often found myself yearning for in Frank. I imagined how much smoother our lives might have been if my husband could channel even a fraction of Malcolm's effortless care. The two were so similar in many ways, but Malcolm just had this way of making everything seem just a little easier, as if he couldn't live with himself if he didn't continuously go above and beyond.

The thought lingered as I took a deep breath, pushing aside the bittersweet mix of admiration and regret.

"Make sure he doesn't forget his homework," I said finally, gesturing toward the staircase that Cam had climbed just moments before. Malcolm saluted with a playful grin.

"All under control," he said, his voice light and reassuring. "*Go!*"

I mustered up a final, grateful smile before slipping out the door. As I walked to the car, I glanced back once more. Malcolm stood in the doorway, watching me with a look that was both supportive and oddly introspective.

With each step, one thing became clearer than ever: we could *never* cope without Uncle Malcolm.

HAYDEN | 9:32 AM

Sitting there, in that tiny office, all I could do was hate myself.

I felt like a fucking rat. And the sterile room, with its harsh fluorescent lighting, only made everything worse. I shifted uncomfortably in the plastic chair, trying to avoid the penetrating gaze of the two police officers sitting across from me. My hands were clasped tightly in my lap, knuckles white.

And Mom being there made everything *so much worse*.

I couldn't talk to the cops without her being in the room— some dumb legal thing about me being a minor. It was fucking ridiculous. She didn't even *want* to be there. She was practically falling asleep in her chair, barely making any effort to make it seem that she had any interest in why we were there in the first place.

I mean, I didn't want to be there, either. But it wasn't like I had much of a choice.

"So, was this a regular thing?" The guy officer—Officer Anderson?—asked, writing something down in his notepad. "You and Brooke going to parties?"

"I guess," I replied dryly, hating myself for even saying it out loud. "She just told her mom that she was staying at my place, or whatever. It wasn't a big deal."

"Run us through what happened on the sixteenth of September."

My nose made this weird crunching sound whenever I inhaled too hard, and it stung like shit. I caught a glimpse of my reflection in the officer's glasses, and I could see the prominent purple bruises spreading from my nostrils, surrounding my eyes. My fists clenched as Allie's face flashed through my mind.

"...Hayden?"

I absent-mindedly ran a finger over the S-shaped bend along the bridge of my nose. Even just lightly touching it sent pain shooting through my face like a thousand needles.

"I came home from school," I said finally, trying to remember exactly how it went down. "Brooke came over around six."

"How did she get to your place?"

"I don't know. I guess her dad gave her a ride." I could've sworn the cops' faces changed slightly when I said that. It was super subtle, but I saw it; Officer Anderson's eyebrows raised less than an inch, and the girl cop's eyes—Officer Hardie—got just a little bigger.

"How do you know that?" Officer Hardie asked. "You live pretty close to the Nicholsons', right? Are you sure she didn't walk?"

"*I* didn't see his car outside." Mom's voice was slurred, the way it always was after noon. Her eyes were half-lidded, bloodshot, and rimmed with smudged eyeliner she hadn't bothered to wash off from the day before. The cops both turned their attention to her, surprised that she was even paying attention. I was too.

"You think Brooke walked to your place that day?" Officer

Hardie asked as Mom flicked her cigarette, practically blowing smoke directly into their faces. I just wanted to die, there and then.

"I didn't see his car outside," she repeated, a bit more clearly this time. Her gaze drifted lazily to the ceiling, then back to the officers. "And I would've known if Frank dropped her off. I always notice when he comes around." She suddenly gave this slow, almost dreamy smile. "That car of his... it's a classic, you know? Real nice. And *Frank*... well, Frank's easy on the eyes, isn't he?"

I sunk further into my chair, my face burning. "Please stop," I muttered, barely making a sound.

"Oh, am I *wrong*? *She* knows what I'm talking about," Mom chortled, gesturing toward Officer Hardie, whose mouth had since contorted into a tight smile. "Any woman with hot blood in her veins would remember if *Frankie Flash* pulled up to her house—"

"Mom!"

"Is there any possibility that Brooke could have gotten a ride from someone else?" Officer Anderson asked, swiftly moving the conversation along. Thank *God*.

I shrugged a little, thinking about it. "Doubt it," I replied. "She wasn't talking to Allie, and her mom was away for the night... and, you know, she was *grounded*. So she wouldn't have asked her mom, anyway."

"She wasn't talking to Allie?"

Their faces changed again, and my face immediately began to heat back up. It hit me immediately: they didn't know. "I-I mean..." I hesitated, reminding myself of what Allie had done to me. Reminding myself that she wouldn't think twice about throwing me under the bus. "They'd had a fight, or whatever. Brooke said they hadn't spoken all week."

The two officers exchanged glances, and Officer Anderson jotted something down. I watched them both, trying to figure out why no one had told them about this sooner.

"Didn't Allie say anything?" I asked, fully aware that I was stirring the pot. A smile almost crept onto my face as I thought about it.

Officer Anderson shook his head slightly before returning to the previous conversation: "Is there anyone else who could've given her a ride? A friend? Or… someone else she was close to?"

My eyes flickered between the two cops, slowly picking up on the fact that—maybe—they knew more than I thought they did. It was a weird question to ask, I figured. Pretty specific. I shook my head, trying to read their faces.

"Not really," I said finally, looking down at my lap as I picked away at my chipped nail polish. "Maybe she *did* walk. I don't know."

"She's not allowed to walk through our neighborhood alone," Mom added with a smirk. "Her mother wouldn't let her—"

"Shut *up*, Mom—"

"—thinks it's too rough around the edges for her precious little girl." She flicked her cigarette ash carelessly, giving the officers a conspiratorial look. "You know, they've got that big house on the hill; fancy cars, *all* the nice stuff. She isn't allowed to come to our place without a chaperone."

"You live in the Reinier projects, right?" Officer Anderson asked, as if he hadn't been to our house just a couple days prior. "Wouldn't consider it to be a bad area."

Mom scoffed, shaking her head. "But it's below *them*, right?" she retorted, poking me in the shoulder as if I was going to back her up. "Lizzie Nicholson thinks she's better than all of us. Always has!"

She was so fucking embarrassing.

I *hated* it.

"So… Brooke got to your place around six," Officer Hardie continued, turning her attention back to me. "What happened then?"

"She was on the phone," Mom interrupted again, jumping in before I even got the chance to open my mouth. "She was in *my* room—"

"Who was she on the phone to?"

I glared at Mom, ignoring Officer Hardie's question for a moment. My face flushed hot as I tried to control my breathing. I mean, I'd been mentally preparing myself for this moment ever since we'd gotten to the station. It was the whole reason I wanted to talk to them.

I just wished Mom could've let me ease into it.

"…Hayden? Who did she call?"

I stared back at my lap, already hating myself for what I was about to say. But I knew there was no other way around it.

"Donnie Booker."

The room fell into a tense silence; the kind that seemed to stretch on forever. My heart raced as I gripped the edge of my chair, my palms slick with sweat. I could feel the weight of their gaze on me, but I refused to look up. Looking at them just made it harder to say the words.

"He was her… *boyfriend*… I guess," I continued, internally wincing as the words came out. "They broke up a couple weeks back. Or maybe longer than that, actually—"

"They broke up in July," Officer Anderson corrected me, catching me off guard. I stared at him, confused.

"You *know*? About Donnie?"

Again, there was something off about their expressions. They were acting super shifty all of a sudden. I watched both of them, trying to figure out what I was missing.

I couldn't understand how they found out.

Brooke didn't want *anyone* knowing about it. Or, at least, she didn't want Allie knowing about it—or her parents. She was super weird about it, like she figured the whole world would collapse if her family found out she had a boyfriend.

"What did she talk to him about?" Officer Anderson asked, clicking his pen. "They'd been broken up for a while at this point, right?"

My mouth completely dried up. Like I said, I had fully prepared myself to talk about this—I knew it was coming, and I'd already basically figured out exactly what I was going to say.

For some reason, now, I was falling to pieces on the inside. I guess I didn't really *want* to talk about it.

"I don't know," I said truthfully. "She went into my mom's room. I didn't hear any of it."

"What did she say after the call?"

"Nothing really." I noticed the skepticism on their faces. "Seriously. I didn't ask. I… well, I didn't *want* to know, I guess. I didn't care. I told her she was an idiot for even talking to him, and she didn't say a whole lot after that."

"Do you know if they had spoken before this?" Officer Anderson asked. "After the break-up?"

"I don't think so… but, again, I don't think she would've told me," I laughed awkwardly. "She knew I didn't want to talk about him."

"Why not?"

It was at this moment that I began to wonder exactly how much they knew about the Donnie situation.

I mean, it was entirely plausible that one of the seniors had slipped up about them being together, but I wasn't sure how many people knew *why* they broke up. And *none* of them knew anything about how fucking depressed Brooke got afterward. There were only so many times I could hear her crying about her perfect relationship falling apart, just for me to remind her what he did to her. What happened with Allie.

I mean, come *on*.

"He's an asshole," I eventually concluded, clasping my hands together. "And… I don't know… I guess I got sick of hearing about him. I just found it super weird, you know… how someone could be so smart but so dumb at the same time. Donnie made her so… *stupid*."

"Did she ever mention him getting physical with her?"

I blinked, trying to figure out if I'd heard him right. "How do you mean?"

Officer Hardie leaned forward, her tone soft and reassuring: "Did Donnie ever do anything to hurt her? Physically?"

"What, like hitting her, or something?" I asked, and they both nodded. "No. I mean, she never said anything. Why?"

"Did she ever mention him being…" Officer Anderson paused, clearly trying to figure out the right way to say it. It was as if they thought I was a little kid, the way they kept rephrasing shit. "…*inappropriate* toward her?"

My mind flashed back to a couple of months before—that one conversation that we'd had. It had been one of the last times that she'd really told me anything about Donnie.

"I-I don't know." I pulled a face, trying to move past it. "I mean, I don't think so—"

"It's really important that you're honest with us, Hayden."

I swallowed hard, the memory coming into sharper focus.

Ugh… it just felt so *weird*, talking about all of it. It was even weirder talking about it without her being there. It felt wrong, like a total invasion of her privacy.

"I, uh…" I pursed my lips out, unsure whether to say anything at all. "I guess… he made a big deal, at the time, about wanting to… do stuff with her. And she didn't want to."

"What do you mean?"

Ugh.

"She was a virgin." The words shot out, causing me to wince internally. "I mean, *obviously*… and, well, she said that he kinda… you know… he *wanted* to… *you know*…"

It just felt so lame. Talking about it. I couldn't get the words out with my mom just sitting next to me, listening to it all.

It was so *weird*.

"Did he force her into having sex with him?" Officer Hardie asked suddenly, and I quickly shook my head. Then I stopped.

"I don't think so," I said slowly, my voice wavering as I fought so hard to remember the exact conversation. "I mean, she didn't *want* to, at first, but… but then, I… I guess she changed her mind. I don't know."

I couldn't even understand how the conversation had shifted so quickly. This wasn't even what I wanted to talk about. This wasn't why I came to the station.

As they exchanged glances, I began putting the pieces together. Figuring out why they were even bringing this up.

"Has someone else said something?" My eyes narrowed. "Did someone say that he did something to her?"

I'd tried so hard to forget that entire conversation.

I just *hated* the person she turned into whenever she talked about him. It was like there was this constant switch of personalities whenever she brought up Donnie. She loved him, then she hated him. He was the love of her life; he was the scum of the fucking earth. She didn't want to fuck him; then she *was* fucking him.

I couldn't keep up with it, and you know what? I didn't *want* to keep up with it.

It was fucking *exhausting*.

"Do you think he did something to her?" I asked finally, causing them both to stiffen up. Their heads turned to me in perfect unison, like two meerkats.

"Do *you* think he did something to her?"

I wasn't sure.

I'd figured she'd been with him the whole time; it made sense that she would've been shacked up with him somewhere, hiding from everyone. She knew how mad I would've been if I'd found out they were back together, and no one else knew about them. It just all felt so *obvious*.

But then, you know... people started dying.

And Donnie knew *all* of them. It was *his* friends being killed... and, well, his friend's girlfriend.

It didn't really hit me until I'd seen him outside the city hall the night before. The way he was running from the building... it was weird, you know? Suspicious. And *that* was when I figured I had to say something.

Someone had to tell them about Donnie.

"I saw him last night," I said through gritted teeth, wishing so bad that I didn't have to be the one to say it. "He was running from the city hall when they were doing that press conference thing for Brooke... and then, you know, I heard about what happened to *Allie*, after, and—"

"You were out *again* last night?!" Mom interrupted suddenly, shoving me hard. "The school's already been on my back about this damn *curfew*—"

"It was before eight!" I hissed, pulling away from her.

Officer Anderson put his hand up toward Mom, attempting to silence her before turning back to me with a more focused expression. "You said you saw Donnie last night?" he asked, and I nodded begrudgingly. "What did you see? What happened?"

"He was just... running." I folded my arms tightly, leaning back in my chair. "I tried to call after him. But he didn't stop. I just thought it was weird, you know... with what happened to Allie, and everything."

Officer Anderson hesitated for a split second before speaking again. "I should let you know that Donnie Booker is currently in custody. We're investigating his involvement in recent events, including the incidents that have occurred—"

"You've *arrested* him?" I wasn't really sure why this surprised me, given the circumstances. If anything, it was a relief to hear it. "Does that mean he did it? *He's* the Madman of Mirrenville?"

"We don't know that yet—"

"I mean, it'd make sense. He's always been so... *creepy*," I muttered, picturing his weird little bald head as I talked. "I never got what Brooke saw in him."

"Did you know him well?"

Further flashbacks from the party flooded my brain.

"Not really," I lied. "He was just... Brooke's weird boyfriend. He was one of the Eezy's, so I guess everyone knew him in a way, you know?"

"What the hell is an Eezy?" Mom asked, and I rolled my eyes. But Officer Hardie jumped in before I could.

"It's what these kids call themselves," she told Mom, and I wondered how she knew that. "There's a group of them... Donnie Booker, Fitzgerald Bird, Allie Nicholson—"

"Oh, he's friends with *Allie Nicholson*?" The words burst from Mom's lips abruptly, followed by a loud scoff. "Well, there we have it! They're probably in on it together."

"*Mom.*"

"She probably lied about the attack yesterday," she droned on, lighting up another cigarette. "Made it all up. I'm telling you— that girl is *bad* news. *Always* has been."

"She didn't lie about the attack, Ms Butler," Officer Hardie interrupted, sounding a little irritated. "I was there."

"You saw her getting *attacked*?" Mom probed, raising an eyebrow. "Or you saw her *afterwards*? She probably used... *fake blood*, or something... *anything* for *attention*—"

"I think we're getting a little sidetracked here," Officer Anderson said suddenly, holding a hand up toward Mom. "Can we go back to the sixteenth? Brooke got off the phone. What happened next?"

All eyes were back on me.

I thought back, remembering everything. Remembering how glassy her eyes were after coming off the phone. How shaken up she was.

"We started getting ready," I replied finally, deciding against giving the smaller details. "We were drinking... we had, like, a bottle of wine, or whatever it was... it was blue flavor. It made our tongues all blue—"

"I *knew* you took my Boone's Farm!" Mom began yelling again, but Officer Anderson held his hand up again, silencing her with a dark look. Then he turned back to me, picking up his pen again.

"You were drinking before the party?" he asked as I actively relived those few hours in my own brain.

"I did her make-up, gave her clothes to wear," I went on, picturing the green plaid skirt that I'd made her put on. "I colored her hair... gave her socks to stuff her bra because, you know, her boobs are *tiny*—"

"You dyed her hair?"

It was Officer Hardie this time. Both of them were giving me really weird looks, but Officer Hardie just looked *really* confused. She just kept staring at me, like I'd said that last sentence in Spanish, or something.

"I didn't dye it," I corrected her. "I... well, I use Kool-Aid— you know, the red stuff? You mix it with a little conditioner, and put it on your—"

"You dyed her hair red?"

"I didn't *dye* it," I repeated, rolling my eyes again. "It barely even came out... her hair was, like, *slightly* red. She didn't want to look like herself at the party, in case she saw Allie, or whatever—"

"She had red hair."

Officer Hardie just kinda kept repeating it, more to herself than to anyone else in the room. Her eyes were glazing over a little. The clock on the wall kept ticking over, filling the silence, and it was as if the sound was really the cogs meshing together in her head.

I stared at her, trying to figure out why she was freaking out so bad. Even Officer Anderson looked a little weirded out by it.

"Hardie," he said, lowering his voice. "What—"

"She had *red hair*," she repeated. "All the missing posters say she's a brunette."

"It barely made a difference," I said quickly, remembering it vividly. "Her hair was so dark that it barely—"

"We've been looking for the wrong girl this whole time?!" Officer Hardie cut me off, her voice rising with agitation. "We've been looking for a *brunette*!"

"Don't you start getting loud with my daughter," Mom suddenly snapped, leaning forward. "She's a *kid*. You don't yell at *my* kid—"

"Yeah, well, Brooke's a kid too," Officer Hardie shot back, making both me and Mom flinch a little. "And *we've* been misled! *That's* Obstruction of Justice!"

"Hardie, calm *down*."

Officer Anderson seemed just as weirded out by this sudden outburst as the rest of us—she'd been all quiet up until this point, following Officer Anderson's lead. It was as if this had suddenly just pushed her over the top.

And it wasn't even *that* big a deal.

"Look, I'm *sorry*, alright? I didn't think—" Before I could finish my sentence, she jumped up from her seat. She stormed toward the door, her footsteps echoing sharply against the floor.

By the time I'd tried to process what was happening, she was already out of the room.

"What the hell was *that* all about?!" I heard Mom saying at the side of me. I just stared at the door, wondering the same thing. "You call this *professionalism*? She can't do that—"

"I'm sorry about that," Officer Anderson interrupted, attempting to soothe the tension in the room. He kept glancing toward the door, his expression a mix of confusion and frustration. "It's, uh… it's a stressful time. This case has been taking its toll on everyone."

"You think that's an excuse for yelling at my daughter?!"

"Well, she didn't *yell*—"

"You cops are all the same," she began shouting, gesturing toward me. "You see a girl like her, and you can't help yourselves!"

"Oh, my *God*," I groaned. "*Mom!*"

Anderson, who hadn't said much yet, shifted slightly. I noticed the flicker of annoyance cross his face, though he kept it locked down. "Ma'am, I assure you, that is not—"

"You see a young black girl and think it's okay to yell at her?" Mom interrupted, suddenly placing her hand on my shoulder. I shoved her away immediately. "I can put a complaint in, you know! This is *discrimination*, and I want to speak to your boss—"

"*He's* black!" I shouted, throwing a hand out toward Officer Anderson. I immediately pulled it back when I noticed his hardening expression, tucking my hand beneath my thigh. Mom scoffed loudly.

"But *she* isn't," she pushed, stretching a finger out toward the door that Officer Hardie had just made her way out of. "Little miss blondie… *white* girl—"

"Ms Butler." Anderson put his hand back up, once again attempting to silence my white, blonde mother. "I can *assure* you that you are misreading the situation. This is a matter of hair color. *Not* skin color."

Jesus *Christ*.

I sunk even further into my chair, wishing I could bolt the room as quickly as Officer Hardie had.

"So, let's just focus on what's important right now," Anderson continued, turning his attention back to me. "We need to get the facts straight, about what happened to Brooke that night. Can we do that?"

Mom huffed, crossing her arms tightly. She still looked like she was ready to argue, but Officer Anderson's calm demeanor seemed to have momentarily subdued her. My eyes continued to dart between him and the door, checking to see if she was going to come back. Wondering what she was doing. Why she left.

"Were there any photographs taken at the party?" he asked suddenly, looking me directly in the eye. "Were there any disposable cameras, or… video footage, or anything?"

"Did you take yours?" Mom asked, once again jumping in before I could speak for myself. "You take that little camera with you everywhere—"

"I've got pictures," I interrupted, wishing she could just stay quiet for longer than ten fucking seconds. "I think."

Officer Anderson gave me a look. "You think?" he repeated.

"Yeah. I think."

"We're going to need a photograph of her from that night," he pressed on, his eyes digging deep into my face. "She was right— we've been looking for a brunette. We need to know exactly what Brooklyn looked like when she went missing."

"Mm-hm."

"You think you can do that for us?"

I wished I'd never gone to that stupid police station in the first place.

It wasn't a big deal. It *wasn't*. The color barely even came out on her hair; her hair was too dark for any of the red to really stick. Sure, it was a little red, but nothing compared to mine. Not enough to make this big of a deal over.

I didn't want to go back through the pictures. I thought about lying, saying that I didn't take any of her that night.

"…Hayden?"

I finally looked back up at him, looking him dead in the eye. I nodded firmly, hoping my face was as blank as his. Hoping I wasn't giving anything else away.

"I'll try."

11 DAYS AFTER THE DISAPPEARANCE OF
BROOKLYN NICHOLSON

ALLIE | 6:56 PM

I woke up to the sound of murmurs outside my bedroom. Light was creeping in through the blinds, but I had no idea what time it was. The way they were whispering in the passage, it was as if it was the middle of the night. It was like they were trying not to wake me.

I shifted under my blanket, trying to make sense of the words filtering through the door. It was difficult to catch everything, but snippets of their conversation reached me:

"*...needs to know...*"

"*...don't wake her...*"

"*...CAN'T be...*"

It took all my strength to pull myself up to sit upright. Pain shot through my abdomen—each movement felt like a fresh tear in my skin. Dark images flashed through my mind, stinging so much worse than the scratches on my stomach. Bile rose from my throat. I wondered how much longer this would last: waking up, forgetting everything for a brief moment in time, just for it to all come flooding back.

I survived.

I should've been more grateful.

The dull throb of pain beneath the bandages wrapped around my torso made itself known with every slight movement I made, mingling with the heavier ache inside my head. The flashbacks came as quickly as the moment itself occurred, flickering into my thoughts in quick bursts. I shut my eyes, pressing a hand to my side, feeling the bandages beneath my fingertips.

But I could deal with the physical pain—I knew I only had a week or two left before it went away completely. It was the mental images I couldn't deal with. All I could think about was the shadow outside my front door. It was so big. So tall.

Outside the door, my parents' whispers continued. I couldn't make out their words anymore, but I could pick up on the mood; Dad sounded scared, but Mom was angry.

Taking a deep breath, I tried to steady myself as I pulled myself from my bed. The room spun as I gripped the edge of the frame, forcing my eyes to avoid Brooke's empty bed, as I did every time I woke up. It was getting harder to move. My legs were weak, my body exhausted from days of lying in bed. The pain in my abdomen flared up with every movement.

I made my way to the door, each step a battle. I hesitated for a moment, hearing my parents clearer as I got closer.

"...*she wouldn't do this...*"

I twisted the knob, opening the door. The hallway light was blinding, and I had to squint against it. As expected, Mom and Dad were standing at the top of the staircase, both their heads snapping toward me as I revealed myself. Their eyes widened at the sight of me.

Misty suddenly darted into the room, rushing through my legs as if I was a door flap. He leaped onto Brooke's bed—a simple action he'd committed countless times over the years, yet the very sight of him curling up on her pillow filled me with a bitterness that I never thought I could feel for an animal.

"You're awake." Dad was the first to speak, but Mom was the

only one moving; his expression remained frozen while hers very quickly shifted from surprise to fury.

My attention turned back to them as Mom tore something from Dad's hand. Paper.

"Liz..." he muttered in a warning tone as Mom began moving toward me, the paper in her hand rustling with each step. It was a newspaper. I gripped the doorframe, holding myself up. It suddenly occurred to me that something had happened. Something had come out.

I stared at the paper in Mom's right hand, unable to look away. "What's wrong?"

Mom just stood there, staring at me. It scared me, the way she was looking at me. I'd never seen this look before. Her eyes were wide and dark, watching me as if she had no idea who I was. It was as if I was a complete stranger, someone who had just broken into the house.

"Mom?" My voice cracked as her name came out. Dad began moving behind her, moving closer to us.

"Let's go downstairs and sit down—"

With that, Mom held the paper up to my face. She held the front page so close to my eyes that I couldn't read it at first. I pried it from her hands, scanning the headline.

"...*what the hell did you do*?"

It didn't make sense. I read it over and over.

It wasn't making sense.

"Let's sit down," Dad said as he tried to link arms with me, moving me back into my room. I wouldn't budge. My feet had anchored into the ground. My body was dead weight.

It didn't make sense.

The words blurred in my vision, a jumbled mess of confusion and horror. My knees buckled, and Dad caught me just in time, guiding me to the edge of Brooke's bed. I bounced back up immediately, realizing what I had done as pain seared through my tender abdomen. I couldn't sit there.

It wasn't my bed.

"How could you *do* this?!" Mom's voice rose to a yell, shaking me to my core. The paper had fallen from my hands somewhere along the way; it had fallen to the floor, facing upright.

The headline was staring at me.

BROOKLYN'S EX ARRESTED FOR ASSAULT AND MURDER.

"He *raped* her," Mom yelled, and my whole body began to tremor. My eyes found Brooke's empty bed. Everything started spinning.

Donnie.

Donnie.

"He wouldn't…" I swallowed, trying to process it all at once. "He wouldn't… Donnie, he wouldn't—"

"Well, he *did*!" she shouted, her voice sharp and pain ridden. "He *raped your sister*!"

It wasn't processing.

None of it.

Donnie's photograph was staring at me from the floor, smiling up at me. Maybe they'd used the wrong picture… I mean, that was *Donnie*. I *knew* Donnie.

He was fucked up—he'd *always* been fucked up—but he wouldn't have done that. He wouldn't have hurt Hurley. *Mandy.*

He wouldn't do that.

"Was he here that night?!" Mom went on, ignoring Dad's pleas to calm down. "During the *conference*?! What, did you… did you *wait* for us to *leave* so you could *sneak him in*—"

"What?!"

"—and then he *attacked you*?! Is that why you haven't said anything?! Because you're *protecting* him?!"

"What the hell are you talking about?!" I began shouting back, barely able to think. It was too loud. Everything was too loud. I wanted them to get out.

I couldn't think.

I couldn't *think*.

"Did she know?!"

"Did she know *what*?!"

"That you were FUCKING HIM!"

Everything stopped.

I felt Dad moving from me, pulling his hands away from my arm. I stared directly into Mom's eyes, desperately trying to figure out what she meant. Denial washed over me as I tried to reword what she had said.

Trying to find some other meaning—*any other meaning*—to

what she had just said.

"I don't—"

"Did you *know* what he did to her?" she asked coldly; her voice lowered but her words were as vicious as ever. Dad tried to say something, but she held a hand up, silencing him. "Did you *know* he'd done this to her when... when *you* were *with him*?!"

My eyes wandered back to the newspaper.

I could barely see it. There was another photograph next to Donnie's. More writing, too. I could barely read it, but the photograph was of a girl's face.

SISTER PREGNANT WITH BOOKER'S BABY (ATTACK HOAX?)

"...Al..." I heard Dad's voice at the side of me. Barely. He sounded a thousand miles away. "...whatever this is, we just need to know the truth—"

"They're saying you faked the attack," Mom interrupted. The room spun faster. "They're saying that you faked the whole thing—"

"We know that's not true," Dad put a hand on my shoulder. "Obviously."

"But do we know that this wasn't *planned*?!"

I stared at my mother through glassy eyes. "Y-you think I planned this?" I asked in disbelief, barely able to get the words out. She laughed, causing my heart to sink further.

"I don't know what I think," she replied coldly. "What I do know is that this... this *Donnie Booker* was in a relationship with my daughter, and during this time, *you* slept with him. *You* got pregnant, and you haven't said a *word*—"

"Liz—"

"You're having a *baby* and you haven't said *ANYTHING*!"

"I'm *not*..."

Of all the ways I'd imagined this conversation happening, I could never have imagined it to have happened like this. I wasn't prepared for it. I wanted it to stop.

I needed it to *stop*.

"Did you get an *abortion*?!" The sourness in her voice made my stomach turn. My face began to crumple as I scrambled to make sense of any of this.

"I—"

"Jesus, Liz, does it *matter*?" Dad was starting to get angry too. I could hear it in his voice.

"Does it *matter*?! Does it *matter* that our first and only grandchild was *killed*?!" Mom shouted back. "I suppose it only matters as much as our grandchild's father being a *rapist* and a *murderer*—"

"Liz, *stop*—"

"We have spent the past *two weeks* wondering why your sister just got up and left!" She held two fingers up to my face. "*TWO weeks*! And you knew *the whole time*?! You and… and *him*—"

"*You think I knew about this*?!" I shouted back, two tears dripping down my cheeks. "You think I had *any idea* about *any* of this?!"

"Was he the one that attacked you?" Dad asked, leaning closer so that I could hear him over Mom's continuous screaming. "Al, if you're trying to protect him—"

"*Why would I protect him*?!"

"They're saying that you're in it *together*!" Mom kept yelling, throwing her arms out toward me. "They're saying that *he* killed those kids, and you made it look like *you* had been attacked by someone else to make *him* look *innocent*—"

"*How would that even make any sense*—"

"*STOP!*"

Dad's voice thundered through the room, cutting through the chaos. The abrupt volume of his shouting stunned both Mom and me into silence.

Dad never got angry. Ever.

His face was red now, his chest heaving as he tried to regain his composure. "We're clearing this up *right now*," Dad said breathlessly, his voice still loud but steadier now. He turned to me, looking me in the eye. "Al, listen to me—"

"How are we supposed to believe *anything* that comes out of her—"

"*Liz*," he snapped, half-turning to face her. She stopped, clearly just as surprised by his sudden outburst as I was. He turned back to me with a blank expression. "Did Donnie Booker attack you?"

"I-I don't know," I stammered truthfully, trying to mask my irritation from him. He didn't deserve my anger: he just wanted the truth. "I didn't see his face. It… it could've been him. I-I don't know."

There was not one single part of me that believed Donnie could ever do that to me.

There was no part of me that truly believed that he could hurt Hurley or Mandy. He wouldn't have hurt Melissa either—he wouldn't have done that to Fitz.

He wouldn't have done that to *any* of us.

"Alright," Dad said with a slight inhale, steadying himself. "So… what they're saying in the paper… that's not true, right?"

"You're asking me if I planned my own attempted murder?!" I said coldly, and he quickly shook his head.

"Al, Al… I have to ask, alright? We've got to get this straight."

My eyes flickered across to Mom. She was watching me over his shoulder, scanning my face. It didn't matter what I said; she'd already made her mind up.

She'd been looking for someone to blame from the start, and now she finally had her reason.

"So, what…" Dad paused, clearly uncomfortable. "What, uh… what was the deal with you and this guy? Were you dating him?"

A laugh escaped my mouth without me even realizing it. Mom's face hardened even further. "It was a *mistake*," I spat, barely holding the tears back. "It was graduation, we were drinking… I don't like him like that, and *he* doesn't like *me* like that… we're just *friends*. We've *always* just been friends. It was… it was *stupid*…"

"Did you know he was dating Brooke?"

I shook my head silently, more tears flooding my cheeks. Dad nodded again, ignoring Mom's scoffs behind him.

"Why wouldn't you tell us, Al?" he asked suddenly, his voice softening. The sudden switch of tone made my heart break into a thousand tiny pieces. "Huh? About the… I-I mean… Jesus, why would you *hide* this from us?"

I shook my head, desperately blinking tears away. "I don't want to talk about that right now—"

"Well, that's too bad," Mom interrupted coldly, stepping closer. "We're talking about it."

"Liz—"

"It doesn't *matter*!" I kept shaking my head, my chin wobbling with each word. "It's *dealt with*, alright?! Please, just... *please* can we not talk about this?!"

"Did Brooke know?"

I shut my eyes, taking a moment before nodding silently.

Two fat tears dribbled down my cheeks so fast I didn't have time to wipe them away. They were streaming down my face now, soaking my shirt. My whole face had crumpled up.

It wasn't as if I hadn't had time to think about that question.

It wasn't as if I hadn't been thinking about this 24/7 since I'd spoken to the cops. I knew what Mom was asking. I knew the answer, too.

Of course Brooke knew. She was the *only* person who did.

She was there when I took the test.

She was there when I cried my fucking eyes out, devastated that of *all* the people that could've gotten me pregnant, it was Donnie Booker. *Donnie fucking Booker.*

I'd kept saying his name, over and over. She'd heard it.

She knew.

And she didn't say a *fucking word.*

"...we're supposed to take her word for it?" I heard Mom asking, exasperated. Dad put a hand on my knee, squeezing it. Despite everything that I felt in that moment—*every emotion* that I felt at that exact second—I felt a sudden rush of relief. *He* believed me.

"It doesn't matter what anyone else thinks," he said finally, turning his head slightly to Mom. "It doesn't matter what they put in the papers, or on the news, or wherever else they put it... *we've* got to stick together now. As a unit. As a *family.*"

"I don't believe this," Mom scoffed.

Dad ignored her, leaning closer to me. He placed his hand on the back of my head, smoothing my hair slightly. "When did it happen, huh?" His voice was soft but filled with concern. "Did you... did you go to the hospital? Have you seen a doctor?"

My throat tightened. "I'm fine, Dad—"

"No, I know, but we need to know if you need to see someone. You should've told one of us."

I rolled up my sleeve, desperately scrubbing it against my face to dry my cheeks. The tears were flowing freely now. I just needed him to let it go. There was too much to think about.

I kept thinking about Brooke. And Donnie.

I just kept trying to make sense of it all.

"I'm *fine*," I repeated through gritted teeth, sniffing hard. "Please, Dad, just… just drop it. *Please*."

"How could you be friends with someone like that?" Mom said suddenly, breaking her momentary silence. "I just… how could you *not know* that someone could be capable of doing something like this?!"

I shook my head silently, praying that she would just stop.

"…*did she tell you what he did to her*?!"

I glared at her. The overflowing tears completely distorted my vision. Dad turned to look at Mom too, and something told me that his reaction was similar to mine.

"You *seriously* think I'd keep that to myself?!" I asked furiously, vibrating with rage. "You *seriously* think I-I wouldn't have fucking *killed* him if I'd—"

"Watch your language—"

"Are you *fucking kidding me*?!" I yelled, trying to stand up but Dad was holding me back. "You think I *knew*?! You think I wouldn't have *done something* if I'd known?!"

"Well, I don't know, Al!" She stepped closer, jabbing a finger in my face. "Maybe she told you and you didn't believe her! You said that he's your friend—*present tense*! You're saying that he's *still* your friend—"

"I am *not* saying that!" I sobbed, still trying to pull away from Dad's grip. "I-I don't know what… I *don't*…"

I'd known Donnie my whole life.

We'd grown up together. He'd done some questionable stuff in the past, sure, and he didn't have the best track record with girls, but… *this* was fucked up, even by his standards.

"How do they know that he… he hurt Brooke?" I asked quietly, and Mom scoffed again. "I'm *NOT saying* I *don't* believe it—I just want to know *how* they know! I-I mean, do they have any *proof*, or—"

"There's security footage," Dad replied quietly, his voice breaking slightly. "They caught it on camera."

The words hung in the air, each one punctuating the gravity of the situation. A cold, empty feeling spread through me.

Security footage.

This wasn't just some rumor or a misunderstanding. This was real.

He really had done it.

"They caught it on camera?" Mom repeated, sounding a little confused. "Where did you hear that?"

"It was on the news."

The image of Donnie from all those years, the friend who had been there through so many stages of my life—all of it had been entirely shattered in just one moment.

And my sister; my 15-year-old sister who weighed just over 100 pounds, who still slept with stuffed animals in her bed. I caught a glimpse of them as my eyes wandered over once more.

My Brooke.

My Donnie.

"I need to see him," I said suddenly, not completely certain that those words had come out of my own mouth. "I-I need to talk to him—"

"You're never going near him ever again," Mom laughed without humor. "You think I'm going to let you *anywhere* near him?!"

"I need to hear it from him—"

"Al—"

I just wanted to scream.

I wanted to lash out, to do *anything* to make this nightmare stop.

The room was closing in around us. My eyes shot around the room, locking onto the final remnants of Brooke's presence—the teddy bears, the scattered books, Misty arched across her pillow.

It suddenly occurred to me that this hurt *so much more* than being physically stabbed.

"*I need to know WHY!*" Further tears streamed down my face. "I-I need to know *why he did this… why* she didn't… *w-why didn't she tell me*?!"

I just lost it.

The cries came out as screams, echoing through the room.

My whole body buckled, and I crumpled onto the bed, my stab wounds burning red as I hit the mattress.

Through the blur of tears, I saw Dad's face twist in anguish.

He got up from the side of me and stormed out of the room, the door slamming behind him. Mom ran after him.

My sobs grew louder, merging with the pulsing pain in my abdomen and the overwhelming confusion in my chest.

It didn't make sense.

It didn't make sense.

The images of Donnie and Brooke kept flashing in my mind; the lines between past and present blurring into one agonizing mess. I buried my face into my bed sheets, screaming in tears.

A brief, blurred memory of Donnie at Fitz's party flashed through my brain, fading as quickly as it had appeared.

I hit my hands against my head, as if to rewire my brain into remembering something—*anything*—of Brooke at the party. *Anything*. Any memory I had from the party was fragmented, slipping through like sand.

Mandy's voice whispered into my ears like a harsh gust of wind.

The car.

The body.

"...*I'm s-sorry...*" I sobbed, not entirely sure who I was speaking to. "*I'm s-s-sorry...*"

A door slammed shut downstairs.

The house was completely quiet now, aside from my shallow, jagged breaths. I rolled onto my back, staring at the ceiling, clutching my chest.

"...*I-I'm sorry...*"

But the room remained silent, offering no answers, no solace. Just the cold, hard truth that nothing could ever be the same again.

FITZ | 7:03 PM

"...and in a dramatic development, authorities are now investigating whether local teenager, Donnie Booker, is connected to the recent string of murders..."

The TV continued to crackle through the silence, lighting up the room with white and blue lighting. None of us said a word as we watched. No one had said a word in what felt like forever.

I couldn't pull my eyes away from the picture on the screen. Donnie's face was staring right back at me.

"...this comes amid shocking revelations about his private life," the news anchor continued as a second photograph faded onto the screen. *"Reports have surfaced that Booker was allegedly having a secret affair with Alexandra Nicholson, the sister of Brooklyn Nicholson, who has been missing for over a week—"*

"Do they get paid to make this shit up?" Joaquin suddenly interrupted, breaking the oppressive silence. His voice was laced with a harsh edge that cut through the low hum of the television. I flinched, my eyes still locked on the screen. The image of Al, now placed directly next to the image of Donnie, made my stomach churn.

It never got any less weird, seeing people I knew on the news. It was like we were watching some kind of documentary based on our lives.

And just when I'd figure it had ended, it just kept going.

"Nichy and Booker..." Freddie said as he walked back into the room, scooping a handful of Doritos into his mouth. "Couple of the year!"

"It's not funny, Fred," I muttered, the irritation slipping into my voice.

"Oh, come *on*..." A laugh broke out as he slumped back onto the couch, just across from me. "It's fucking *hilarious*, dude! I mean, of all the men in the world, who would've thought Donnie would be the one to tie her down? Kid's got more game than I gave him credit for." The sarcasm was dripping from his mouth, along with bright orange crumbs. He'd been at it all day—talking shit.

"Game?" I repeated, shoving his hand away as he waved the

chip packet in my direction. "He raped a fucking freshman."

"He killed our friends."

Joaquin's jaw had tightened, his gaze fixed firmly on the floor. He hadn't touched the food Freddie had shoved in front of us earlier, nor had he said much since the news broke about Donnie. Whenever he did speak, it was something dark. Something that hurt to hear. I could feel the pressure building, the silent clash between Freddie's desperate attempts to lighten the mood and Joaquin's quiet, simmering grief. And I was stuck somewhere between them.

"We don't know that," I replied quietly, turning my attention back to the TV. In the corner of my eye, I watched Joaquin's head snap toward me.

"What do you mean? They've got... fucking... *evidence* that he did something to Allie's sister," he argued, raising his voice just enough that I could sense his anger building. "If he could do *that* to her, you think he couldn't do the rest of it?"

"Why would he hurt Hurley? Or Mandy?"

That was the one thing I couldn't get my head around.

Donnie was an asshole. He always had been. The way he talked about girls like they weren't human, and the way he just used people, stepping on anyone who got in his way... he had a fucking dark side. And we all knew it, even if we didn't talk about it.

But *murder*?

I just wasn't sure if he had it in him.

And above all else, there was *no way* he was smart enough to get away with something like this for so long. It just wasn't adding up.

Freddie suddenly raised his cup. "A toast to us, gentlemen," he announced; the tone of his voice alone told me that we weren't going to like what he was about to say. "To the last men standing."

Something flew across the room, missing my head by an inch.

I flinched, my head spinning at the exact moment to catch Freddie getting lobbed in the face with a half-empty soda can. It bounced off his forehead with a dull thud.

"The *fuck* is wrong with you?!" Joaquin snapped as Freddie grabbed a pillow, using it to wipe away the orange soda that had dribbled all over the front of his shirt.

Before Freddie could respond, Scruff suddenly stirred to life. I'd almost forgotten he was even in the room, sprawled out like an old rug in the corner. His movements were slow and stiff, his joints creaking like they hadn't been oiled in years, but his tail was now thumping against the wooden floor as he struggled to jump up on Freddie. The sight and scent of something sweet was enough to get him going.

"What?!" Joaquin laughed, attempting to push Scruff away with one hand. "Oh, come *on*, guys—what are we supposed to do right now? Seriously? Do you just wanna sit here and fucking cry about it?"

"They're *dead*," Joaquin exploded, edging forward in his seat as if he was about to launch at Fred. He began gesturing toward me: "*Melissa's* dead. Allie *almost* died—"

"It's a fucking *joke*, man," Freddie muttered, his smile faltering slightly. "*Jesus*... just trying to lighten the mood..."

My heart started pounding again, just like it had several times over the course of the day. It just came out of nowhere, every time. The pressure in my chest tightened; it was like a fist closing around my lungs.

"*...we're yet to hear any confirmation from the Nicholson family*," the news anchor continued in the background, "*but close sources have revealed that Alexandra Nicholson is pregnant, adding another layer of complexity to this already tragic situation...*"

I moved forward, sitting on the edge of the couch. Staring at the screen in total disbelief.

"Nichy's *pregnant*?" Freddie's voice cut through the fog of my mind. His words barely registered; they all seemed to merge together.

"*...speculation is already rife, with some sources suggesting that Donnie Booker could be involved, given the recent allegations about their relationship... however, it's important to note that these are unconfirmed reports, and the investigation is ongoing...*"

I felt my breath hitch as the anchor's words sank in. I thought about the last time I saw her, at the memorial.

She hadn't said anything.

"Did you know about this?" I heard Joaquin asking; he was

fully turned to Freddie, asking him directly. Fred shook his head, unusually silent for once. Joaquin's attention turned to me. "Did you?"

I shook my head, unable to say a word.

"That's *crazy…*" Freddie finally muttered, shaking his head as if trying to shake off the weight of the news. But then, true to form, he couldn't resist. "At least it's none of ours, right? I ain't got the money for fuckin' child support."

My head snapped toward him.

"Dude," I started to say, but he was already grinning again. His whole demeanor felt like a punch to the gut.

"Can you imagine if *I'd* gotten her pregnant? I would've been, what… a fourteen-year-old dad?"

"Fred." His name shot out like a warning.

"Oh, *relax*, will you? Just because *you* never got to fuck her—"

I jumped up, storming toward the light seeping through the crack in the door. The room fell into a heavy silence as I swung the door open, stomping into the hallway.

"*Fitz, come on—*"

I slammed it shut behind me, the sound echoing down the empty corridor.

Scruff immediately began whining from inside the room, pawing at the door. I barely heard him through the ringing in my ears. Leaning against the cool wall, I struggled to steady my breathing, each inhale ragged and unsteady.

Allie was *pregnant*.

The hallway stretched out before me, the silence amplified by my heavy breathing. My heart pounded so loudly I could almost hear it echoing in my ears, each beat feeling like a drum driving me into a further state of panic.

I pressed my back against the wall in an attempt to ground myself, but the world seemed to tilt and sway. Everything moved around me.

I couldn't stop it.

The shadows of the hallway danced and flickered, the distant hum of the house's old heating system growing louder, almost deafening. I squeezed my eyes shut, trying to shut out the noise— the images of Allie and Donnie on the news flashing behind my closed lids. Mel's face was there too. And Hurley's. Hurley's face, covered in blood.

My hands, covered in blood.

A sudden noise from the living room—a door creaking open or someone calling my name—seemed to pierce through the fog of my panic, just barely.

"*Fitz?*" Joaquin's voice called from the other side of the door.

I didn't answer.

I couldn't.

With that, the door creaked open. He made his way out into the hallway, shutting the door once Scruff had squeezed his way out of the room behind him. I couldn't even look at him. I couldn't look at either of them. I wasn't even sure why.

Joaquin stood a few feet away, his presence both comforting and unsettling. He waited a couple seconds before speaking. "Don't listen to him, man. He's an idiot."

I nodded, forcing a laugh. It sounded like a sob. "It's cool."

"Fuck him," Joaquin said, his voice carrying a rare edge of anger. Then he paused again. "And fuck Donnie."

It didn't feel right, hearing it. Feeling it, even.

These were the people I'd grown up with, you know? The people from my childhood.

Donnie was a part of the tapestry of my life, woven into my memories the same way Hurley and Mandy were. Same as Joaquin and Fred. And Allie. No matter what fucked up shit Donnie did, or said, he was a huge fucking part of who I was—who we *all* were.

And I couldn't shake the feeling that whatever I was going through, it was nothing compared to what Al was going through.

Her sister was gone. Donnie... he did what he did to her sister. And she was *pregnant*.

Why the fuck didn't she say anything?

"What do we do now?" I asked, not entirely sure whether I was asking Joaquin or just speaking my thoughts out loud. "I mean... what do we do with this?"

He stepped forward, putting a hand on my shoulder. "We're still here, right? We just... we get through it."

"I should call Al."

"We could go see her," he offered. "Maybe not *right* now, you know... she's probably going through it. I mean, this is all happening *right now*. We've got to give her some time, right?"

I nodded, trying to figure out what to say next.

Joaquin squeezed my shoulder before pulling away, taking a step back. "We've got this, brother," he said, his tone steady and reassuring. I just kept nodding. "It's going to be alright."

"Yeah."

Scruff's heavy head gently nudged against my leg, seeking some sort of acknowledgment. I absentmindedly reached down and scratched behind his ears, feeling the softness of his fur between my fingers. The softness of it grounded me for a moment.

Joaquin didn't push any further, and I appreciated that. He just stood there, giving me space, like he knew I needed a moment. The hallway felt suffocating. It was squeezing the fucking life out of me. Scruff let out a low, tired sigh, like the old dog could feel it too. He leaned his weight against my leg, steadying me in a way I didn't even know I needed.

But I needed to move.

"I'm getting another drink," I mumbled, nodding toward the living room. "I'll be back in a second."

"Sure thing." He wandered back through the door, and I began making my way down the hallway. Scruff hobbled after me, his nails clicking against the wooden floor.

As I heard the living room door shut behind Joaquin, I turned toward the front door, shoving it open and stepping outside. The cool night air hit me like a splash of cold water, and I inhaled deeply, filling my lungs. Standing there in the dark, everything felt quieter; just the sound of the wind rustling through the trees and the distant hum of traffic. It would've felt peaceful, almost comforting, if it wasn't for the constant images flushing through my thoughts. I saw all their faces, all at once.

Donnie.

Hurley.

Mandy.

Mel.

Allie.

I pressed the heels of my hands against my eyes until I saw flashes of light, trying so fucking hard to push their faces away.

The air pressed cold against my skin as I spiraled. They were all I could see. All I could think about. The images washed in and out in forceful waves. Everything that had happened. Everything that was still coming.

I just had no idea what the fuck we were supposed to do now.

FRANK | 7:23 PM

I slammed my foot on the gas, pushing the car harder than I ever had before. The road stretched out before me, empty except for the occasional flash of headlights that blurred as I shot past. I didn't know where I was headed. I just knew I couldn't go back. That house was a fucking prison, and I couldn't stand it anymore.

Liz's voice rang in my ears—sharp, cutting, relentless. And Allie's screaming. I had to make it stop.

What the hell had happened to us?

I took the second turn off the highway without thinking, my hands moving before my mind could catch up. The streetlights flickered as I passed, growing sparser until they disappeared altogether. As my eyes adjusted to the darkness, I gripped the steering wheel tighter, telling myself that I had no idea where I was going. Telling myself that I had no idea what I wanted.

But it was all a lie. The wheel spun almost all on its own, taking me down a path I knew I should not be taking.

Who was I kidding?

I knew exactly where I was going.

The familiar road felt both comforting and suffocating—every corner, every landmark, brought back memories I'd fought so hard to bury. It felt like it'd been a lifetime since I'd last driven this route, but in reality, it hadn't been very long at all. These past two weeks had felt like two years, and time was becoming less and less a reliable measure of anything. I couldn't shake the feeling of being trapped in a loop, reliving the same moments over and over. It almost felt as if none of it mattered.

The blur of streetlights and the hum of the engine provided a strange sense of continuity, but it was fleeting. Each passing second seemed to stretch into eternity. The events of the night replayed in my mind as I drove, and the weight in my chest refused to lift.

I just kept my eyes on the road. It was all I could do for now.

The tires screeched as I slammed on the brakes, sending the car skidding into the parking lot. The smell of burning rubber flooded the car. I switched off the engine and just sat there for a second, staring up at the building. I looked up at the top row of windows, zeroing in on the third one from the right. The lights were on; a few bars of orange shone through the blinds.

With a deep breath, I jumped out of the car and made my way toward the building before I could change my mind.

The heavy oak door loomed before me, its brass handle glinting under the dim streetlight. I reached out, the cold metal shocking against my warm skin as I pushed the door open. The lobby was eerily silent. It wasn't even that late; it had to be, what, sometime after seven? But there was no one else around. Not a soul.

I was more than grateful for that.

I'd spent the whole car journey scanning the roads for anyone who might've followed me. The media attention had amped to the max since the conference; they now hid behind our cars, behind the fence, waiting to jump out at us like vultures. I was surprised that they hadn't already begun lining up outside the house the moment the news broke about Donnie Booker. I guess I'd gotten lucky. I'd made it out just in time.

I made my way to the elevator, pushing the button so hard that my finger bent back awkwardly. The doors opened almost immediately, and I jumped inside. The anxiety crept up on me, sticking to my limbs like a wet blanket as the doors closed behind me. I pushed the button for the third floor and leaned back against the wall, my mind racing as I tried to figure out what was about to happen. I hadn't thought that far ahead yet.

What was I even doing here?

The elevator jolted to a stop, and the doors slid open to reveal an all-too-familiar corridor lined with faded floral wallpaper. My footsteps echoed unnervingly as I counted the doors, making my way to the very end of the corridor. I tried to remember how long it had been since that first night here; a night I barely remembered through a thick haze of whiskey and regret.

Aside from being sober, all those emotions from that first night came rushing back to me as if nothing had changed.

As if *everything* hadn't changed.

I stopped outside the third door from the end, staring at the faded olive-green door with its peeling paint and chipped gold lettering. I used this moment to quickly scan my surroundings once more, checking that no one had actually followed me. That would've been the last thing that any of us needed.

With that, I lightly knocked on the door.

I could hear the buzz of a television inside the apartment, but no other voices. It suddenly hit me that she may have had someone over, and I wished I'd thought of that sooner. I'd been so concerned about checking who was following me that I hadn't even stopped to think about who could've been *inside* the apartment. But it was too late to think about that now. I'd already knocked.

I was about to knock a second time when I heard the click of the lock turning from inside. The door creaked open, the dim light from inside spilling into the hallway.

And there she was.

She didn't say anything at first. Not a word. She just stared at me blankly, almost as if she didn't recognize me. We stared at each other for the longest time, in complete silence, and I had no idea what I was supposed to say. Every thought that had been rushing through my brain suddenly ground to a halt at the very sight of her.

"Can I come in?" I asked, and it was as if something clicked in her brain. She unfroze, poking her head from the door to scan the corridor left, right, left again, right again. Then she turned back to me. Her eyes were a little bigger this time.

Before I could say anything else, Lucy grabbed me by the collar and dragged me into the apartment, slamming the door shut behind us.

I stumbled into the room, barely catching my footing. She spun around, pressing her back against the door. She was glaring now. *Oh*, she was pissed.

A finger stretched out toward my face as she pulled herself from the door. "What the *hell* are you thinking?!"

"Luce—"

"You are *all over* the news," she hissed, gesturing toward the television. Sure enough, one of our family photos flashed onto the screen as she said it. "*Everyone* is talking about you, and you think you can just... just *show up here* and *no one will notice*?!"

"No one saw me—"

"*Bullshit!*"

"I checked!" I put my hands out toward her, trying to calm her down. She was mad. Really mad. I suddenly realized, despite all else that was going on, that she was wearing my shirt.

She was wearing an old Unrest Stand shirt that I thought I'd lost a while back. It was so big on her that it draped past her knees, almost completely covering her gray sweatpants. It was weird, seeing her like this; I'd gotten so used to seeing her all buttoned up and professional in her bulky, blue uniform. *This* was the real Lucy. My heart began picking up speed and I almost forgot why I was there.

She followed my gaze down to the shirt, and her cheeks flushed with embarrassment. She crossed her arms over her chest, trying to cover the shirt, but it only made it more obvious. "I haven't done laundry this week," she muttered, her voice softer now. "This was all I could find... it's just a shirt—"

"It's *my* shirt."

A small, involuntary smile tugged at the corners of my mouth. She rolled her eyes, immediately turning her attention back to the matter at hand. "What the hell are you doing here, Frank?"

Her attempt to deflect didn't go unnoticed, but I let it slide. I wished more than anything that I could forget why I was really there. Seeing her in an old t-shirt and sweatpants, hair tousled, no make-up on—I almost thought for a moment I could just pretend that nothing else was going on. We could've pretended, just for a moment.

But we couldn't.

I couldn't.

"Did you see the footage?"

Her face fell the second she heard those words. My throat tightened, suddenly unsure if I really wanted to hear her answer.

She was the one who had told me about the security footage in the first place, but I hadn't asked her if she'd watched it herself.

"I can't keep doing this," she replied, suddenly freezing over. "I could lose my job—"

"Allie wants to see him," I interrupted. "She wants to ask him herself, if he really did it. I don't think she believes it."

Her face hardened. "Well, he did."

The look on her face gave it all away.

I'd never seen her like this before, and it scared the shit out of me. A cold sweat broke out on my forehead. "You saw it," I whispered, more to myself than to her. She nodded silently, and it felt as if the floor was falling from beneath me. "What... I mean... what actually happened? Did he—"

"Frank." Her voice was hard; cold. "You don't want to hear it. Please just... please don't ask."

The world tilted, throwing me into a violent, nauseating spin that left me grasping for something to hold onto as my mind struggled to process the enormity of what she was saying. I knew she wouldn't have lied to me; there had never been any doubt in my mind that she had been telling the truth. I had just wished, with my whole being, that maybe she'd gotten it wrong.

Images of Brooke as a little girl flashed before me; her first day of school, her birthday parties, her laughter. I'd begun to forget what that sounded like.

"Sit down..." Lucy guided me over to her couch. My legs almost gave out before I could make it there. "Stay here for a while to calm down... but then you've got to get out of here," I heard her saying. "You can't be seen here—"

"I can't go back."

"Frank—"

"It's broken." The words slipped out before I could make any sense of them. "All of it. Without Brooke... and now, with everything with Allie... and *Liz*... she just... she... she blames Allie for *all* of it... and the way she *talks* to her, I just..."

I shut my eyes, fighting so hard to block it all out.

"She's not thinking straight," Lucy replied, almost entirely emotionless in her tone. "None of you are. No one is expecting any of you to be in a good place right now."

"We were never in a good place."

"What are you—"

"I don't want to be with her."

This was the first time I'd said it out loud.

It had been floating around in my mind for some time, but I'd never had the guts to bring it to light before this moment. But it was the truth. I couldn't keep ignoring it, not when it continued to gnaw at my thoughts, every single waking moment.

"I don't think I love her," I went on, hardly believing that I was actually saying it. "I don't think I have for a while."

"You're both going through a lot," Lucy said stiffly, sitting down on the coffee table opposite me. "It's not like you're supposed to be having fun right now—"

"It's not like that."

"Come on, Frank—"

"I know you don't believe me, but I swear, I never would have gone anywhere *near* you if I felt anything for her," I admitted, a brief laugh following my words. "I never have before. Never did. We've been married almost thirty years, and I've *never* looked at anyone else... except for you."

She laughed without humor. My chest tightened.

"Luce, I'm serious."

"So..." She shook her head, still laughing. "*We* happened because you were bored? Because things aren't working out right now?"

"That's not—"

"You used me."

"I didn't!" I stood up from the couch, pleading with her. "Okay... okay, maybe it started off as something less serious, but... but, then things changed! I never lied to you—"

"You never *lied* to me?" Her tone completely shifted. I regretted it as soon as I said it. She was getting angrier, and I couldn't even blame her. "You didn't lie to me about being *married*?" Her voice got louder and louder. "About having a *family*?!"

"I didn't lie about how I felt about you."

"Oh, just *stop*—"

"You want the truth?" I shouted back, starting to shake. "I liked *talking* to you! In the beginning, that was *it*. I talked to you, and you listened to me, and it felt fucking good to be listened to!"

"Yeah, I had to listen to every *lie* that came out of your mouth—"

"They weren't lies," I groaned, covering my face. "Not in the beginning. You listened to me talking about work, about leaving the band, about everything... *you listened to me*! I needed a *friend*. *All* I wanted was a friend... I-I wasn't the one suggesting we got a room at the motel—"

"Don't you *dare*—"

"*You're* the one that said it," I jabbed a finger at her. "*You* kissed *me*! *You* said, "Hey—let's get a double suite"! What the hell was I supposed to do?!"

"You were supposed to say, "*I can't—I'm married*"!"

"I said *no*—"

"If you'd told me the truth, I *never* would've said it," she shouted, moving closer to me. "You weren't even wearing a wedding ring, Frank! You're telling me it *magically* slipped off your finger whenever you saw me?! You knew *exactly* what you were doing!"

I scrambled through each and every deep corner of my brain for any excuse, any justification. But I knew it was useless. We both knew the truth, no matter how I tried to reshape it.

This whole situation was fucked up beyond repair, and neither of us knew how to fix it.

"Alright," I turned back to her, preparing myself. "All cards on the table?"

She just stared at me blankly, barely moving.

"You were the *only* good thing in my life."

Even saying that out loud felt wrong. Her face fell, and I knew I shouldn't have said it. At the same time, I knew saying the truth was my only option at this point. It was the only way I could make her understand, no matter how fucked up it was.

"I gave up everything," I went on, fighting so hard to hold back my frustration. "I was a fucking *rockstar*, Luce. People *knew* me. People *respected* me. I gave it all up for a wife and a family... and I love my kids, alright? I love them more than *anything*, but I..." I paused, trying to figure out how to say it. "I gave up my *whole life*. I worked *so fucking hard* for it—*all* of it—and it just... it was all over in a *second*. No one cared anymore. I didn't mean *anything* anymore."

"Am I supposed to feel bad for you?"

"No—"

"*You* gave it up," she said frostily, looking me dead in the eye. "*You* chose to get married. *You* chose to have a family—"

"No, I didn't," I laughed, regret and guilt building up inside my chest like a pressure cooker. "I never got to make that decision. It was made for me. Liz made it for me."

Lucy shook her head, unable to hide her disappointment. I could see it on her face. She didn't get it. I had to make her understand. Or, at least, I had to try. At this point, I had nothing left to lose.

"I never wanted this life," I continued, realizing how pathetic it all sounded. "I don't regret the kids, and I'd *never* change that part, but I... I was *Frankie Flash*. Now I'm some guy in an office. And, then, one day, *you* show up. *You* listen to what I'm saying. You *hear* me. I never, *ever* meant for things to end up the way they did, but I can't... I *can't* bring myself to regret anything that happened between us. I know I should, but I can't. *You made my life worth living.*"

The coldness in her gaze cut straight through me. "So, what? I was your escape? Your *break* from *reality*?"

"You made me feel like a person again."

"You're not a person, Frank." Her words sliced through me like a knife. "You're a fucking cliché. You used me to feel important again—"

"I didn't use you. I *needed* you."

"And was it worth it?"

Those words hung in the air; a brutal echo of my own self-doubt.

I opened my mouth to respond, but nothing came out. I wanted to tell her that it was worth it, more than anything. And I think a part of her wanted to hear it.

My daughters' faces flooded my thoughts.

"You can't just show up here and rewrite the narrative to make yourself the good guy," she added, her voice raising a fraction. "You can't just... just *justify* everything because you felt unfulfilled in your life. You haven't been Frankie Flash for a long fucking time—*long* before you even met me!"

"I'm not trying to justify it," I said, my voice cracking. "I never wanted to hurt anyone. Least of all you."

Her face softened, just a little. Just for a moment. Her eyes glossed over, and I watched as her thoughts spun like a whirlwind behind them. For a second, it felt like the distance between us was closing—like we were back to being just us. Just like it once was.

Then something clicked. The anger resurfaced. "I have to see your family every day," she said finally, glaring at me. "I have to look them all in the eye *every single day*, knowing that… that I… that *we*…"

I looked away.

"…every day, I have to listen to your wife *thanking* me. *Every day*, she *thanks* me."

The words stung, each one like a needle piercing my skin.

"You said at the coffee house that you weren't changing your alibi because you didn't want to hurt her."

"I don't want to hurt her—"

"*THEN WHY ARE YOU HERE?!*"

Her shout echoed through the tiny apartment, the raw emotion in her voice hitting me like a physical blow.

I had no answer for her. Not at first. The silence stretched between us, heavy and oppressive, as my mind scrambled to fix this. I'd never seen her like this. I could never have imagined it.

"You didn't want to *hurt* me…" she spat, repeating my own words back to me. She began pacing the floor between us as the sentences flew out like wildfire. "God… do you have *any idea* what you've done?! To *me*?! To *my* life?!"

"I'm sorry—"

"You made *my* life worth living!" she screamed, throwing her arms out toward me. "You made *me* feel like a person again! And *now*… now, I have *no idea* who the *fuck* I am! Did you even think about that?! Even *now*?! Did you ever stop to think how *you* broke *my* heart?!"

Her eyes were filling up, and I completely froze to the spot.

The worst part was, she was right: it'd never even occurred to me how much any of this had affected her. Not until after she found out. I just didn't think she cared that much. She didn't deserve this. Any of this.

She'd done nothing wrong.

"Luce, I—"

"*Stop!*" she interrupted, her voice breaking with each word. "*Jesus*, just… just *stop*, alright?!"

"I know I've fucked this up," I said, my voice barely above a whisper. "And I'm not asking you to forgive me. I just… I needed you to know how much you meant to me."

"How much I *meant* to you?!" she repeated, her laugh bitter and hollow. "I was your *escape*, Frank. Your *convenient* distraction. And now, *I'm* left picking up the pieces while you run back to your *perfect little family*—"

"It's not perfect."

"And that's supposed to make me *feel better*?!" Her eyes flashed with anger. "That *your* life is just as fucked up as mine?! Well, *congratulations*, Frank! Misery loves company—"

"I never wanted any of this."

She slumped onto the couch, burying her face into her hands. I just stood there, watching her. Utterly helpless.

"…*why are you here?*" she repeated, and a tear rolled past her cheek. She shakily wiped it away as another one fell.

It took all my strength to just stand there, not making any sudden movements. The silence stretched between us, thick and heavy. Each second felt like a lead weight dragging me deeper into the swamp of my own making. The weight of my own guilt pressed down on my chest, suffocating me.

My body began moving before I could even think about it; I sat down next to her, not saying a word. My hand moved onto her shoulder, sliding across her back. Pulling her in. I'd expected her to fight it, but to my surprise, she didn't hesitate to bury her head into my chest, crumpling into me. My arms tightened around her. She began sobbing onto me. I shut my eyes, just letting it happen.

I honestly couldn't remember the last time I felt this way about Liz. Not just the physical closeness but the emotional intimacy; the sense of being completely seen and heard.

"…*you have no idea how much you've fucked my life up…*"

I began to stroke her hair gently, trying to offer some semblance of comfort. It felt strangely soothing, like a small act of redemption amidst the chaos. A while passed in that silence, punctuated only by her soft cries and my occasional whispers of reassurance.

Slowly, her crying subsided into quiet, ragged breaths. I felt her body relax against mine; her sobs turning into the occasional shudder.

I leaned down, gently kissing the top of her head, my lips brushing against her hair. As I pulled back, my eyes met hers. There was something fragile and raw in her gaze; a vulnerability that mirrored my own. Without thinking, I cupped her face in my hands, my thumbs brushing away the tears that still lingered on her cheeks. For a moment, it felt as if nothing had changed. Time stood still. She stared into my eyes, and something flickered across her face. It was a softness that I hadn't seen in what felt like a very long time. Almost instinctively, our lips met.

I'm not entirely sure who instigated it, but neither of us pulled away. Her lips were soft and warm against mine, and for a brief moment, everything else fell away. The pain, the regret, the guilt—it all seemed to dissolve into the moment; a single flash of clarity amidst the chaos.

Her arms slowly moved around my neck, pulling me closer as the kiss grew more intense. Her hands tangled in my hair, and the heat of her breath mingled with mine.

When we finally broke apart, the world seemed to come back into focus. We both froze up—the consequences we'd both been trying to escape crashing over us like a cold wave. It shouldn't have happened. We both knew it. My heart pounded as I desperately tried to figure out what to say next.

Before I could, she pulled me back in, her lips crashing against mine with an intensity that stole my breath.

My hands found her waist, pulling her closer. Her legs wrapped around me as I lifted her effortlessly, her fingertips digging into my shoulders and neck. We staggered slightly, our movements frantic, almost primal. I stumbled toward her bedroom, our kiss unbroken; each step a defiant act against the gravity of our situation. It was as if the world outside had ceased to exist. None of it mattered anymore.

It all came flooding back; the whole year we'd spent together. Each shared secret and stolen moment. It all made sense again. Our breaths mixed, ragged and urgent, as if we were trying to merge our shattered worlds into something whole and defiant.

For a brief moment, Liz reentered my mind.

My wife.

My daughters.

My family.

Lucy's fingers dug into the back of my neck, tangling into my hair, dragging me back to the present. She flooded every corner of my mind. All I could feel was her; her touch, her warmth, her presence. Every fragment of my consciousness was consumed by her.

I kicked the bedroom door shut, plunging us into darkness.

Tonight—just tonight—I wanted to forget.

LIZ | 9:57 PM

"…I can't believe how much can change in just three weeks…"

I handed Vic her coffee, sitting down on the couch opposite her. She'd made herself comfortable on Frank's chair; legs crossed, a blanket draped over her shoulders. Her eyes were dropping ever so slightly. So were mine. I'd been getting ready for bed when she showed up.

"You're telling me," I muttered, my thoughts heavy.

"And, jeez, the *weather*…" She ran her hands through her hair, still damp from the rain. "I'm seriously thinking about moving away. Permanently. I'm serious, Liz. Why is it always so *cold*?"

I found myself staring at the cup in my hands, the warmth seeping into my skin. The small talk was a welcome distraction, but it couldn't drown out my thoughts entirely. I was glad to see her, sure, but I hadn't expected her to be at my door at this time of night. I had been so sure it was going to be Frank.

It'd been almost three hours, and he hadn't even called.

"And what the hell is up with the paparazzi?" I heard her say as lights flashed outside the window, seeping through the curtains. "Do they think Princess Diana's in here or something? Do they just camp out there all night? In the *rain*?!"

I glanced toward the window, watching the persistent flicker of cameras and flashbulbs. Someone must've walked past the house. For a moment, I wondered if it was my husband. I kept waiting for the front door to open.

"...anyway, you wouldn't *believe* the flight," Vic went on, returning to her story. "It... was... a... *nightmare*. Delayed for *six hours*, and there was turbulence the *whole* flight. I haven't slept!"

"You could sleep *now*."

"No way." She shook her head erratically, taking a quick sip of her coffee. "I haven't even told you about the hotel yet—"

Maybe it was because she'd never had kids of her own, but an early night never seemed to interest my little sister. And being the baby of the family, she had a knack for talking about herself for hours. Days, even. It was my father's fault—he'd never had an issue with telling me or Lottie to be quiet for five minutes.

Vic, on the other hand, had *never* been told to shut up.

"Oh, it was *beautiful*," she continued, waving her arms dramatically as she spoke. "I shit you not, the pool *alone* was the length of this house... oh, Liz, *we* should go sometime! *All* of us! There's a spa for us, and you and Frank can go for a nice meal on the beach, and the girls would *love* the... the..."

Her voice trailed off when she realized what she'd said. She paused for the first time since arriving at the house, allowing her words to sink into the atmosphere around us. I stiffly shook my head. "Don't worry about it."

"It's just—"

"Vic."

"I didn't even hear anything until I got to the airport." Her voice wavered a little. "It came up on the news, and I saw her face, and I... I didn't know, Liz."

"Right."

"I would've come straight back. You know I would have."

For once in her life, Vic's tendency to talk about herself had become a blessing to me. She could spend hours recounting her adventures before ever asking about the family. It wasn't that she didn't care—she loved her nieces and nephews, and even Frank— but it was just her nature to dive into stories of her own exhilarating, child-free, single life before turning the conversation to me. And in her defense, my life rarely changed, so there was seldom much to update her on.

Now, for the first time in a very long time, my life *had* changed. But I didn't want to talk about it. I would've preferred to hear her talk about pools and hotels and flights for the rest of the night rather than repeat the same few sentences that I had been regurgitating for the past 11 days.

"How long has it been?" She asked the one question that most people, at this point, already knew the answer to. "I mean, when was the last time you actually *saw* her?"

"September sixteenth. We reported her missing on the eighteenth."

"Why'd you wait so long?"

It took *everything* not to snap at her.

It was a valid question, of course, but it didn't make me feel any less useless. It was my one regret: not reporting her missing sooner. And yet again, Frank was to blame.

Thankfully, Vic moved on to the next question before I could answer the last: "God... so this is serious?"

I stared at her in silence. She quickly shook her head, about to explain herself, but even I couldn't believe that she'd said that out loud. "Yes, Vic," I replied coldly. "This *is* serious."

"I just figured because, you know... I mean, how many times has *Allie* run away in the past? And, you know, everything with Mickey—"

"This isn't like that."

The words flew out with such hostility that I even caught myself off guard. She just sat there for a moment, allowing that sentence to linger in the air. I watched as the severity of the situation flooded her expression. This wasn't like the other times. She should've worked that out sooner; after all, every other time one of my kids had run away, the first place they usually showed up at was her place.

"And, well... it's *Brooke*." She stared ahead as she took it all in. "This isn't like her. At all."

"Glad you're finally caught up."

"How are *you* feeling?" she asked, leaning forward and taking my hand in hers. "How is everyone coping?"

"Cam's fine. Allie's..." I stopped, shutting my eyes. "Allie's fine."

The fact that she didn't immediately start questioning that response confirmed that she hadn't watched the news for longer than ten seconds. She clearly knew nothing about what Allie had done.

"What about Frank?"

I laughed slightly, diminishing any hope I'd had of lying in her face. It was all too fresh to hide. Her eyebrows furrowed a little, and I knew I had no chance of taking it back. "He left," I said finally, shrugging. "Walked out a couple hours ago."

"What? Why?!"

"We had a fight."

"Why?!"

More often than not, a conversation with Vic would feel very similar to having a conversation with Cam. There were always a lot of questions. A lot of *why*'s.

"I guess things have been a little stressful since our child disappeared off the face of the fucking earth." Another laugh escaped my mouth. "And now that everything's come out about that... that *Donnie Booker*... I don't think either of us know how to deal with it."

"What did he do?"

I just shook my head again, still chuckling. I'd drank half a bottle of red before she'd showed up, and I hadn't realized how much it had affected me. It had almost slipped my mind. I was about to delve deep into what had really happened that day when it occurred to me that Vic had asked the wrong question.

Surely my highly inquisitive sister should have asked "Who is Donnie Booker?", not "What did he do?".

"Do you know him?"

She didn't answer at first. Her expression glazed over, and I watched as she scrambled to give me a good answer. "Who?"

"Donnie Booker."

She shook her head, avoiding eye contact. "Donnie *Booker*... no, uh, I don't think so—"

"You sure?"

Vic was a lot of things, but she'd never been a good liar. She just didn't have it in her.

I put my cup down on the table, leaning closer to her. Seconds passed like hours. The longer it took for her to open her mouth, the more agitated I became. "Vic, I swear—"

"*Alright*, alright!" Her head twitched slightly, as if she was unsure whether to shake her head or start nodding. "Brooke might've mentioned a... a *Donnie*, or whatever. Some guy."

"What did she tell you?"

She groaned slightly, utterly defeated. "Barely *anything*! Just that she had a boyfriend, I guess. I don't know!"

"And you didn't think to tell me?!"

With that, she burst out laughing. I couldn't even begin to comprehend her reaction. She was grinning from ear to ear, all the rage that I had suppressed from earlier that day came flooding back.

"No, I didn't *think to tell you*," she replied in the most condescending tone I'd ever heard, "for the same reason *she* didn't *think to tell you*... which, matter of fact, is the same reason I didn't tell Mom when *I* had boyfriends, or *you* didn't tell her about Frank for, what, six months—"

"Oh, stop—"

"—for the same reason *any* of the kids tell me *anything*! Brooke, Allie, *Mick*... and I'll bet *anything* that I'll find Cam on my doorstep by the time he's in middle school, because *that's my job*! They talk to *me* because they can't talk to *you*!"

I sat back, stunned. She just kept smirking, driving the knife even further into my chest. "My kids can talk to me," I murmured, and she groaned again.

"Of *course* they can! But, you know... they don't want to disappoint you. Or stress you out. You're their *mother*, Liz—you can't take it so personally."

"He raped her."

Her face paled almost immediately. Her confident demeanor shattered in an instant. Her mouth opened and closed as she struggled to find words, but none came.

I watched as the horror of the situation fully dawned on her, but for some reason, I couldn't bring myself to share her emotions. Maybe the toll of all that had happened had drained the little emotion that I had left. I was fucking exhausted. I had little left to give.

"He's been arrested for killing those kids too," I added, staring blankly ahead. "They say he's behind everything. All of it."

"What kids?!"

She really hadn't heard anything.

I found myself absent-mindedly reaching for the bottle of wine that I'd tucked away beneath the coffee table when Vic first arrived. I unscrewed the lid and took a long, hard gulp straight from the bottle, swallowing the dull ache remerging from the pit of my stomach. "You knew that she was with this... this *monster*," I continued, wiping my mouth. "You could have said something."

"I didn't *know* that he was a monster—"

"Well, what *did* you know?"

It wasn't often that my sister found herself lost for words. My baby sister was visibly shaken, clearly struggling to process all that I had said so far. And she didn't even know the full reality of the situation yet. This was just the beginning.

"...she thought she was pregnant."

The bottle fell from my lips, hanging limp in my hand.

My face contorted as I stared at her. I thought maybe I'd heard her wrong. I wasn't sure I'd heard that right. The wine in my stomach began to curdle, bubbling up until I was certain that I was going to vomit all over the coffee table. Vic's face was completely white. Translucent.

I leaned forward, unable to look away from her face. "...what?"

She nodded slightly, staring down at her lap. "I got her a test," she went on, her voice getting quieter and quieter with each word. "She was really scared, Liz—"

"When?!"

Her eyes darted from left to right, unable to bring herself to make direct eye contact. "Just before I left."

A *month* ago.

The room seemed to close in on me, the walls pressing against my thoughts. The silence that followed was deafening, filled only by the sound of my ragged breaths. Vic had very slowly regressed to being 13 years old again, cowering from me with her knees up to her chest, hiding her mouth with her right hand.

I breathed deeply through my nose, working out what to ask next. Working out where to even begin. "Did she take it?" I asked finally, and she nodded her head in silence. "And?!"

"She wasn't."

The smallest amount of relief rinsed over me, so small that it barely made a difference.

"Did you know about Allie?" I asked next, and her eyes narrowed ever so slightly. Her reaction was enough to convince me that she didn't. "Well... she *was* pregnant. With Donnie Booker's baby."

"*What*?!"

"A lot can happen in three weeks, huh?" The sarcasm dripped from my words, and I wasn't sure how to reign it back in. I wasn't sure if I wanted to. Bitterness oozed from my every pore. I took another gulp from the bottle before, for some reason I can't explain, offering it to Vic. She grabbed it without hesitation, forcing it to her lips.

"You had no right to keep this from me," I said coldly, watching the wine stain her chin as it dripped down. "*No* right."

She wiped her mouth, shaking her head. "Brooke's fifteen," she replied finally. "She made me promise not to tell you... and, you know what? I thought you of all people would understand—"

"I've never done anything to make her feel like she can't talk to me."

"Are you kidding? She thought you were going to kill her!"

"Because she's a *kid*!" I shouted. "Of *course* I would have killed her! Just like *Mom* would've killed *us* at that age—"

"Okay, do you want me to be honest right now?" She held her hands up, halting me mid-sentence. "Seriously? Everything else aside, I think you're focusing too much on the pregnancy thing. With Brooke. You're not seeing the full picture—"

"The *full picture* is that my daughter has been missing for *eleven days*," I spat, "and she thought that her boyfriend—who *raped* her—had gotten her *pregnant*!"

"I didn't know anything about that!" she shouted back. "My niece came to me with a problem, and I helped her! I made sure that she was *safe*, and felt like she could talk to me about *anything*—"

"Clearly not *anything*—"

"And you know what?! If you'd just *talked* to her about this kind of stuff, she wouldn't have *had* to have talked to me! I'd like to take this opportunity to congratulate you on educating your kids, Liz, because she didn't even know how to use a fucking *condom*—"

"*SHE'S FIFTEEN!*"

"*EXACTLY!*"

"You remember *Mom* talking to *us* about that stuff at her age?! *No*, because she *didn't*—"

"And look how *that* turned out!"

I grabbed her wrist, digging my nails into her skin. She tugged herself away with such force that she almost pulled me onto my feet. She knew she'd hit a nerve; I could see it on her face.

"I *know* they're your kids..." She stood up, pointing in my face. "And I *know* it's not a conversation you want to have with them, but *Jesus fucking Christ*, Liz! You're telling me *both* your *teenage daughters* thought they were pregnant *at the same time*?! Do you not think that maybe—*just* maybe—that could be a *you* problem?!"

"How *dare*—"

"Mick had different girls back here *every weekend*! And oh my God, the *shit* I've heard about *Allie*—"

"Brooke *isn't* Allie!"

"And that's *exactly* what she said to me!" Her finger was mere inches away from my nose. "You *really* want to know why Brooke didn't tell you?! Because she *knows* what you think about Allie! *Everyone does*! You never say a fucking *word* but you *know* who she is, you *know* what she does, and you just... *just*..."

I stood up too, turning away from her, trying to calm my racing thoughts. A slight *creak* from above us made me jump, drawing my attention back to Allie's presence.

I wondered if she could hear us.

"...you try and keep up this perfect family image," I heard Vic saying behind me, "but *everyone* knows that you gave up on Allie a *loooong* fuckin' time ago... *that's* why your daughters come to *me*! *Not* you!"

I grabbed her wrist again, wrapping my fingers so tightly around it that she couldn't get away this time. I tore her hand away from my face, her finger still outstretched. My fingernails sunk into her skin. She tried to pull back, grunting. "Get *off* me—"

"And what do *you* know about raising kids?!" I yelled as her bones clicked beneath my palm. "You think you know it all?! You have *no idea* what it's like holding a family together!"

"And you're doing such a *great job*—"

"*Oh, YOU DO BETTER!*"

My grip on her wrist was so strong that one of her bracelets dug into my palm; the tiny beads cut into my skin. I didn't even notice at first.

When I did notice, however, it pulled me back to the present. It wasn't like her other bracelets, all gold chains and jewels. This one looked so flimsy that I thought it would snap under my grip.

I'd seen it before.

I instinctively tugged her sleeve up her arm, fully revealing it. The very sight of it triggered a memory I didn't even know I had. I must've loosened my grip because she jerked backward, tugging it away from me. "Liz—"

"Where did you get that?"

There was something so eerily familiar about that loosely tied string of cotton. The beads were black, white, and gray, contrasting against the gold jewelry draped along her forearm.

"Where did you get that bracelet?" I asked again as she kept trying to pull away from me.

"I got it in Sacramento! Jesus, Liz, *what*—"

The more I thought about it, the less it made sense.

I stared at the bracelet, partially visible beneath her sleeve, and everything came flooding back. I'd been transported back in time.

It made absolutely no sense that Vic had one of them.

"Brooke made that." My voice was so quiet that I barely even heard myself. "She made them in school, for the kids. One for all four of them."

Vic shifted awkwardly, folding her arms. Her eyes darted around the room, looking anywhere but at me. Her usual bravado seemed to crumble under my gaze. Her silence made me even angrier.

"Where did you get it?!"

They were made up of their favorite colors.

Cam's was yellow; all his clothes and toys were yellow when he was a baby, so Brooke thought that was his favorite color. My mind raced back, trying to remember the others. I could've sworn Allie's was a dark blue, almost navy.

I could still remember the day she brought them home. It was as if no time had passed.

Frank and I had been so impressed that she'd done that for her brothers and sister. She'd gone through the effort of making four identical bracelets, and they were all so neat and professional-looking. I was so proud of her. No matter where she was in the world, she always thought of them. Her siblings.

Allie's was purple.

The thought popped into my head suddenly—that was her favorite color. It was a dark purple. She went through this obsessive Prince stage just after *Purple Rain* came out.

I couldn't remember the other two colors.

"Okay…" Her voice trailed off as she thought what to say next. "Liz… just listen to me for a second, alright—"

"Where is she?"

"What?!"

I grabbed her, digging my fingertips deep into her shoulders. "*Where is she*?!"

She tried to wiggle away but I wouldn't let go. I couldn't.

"It's not Cam's, and it's *not* Allie's," I began shouting again, my voice getting shakier by the second. "And it's *obviously* not Mick's!"

Her eyes widened.

With the last word, the last name, her entire composure shifted.

My eyes darted back to the bracelet; her right arm was now slumped at her side, completely limp. She wasn't trying to hide it anymore. My gaze switched between the bracelet and her face a couple of times until it clicked.

I grabbed her wrist again, running my fingertips along the thread. I gently pinched the one tiny white bead that stood out from the rest, spinning it around so I could see it clearly.

Nothing could've prepared me for seeing the letter M.

Her hand dropped from my grip, falling back to her side. Gravity felt stronger than ever, dragging me down into Frank's armchair. My limbs felt heavy, as if they were made of lead. I could barely hold my head up.

Vic was saying something, but I couldn't hear her through the buzzing in my ears. Her mouth was moving, but I didn't catch a word.

"…you…" The words slipped from my mouth, but I wasn't

entirely sure what I was saying. "...you..."

"...*I promised I wouldn't say anything...*"

I finally turned my head to face her. She had sunk down onto the couch, covering her face with her hands. My whole body had become numb. I licked my lips, attempting to moisten my mouth before asking the next question: "...is he okay?"

A moment passed before she could bring herself to look at me. She looked terrified. When she finally nodded her head, my eyes began filling up before I could fully grasp what any of this meant.

"Yeah, he's..." She paused, sighing in defeat. "He's good."

A wave of relief washed over me, so overwhelming that it left me dizzy. My body, which had felt heavy and immobile, now seemed lighter, almost buoyant. My vision gradually cleared as I blinked away the tears that had welled up.

He was good.

"He didn't want me to say anything. He... well, he specifically told me not to tell you or Frank. I'm sorry, but I had—"

"When?!" I could barely hide the excitement in my voice. "When did you... oh *my*... he's in Sacramento, isn't he?"

For three weeks, I'd thought Vic was away on business.

Never in a million years would *this* have ever crossed my mind.

Her blank expression confirmed my suspicions, and my eyes filled up faster and faster. I wasn't entirely sure how I was supposed to feel: happy or mad. I think I experienced a little of both at that exact moment.

"Where is he now?" I asked frantically, the questions overflowing from my mouth before I could stop them. "What was he like? What did he say?! How—"

"Liz."

The sudden sharpness of her tone brought me back to the moment.

The realization hit me like a punch to the gut: Mick had reached out to Vic. Not me.

The excitement quickly drained away, leaving a hollow emptiness in its place. "Of course he got in contact with you." I forced a smile, trying to hold it together. "I-I mean... of *course* he did."

He had just turned 30.

She would've been there for his 30th birthday, celebrating with him. He had consumed my thoughts that whole entire day—September 12th—and little did I know Vic had been with him. She'd been with him the whole time.

She stood up and sat on the arm of the chair, putting her arm around my shoulder. I really didn't want her to. I knew it wasn't her fault, and I didn't blame her for any of it, but... well, it had been eight years.

Eight years.

"I found him," she said finally, rubbing my shoulder. "He owns this hotel business, and Andy worked with him for a little while—"

"Andy?"

"The construction guy, remember? I... forget it," she laughed slightly, flapping her hand as if to shoo the thought away. "You're never going to meet him... anyway, he was telling me about the big guy in charge—the one building the hotels—and he said his name. Michael Nicholson."

It had been so long since I'd even heard his name out loud.

"Andy gave me his number, and, well... I went for it. Figured I had nothing to lose."

"I'm surprised he agreed to see you," I muttered, and she froze up a little. The hatred began to set in, and it was quickly seeping into my tone. I wished I could've stopped it.

It *wasn't* her fault.

"Yeah, well, so was I," she replied, laughing without humor. "But he did."

But he didn't want to speak to me.

Eight years.

I wondered if I would even recognize him now. Would he recognize *me*? Would he recognize his siblings? I thought back to the last time I saw him, picturing his face perfectly. I could see what he was wearing. His hair. The look on his face.

"Look, he's fine, Liz," she went on, hugging me tighter. "He's really made it! The kid's done us proud..."

I nodded, trying to force a smile. It wasn't working.

"...and, well... he's got a family of his own."

My head spun toward her as I snapped out of my thoughts. She was smiling now, nodding to confirm what I thought I'd heard.

My mouth opened but nothing came out.

"A boy and a girl," she confirmed excitedly. "Twins."

Twins.

The word echoed in my mind, slowly sinking in. The overwhelming surge of emotions that followed left me breathless. Love, happiness, and an unexpected sense of completeness flooded through me.

My son—my *Mickey*—was a father. The realization filled the emptiness that had been gnawing at me moments before.

I clutched Vic's hand, my eyes wide with a mixture of shock and joy. "Twins," I repeated, a genuine smile breaking through. Vic nodded, her own smile broadening.

"If there was ever any doubt that he was Frank's, huh?" she smirked a little, dampening the moment ever so slightly with that out-of-pocket comment that she knew would trigger me. "You know… because he's a twin too, right?"

"Vic—"

"They're great, Liz…. and they're so *blonde!*"

A tear rolled down my cheek, but this time it was from happiness. My heart swelled with a love so profound it made my chest ache. I never would've imagined that I could've felt so strongly about anyone that I had never met.

"I'm a *grandmother…*" I murmured, my voice trembling. "I've got a grandson… and a grand*daughter…* I-I can't believe this…"

"And, hey—now that he's talking to me, I'm sure he'll come around to seeing you at some point!"

Just like that, I remembered why I was mad.

The sadness came flooding back, reminding me that none of this mattered. My son still didn't want to see me. He didn't want me to meet my grandchildren.

I remembered Allie, and how she'd denied me from meeting another grandchild.

I remembered Brooke.

Vic's hand on mine was a faint anchor, but I was drifting away as I remembered how much I had lost. "…he's just not there yet, you know? With you and Frank. But he will be! I know he will!" Vic's voice was full of hope, but her words only brought back the sting of reality.

"And yet, he's forgiven you," I finally replied, my voice cold and shallow. She pulled away, sighing a little.

"He wanted answers. *Real* answers. He knew he'd get them from me."

"Sure… it's like you said, right?" I shrugged, attempting to appear indifferent. "My kids would rather speak to you. Aunt Vic's the one with *all* the answers—"

"It's not like that."

"I bring them up, *I* take them to school… feed them… *clothe* them," I began ranting. "I dedicate my *whole life* to them just for you to swoop in and save the day by… by giving them *condoms…*"

"Well, maybe if *you'd* given them condoms, they wouldn't have to buy pregnancy tests."

I glared at her. Her eyes widened again. Her hands quickly went up, covering her face as if she thought I was going to smack her. Maybe I was. Maybe I hadn't decided what I wanted to do to her yet.

"I just…*ugh…*" She took hold of my hands again, squeezing them gently. "Let's just take this one day at a time, alright? And I mean this in the best way possible, but… maybe you could see this as a silver lining. I don't think he knows that Brooke's missing yet. When he finds out, he'll *have* to come back!"

"There's a silver lining to my daughter going missing?" I asked dryly. She nodded enthusiastically, not taking the hint.

"This could be the *only* good thing to come out of this shitty situation," she smiled, still somehow unaware of the insensitivity of her words. "His *sister's* missing! He'll *have* to come home when he finds out, and then you and Frank can patch things up with him, you know? He just… he needs some time to figure things out for himself. That night… it was traumatic for him, Liz—"

"You think I don't know that?"

"I don't think you understand how badly it's affected him."

I laughed loudly, utterly mystified by how wrong she could get the situation. "You think I haven't thought about it *every day* since?"

I was his mother, for goodness' sake.

I'd done all I could that night. I knew what he'd gone through, and I tried to help in every way I could. But nothing had been enough. Nothing helped.

Well, aside from him wiping our savings and fleeing the state.

"You can't afford to think about this right now, alright?" Vic brushed a loose strand of my hair from my forehead, tucking it behind my ear. "It's out of our control. You need to focus on Brooke… and, well, Allie and Cam, for that matter. *They* need you right now."

Her words were meant to be comforting, but they only seemed to highlight the enormity of all that was going on. My heart ached with the weight of all the missed opportunities and unresolved pain; almost an entire decade of agony.

The love I felt for my children—all four of them—was all-consuming, but so was the grief.

My eyes flickered toward the clock, realizing that Frank still hadn't come home. My anger rerouted toward him; he should've been there. *He* had grandkids too, and he had no idea.

He should have been there to hear that news with me.

There had been a time when this house was filled with life, when laughter and noise filled every corner, and the rooms were never empty. There was a comfort in knowing that we were all together, under one roof, a comfort that I had taken for granted.

Mick leaving had left a void that continued to reverberate through the house almost a decade later, and Brooke's absence now cast a heavy shadow over every room. Allie… well, Allie hadn't been Allie for a long time. And Cam—my baby boy—was growing up and changing every day. It was only a matter of time before I lost him too, and all I could do was count the days.

The house was slowly emptying itself out, and it felt like the very walls were mourning the loss of the family that once filled them.

I shut my eyes, allowing the memories to wash over me.

"Do you have Mick's number?" I eventually asked, and it took her a moment to reply. She hugged me tighter, clearly overthinking her answer.

"…*I'll call him tomorrow… I'll see what I can do…*"

I leaned into her, allowing myself to finally accept her embrace. The road ahead was uncertain, but Vic's presence was a small comfort amid the chaos. Despite everything, I was glad she was home.

It was just one small step toward some semblance of normality, but one that I had so badly needed.

And despite her occasional thoughtlessness and lack of boundaries, she was right about one thing: for the sake of my children—or at least the family that remained—I had to find some way to navigate this living nightmare and come out the other end unscathed.

I just needed my family home.

All of them.

12 DAYS AFTER THE DISAPPEARANCE OF
BROOKLYN NICHOLSON

LUCY | 6:12 AM

As the first birds began to chirp outside my window, I came to terms with the fact that I wasn't going to get any sleep.

The sky behind the curtains was gradually lightening, and I knew the alarm clock would ring soon. Despite my exhaustion, a sense of relief washed over me. I had been counting down the hours, eager for the moment I could finally get out of bed. I wasn't entirely sure how long I had been staring at my ceiling, trapped in the space between being asleep and awake, unsure if I had gotten any sleep at all.

All I could do was wait for the sun to rise.

By the time the light had begun to illuminate through the

crevices in the curtains, I couldn't wait any longer. My legs moved before I could mentally catch up, throwing themselves over the side of the bed and pushing myself onto my feet. I flicked the button on my alarm clock, grabbed my shirt from the floor and pulled it over my head, quivering. I'd left the window open all night. My whole body was vibrating uncontrollably, and I tried to convince myself it was just the cold. But I knew that wasn't completely true.

I wandered into the bathroom, flicking on the light and shutting the door behind me. That's when I heard movement from the bedroom—the bed creaking just a little. I ignored it. I wanted to buy some time before facing it.

I stepped into the shower. Rinsed my face. My body. I stood under the semi-warm water a little while longer than usual, just to kill time.

I couldn't escape the tension knotted in my chest or the pit in my stomach. I tried to focus on the water trickling down my skin, hoping it would wash away the unease. But it didn't. As I leaned against the shower wall, I let out a shaky breath. The steam enveloped me, but it couldn't blur the sharp edges of my thoughts.

Snippets of the night before ran through my mind in an endless loop, no matter how hard I tried to push them out.

My hands trembled as I turned off the water and reached for a towel. Drying off slowly, I caught my reflection in the mirror. My eyes were black, haunted by the memories I couldn't shake. I rubbed my face, trying to scrub away the remnants of the night that clung to me like a second skin. The horror began to set in.

I'd fucked up.

I violently ravished my hair with the towel, desperate to distract myself. The rough motion felt oddly satisfying, and a small relief came from the reminder of how much faster my hair now dried since I'd cut it short. Once it was half-dried, I hung the towel back up and slipped into my uniform while avoiding my reflection in the mirror. It'd taken me so long to start feeling better about myself. It'd taken *so long* to stop hating the person that stared back at me.

This time, I couldn't even blame anyone else.

This time, it was all on me.

I smoothed out my shirt across my chest; each movement felt

mechanical. Stiff. This had been my routine for a long time, but this morning felt different. It *was* different. This morning, I would've done anything to avoid venturing back into the bedroom.

But I knew I couldn't delay any longer. I had to get to work.

I pushed the bathroom door open. The bedroom felt cold. Unwelcoming. The creak of the floorboards seemed louder than usual as I moved toward the dresser, grabbing my watch and shakily fastening it around my wrist. I could hear my own heartbeat, a rapid drumbeat in my ears. I found myself gripping the dresser as my heart hammered in my chest, and another *creak* came from the bed behind me. I felt a sudden urge to run.

You did this, the voice inside my head stated with an audible sneer. *Now you deal with it.*

I sat on the bed, pulling my shoes onto my feet. Tying my shoelaces. Within a second or two of sitting down, I felt him stirring beside me. My fingers locked up immediately. In my peripheral vision, I saw him rolling over. He was barely visible in the darkness. The birds continued to chirp outside, barely filling the silence as a million and one thoughts ran through my brain.

Had he been drinking the night before? He'd said he'd driven here. He didn't seem drunk. What if he couldn't remember anything?

What if he thought that this had been *my* idea?

He slowly sat up, not saying a word. The rustling of sheets and the creak of the bed frame only made me feel more nauseous. I focused on tying my shoes; the laces felt like lead in my hands, and I had to concentrate to make the simple knots.

The silence stretched on. It was as if we were both too afraid to speak, fearing that any words might shatter the fragile peace we clung to.

He finally stood up, moving slowly, deliberately. I glanced up, barely catching a glimpse of the same haunted look in his eyes that I had seen in my own reflection in the bathroom. The guilt, the confusion, the regret—it was all there, mirrored back at me through the darkness. He picked up his own shirt from the floor, slipping it on without a word. The sight of him getting dressed drove home the reality of what had happened.

"*...you working today?*"

The sudden sound of his voice made it impossible to ignore the horrifying reality that we were now facing. I had unrealistically hoped that we could've gotten through this without having to actually speak to each other. I cleared my throat, trying to steady my voice. "I'm leaving in five minutes."

He didn't say anything else.

Once my shoes were on, I found myself frozen on the bed. I knew I had to stand up and get moving, but my legs weren't cooperating. I just sat there as he moved around me, collecting his things. Then he sat down on the other side of the bed, slipping his own shoes on. My thoughts raced to catch up with the moment as I realized that we did need to talk. We had to work out what happened next.

"You slept in your car all night," I finally spoke, staring into the darkness ahead of me. "You got drunk at the bar and you didn't want to drive home. You parked here because all the spaces at the bar were taken."

It felt odd—as an officer—giving someone an alibi rather than taking it. I felt him shuffling behind me. The mattress moved with him. "*Good thinking.*"

"And we did *not* see each other last night," I added, my throat tightening. "You didn't see me at the bar. You didn't even see me through the window."

"*Okay.*"

The words hung in the air; a fragile pact forged out of necessity. I turned back to look at him. His silhouette was barely visible in the dim light. His shoulders slumped, and he looked older, wearier than I remembered. His current demeanor was a stark contrast to what it had been the night before.

Further flashbacks came flooding into my head, and I wanted to smash my hands against my skull.

"*Luce—*"

"Don't." The word slipped out before I had the chance to stop it. Despite not knowing what he was going to say, I had a strong feeling that he was about to say something stupid.

The worst part of it all was that, despite the crushing guilt, a small, insidious part of me was ecstatic. I'd missed him more than I'd admitted to myself, and for those fleeting hours, everything seemed to make sense. In the moment, I'd justified it. This wasn't some cheap, heat-of-the-moment fling—this was *us*. It felt natural. Normal. That night, I felt more myself than I had for almost two weeks. It was a sanctuary I hadn't known I needed.

As the weight of what we'd done sank in, the exhilaration was slowly being suffocated by an oppressive blanket of guilt.

We'd fucked up.

The last thing I'd expected Frank to do was move over to my side of the bed, sitting down next to me. I should've moved away from him, but I didn't. Of course I didn't. We both sat there for a moment, the silent acknowledgment of our actions hanging heavily between us.

His hand found its way onto my knee. "*I missed you.*"

His words broke my heart in ways that I'd never deemed imaginable. They cut deeper than I'd ever thought possible, reopening each and every wound I'd fought so hard to sew up.

The room felt too small, the air too thick. I wanted so badly to escape, to bolt from the painful truth that even then—even knowing what I knew—there was a part of me that still longed for things to return to what they had once been. It was a brutal reminder that, despite everything, I wasn't over it.

I stood up before I could fully process my actions. His hand jerked from my leg as I moved. "I'm going to tell them."

I could barely make out his confused expression in the darkness. "*What?*"

"I'm coming off the case," I said firmly, hearing the wavering in my own voice. "I can't do this anymore."

"*Hey—*"

"I'm supposed to be coming by your house later," I continued, my voice getting louder. "To check up on Allie. To check up on *all* of you. I can't do it... I-I... *how* am I supposed to—"

"Luce, it's okay—"

"No, it's *not* okay—"

"You can't give up on the case." He stood up too, moving closer to me. "Please, you... you *can't...*"

The guilt quickly washed to anger as I realized what he was saying. Or, at least, what I'd assumed he was saying.

I stared at the desperate expression on his face. "Is that what this was all about?" I demanded as the sudden realization set in. "Was... *this*... just a way for you to get information from me? So you could find out more about the case?!"

His face hardened. "What the hell are you talking about?"

"Is that why you came here?"

"You can't be serious—"

"You show up here, asking about the security footage," I began hissing, trying to keep my voice low. "And then... is *that* what this is all about?!"

"You think I *planned* this?!"

"It'd be easier to explain to Liz, right?! Using me for *information*—"

He started laughing, pulling his coat on. He began walking toward the door, shaking his head. "Fuck you, Luce—"

"Why do you care if I stay on the case?!"

"*Because I like seeing you!*"

He spun back around as he yelled it, his anger mingling with a deep, disoriented sadness. I stared at him, searching for any sign of dishonesty, but there was genuine remorse flooding his expression.

"At the start, I hated it..." he went on, his voice still laced with resentment. "I fucking *hated* seeing you, but then... God, I don't know... I'd see you, and *I felt better!* Even just you *being* there—at the house, at the conference—it gives me this... this small, *fucked up* sense of relief, just being in the same room as you... *even if Liz is there!*"

Despite still being unsure of the legitimacy of his words, they struck a chord deep inside me.

He was describing exactly what I'd been feeling; the bizarre, twisted sense of relief that I felt just sharing a room with him, amidst the raw, inescapable guilt.

"And I know it's wrong," he continued with a groan. "But... *Jesus*... what's *right* about all of this?!"

I just stood there, taking it all in. Understanding everything that he was saying, more than I cared to admit.

"And for the record, I did *not* think last night was going to happen," he added angrily. "I came here to ask about the footage... and I guess... I don't know... I guess seeing you made it harder to leave. I didn't plan it, but *yeah*, I wanted it. I *still* want you. I *never* stopped wanting you."

My chest tightened, my throat constricting as I fought to keep the tears at bay. It was as if he was speaking my own thoughts out loud. It was like he knew exactly what I felt at that moment. His saying it out loud made it all the more real.

Liz's face flashed through my mind, drawing every last breath from my lungs. I wished—more than *anything*—that I could forget her. I wished I could pretend she didn't exist.

But she did.

"This never should have happened," I muttered, struggling to mask my devastation as I attempted to reclaim control over the situation. "You shouldn't have come here."

"You think I don't know that?"

The last time this happened, I didn't know he was married. I didn't know he had a family.

I'd convinced myself I hadn't done anything wrong—that all of this was his fault for keeping that part of his life a secret, and that I *never* would've crossed that line if I'd known the truth. I thought I was a better person. A good person.

But I wasn't.

That realization hurt more than anything.

"It never happened," he added, and I hadn't anticipated how hard those words would sting. "We just... we pretend it never happened—"

"Just like last time," I interrupted coldly. "And every other time."

"What else is there to do?"

"You know she's going to find out, right?" I asked, looking him dead in the eye. "It's going to come out at some point. And the longer we hide it, the bigger this is going to become."

He didn't say anything. But his silence told me all I needed to know; he knew I was right.

All I could do was hold myself together at that moment. I'd already grappled with what I was going to face when it all came out. This wasn't just about Liz—the whole *country* was watching the Nicholsons at this point. Everyone and their mothers were readily tuned in, waiting for the next shitshow to transpire. It was a public spectacle—a story that had captured the imagination of a nation. And little did they know yet, but I was a primary piece of the Nicholson puzzle. All I could do was prepare for the fallout.

My eyes flickered toward the clock on the wall, above my bed.

Time was running out. "I've got to get to work."

"Luce—"

"Someone's got to go deal with Donnie Booker."

The words shot out like venom, and I regretted saying his name as soon as it left my mouth. It was a cheap shot. An unforgivable one. Frank's eyes widened in shock, clearly surprised that I went there. I'd surprised myself. The sting of my own words hung heavy in the air.

My emotions were a maelstrom—conflicted between the urge to comfort him, to apologize for my own harshness, and the burning anger that made every word feel like a knife. The guilt and anger clashed inside me, making it nearly impossible to figure out what I should do next. "I'm sorry," I said quietly, almost as an afterthought. "I shouldn't—"

"No," he interrupted, barely lifting his head. "I'm sorry."

I wondered what he was sorry for. I also wondered if he'd truly meant it.

The silence between us grew even thicker. There was nothing left to say that could fix what had happened or undo the damage. The world outside was waiting for the both of us, and we had to face it at some point. It occurred to me that we were, perhaps, both stalling for time, trying to avoid it for as long as possible. There was no other reason we were still there, picking fights with each other.

"I want to kill him," Frank said finally, barely moving his lips. "I've never wanted to hurt someone more in my life."

I had been consumed by the image of Donnie Booker on that security footage ever since I'd watched it; an image that had burned itself into my brain, replaying over and over.

"I know," I managed to reply, unsure of what else to say.

"Did he kill her?"

The question completely caught me off guard.

A lump rose in my throat. He hadn't asked anything that hadn't already been floating around the town for the past 24 hours; it was the most obvious question that anyone could've asked at that point. But that didn't make the question any easier to answer.

As far as I was aware, around 90% of the officers I worked with shared the same opinion on Donnie Booker's innocence—he had to have had *something* to do with her disappearance. It just made too much sense.

"There's no evidence to suggest it," I said semi-truthfully, and his head dropped. "We're still considering all possibilities—"

"So, you're considering that she's dead."

She'd been missing for almost two weeks. Of course we'd considered that she was dead.

I wasn't about to tell him something that he already knew, especially when I didn't necessarily believe it to be true myself. Maybe she was still alive. Maybe she wasn't. Until we found her, *considering that she was dead* wasn't going to help anybody, and it certainly wasn't going to make Frank feel any better.

"I can't stop thinking about her, Luce." His voice broke; exhaustion and pain etched his face. "Every day I wake up in that house, and... and every day, she doesn't come home. Cam's confused. Allie's falling apart. I-I don't even know what to say to any of them, *or* Liz..." He paused, shaking his head stiffly. "I had to get out of there... that house... I can't *breathe* there. I can't think about anything else."

Despite everything that had happened, a part of me wanted to comfort him. I just wanted to take his hand or put my arms around him. The conflicting emotions swirled in my mind—anger, guilt, sympathy. It was just a mess. All of it.

"When I'm with you..." He stopped himself again, laughing suddenly as if he couldn't believe what he was about to say. "When I'm with you, *you're* all I think about." A faint, conflicted smile tugged at the corners of his mouth, but it didn't reach his eyes. I was locked in position, barely breathing. Not knowing where to look, or what to do.

I was slipping.

I really, really did not want to, but it was already happening.

"I wish I'd never met you," he continued, his laugh devoid of any real humor. "I wish you weren't a part of this... because you don't deserve any of it..."

I wanted to argue—to tell him that I'd made my own choices the night before, that I was responsible for my own actions. The consequences of our actions had wrapped around us both, and it was impossible to untangle the mess we'd made.

But I would've been lying if I'd said I didn't hate him for putting me in this situation.

And I certainly hated him for making me feel the way that I did.

"...and I hate that you're the only thing in this fucked up world that makes me happy." He looked at me, tears in his eyes. "I hate that more than anything."

I'm not sure how my hand ended up on his face. My thumb struck his cheek, wiping away a tear that had slipped out at the end of his sentence.

"...I-I know it's selfish, and I... I shouldn't even be here, but—"

I cut him off with a kiss.

He froze for a moment, caught off guard, before his lips softened against mine. The kiss was hesitant at first, like we were both trying to gauge if this was real. If this was really happening again.

But then something shifted. He deepened the kiss, and I felt his grip on my waist tighten, pulling me closer. I let myself fall into it, letting the warmth and familiarity of him flood over me. All the pain, the guilt, the turmoil—everything seemed to dissolve in that one, intense moment of connection.

When we finally broke apart, breathless and shaky, I saw both relief and desperation in his eyes. He opened his mouth as if to say something but then just closed it, shaking his head slightly. Guilt flooded my entire body once more.

I don't know why I did it.

I *shouldn't* have done it.

His forehead gently pressed against mine; his breath mingled with mine in the stillness of the room. For a moment, time seemed to pause. Frank's eyes searched mine with an intensity that spoke of everything unspoken between us.

Then, he leaned in again; our lips met in a gentle, almost reverent kiss. It was slow and soft, filled with the weight of all the words we couldn't say out loud.

I wanted to hate him.

I *really* wanted to hate him.

As we pulled away slowly, I felt my bottom lip begin to quiver. I could feel the tears welling up, threatening to spill over. Frank's gaze remained locked on mine. His hand reached out, hesitating before it gently brushed a stray tear from my cheek.

KNOCK-KNOCK-KNOCK.

Our heads span to the bedroom door, leading into the living room. The sound was sudden and jarring, pulling us both back to the present. We both completely froze, staring in the direction of the knocking.

As the silence that followed drew on, I turned back to Frank. His face paled as the reality of the interruption sunk in.

"*Who…*" His voice was barely a whisper, and he couldn't finish his sentence.

I swallowed hard, attempting to gather my thoughts as I slowly moved toward the living room. Frank stayed put, watching me through the bedroom door as I approached my front door cautiously, my heart racing.

I had to be calm. I had to be cool.

The last thing I needed was for whoever was on the other side to suspect anything was wrong.

I slowly opened the door a crack, peering out. The dim light of the hallway flooded my apartment. I leaned out, scanning left and right. There was no one there. The hallway was completely empty. My heart hammered against my chest as I silently confirmed that we were alone.

I was about to close the door and return to the living room when something on the floor caught my eye: an envelope on the ground, half hidden by the door frame.

My breath caught in my throat as I crouched down to pick it up, careful not to make any sudden movements. The weight of it felt strangely heavy. I glanced nervously at the hallway again before pulling the letter inside, shutting the door quietly behind me.

"*…who was it?*"

I reached for the switch on the wall, finally flipping the lights on. Frank was stood in the bedroom doorway now, squinting against the sudden glare of the lights. I examined the envelope.

"What's that?" I heard Frank ask as I flipped it over. The envelope was plain, unmarked by any identifying information. On the back, I found a small sketch of an apple, crudely drawn but unmistakable. There was no name, no address; just that strange drawing.

I studied the envelope, a sense of unease settling over me. My instincts kicked in before I even had time to think about it; I rushed into the kitchen, pulling some rubber gloves out of the drawer.

Frank's footsteps followed me closely. *"What's going on?"*

I snapped the gloves on, my movements precise despite the whirlwind of thoughts racing through my mind. With careful hands, I tore open the envelope. As I slid my fingers inside, I felt something rigid and slightly textured.

I pulled it out, revealing a Polaroid photograph.

"...Luce?"

I held it up to the light. The image was still forming; the colors and details gradually emerging. I began flapping it violently, much to Frank's rapidly growing confusion.

"What the hell is going on?!"

I pulled the Polaroid to my face, scanning the image.

My heart stopped.

I felt Frank leaning over my shoulder, following my gaze. A guttural noise escaped his lips as he saw what I was seeing. *"...what... how..."*

I ran back through the hallway, back into the bedroom.

As I came to a halt, my eyes fixed onto the slightly ajar curtains, barely covering the window that led out to the fire escape. Daylight was now seeping through, filling the room. I looked back at the Polaroid, my heart sinking as the image came fully into focus. Then I glanced at the window, the open space that had exposed us.

It was us.

The photo captured the exact moment we had just shared. We were sitting on the bed, just moments before—the same bed, the same room. Frank's hand was gently touching my face. My lips were pressed against his in that tender, desperate kiss. The photo had frozen that moment in time, preserving every detail.

The realization hit me like a cold wave.

Frank was now yelling in the next room, his voice a raw mix of terror and fury. His words were muffled but unmistakably enraged.

I was frozen in place, my heart pounding as I clutched the Polaroid—the clear, unfiltered evidence of our mistake. The room felt like it was closing in on me, each breath becoming more labored as my thoughts spun wildly. Frank's shouting grew more frantic.

I shakily turned the Polaroid around, desperate to make sense of it. That was when I saw the writing:

$5000
808 BAR
NEXT WEDS 9PM
THANKS FRANK!

The last part was underlined three times, with a smiley face etched next to his name. The realization of what this meant slowly sank in.

Someone had been watching us.

Maybe they'd followed Frank to my apartment. My eyes shot back to the window as I realized that there was no way someone accidentally got up onto the fire escape outside my room— whoever it was, they knew we were both there. This had been planned out. This wasn't an accident; they knew we'd spent the night together.

And this wasn't just some personal vendetta.

This was a transaction.

Frank's yelling in the next room faded into the background as I struggled to process the implications of the message. There was a small, unsettling relief in realizing they were demanding money; if this was just blackmail, it meant they might not necessarily leak the evidence of our affair if we followed their instructions. My initial fear that this might be connected to Brooke's disappearance—which had crossed my mind when I first saw the envelope—seemed less likely now.

The sinking feeling in my stomach grew bigger as I wondered how long they had been watching us. If they knew Frank was there that morning, they must've seen him arrive the night before.

They could have been watching us all night.

Frank burst into the room, his face pale but set with determination. My eyes wandered toward him, my mouth dry as I imagined what other pictures they could've taken of us. We stared at each other in horror. I shakily passed the Polaroid to him, revealing the writing on the back. He grabbed it from me, reading it, muttering the words out loud.

"We should tell the police," I mumbled emotionlessly. Frank scoffed angrily, tossing the photograph across the room.

"No way—"

"Frank—"

"*No fucking way!*" His voice was raw with desperation and anger. As my eyes followed the direction of the fallen Polaroid, the whole world seemed to churn. The photograph landed face-up on the carpet.

"If this gets out, Liz, the kids—*everyone*—will be dragged through the mud." He ran a hand through his hair, pacing frantically. "It'll be a fucking *circus*. We've got to find another way."

A numbness settled over me. It occurred to me that Frank hadn't considered every possibility; these people might not have been interested in negotiating at all. They could leak the photographs no matter what we did. And we weren't even entirely sure *what* they had taken pictures of. That kiss was the least incriminating leverage they could've had on us.

At that moment, I felt nothing but hopelessness. I knew the reality of the situation. We may as well have gone straight to the press ourselves, handing ourselves in.

But Frank wasn't ready to accept that.

He was pacing back and forth uncontrollably now, too focused on fighting this. Clinging to the hope that he could still, somehow, control the situation.

Knowing that it didn't matter either way, I offered the final option:

"You're going to need five thousand dollars."

16 DAYS AFTER THE DISAPPEARANCE OF
BROOKLYN NICHOLSON

ALLIE | 4:04 PM

"How are you feeling today, Alexandra?"

I stared down at my boots, which now had a layer of fluff spread across the soles from when I'd entered the room. The dark purple carpet was weirdly sticky. It was so gross. And ugly. I couldn't look away from the subtly striped pattern running through it, wondering what the hell would possess someone to think that it was attractive in any way.

"...Alexandra?"

I looked up at the strange man behind the desk. "No one calls me that," I said finally, folding my arms.

"Okay. What should I call you?"

He was this middle-aged guy with grayish hair, thick glasses, and a pot belly. Sweat patches were seeping through his shirt, under his arms. He smelt like blue cheese. My eyes wandered to the clock on the wall just above his head, like a rusty three-dollar halo, counting down the seconds until I could get out of this god-fucking-awful room.

"Allie. It's Allie."

He clicked his pen, writing it down. "Okay… Allie… how are you feeling?"

Three-thousand, three-hundred seconds.

"I'm good."

He nodded, clearly not buying it, but playing along regardless. "That's good to hear."

Judging by his silence, I think he was waiting for me to continue the conversation. But I had no intention of doing so. I shifted in my seat, eyes wandering around the office. A name was scrawled on a gold-plated sign on the desk in front of me: *Dr. Dibson, M.D.* A shelf behind his desk held an assortment of books and knick-knacks—items that were clearly intended to make the room feel warm and inviting but failing miserably. The walls behind him were lined with framed certificates and a few generic landscape paintings.

That's when I saw my dad.

Among the awards and pictures on the wall, there was this tiny Unrest Stand poster. It was so small that I probably wouldn't have noticed it if one of the band members hadn't been my own parent.

His face caught my eye right away, which kind of freaked me out. It was back when he had his perm. It looked ridiculous. The lyrics, "*Good thoughts get me through; Nothing else'll ever do*" were scrawled across the poster in purple glittered writing, circling above my father and uncles.

It was at that moment that it hit me—recent news stories aside—that there was *no way* this guy didn't know who I was.

I could already picture him calling everyone he knew the second my session was over: "*Guess who my new patient is? FRANKIE FLASH'S DAUGHTER!*"

"So," Dr. Dibson, M.D. clapped his hands together softly, sitting forward in his chair; "what brings you here today?"

It took all my self-restraint to stop myself from rolling my eyes. I mean, come *on*—what was he expecting me to say? He knew damn well why I was there. "My parents think there's something wrong with me."

"Really? That's not the vibe I got from them," he replied, his pen poised over his notepad. "Seemed to me that they were worried about you because you've been through a lot recently."

I sat back in my chair, avoiding eye contact. "They think I'm depressed."

"Well… even if that is true, that wouldn't mean that there's anything wrong with you. It just means you might need a little help to get back to your usual self."

I scoffed slightly, picking at a loose strand of cotton hanging from my jeans. As the denim unraveled, I wondered who my "usual self" even was. I couldn't remember a time when I didn't feel the way I felt at that moment. This *was* my usual self. Not a lot had changed in that aspect.

"…am I right in saying that some of your worries are family-related?" he asked suddenly, and I tugged the thread harder. "I tell you what—I'm going to make a little sketch of your family tree, just so I can get a little insight into your home situation… what are your parents' names?"

My eyes zoned back to Frankie Flash and his god-awful hair. "Frank," I replied, cringing internally as my dad winked at me from across the room. "And Elizabeth."

Dr. Dibson drew out three squares, two above one. He wrote my name in the bottom square—*A-L-L-Y*—and then my parents' names inside the other two. I could've sworn he almost wrote the letter *'I'* at the end of my Dad's name; there was a slight scribble from where his pen had touched the paper after the *'K'*.

"Are they together?" he asked as he scrawled Mom's name on the paper. I nodded. "Great. Any siblings?"

I shifted in my seat, struggling to get comfortable. "Two brothers and a sister."

He drew three more squares before looking back up at me. "Your brothers? What are their names?"

"Michael and Cameron," I answered, feeling a little funny using their full names. "Mick and Cam."

"And your sister?"

There was no way in hell he didn't know her name.

"Brooke."

He nodded, scribbling her name with an infuriating calmness. "How old are they? Your siblings?"

"Uh, I don't know… Cam's nine or ten… Brooke's fifteen…" I hesitated, having to think backward to work out the final equation. I couldn't remember the exact year my oldest brother was born, but I knew he was around ten years older than me. "Mick's thirty-something."

"That's a pretty big age gap between you and your older brother," he stated, scribbling numbers next to the squares. "Were you close? Growing up together?"

I shrugged slightly, unsure how I was supposed to answer that question. Maybe I just didn't want to answer it.

He must've taken the hint because he swiftly moved on to the next question: "Are there any other family members you're close with? Grandparents? Cousins?"

"My Mom's sisters, Vic and Lot." I shrugged again, trying to remember the last time I'd actually seen Mom's older sister. "My Nanna and Grandpa live in Oregon, but we see them at Christmas. My mom's parents."

"And your father's?"

I knew little to nothing about Dad's side of the family, but I'd never questioned it.

His dad died when I was a baby, and the little that Dad had told us about him had been enough for me to understand why he didn't want us knowing him. He was this big, scary dude who hated kids. He was a general—or maybe a sergeant—in the Second World War, and he'd never really gotten past it. And my Nonna died long before I came along, so I'd only ever seen her in pictures. I just knew she looked a little like Brooke. That's what Dad always said, at least.

He had a sister too, but I wasn't sure if I'd ever met her. I think she was his twin. But again, all I had for reference were photographs; I had no idea who any of these people really were.

Instead of saying all that out loud, I just shook my head again.

Dr. Dibson put down his pen, taking a look at his freshly sketched Nicholson/Crowe family tree. "This will come in handy," he said with a smile, picking it up and showing it to me. "Always does with big families."

"Dope."

"Who else is important in your life, Allie?" he asked, and I laughed awkwardly. "Any close friends? A boyfriend?"

The atmosphere suddenly switched up.

My stomach twisted, and my hands clenched into fists as I fought the urge to bolt out of the room. Why was I even surprised? He'd seen the headlines. He'd read all the stories about me and Donnie. I wondered if he'd read the one about us planning to elope in Canada. Or the one about me secretly carrying triplets, planning to name one after Brooke. Or maybe he'd read some other bullshit story that had been freshly printed that morning.

"What are you asking me?" I forced a tight smile. "If I've got a boyfriend in prison?"

His expression barely moved. "Do you?"

"Well, you tell me, Doc." My voice dripped with sarcasm. "You watch the news, right? You're up to date with current events?"

"I'm not sure what you're saying, Allie."

"Okay…" I leaned forward, resting my elbows on the desk. "How about we both cut the bullshit from this point onwards? I'm Allie fucking Nicholson. I'm eighteen years old. My sister is *Brooklyn* fucking Nicholson, my *father's* Frankie fucking Flash, and *you know* who we are. *Everyone* does."

His eyes flickered with something—perhaps curiosity, or maybe just an attempt at maintaining professionalism. It was a pretty solid attempt, to be fair. He wasn't giving much away. "I understand there's a lot of media attention surrounding you and your family at the moment—"

"Oh, I'm *sure* you do!" I interrupted loudly, throwing my arms in the air. He maintained his calm demeanor, barely reacting.

"But," he continued, "my focus here is on you and your well-being. Not everyone is gullible enough to take newspaper headlines as fact… Allie-fucking-Nicholson."

The curse slipped out so unexpectedly that it took me by surprise. For a moment, I was caught off guard, my frustration momentarily overshadowed by the sheer audacity of hearing such words from a man who looked like he'd never seen anything more scandalous than a misplaced paperclip.

He took off his glasses, wiping them against his sleeve as he asked the next question: "So, where do you want to start?"

Good fucking question.

I shuffled back in my chair, my arms tightening across my

chest. I wasn't sure where I was supposed to start. Or where I *wanted* to start. So much had happened and I wasn't sure which part made the most sense to begin with.

"I'm not in love with Donnie Booker." The words came out of nowhere. They surprised me just as much as they'd likely surprised him. "I don't even like him in that way. Never have."

He barely nodded. "Alright."

"We got drunk and slept together after graduation. I got pregnant. That was *it*," I laughed awkwardly. "Nothing exciting about any of it."

"Would you like to talk more about that period of time?"

"What do you mean?"

"When you discovered you were pregnant," he clarified, noticing my tension. "We don't have to if you're not ready—"

"No, no... sure." I pursed my lips, blowing a small raspberry as I stumbled to find the right words. It occurred to me that I hadn't actually addressed this whole thing out loud in a pretty long time. "It was all pretty straightforward. I, uh... I took a test. There were these two pink lines, which, you know... means you're... *with child*. They came up right away."

"How did you feel when you found out?"

"How do you think?" I laughed, scratching an itch on my forearm. "Fucking *terrified*. My mom was going to *kill* me."

"Did you tell anyone?"

"Just my sister."

I remembered every tiny detail from that day.

After taking the test, I jumped into the car to pick up Cam and Brooke from school. I'd figured I could keep it together for the 20-minute car ride, but I broke down the second we pulled up outside the house. Brooke told Cam to go inside. She stayed with me.

I hadn't exactly planned on telling her, but it wasn't as if I really had a choice at that point. It was the first time I'd cried in front of her since we were little kids.

"You didn't tell Donnie?" he asked, pulling me back into the room. I shook my head stiffly. "Why not?"

It was insane how just hearing his name—a name I had known my whole life—could suddenly flood my senses with pure anguish. It was as if I was now thinking of a completely different person. That was how it felt, at least. *He* wasn't the same person.

"I wasn't planning on keeping it," I replied, realizing that this was the first time that I had actually said that out loud. "So there was no point."

"Did you have an abortion?"

I remembered how Mom had asked that exact question just a few days before. There was a huge contrast in the way they each asked that question; Dr. Dibson's voice was calm and measured with an almost cooling effect, as if he didn't really give a shit about my answer. Mom's words were like bullets.

"We don't have to speak about this if you're not ready—"

"It's fine," I interrupted, tapping my fingers against my knee. "Uh, no. I was *going* to, but... yeah. I didn't."

Up until this point, he'd managed to keep his expression neutral. But now, a flicker of confusion crossed his face; just a slight shadow of uncertainty. This was breaking news, after all. He was getting the real inside scoop, straight from the source.

"I lost it at twelve weeks, so it didn't matter in the end anyway." A laugh, hollow and sharp, escaped me. "I should've just gone through with it. Should've saved myself the trouble."

The air suddenly felt heavy around us. No one else knew this part, not even Brooke—just me and the doctors. I thought I'd feel something more, saying those words out loud for the first time. Maybe it was because of everything else that had happened since then, but at that moment, I felt nothing.

Dr. Dibson's eyes softened, his professional demeanor giving way to a more compassionate look. "I'm sorry you had to go through that."

I pulled a face, trying to lighten the mood. "Nah... don't worry about it," I said quickly, smiling a little. "So much has happened since that I don't even think about it anymore, you know? It's just... whatever."

"When did the miscarriage occur?"

"September 12th." I surprised myself that I remembered the date so quickly. "It was the week my sister went missing, so, you know... I didn't have a whole lot of time to dwell on it."

"The timing of those events must've made it even harder to process everything."

"Not really," I lied, nibbling on my thumbnail. "Shit happens."

"Do you want to talk about your sister?"

Another laugh slipped out. I wondered how long he had been waiting to ask that question. Hundreds of reporters would've killed to have been in his position. "Not really."

"That's okay." His tone remained cool. Gentle. "If it helps, we can explore other aspects of your life and how you're managing day-to-day. How does that sound?"

"What do you want to know, Doc?"

Dr. Dibson looked up from his notes. "Are there any particular challenges you're facing... or, well... anything that's been on your mind lately? Anything you're struggling with?"

"Well, I haven't been getting out much recently... you know, since someone tried to kill me last week."

I studied his face, waiting for some kind of reaction. If I'd said that in front of anyone else, there would've been gasps, yet he barely budged. In fact, he didn't even say anything—he just sat there, waiting for me to continue. I wasn't giving in. We stared at each other for a little while, participating in a psychological game of Chicken.

He broke first.

"Do you want to talk about that?" he asked, his tone as steady and professional as ever. I smirked a little, running my fingertips over my now jagged thumbnail.

"Why? You saw it on the news, right? You know what happened—"

"My focus here is on *your* personal experience and feelings," he reminded me, and I rolled my eyes. "We don't have to go into any details... just whatever you're comfortable with sharing. I'm here to listen."

"Well, there's not a whole lot to say." I'd begun tugging at the loose strand on my jeans again. "I survived."

"Did you know the other victims?"

"You know I did," I replied coldly, not looking up.

"I can imagine that being the only survivor must be incredibly difficult."

I stared at the thread I was picking at, feeling the all-too-familiar lump re-forming in my throat.

"...not only are you dealing with the trauma of the event itself, but you're also carrying the weight of losing friends," he continued. "These past few weeks can't have been easy for you."

I looked up, smiling tightly.

"I survived," I repeated. "I'm still here."

He leaned forward. "And how do you feel about that?"

"About what?"

"Still being here."

Fuck.

The question dug deeper than I wanted to admit, and I tried not to show it. I didn't want him to think that he'd gotten me.

I mean... I had a *lot* of thoughts on that.

I thought about Mandy a lot. I mean, she had college, ambitions, a future with Hurley. And I figured Melissa MacKenzie had her future all planned out too. Their lives were only just beginning, you know? Same as Brooke.

And here I was—trapped in a room with some greasy old guy who thought I was crazy. I had all the time in the world, but I had no big future planned out.

It just felt kind of a waste.

"It is what it is," I replied, clasping my fingers together. "Can't change any of it."

Dr. Dibson leaned back in his chair, his expression thoughtful. "You're right. But talking about how you feel about these... events... can help you to start processing and understanding those feelings."

I readjusted in my seat, suddenly hearing a crinkling sound under my butt. My heart stopped.

I reached into my back pocket, feeling the familiar texture of the paper that had been crumpled in there for days. My fingers brushed against the edges.

I'd forgotten they were in there.

"...sometimes, when we're faced with such profound loss and survival, it's hard to reconcile our own feelings with the reality of what happened," he went on as I focused solely on not breaking down. My eyes began filling up dangerously fast. "It's okay to feel conflicted or to question why you're still here. Those feelings are valid and, in my opinion, worth exploring—"

"I wrote poems."

It was as if a third person in the room had spoken. My mouth was moving before my thoughts could catch up. Dr. Dibson's attention shifted, his eyes glimmering with a hint of curiosity. "Poems?"

What the fuck was I doing?

"I-I wrote poems," I repeated, pulling the papers out of my back pocket. "They're about my friends. The ones that died."

My heartbeat quickened as I fumbled with the letters, unfolding each of them. They crinkled in my hands, the sound somehow grounding me in the present moment.

This was insane.

This was *actually* insane.

"Writing poetry can be a great way to process what you're fee—"

"I wrote them from the killer's perspective," I interrupted shakily, causing his eyebrows to raise a little. "To, um... to understand how he may have tried to... *silence* them, I guess. Before he killed them. Or... maybe how he wanted to warn them about what was about to happen to them."

I wasn't even sure if any of that would make any sense.

It barely made any sense to me, and *I* was the one saying it out loud.

"Seeing things from a different perspective can be a good way to process difficult emotions," Dr. Dibson offered, and I quickly nodded.

"Right."

"Are these your poems?" he asked, gesturing toward the letters that Mandy had given me. I stared down at them, still crumpled up in my hands. I'd read all three of them so many times that I knew every single word, front to back. I had every line memorized. "Would you like to share them?"

I really didn't want to. Or, at least, I didn't *think* I wanted to. Maybe I did, deep down.

Once again, my body began moving before I got the chance to stop myself; I uncrumpled the first letter, clearing my throat. It was Hurley's letter. *Good.*

It made sense to start with the first one.

"...*Patrick, Patrick, you should have known better*," I read out loud, my vision blurring as I moved on to the next sentence. "*Now it's too late, so here is your letter...*"

I licked my lips, attempting to moisten my mouth before

continuing:

> *"Your careless words are the reason you'll sink,*
> *And here is your warning written in ink.*
>
> *Your girlfriend will miss you, but never you mind;*
> *I promise that she won't be too far behind.*
>
> *I promise you two will always be together—*
> *Just make sure this letter stays secret forever."*

My hands trembled as I folded the letter back up, moving it to the back of the pile. My eyes wandered up, moving from the second letter up to Dr. Dibson's face. He wasn't giving anything away. He just sat there, waiting for me to continue.

I nodded slightly, swiftly moving onto the second letter:

> *"Amanda, Amanda, and Patrick too—*
> *Sitting on a bench, looking so blue.*
>
> *Patrick fell and left you alone,*
> *And now you're left with no one else home.*
>
> *Do you miss him? I'm sure that you do,*
> *But don't worry—soon you will be with him too.*
>
> *But don't tell the cops! No, don't you dare,*
> *Or your sister will also be joining you there."*

I was about to move straight on to the final letter when Dr. Dibson put a hand up, stopping me.

"Can I say something before you move on?" he asked, and I nodded. "These poems are… intense. Could you tell me a little bit about your thought process while writing them?"

I froze up, having not thought that far ahead. I wasn't entirely sure what I'd expected to happen. My mind raced backward, going through each line over and over.

"I'm not sure."

Great thinking, Al.

"Please tell me if I'm completely missing the mark," he went on, gesturing toward the crumpled pile of paper in my hands. "But... it feels almost as if you wanted to turn the killer into a character... you know, a villain with a motive, like... like Hannibal Lecter! It's almost as if you're giving a backstory to something that's otherwise faceless and terrifying." He paused. "Am I close?"

I nodded immediately. "Yes."

"You've turned the killer's actions into a narrative. By trying to understand his intentions, it feels like you're attempting to process the fear and helplessness you've felt over the past few weeks. It feels like you're trying to find some order in the chaos by spinning these experiences into something you can control... do you agree?"

"Absolutely."

"Do you believe any of it? What you've written?" he asked suddenly, catching me off guard. "This character, he—or she, I suppose—seems to be toying with your friends, almost laughing at them. He's... *reveling* in the control he holds over the fates of his victims. Is this really how you view this person?"

I found myself nodding again, recalling the first time I'd read those letters; remembering how I had gone over each line a thousand times, analyzing every word like it was one of those Shakespearean plays they made us read in school.

"I think he saw it as a game," I concluded. "I think that's why he wrote the letters... to make them all paranoid before he actually... you know..."

"That makes sense." He leaned forward slightly, his gaze steady but empathetic. "You're trying to make sense of a situation that's inherently senseless and terrifying."

"*Right.*"

"Did you write one for the third victim?"

"No, uh... well, actually, I didn't really *know* Melissa MacKenzie, so I didn't write one for her," I lied, stumbling over my words. "But I've got *my* letter... the one I wrote for myself. *About* myself."

"Go ahead."

I cleared my throat, skimming over the words of the final letter. My letter. I began shaking even harder, vividly remembering the moment Dad handed me the envelope, just moments before he told me that Mandy was dead.

"*Allie, Allie,*" I began. "*Victim of amnesia...*"

For a second, I thought I was going to throw up.

"*Lying or not, I'm here to teach ya.*

What happened that night changed who you are,
It took your sister away somewhere far.

Maybe you know where, but you say that you don't—
If you did, I'm sure that you won't.

Do I know what happened? I'll never tell—
I'll be seeing you, Allie..."

My mouth dried up. I stared at the final line, once again questioning everything that I had just read out loud.

"*...seeing you in hell.*"

My knuckles flushed white as I immediately crumpled it up after reading the final line, holding the paper in a ball in my fist. The room seemed to spin out of control around us, the walls moving in with each passing second.

"Before we go any further," Dr. Dibson said, "could you explain what you meant by being a "victim of amnesia"?"

I squeezed my eyes shut, trying to steady my breathing.

"I went to a party the night before Brooke went missing," I said through gritted teeth. "Someone spiked my drink. I can't remember anything... and they think I'm lying about it. The killer..." I paused, rushing back to correct myself: "Or, I mean, that's... that's what *I* wrote."

"I'm sorry that happened to you." Dr. Dibson nodded sympathetically. "That must have been a frightening experience. Was Brooke there that night? At the party?"

"Apparently," I said, my voice trembling. "I don't remember seeing her, so... I don't know for sure. I'm sure you've read all about it in the papers, or whatever—"

"Do you believe that if you hadn't been drugged, you might have been able to have stopped her from going missing?"

I hesitated, my throat tightening. "I don't know."

He began writing something down, the sound of the pen scratching against paper felt deafening. The clock began ticking twice as loud, filling up my ears. "…it seems…" he said slowly, finishing his writing, "…that… you are putting a lot of the blame on yourself for Brooke's disappearance."

A sharp, uncomfortable heat rose to my face. "But it's not my fault," I replied frostily. "I *want* to remember what happened. I-I wish I did—"

"I'm not saying it is your fault—"

"Good, 'cause it's *not*," I cut him off again, my voice tinged with frustration. "This is *his* fault! The *killer*!"

"You think that the killer has something to do with Brooke's disappearance?"

I wanted to scream at him that *yes, obviously* the killer had something to do with it. They said it *in the letter*.

In the midst of my breakdown, I reminded myself why I couldn't say that. He already thought I was crazy enough—I could tell by the way he was writing.

"What do the apples mean?" he asked suddenly. "On the letters. I noticed you've sketched little apples on each one."

I'd already crumpled the letters up beyond recognition, and I had no intention of opening them back up. I knew what he was talking about, though. The apples.

I didn't get it either.

"What do you think?" I asked, trying to keep my cool. "You're the expert. What do *you* think it means?"

He was quiet for a moment, shaking his head. Chewing on his pen. I watched him, hoping that he would actually have the answer. I'd been completely clueless up to this point. And I'd thought about it.

I'd thought a *lot* about it.

"Well… apples can represent a whole range of things, in literature and psychology," he pondered. "They might symbolize temptation, like the forbidden fruit… would you consider yourself to be religious?"

I blew another raspberry as my thoughts flooded back to Mom. "Not particularly. My mom's family are Catholic, and she, you know... she made sure we were all baptized, and whatever."

"Do you believe in God?"

"No." I hesitated slightly as a familiar pang of guilt settled in the pit of my stomach. Catholic guilt, Dad called it.

I didn't believe in God, hadn't in years. But somehow, admitting that out loud still made me feel like I was going to get struck by a bolt of lightning. Maybe it was Mom. Maybe it was the way we were raised, sitting in pews every Sunday, hands folded like good little soldiers, repeating words that never really sank in.

It helped that Dad grew up in a similar situation—his mother was Catholic, and she'd raised him that way, but he grew out of it as he got older. He never tried to guilt me into it like Mom did.

And moving schools had been a *major* game changer. It's kinda hard to question your faith when you're being taught by fucking nuns.

"Apples could also symbolize knowledge," Dr. Dibson went on, taking my reflective silence as a sign to continue his theories. "Or... well... well, what do *you* think? Do you have any personal connection to apples?"

"No," I sat back, becoming more and more frustrated. "They're just... *apples*. What's special about an apple?"

"You tell me."

I honestly had no idea.

"More often than not, the process of uncovering meaning is gradual and involves exploring different angles," Dr. Dibson continued, putting his pen down on the desk. "Whether we're looking at poems, drawings... *or*, you know... our real-life feelings and emotions."

My eyes rolled back in my skull, remembering where we were. What we were doing.

"Sometimes understanding comes from examining different facets of our experience," he said, his voice gentle but unwavering. "Even if it feels disconnected from the immediate reality of our situation."

I covered my face with my hands, groaning.

What a fucking waste of time.

"I'm sorry…" I struggled to get the words out as frustration built up inside me. "I know this is your job, or whatever, but I… I really don't think this is going to work. I don't really buy into this therapy shit, alright?"

"I understand—"

"I'm depressed because my friends are dead," I cut him off, laughing. "And my sister's missing, *and* there's a serial killer out there somewhere, and they want me *dead*. That's it… alright? Sometimes an apple's just an apple, you know?"

Dr. Dibson nodded thoughtfully, his fingers stretching toward his pen. "I hear you," he eventually replied, clapping his hands together. "A lot has happened. And you're dealing with an immense amount of pain and uncertainty—"

"*Duh*—"

"And therapy isn't going to fix all of your problems."

I scoffed, the sound sharp and bitter.

"*But*… it might help you find ways to cope with them," he continued, undeterred by my sarcasm. "It can give you tools to manage the stress and fear, to process your emotions, and to find a way forward. I think you'll find it helpful if you give it a chance."

My life was hell enough without having some balding dude with armpit stains picking apart my every word. And I needed more than "tools" to "find a way forward".

My parents hated me. Hell, the whole fucking *world* hated me. My friends were dead, Brooke was gone, and Donnie… *Donnie*… I wasn't even allowed to *see* him. I couldn't even look him in the eye and ask him all the questions that the rest of the world had already answered for themselves. I just had to accept that he was this evil, twisted monster, and that I was the world's *biggest fucking idiot* for not seeing it.

And on top of that, *I* was just as evil and twisted as him for just wanting to *talk* to him. I was supposed to be content with what I had already been given: rumors of a security tape.

My eyes flickered back to my father's face, seemingly mocking me with his sparkly outfit and huge, creepy smile.

Good thoughts get me through;
Nothing else'll ever do.

"You have no idea what you're dealing with, Doc," I said icily, making direct eye contact with Frankie Flash and his stupid hair. I heard Dr. Dibson chuckle.

"...well... let's find out, huh?"

LIZ | 4:31 PM

I could hear my husband and my sister making conversation in the hallway as I finished folding our freshly ironed towels. I couldn't quite make out what they were saying, but I figured I wasn't missing anything important. Their conversations rarely were.

When Frank and I first met—when Vic was just a little girl— she immediately took a liking to him, seeing him as the big brother she never had. The two of them bonded over football and music, and it wasn't unusual to find them engrossed in animated discussions about last weekend's game or the latest album by some band I'd never heard of. Vic had always been "one of the boys", and their conversations often drifted into topics that never really caught my attention. I'd just leave them to it.

Despite my lack of interest, there was something comforting about the familiar sound of their camaraderie; a small piece of normalcy in our new set-up of a life. Since Vic had returned to Mirrenville, it had almost felt like things were back to the way they had been before Brooke left.

As I finished the last towel and placed it on the stack, their conversation suddenly grew louder, punctuated by Vic's laughter. I glanced toward the hallway, wondering what could have sparked such amusement. Frank's deep voice followed. He was laughing too; it was the first time I'd heard him laugh since everything had happened.

If I hadn't been so angry with him, maybe I would've been happy to have heard it.

It had almost been a week since he'd walked out, and he still hadn't given a clear answer on where he'd gone... or, at least, why he was gone for so long. And I'd spent the past five days trying to convince myself that I didn't care. But the truth was, every time I heard his laugh, a pang of something—resentment, bitterness, disgust—rippled through me.

And I was more surprised at Vic's reaction than anything else. Or, rather, her lack of a reaction.

Despite her closeness with Frank, she usually never gave up an opportunity to knock him back into place if she knew he'd upset me. This time around, it was as if nothing had even happened; he came home the next morning, and they were happy to see each other. I just continued on with my life, not wanting to waste any more energy on the matter. I had bigger fish to fry.

When I carried the laundry into the hallway, the two of them were still standing there, gossiping like a bunch of teenagers. The laughter had died down by the time I got to them, and Vic appeared almost concerned. They hadn't noticed me entering the room at first. "Why would they ask you to do that?" she'd asked him. "It's only been two weeks—"

"If I stay here, I'm just going to be sat around, dwelling on everything," he replied as I noticed his black duffle bag laid out at his feet, half-zipped. I folded my arms—once again, attempting to show that I didn't care.

"Where are you going?"

They both turned to me, surprised to see me there.

Vic began gesturing toward the bag on the floor, animatedly moving her arms around. "They're making him go to this conference thing! I don't get it," she continued, her voice rising with frustration. "I mean, there's so much going on *here*... why are they making you go back so soon?"

Frank sighed, running a hand through his hair. "The company's insistent. And I've missed a lot over the past few weeks, so it'd be easier for me to jump back in sooner rather than later."

I could feel my anger simmering beneath the surface, my arms still crossed tightly over my chest.

"Thanks for letting me know," I said coolly. Vic's face softened a little, her eyes anxiously darting between the two of us. Frank shifted slightly, avoiding eye contact.

"I didn't think you'd notice. I'll be back first thing in the morning—"

"You didn't think I'd notice?" I repeated. "Is this what we do now? We just take off and do our own thing without telling each other?"

"It was a last-minute—"

"Are you still giving Allie a ride home from her appointment?"

He sighed slightly, shaking his head. Rage bubbled up inside me until I could barely see straight. The sheer arrogance of his actions astounded me. The *selfishness*.

"I gave her cash to get a cab," he said, and I scoffed loudly. "She'll be fine, alright? It's a ten-minute drive from here."

"This is a huge deal for her, and you're going to make her get a *cab* home? Are you kidding me?"

"*You* could always go get her," he suggested. "Or Vic."

I turned to Vic. She was covering her face slightly, avoiding looking at either of us. The whole atmosphere had changed the second I'd walked into the room. I'd ruined their fun. As usual.

My eyes wandered to his half-open bag. I could see most of the contents inside—a crumpled-up shirt, his wallet, a pair of underwear. No pajamas. "Whatever," I muttered, unable to mask the bitterness in my voice. "Have a great trip."

I turned on my heel and marched down the hallway, my vision blurred with anger. I heard Frank calling after me, but I didn't stop. I couldn't. I didn't want to see his face, let alone dignify him with a goodbye—after all, he hadn't planned on giving me one.

As I reached the kitchen, I grabbed the counter for support, my knuckles turning white from the grip.

In the hallway, I heard Vic and Frank muttering goodbyes, followed by footsteps and the front door opening and shutting. To my surprise, my heart shattered. My vision blurred further, causing everything in front of me to merge into one big blob.

Then I heard footsteps behind me. They stopped at the doorway. I finally turned to see Vic standing there. She didn't see me properly at first. She couldn't see my face.

"...paparazzi bastards," I heard her moaning as she slumped into the room. "I *swear*, if they got a picture of me without my makeup on, I'm going to fuckin' sue... hey, what's wrong?"

Before I could respond, she nearly tripped over Misty, who had darted out of nowhere.

"*Stupid cat…*" she muttered under her breath, brushing him aside with her foot. He hissed before scarpering back out of the room. I quickly wiped my eyes, becoming increasingly frustrated that she hadn't left with him. I heard the car moving out of the driveway and a tear slipped past my cheek.

"Hey…" Vic ran over to me, trying to wipe my face. I pushed her away angrily. "What's going on?!"

I took a deep breath, straightening up. Facing up to it.

"He's seeing someone," I announced, forcing a laugh. Vic's face hardened as she pulled her hands back.

"What are you talking about?"

"He didn't pack pajamas," I added, almost choking on the words. "And this isn't the first time he's just… just *gone*. Staying out all night. He's doing a pretty shitty job at hiding it—"

"Wait, *stop*." She pulled up one of the stools at the counter, trying to pull me down with her. I refused, remaining on my feet. "He said he was with Malcolm the other night. You had a fight. It's not a big deal!"

"He wasn't with Malcolm," I sneered, starting to pace the kitchen floor. "He's lying."

"How do you know? Have you talked to him?"

"He's *lying*!" I repeated angrily, throwing my arms into the air. "He's not going to tell me the truth about this—"

"Not *Frank*…" Vic cut me off, rolling her eyes. "*Malcolm*. Did *he* say that he was with Frank the other night?"

I stopped pacing, my breath catching in my throat.

The thought hadn't even crossed my mind, to verify Frank's story with Malcolm. My thoughts sped forward, immediately figuring out—in my head—if Malcolm was at work or not. Wondering if he would answer if I called him, there and then.

"No," I shook my head almost immediately. "I mean… no… I could call and ask, but what if he tells Frank? How would that make me look?"

"Look… *I* personally think you're overthinking this whole thing." She reached across the counter, picking an apple out of the fruit bowl. "I mean… this is Frank we're talking about! He's not *seeing someone*—"

"We haven't slept together in months." The words began pouring from my mouth. "Maybe even longer. We've barely even *touched* each other since... since... gosh, I don't even *know*..."

"So?! No one's expecting you to be horny teenagers right now," she replied, her mouth half-full. "Your fucking *daughter's* missing!"

"No, no, you're not *getting it*! We haven't been close for *years*, and I..." I paused, questioning why I was saying all of this to my little sister. I questioned why I was saying it at all. "I don't feel *anything* for him anymore. Things haven't been good for...well... a while."

Vic chewed slowly, digesting both the apple and my words. Then she placed the fruit down, her expression turning serious. "Do you still love him?"

I glared at her. "Of course I do."

"Do you still find him attractive?" she asked, pulling a face. "I mean, he's no Tom Selleck, but he's still got a certain... *charm* to him, I guess... even if he's gained, what, thirty pounds—"

"It's nothing to do with that," I interrupted, leaning against the counter.

"Well, what is it?"

I took a deep breath, searching for the right words to explain the tangled mess of emotions. I wasn't entirely sure how to word it.

I'd spent many nights questioning what I felt and why, but I could never come up with a concrete answer. The distance between us—it had just *happened*. It'd been this painfully slow, drawn-out process of slowly falling out of love with each other.

"We're different people now," I said finally, staring ahead. "We've both changed so much that... I don't know... it doesn't feel right anymore."

She picked the apple back up, taking another bite. As she nonchalantly chewed on the fruit, I thought back to when I first met Frank. How different it all felt. How easy it was before the kids, and the house, and our jobs. He wasn't Frankie Flash anymore. And I wasn't 19 anymore.

There had been a time when I'd wished more than anything that I could spend the rest of my life with Frank Nicholson—*not* Frankie Flash—and now that I had it, it all felt hopeless. My thoughts fled back to the early days when Frank was full of energy and dreams, a far cry from the empty shell he'd become. We were young, and the future seemed endless, filled with possibilities and excitement. I loved his spontaneity back then; his *passion*, the way he made every moment feel larger than life. And yet, all I wanted back then was a family. I wanted a husband. A father for my kids.

The life we had built since was solid and stable, but somewhere along the way, Frankie Flash had died a horrible death.

And Frank Nicholson had never forgiven me for killing him.

"Okay, so…" Vic's voice pulled me back to the present. "Don't take this the wrong way, but… if you don't love him anymore, why do you care if he's seeing someone?"

"I *do* love him," I corrected her once again, becoming more and more irritated. "And I care because he's my *husband.*"

"But you don't want him to be your husband."

"He's still *their* father, no matter what," I began shouting, pointing up at the ceiling, momentarily forgetting that Cam was at school and Allie was at therapy. "I can't just *go back to work*, or… or go out *fucking* other women!"

"We don't *know* that he's—"

"He went to the bar a lot last year." I thought back, remembering everything. "The bar on the square… the one you liked. The 808 Bar. He went there *every night* after work, and he stayed out *so* late… *oh*… what if he met her there?!"

"Liz, *stop!*" Vic grabbed my hand, laughing slightly. "You're getting all worked up over someone who probably doesn't even exist!"

"I've got this feeling, Vic."

I really did.

It was this guttural sense of unease that I just couldn't shake. The more I thought about it, the more everything seemed to fall into place. The thought of it made me want to throw up.

"Okay, you know what?" She clapped her hands together, shuffling closer to the landline. "*I'm* going to call Malcolm."

I stared at her, thinking it over. Considering all possibilities.

"I'm just going to ask him about Frank staying over last week," she went on, flicking through the phone book in front of her. "If Frank *had* stayed with him, he'll tell me all about it… and if he *didn't*… well… wait, is this still his number?" Her finger jabbed the digits scribbled next to Malcolm's name.

I nodded silently, still trying to process that this was actually happening.

Vic picked up the receiver, her movements deliberate but quick, as if she were trying to get it over with before her own nerves got the best of her. I watched her dial the number, the sound of each digit pressing down echoing loudly in the quiet kitchen.

I quickly spoke up, already knowing I was too late as Vic pressed the phone against her ear: "Maybe we shouldn't—"

"Malcolm!" Vic suddenly yelled as a big smile spread across her face. "*Hey*! It's Vic... Vicky Crowe? Liz's little sister?"

I heard a muffled buzz on the other side of the phone. I couldn't hear a word. All I could go by was Vic's reactions, and they were off to a positive start. She started giggling, twisting the phone cord around her finger like she was 16 again.

"...yeah... yeah, I'm good! How are you doing?"

I widened my eyes at her, attempting to telepathically convince her to move the small talk along. She put a hand up to me, gesturing for me to stop. She just kept laughing, nodding along to whatever he was saying to her. My heart was about to crack through my chest.

"...yeah, sure! I just got back from Sacramento..."

I'd almost forgotten that Vic and Malcolm had known each other for a long time.

They'd known each other just as long as me and Frank had known each other; we'd all met around the same time, back when Vic was a teenager and had dragged me to one of their shows. She was a *huge* Unrest Stand fan at that time. That night they first played in Mirrenville marked the beginning of a tangled web of relationships that would span years, continuing long after the band itself fell apart.

There had even been a period when Vic and Malcolm were more than just friends. I'd tried my hardest to erase that chapter from my memory. Seeing Vic giggling over the phone and kicking her feet under the table brought it all flooding back.

"...so, hey, I wanted to ask you something," she said finally, straightening up in her chair. "Did Frank leave his tool kit at your place last week? I need to use it."

I stared at her, in complete awe at her genius.

She shot a subtle wink in my direction before maintaining her composure, falling silent as she listened to the response. I leaned closer, trying to hear what was being said. I couldn't pick up on a thing. I moved even closer, but Vic started swatting me away, hissing under her breath.

"…uh-huh… okay…"

Her eyes flickered between the phone and me, her face an unreadable mask. My anxiety continued to climb as I watched her, rising until my face felt as if it was on fire.

"…really?"

My heart stopped.

Her face barely changed, but the tone of that one word sent electric shocks through my body. She quickly caught my eye, shaking her head slightly. I had no idea what that meant.

"…well, sure… we'll have to catch up and talk about it," she added with another short, sultry giggle. "Next week?"

My eyes almost popped out as I scowled at her, hardly believing that she was doing this now. Vic shot another quick glance in my direction and waved her hand in front of my face, a gesture that seemed more to distract me than to give any real information.

"…sounds great," she smiled again, nodding. "Buh-*bye!*"

She blew a kiss down the phone before hanging it back up.

I could've sworn I noticed her hand shaking ever so slightly. I searched her face for answers. "Well?"

She sighed slightly, shaking her head. "He was with him,"

A cool wave of relief washed over me.

"He stayed the night," she added as I collapsed onto the stool next to her, covering my face with my hands. "Last Wednesday."

For the first time in a very long time, I almost experienced true happiness. I started laughing. "Good," I smiled, taking a deep breath. "Good… *oh my*… I would've killed him, you know. I would've *murdered* him."

"Well, now you don't have to!"

"This doesn't mean anything though," I suddenly said, reminding myself more than anything else. "This still doesn't mean that—"

"Liz, *Liz*…" She took both of my hands, squeezing them. "You *need* to stop stressing out, alright? You've got more important things to think about, remember? Just leave it to me."

I stared at her, confused. "Leave what to you?"

"Well, I'll call his work later if I have to," she explained, seeming a little breathless. "Whatever I need to do to make you relax. Just promise me you'll stop thinking about this now, alright?"

I nodded, squeezing her hands back. "Thank you."

We both stood up, and she picked up her half-eaten apple. Instead of taking another bite, she threw it into the trashcan at the side of the door. Then she began pushing me out of the room.

"Go sit down," she instructed me with a smile, playfully shoving me away. "I'll make coffee."

"I owe you."

She nodded, not saying anything back. A thin smile had stretched across her face.

I did what she said and made my way into the living room, unable to shake the immense feeling of relief. Thank *God*. For a moment there, I thought our lives were about to go from bad to worse.

Memories of Frankie Flash flickered through my mind. I recalled the wild energy of his performances, the way girls would leap onto the stage, throwing themselves at him. He'd always pull away, searching through the crowd until his eyes found me. I could still see that stupid, crooked smile. I felt myself smiling back at him, 30 years in the future.

Thank God Frank wasn't that stupid.

FRANK | 6:18 PM

My fists hammered against the door as I scanned my surroundings. I'd grown so used to reporters following us that I now constantly felt that there were eyes on me—they were *everywhere*. And with the blackmailer added to the mix, it felt like I was never alone.

I couldn't let my guard down anymore. Not even for a second.

When the door didn't open after the first few knocks, I leaned sideways to get a clearer glimpse of the driveway. The light blue Beemer was parked up in its usual spot, clean as ever, as if it had just rolled off the lot. The chrome was so bright it practically blinded me in the afternoon sun. I stepped back to the front door, ready to knock again when I heard footsteps inside.

A second later, the door clicked open, and there was Malcolm, standing in the doorway with a half-eaten sandwich in his hand.

"Frank?"

He looked surprised to see me. The confusion quickly morphed into something else—fear. His eyes flickered to my face, and I realized I must've looked worse than I thought.

"Has something happened?" he asked, almost immediately springing into action as his free hand moved toward his coat, hung up at the side of the door. I shook my head, already struggling to find the words.

"No, no…" I took a deep breath, looking him in the eye. "I just needed to talk to someone."

Without saying another word, he widened the door so I could make my way inside. I followed him into the house, shutting the door behind me.

I loved Malcolm like a brother—he was the best person I knew—but that never eased the bitterness that I experienced every single time I walked through his home. The mid-century furniture, the abstract art on the walls, even the vinyl collection neatly organized next to a state-of-the-art sound system; everything was carefully curated, just like the man himself. It was exactly the kind of place I used to imagine for myself, back when we were on top of the world. There were no toys scattered around, no piles of laundry or crumpled clothes shoved in a corner. No chaos.

No signs of life beyond his own.

"Ignore the mess," I heard him say as he picked up a single empty coffee mug from the kitchen counter, swiftly setting it down in an empty sink. It clattered against the stainless steel, the sound echoing in the otherwise pristine kitchen. "I just got back last night, after the shoot in Tacoma. At the orchard."

I glanced around, taking in the sleek countertops and perfectly organized shelves. My chest tightened, and I forced myself to swallow the resentment. It took all my strength to push it down,

278

especially now. Especially with everything that was happening.

"You want any?" he asked suddenly, snapping me out of my daze momentarily. He gestured toward a plate of leftovers sitting on the kitchen island; a neatly arranged plate filled with cheese and meat, and a bowl of olives. "I've got some prosciutto, mozzarella—"

"I'm good, man. Thanks."

"You've got to make sure you're eating," he went on, pulling up a chair for me to sit opposite him. "Got to keep your strength up."

I sat down, feeling the plush cushion beneath me. Desperately trying to figure out how I was supposed to say what I was about to say. Malcolm watched me closely, his casual demeanor giving way to genuine concern.

"Before you say anything," he said, tapping his fingers against the counter, "uh... Vicky called around an hour ago."

I stared at him, confused. "What, Vic? Liz's sister? Vic?"

"Yeah." He shifted uncomfortably. "She said something about you staying here last week, and... look, man, I wasn't thinking straight. She thought you stayed here last week, and I said you hadn't."

My blood ran cold.

"I thought she'd gotten the date wrong, or something... or you'd gotten confused." My whole body froze up further with each word he said. "I... I was going to call you. It didn't hit me until afterward that maybe... I don't know—"

"Why would she call you?" A million questions ran through my mind at once. "I mean, why would she... what did she say exactly? Why did she ask?" The questions spilled from my mouth, each word running into the next.

"I don't know... something about you leaving something here," he said, shaking his head a little. "Your tool kit?"

Why the fuck would Vic ask about my tool kit?

She knew something.

"Why would she think you stayed here?" he asked, his voice lowering a little. He sounded unsure. "I mean, I haven't seen you in over a week."

My mouth went completely dry. The crazy thing was, I had come here with the full intention of telling Malcolm everything.

That was why I showed up—to come clean.

But now, the notion of Vic being onto me threw everything into chaos.

"I fucked up." The words tumbled out before I could stop them, my voice heavy with frustration and panic.

"What do you mean?"

I stood up, beginning to pace back and forth. Making my way up and down the kitchen. Malcolm's eyes burned into my head as I scrambled to make sense of it all.

"Frank, what—"

"I'm having an affair."

I waited a second before turning back to him. I didn't want to see his reaction; the sudden silence was enough to tell me exactly what he was thinking.

When I finally turned to him, I saw it. His face was white as a sheet. He just stared at me, his mouth slightly open as if he was unsure how to respond. For a moment, the room seemed to freeze, and the weight of my confession hung heavily in the air.

"Well, I'm not..." I paused, hesitating before correcting myself. "I'm not anymore. I... I *was* having an affair. But not anymore."

I wasn't lying. Not really.

I *was* heading to Lucy's after speaking with Malcolm, but that was purely to come up with a plan for the blackmailer. She was helping me through it. And we'd both agreed that we *couldn't* let anything else happen between us. I was going to sleep on the couch, for Christ's sake.

Malcolm ran a shaky hand through his hair, his expression a mix of disbelief and anger. I stopped in my tracks, just watching him. Waiting for him to say something.

"You..." He shook his head slightly, scoffing. "*What*?"

"I fucked up," I repeated. "I didn't mean for it to go so far, and I... I-I just... things haven't been good with Liz for a while, and I—"

"How could you do this to her?"

I covered my face with my hands, groaning.

I wasn't sure what I had expected. I guess a part of me had hoped that he would be on my side—that he'd, at least, hear me out. He was my best friend. He *had* to hear me out.

But this was Malcolm. He was a good guy.

He was *the* good guy.

"I ended it," I said quickly. Then I began backtracking, remembering that I didn't want to lie to him. That was the whole point of all of this. I wanted to be honest. I wanted it off my chest. *All* of it. "Well, *she* ended it... it's over. It's been over for weeks—"

"*Weeks*?" he repeated, his eyes widening. "Shit, Frank... how long has this been going on?"

"A while," I replied, becoming more and more fearful of his reaction as the conversation went on. His disappointment was killing me far more than any form of anger would have. I figured my best option was to ease him into it. "But it's over now—"

"Who is she?"

"It doesn't matter," I said, closing my eyes in an attempt to block out the reality of the situation. "Look... that's why I came here. I need your help and I don't know who else to turn to, alright?"

"Frank—"

"I'm being blackmailed!"

Malcolm just watched me for a moment, his eyes narrowing. He shook his head slightly, as if trying to process the gravity of what I'd just said. It felt surreal, even just saying it out loud. It was the first time I'd said it out loud to anyone aside from Lucy. It suddenly felt more real. More terrifying.

"You're being blackmailed?" he repeated, his face barely changing. "What are you—"

"Someone found out about us," I cut him off, desperately trying to explain before he could completely turn against me. "They've got a picture of us, and they're going to tell Liz if I don't give them $5,000."

He shook his head, laughing awkwardly. I decided to keep going.

"I'm not asking you to take my side," I added, to which he laughed again. "I'm not even asking you to understand where I'm coming from, but—"

"How the hell could I understand where you're coming from?"

"These past few years haven't been easy, Mal," I said coldly, trying so hard to make it make sense. "My life is a... it's a fucking *nightmare.* Me and Liz aren't in a good place—"

"Brooke's been missing two weeks, and you're cheating on Liz?" The mention of Brooke's name was like a punch to the gut. "You couldn't make it past *two weeks*?"

"It started before she went missing."

His jaw dropped, and I knew I shouldn't have said it. I should've kept it simple, like I'd planned on doing. "What the fuck, Frank?!"

"I know," I said quickly, trying to smooth it over as quickly as I could. "I *know*... please, Malcolm, I just need your help. I know I've fucked up. I just need your help."

"How the hell am I supposed to help you?" I watched as the sudden realization hit him. A scoff escaped his mouth as he worked it out. "You want the money."

I couldn't speak.

I couldn't even bring myself to nod in confirmation.

All I could do was watch as all the respect he had for me seemed to drain from his face.

"Frank..." He began shaking his head, barely able to look me in the eye. "No—"

"No, no, listen, alright?" I moved closer to him, clutching the counter. "Malcolm, *please*. You don't understand. This is going to destroy my family—"

"You can't be serious."

"You know I wouldn't ask if I wasn't desperate," I pleaded, moving closer in an attempt to make eye contact. "You know I wouldn't, but I... *I don't have the money.* I need to stop this!"

"I'm not doing that to her," he said, causing anger to flare up inside me.

"But you're *my* friend!"

"I'm your *family*!" His voice got a little louder. "And as part of that package deal, I'm *her* family! And your *kids'* family!"

"What do you think this will do to the kids if they find out like this?!" I pressed. He took off his glasses, rubbing the bridge of his nose. "They don't deserve to find out like this. *None* of them do."

"They don't deserve *any* of this," he replied frostily. "I just... I don't understand why you would do this."

"Me and Liz haven't been good for a long time," I tried to explain, wishing that I didn't have to say it out loud. "And I *know* that's not an excuse, and I... I wish it hadn't gotten this far. I shouldn't have done it. I *know* that. But she does *not* deserve to find out this way! Neither do the kids. This will *destroy* the *family.*"

He slid his glasses back on, sighing quietly. I could see the conflict on his face, clear as anything. "How am I supposed to see her again, Frank? I mean, how am I supposed to be in the same *room* as her—"

"I wouldn't ask this of you if there was any other way."

"I can't do this to her," he said quietly, barely able to glance in my direction. "She's my friend too."

"No, she's not!" I laughed suddenly. "You don't even *like* her!"

"What the hell are you talking about?"

"She refused to be in the same room as you for *years*," I reminded him, and his face fell. "*She's* the reason you and Vic didn't work out—you know that, right?!"

"Yes."

"She didn't think *twice* about lying to you when Vic was seeing other people! Why can't you do the same for me?!"

"It wasn't that serious with Vicky," he mumbled, turning away from me. "It wasn't the same, and you know it. And obviously she was going to side with her sister—"

"And I'm your *brother*," I said, trying to soften my tone. Trying not to get angry with him. "I'm at the end of my fucking rope here, Mal. I don't have anyone else I can turn to."

His eyes darted around the room as if seeking a way to escape the conversation. "It's not just about Liz," he said quietly. "It's about everything that's happened... and the consequences. It's not just about the immediate fallout. It's about what comes after. If this goes public... if the kids find out—"

"You think I'm not aware of that?!" I cut him off, my voice cracking. "*That's why I'm asking for your help*! I'm trying to *stop* it from blowing up! They don't *need* to find out!"

"I can't do it," he said finally, crossing his arms against his chest. "I'm not doing it to her. Or the kids."

"Allie is in *therapy* right now!" I began to shout, suddenly unable to control myself. "Someone tried to *kill* her last week, and she's... she's in a bad way, Mal—she's in a *bad fucking way*! *This* would kill her! And what do you think this would do to Cam?!"

He flinched at the mention of Cam, and I saw the pain flicker across his face. In a twisted way, I knew that would get to him more than anything else. Malcolm had always been closer to Cam than the other kids—at least, since Mick left. He'd always been close with the boys. He loved the girls too, of course, but he had a different bond with the boys. Especially Cam.

"You'll work it out, Frank," he replied firmly, shaking it off. I stared at him in complete disbelief. "You are my brother, and I've always got your back—"

"Then *help me!*"

His face fell, and I already knew there was no way out of this. He'd already made his mind up. "I've got your back," he repeated. "No matter what. But I can't help you out of this one. I'm sorry, Frank. I *won't.*"

The silence that followed was suffocating.

The weight of Malcolm's decision pressed down on me, each breath coming harder than the last. The reality of my situation settled over me like a cold shroud. And he couldn't even *look* at me. The heavy weight on my shoulders felt even more crushing than before.

I genuinely thought he would've helped me. I thought we could've fixed this.

All I'd done was make it worse.

RING-RING—

The phone on the kitchen counter broke the silence with its shrill tone. The sound felt jarring and out of place, like a cruel reminder that life was moving on while my entire world was falling apart.

Malcolm glanced at the phone, then back at me, his expression unreadable. My whole body trembled under his penetrating gaze. After a few seconds, he stood up and made his way over to the phone, turning his back to me. I took a moment to try and compose myself. All the hope I'd held that Malcolm would come through for me had evaporated.

Now, as I sat there, it hit me that I was all the way back at square one. It wasn't over.

And I wasn't sure how it could ever be over.

"...Malcolm speaking."

Malcolm's voice was upbeat at first, masking the tension that had been clear just moments before. But as he continued, his tone faltered, and the anxiety returned.

"Oh... hey..." His eyes flickered back to me, widening in alarm. "...no, uh... no, he's not here."

My stomach clenched.

"What's going on?" Malcolm's voice edged with panic, and the sharpness of his tone jolted me upright. "What?! Wait—what happened?!"

I was already on my feet.

I couldn't hear the voice on the other end of the phone, but the distress in Malcolm's voice was enough to send shockwaves through me. I paced the small space, unable to stay still as a knot of anxiety tightened in my chest. All I could do was watch him, waiting for an explanation.

"...I'll try and get hold of him," Malcolm said, his face hardening with fear. "I will... I'll tell him... and I'll come straight over. Tell Cam I'll be there as soon as I can."

With that, he slammed the phone down.

His eyes shot to mine, filled with concern and resolve. I could tell something was seriously wrong, but the urgency in his voice and the intensity of his expression made it clear that he had other responsibilities now. "We need to go."

I hadn't even waited for him to finish his sentence. I had already started making my way toward the front door.

"Get to the hospital," I heard him say as he moved at the side of me. "I've got to get to Cam—"

"What's happened?" My voice was barely audible. The blood had completely drained from my face. "Who was that?"

His words barely registered as we rushed out the door, heading to our cars. I moved on autopilot as we headed separate ways, preparing to drive in the same direction.

He pulled out first. I followed him, matching his speed as our cars flew down the road.

My legs began to numb as I pushed down on the pedal. I focused on the blue BMW ahead of me, my mind racing to keep up with the unfolding nightmare.

The road stretched out before me, but the landscape was a blur as I pushed down harder on the accelerator.

I tried to focus on the road.

I just kept going.

As I spun onto the highway, all I could do was attempt to push away the crushing realization that this was never going to end.

HAYDEN | 5:23 PM

The air felt thick as I drove down the high street, moving at roughly 10 miles per hour. Every little noise made me jump—a dog barking, a car door slamming, even the rustle of leaves in the breeze. I glanced at the rearview mirror every few seconds, checking who was behind me. Making sure I wasn't being followed.

I was pretty sure I was in the clear at this point—like, 99% sure. I'd been sneaking out with Mom's car every day after school, and no one had stopped me yet. I figured I must've been doing something right if nobody had figured it out yet.

And, besides—I was a fucking natural.

The car hummed softly as I turned onto Oak Street, edging away from the busier streets heading toward the square. This part of town was quieter, all lined with old houses and tall trees. I felt safe enough to turn the radio up, playing the music just a little louder as I cruised past all the houses. It crackled through the car, playing some old rock song. My fingers tapped on the steering wheel, matching the beat.

Turned out, I didn't even *need* driving lessons. Mom's old boyfriend had taught me the basics, but he hadn't been around for months. This was *all* me.

And I was *killing it*.

"*...alright folks, that was* Echoes of a Silence *by Unrest Stand, and wasn't that a blast from the past?*" the radio presenter chimed in, his voice full of energy. "*If you're old enough to remember Frankie Flash BEFORE his little girl went missing, you're probably feeling pretty nostalgic right about now—*"

I jammed my finger against the radio tuning button, holding it down until another song started coming through. The car went silent for a moment as it searched for another channel.

"*...Brooklyn Nichols—*"

Skip.

"*...over two weeks since Br—*"

Skip.

"*...taught there for 4 years bef—*"

Skip.

"*...we haven't even mentioned ALLIE Nicholson yet—*"

God *damn* it.

I hit the off button angrily, flooding the car with silence.

I reached across the seats, feeling around for a loose cassette tape; there were a bunch of them on the floor, all unlabeled. They'd all been pretty shitty so far, but I wasn't losing hope just yet. There *had* to be good music somewhere in this car.

I continued to feel around, my fingers brushing against endless plastic bottles and crumpled receipts. Something sticky touched my fingers and I jerked back, pulling my hand away.

Before I could even react, the radio blared back to life:

"*...do you think we'll EVER find out what happened to Brooklyn Nicholson?*"

A sudden thud jolted me back to reality.

I slammed on the brakes, the tires screeching in protest as I came to a stop. My breath came in short, panicked bursts as I looked up.

There was a person on the hood of my car.

A *person*.

Everything seemed to slow down as I watched the figure—a girl—sprawled across the front of my car. There was no sound except for muffled background noise coming through the radio.

My hands gripped the steering wheel as if it could somehow steady the world around me. Oh, shit. Oh, *shit*—

She was moving.

She moved *very* slowly, but she was moving.

She was *alive*.

I just sat there and watched her in terror, trying to figure out what to do next. If she just *stood up already* I could've bolted, speeding back down the street before anyone noticed.

But, no—she just continued moving at the speed of a disabled snail, as if she hadn't just been hit by a fucking car.

My head spun as I frantically scanned my surroundings, my eyes darting from one house to the next, searching for anyone who might have witnessed what happened. I checked the sidewalks and doorsteps, hoping to see no one watching or rushing to help.

My head locked back into a forward-facing position, watching in horror as the girl lifted her head. I knew her face.

I knew her fucking face.

"God *fucking* damn it," I groaned as Diarrhea Darlow peeled herself from my hood, trying to balance on her feet.

Her head lifted. Her eyes locked on mine. We stared at each other for what felt like hours, the world around us fading into a blur. Her initial expression of shock quickly faded to surprise. Then to anger. She began mouthing something at me, wriggling her arms around.

I began mouthing back at her:

"*Get in the car!*"

She shook her head, pointing to her ear. She couldn't hear me.

I groaned even louder before rolling the window down. She walked over to the window. She wasn't limping, at least. She seemed good to go.

"*Get… in… the… fucking… car,*" I hissed, reaching forward to open the door. She pushed it shut again.

"No *way*—"

"Rhea, I swear to *God*—"

A loud and long *beep* made me jump a freaking mile. My eyes zoned in on my rearview mirror, catching a glimpse of another car behind us. Shit. *Shit.*

I turned back to Rhea, practically begging her with my eyes. "*Please… GET in the CAR…*"

It was going to be all over.

If anyone we knew saw me in the front seat, it would be *all* over.

Rhea started moving her arms again, gesturing for the car behind to go around me. I held my breath as they zoomed past, turning my head slightly so they couldn't see me. They didn't stop. They kept going, slowly becoming a tiny blur down the road.

Rhea took this moment to finally do what I'd asked of her; she reopened the door, stepping inside.

I glared at her. "What are you doing?!"

She glared back at me. "You *told* me to get in—"

"Because *they almost saw me*," I hissed, pointing at the car that had pretty much disappeared into the distance at this point. "You were drawing too much attention!"

"*Drawing too much attention*?! I... y-y-*you*..." She couldn't even get her words out without fucking stammering. Classic Rhea. "*You ran me over*!"

"Come *on*—"

"You smashed my retainer!" she gasped, pulling a plastic case out of her pocket. Some of it had chipped off, crumbling onto her lap. I was still struggling to catch my breath.

"Oh, I think you'll survive," I said slowly, each word dripping with sarcasm. "Look at you! You're *fine*!"

Rhea shot me the evilest look I'd ever seen from her. In fact, this was the most expressive I'd *ever* seen her. Seeing her like this—all mad and loud—was both surprising and unsettling.

Maybe it was the adrenaline.

My teeth were clattering as my heartbeat pounded through my ears, pulsating through my head. "*Are* you hurt?" I asked, trying to get a clear view of her legs. I could tell she was shaken, but it didn't look like she was seriously hurt.

"I'm fine," she replied, erratically shoving the broken pieces of her retainer back into the case. "How are you driving? You *shouldn't* be driving—"

"Don't be a narc, Rhea."

"You could get arrested, you know. You're *fifteen*. You could go to *jail* for driving without—"

"Get your feet *away* from that," I snapped suddenly, grabbing my camera from the floor beneath her legs. She suddenly flinched, moving to the side as I tossed it onto the back seats. As I moved back into position, twisting the key in the ignition, she immediately grabbed her seatbelt, dragging it across her body in the *most* dramatic fashion.

"Where are you taking me?!" she practically shouted, her voice filled with panic as if I'd just tied her up and thrown her into the trunk. I shifted into first gear, easing the car forward.

"Back to your house, you fucking moron." I checked the rearview mirror again. "Where do you live?"

Rhea hesitated, barely even glancing in my direction. Her hands were still gripped around her seatbelt, pulling it tighter as if that would make a difference. "Just… take a right at the next stop sign," she finally muttered, her voice a little quieter now.

"Dope."

The road stretched out in front of us, the houses blurring together as we drove in tense silence.

Rhea stared straight ahead, her knuckles white as she gripped the seatbelt. My knuckles were the same color, tightening around the wheel. Of all the people I could've imagined giving a ride, Rhea Darlow was the last person on my list. This was *social suicide*. I kept glancing out the window, now hoping the two groups of people wouldn't catch me driving: cops, or *anyone* from our school.

"You're not going to tell anyone, right?" I asked, trying to sound casual but unable to hide the edge in my voice. "You can't."

"You could've killed me, Hayden!"

"*Oh…*" I scoffed loudly, staring straight ahead. *Fucking drama queen.* "I barely even *touched* you—"

"You shouldn't be driving," she repeated. "Who's car is this?"

"Mine," I lied, watching her through my peripheral vision as she picked up a half-empty box of diapers. I felt her watching me, but I didn't have the energy to argue with her, so I just decided to ignore her.

Neither of us said anything for a while after that.

The silence between us was thick and awkward, like we were both stuck in some uncomfortable waiting room. I kept my eyes glued to the road, scanning for any cop cars that might suddenly appear. Out of the corner of my eye, I saw Rhea fidgeting, her fingers tapping nervously against the seatbelt. She reached over to switch the radio on, and without thinking, I slapped her hand away.

"No," I snapped, the words coming out harsher than I intended.

She flinched, pulling her hand back like I'd burned her. If I had to hear Brooke's name one more time, I might have driven this car straight into a wall.

Rhea shifted in her seat, folding her arms tightly across her chest. It just all felt so fucking weird; we'd never spent this much time alone together, and honestly, I wasn't sure how to handle it. She was Brooke's friend—*not* mine. Everything about her made me feel icky. Gross.

"Turn left at the light," she mumbled, breaking the silence. I nodded, grateful for something to do other than wallow in my own thoughts.

The turn brought us into a quieter neighborhood, where the houses were more spaced out and the streets less busy. I could feel Rhea watching me again. I wanted to snap at her to stop being so fucking weird.

"...did you know about Donnie Booker?"

Those words shook me to my core.

Of all the things I'd expected her to say, that wasn't one of them. I thought about ignoring her, pretending that I hadn't heard her, despite the killer silence engulfing us inside that car.

"I knew they were together," I said finally, staring at the road. "*Obviously.*"

"*No*... I mean... did you know about her sister?"

"Well, yeah. Duh."

She'd told me right away.

I think she'd just found out, maybe a couple of hours before, and *then* she told me.

I was convinced that Allie had done it on purpose. I mean, come *on*—what were the odds of her waiting to fuck Donnie until he was dating her *sister*? They'd been friends for *years*, and she waited *that* long to make a move? I mean—*seriously*?

Brooke was totally adamant that Allie had no idea, but I didn't believe it for one second. It was just *way* too much of a coincidence.

"Do you think he killed her?"

"What kind of stupid question is that?" I snapped, feeling her jump at the side of me. "What the fuck are you talking about?"

"It's just... well, I heard—"

"She's *not* dead." The blatant indifference of her question had completely thrown me. "How could he kill her if she's not dead?"

She went quiet.

I knew what she was thinking though. She was thinking the same as everyone else—Hurley and Mandy and Melissa MacKenzie were all dead, so surely Brooke was too, right? She *had* to be.

It was like none of them had a fucking brain cell between them.

Hurley, Mandy and Melissa MacKenzie were *found dead*. The police found their bodies. Why the hell would someone kill three people and leave them there to be found, but go through *so much effort* to hide Brooke's? It just didn't make sense, and it made me so mad that people thought it. It was as if they'd never seen a crime show before.

"Why haven't you been at school?" Rhea asked suddenly, changing the subject. I wished she would just shut up for five seconds. I couldn't understand why she was so insistent on making conversation.

We didn't even *know* each other.

"Why do you care?" I shot back, my voice laced with annoyance. Her previous question lingered in the air like a bad smell.

She sighed, and out of the corner of my eye, I saw her shaking her head. It was an irritated sigh. "Next right," she said instead, her tone a little gentler now.

The houses were getting bigger the further we moved away from town. They weren't as nice as the ones in Brooke's neighborhood, but they were still pretty nice. I'd never thought about Rhea's family before—or, well, *anything* about her—so I'd never considered that they had money. Her dad must've had a decent job for them to live in this area.

The streets were pretty much empty, so it caught my attention when one person walked out of a drug store at the side of the road. They had their hood up, but small tufts of red hair were poking through.

And I would've recognized that hair anywhere.

"Shit…" I pulled up to the side of the road, staring at her. Watching her making her way down the street, clutching a paper bag.

"What are you doing?" I heard Rhea ask. I shushed her before turning back to the window, practically pushing my nose up against the glass. "...is that Brooke's sister?"

My hand slowly moved to my nose, lightly touching the bridge. It still stung like hell. I embraced the pain as my eyes locked onto the very person who had broken my nose just days before.

This was the first time I'd seen her since.

She practically jogged up the street, her eyes darting back and forth as if to scan her surroundings. I quickly slumped into my seat, pushing myself down as far as I could go. Rhea—clearly not understanding the severity of the situation—remained as upright as ever, as if there was a stick up her ass holding her straight. Like a kabob.

"Why are you hiding—"

I grabbed her shoulder, pulling her down with me.

A gasp escaped her mouth as I dragged her down to my level. A group of boys had started walking down the street now, heading toward Allie. One of them shouted over to her. I moved closer to the window, trying to see who they were.

"Why are we *hiding*?!" Rhea hissed.

I pointed out the window, watching them. "She attacked me last week," I said finally, not taking my eyes away from Allie. "Just showed up at my house. Beat the shit out of me."

"What? Why?!"

"She thought Brooke was with me at the party."

She went quiet for a moment. The group of boys were now standing around her, talking to her. She just stood there, wrapping her arms around the paper bag like it was a baby.

"But... *wasn't* Brooke with you? At the party?" Rhea asked, but I ignored her. Things were getting weird. One of the boys put his arm around Allie but she was pulling away. She'd pushed him away from her.

"What are they doing?" I asked under my breath, watching the scene unfold. There had to be ten of them altogether, all crowding around her.

Suddenly, Allie was on the floor.

I'm not sure what happened. It happened too quickly. She was on the floor, and the circle got smaller as they moved together, moving in toward her. They were covering her.

"What—"

They started kicking her.

"*Hayden*," Rhea started shouting but I couldn't move. I just watched them, my body frozen in shock.

The sound of their kicks thudding against Allie's body echoed in the car.

"Hayden, we have to help her!" Rhea's voice broke through the haze, high-pitched and frantic.

Allie was trying to shield herself, her arms curled around her head as they kept kicking. And they were *laughing*. I could see the panic on her face, the sheer terror as she curled up tighter, trying to make herself as small as possible.

But there was nowhere for her to go.

There were too many of them.

Rhea unbuckled her seatbelt with a sharp click and reached for the door handle. I grabbed her arm. "What the hell are you doing?!"

"We have to do *something*!"

"And what are *you* going to do?!" I shot back, suddenly becoming very aware that a smile was creeping across my face. It weirded me out at first. When I turned back toward the window—witnessing Allie fighting for her life—I suddenly realized that I was *enjoying* what I was seeing. The sting in my nose got stronger as I inhaled deeply.

Allie had attacked me, humiliated me, and for *weeks* I had fantasized about getting back at her. Now, seeing her in this position, part of me was satisfied. Part of me wanted it to go on forever.

I wondered if I'd made it happen.

Maybe I'd wished for it hard enough that it had actually come true.

"We've got to *stop* them," Rhea was shouting, but I could barely hear her. All I could do was take in the moment. Relish it.

The way Allie struggled against the blows, the way she looked so small, so powerless—just like I had felt when she came after me. My breaths came in slow, measured gulps.

For the first time in weeks, *I* felt like I had the upper hand. *I* was finally in control.

"They're going to *kill* her!"

Kill her.

The words snapped me back to reality, the dark cloud of satisfaction lifting just enough for fear to creep in.

My heart started pounding for a different reason; not from the rush of vengeance, but from the terrifying thought that things may have gone too far. Allie was barely visible under the crowd, their fists and feet flying in a frenzy.

Blood was pooling on the pavement, swirling with a brown, sticky liquid pouring from the paper bag that had smashed all over the floor.

They really were killing her.

My hand slowly reached toward the door handle when suddenly, some guy came running out of the drug store. He had a broom in his hand. I watched as he started swinging at the group of boys, hitting them away. They started running up the street, pulling their hoods up. One of them shouted "*SLUT!*" as they ran.

We saw Allie for the first time, all crumpled up on the ground, covered in red and brown stains. The man from the store was leaning over her, picking up her arm. Checking her pulse, I figured.

My brain hadn't even caught up with what was happening before my foot slammed down on the gas pedal.

"*Stop*," Rhea was shouting. "*We can't—*"

The tires screeched as we shot out of the street.

"He's helping her!" I shouted back. "She's *fine!*" As we moved further from the scene, I continued to question that statement.

The image of her folded on the ground like a pile of bloodied clothes stuck in my brain as a still image, visually becoming more and more disturbing as my imagination ran wild. She wasn't moving. She just... lay there. Motionless.

I swallowed hard, reminding myself of what she had done to me. She'd beaten *me* to a bloody pulp, leaving *me* on the floor as I bled out.

Except... I wasn't bleeding out. Not really.

She broke my nose. I didn't even fully lose consciousness.

She had.

"...I-I'm going to tell my mom," Rhea was saying, panic and

terror rushing through her words. "W-we have to call the police—"

I wondered how differently this all would've played out if Brooke had been in the car instead of Rhea.

She would've gotten out. She would've tried to stop them.

I wondered what she would've thought if she'd known what Allie had done to me.

I wondered if she did know.

Flashes of blue and red shone across the road, and I ducked my head as two police cars shot past us, moving in the direction we had just come from. A light sense of relief washed over me. They were going to help her. It was all going to be *fine*.

I still couldn't shake the satisfaction I got, seeing her being kicked. For the first time in a long time, I had felt something other than dread. Something *other* than misery.

I didn't want Allie Nicholson to die. Of course I didn't.

But it sure felt good seeing her hurt.

FRANK | 8:47 PM

Traffic was building up. Every car in front of me was a solid wall between where I was and where I needed to be.

My line of sight kept getting pulled toward the clock on the dashboard. I watched as the numbers changed, but the car barely moved an inch.

My mind was racing, filled with images of my eldest daughter.

I'd had to switch the radio off. It was all they were talking about. And they knew *nothing*. Not a damn thing.

But that didn't stop them from filling the airwaves with speculation and half-truths, as if they were all in on some secret that the rest of us weren't privy to; grasping at straws, piecing together a narrative out of scraps. It was just another story to them.

My jaw tightened as I thought about the reporters camped

outside the hospital, waiting to shove a microphone in my face in the hope of a soundbite, any scrap of information they could twist into something sensational.

They were fucking *vultures*—circling a situation they barely understood, waiting to pounce on any detail they could sink their teeth into and spin into a story.

And the worst part? Everyone was *eating that shit up* with a knife and fork. Every word, every baseless theory, was being absorbed by the public like it was gospel. They didn't care about the truth—they just wanted a story, something to talk about at dinner, while it *tore my fucking family apart.*

The traffic inched forward, and I slammed my hand against the steering wheel in frustration. I was trapped in this slow-moving hell, all the while scraping my thoughts together to figure out what the hell I was going to do about the money.

Five thousand dollars.

My thoughts had somehow spiraled even further than they had just an hour before. But if anything, the idea of scrounging up the cash had somehow become a twisted distraction from the real problem, keeping my mind occupied while I sat motionless in traffic.

Malcolm wasn't going to help. It didn't make me feel any better, but at least I could understand why—I'd spent the past two hours in the car thinking about it, justifying his actions. He was a part of our family. He was scared of what would happen if it all got out and he had been a part of it. He didn't want the blame. I got that.

I just wished I could have the same luxury; the luxury of backing out, pretending it wasn't happening.

But this wasn't his burden. It was mine.

My mind raced to find solutions. I could sell something, but what? The car? No—that would only raise more suspicion, and besides, I needed it to get around, to keep up the appearance that everything was fine. I couldn't risk tipping anyone off, least of all Liz. I couldn't get a loan, either; Liz would find out. I could try to borrow from someone, but who? And how would I explain why I needed it?

I could already hear the questions, the suspicions, and I knew that if anyone started digging, it wouldn't take long for everything to unravel. The affair, the lies, *all of it*—it was all hanging by a thread, and one wrong move would cut it clean through.

The longer I sat there, watching the minutes tick by on the dashboard, the more I realized that I was cornered.

As I edged closer—the hospital finally in sight—I envisioned how much bigger the media explosion would become if news of the affair got out. The thought was almost paralyzing.

I gritted my teeth, fighting the urge to scream. The pressure was suffocating, and I was running out of time.

I tapped the steering wheel impatiently, my foot hovering over the gas pedal, ready to floor it the moment the traffic opened up. We were moving along, slowly but surely, but every second stretched on for a lifetime. And images of Allie kept flooding my brain. I didn't have enough information to prepare myself.

I knew she was okay, that she was stable, but that was it. They'd hurt her enough to put her in hospital. She'd only just gotten *out* of the hospital after the last attack.

It wasn't fair. None of it.

I swerved into the parking lot at my first opportunity, barely squeezing past the Jag in front of me. The beeping echoed into the distance as I sped toward the hospital, skidding into a spot with more force than necessary. The screech of tires and the abrupt stop jolted me from my spiraling thoughts, just for a moment.

I took a deep breath, trying to steady my racing heart, and quickly leapt out of the car. I didn't have time to think about it.

Before my brain could catch up with my body, I had already begun storming toward the main entrance. As expected, the media had already found their way to the hospital; a cluster of reporters with cameras and microphones crowded the entrance, their voices rising in a cacophony of intrusive questions and flashing lights every time someone so much as moved past them. A sinking feeling settled in my stomach as I quickly tried to figure out a way around them.

As I got closer, I spotted a tuft of bottle-blonde hair. The hairdo alone was enough for me to recognize the tiny figure flicking a cigarette in a tucked-away corner aside the entrance, hiding from the reporters.

Fuck.

My footsteps slowed as I caught sight of my sister-in-law,

realizing that there was no way around it. I had to move past her to get to the front entrance. The anxiety gnawed at me, and I could feel the weight of what was coming. There was nothing else I could do other than walk straight into what I now knew was a trap.

But none of that mattered.

Not now.

She didn't notice me until I got a little closer. When she did, she limply waved with one hand, flicking her cigarette with the other. She didn't look upset. She hadn't been crying. That was a good sign.

I shuffled over to her, slipping past the crowd of flashing cameras, my breaths coming in fast, shallow gasps. "Where is she?!"

"She's fine," Vic replied with a calm that seemed almost out of place given the circumstances. Her demeanor was a stark contrast to the panic I felt. I put both hands on my knees, gulping the air.

"What happened?!" I asked, and she took a drag from her cigarette. The pace of the conversation made me even more anxious. Any other time, Vic wouldn't have been able to get her words out fast enough. She took her time, exhaling a cloud of smoke in my direction.

"They beat the shit out of her," she finally replied. "She's got a broken arm, fractured ribs. Bruised all over, and her face is pretty swollen. They had to give her some stitches, too."

"But she's going to be okay?"

Vic nodded, her expression serious but not alarmed. "Just in a lot of pain. She might be in rough shape for a while, but she'll be fine. Physically." I rubbed my face with both hands, trying to absorb the news.

I just had to see her.

Once again, my legs began moving before I could take control of them mentally. I started making my way toward the entrance of the hospital.

"We need to talk," I heard Vic saying behind me. I tried to ignore her, quickening my pace.

"Vic, not now—"

"Where were you?"

Shit.

I slowed to a stop, wincing. We didn't have time for this. *I* didn't have time for this. As I turned back toward her, she was watching me with a look that was more unsettling than I'd anticipated. Her gaze was sharp, almost penetrating. She took another drag from her cigarette, waiting for my response. I swallowed.

"I was at Malcolm's, alright?" I admitted exasperated, realizing this minor confession would mean nothing compared to the others. "I was there when you called. I told him to tell you—"

"Why would you tell Liz you were going to work?" she cut me off, her eyes lingering on me a moment longer than comfortable. Her expression shifted to something more contemplative, though still inscrutable. "And why would you take an overnight bag?"

My mouth opened, but nothing came out.

She continued to speak before I had the chance to reply: "Were you *really* with Malcolm? Because you weren't with him last week."

Her question was direct, and the intensity of her stare made me uneasy. I tried to brush off my intensifying paranoia, attempting to convince myself that I was overthinking the tone of her voice.

She didn't *know* anything.

"Why did you call him?" I asked, attempting to pull back the reigns. It was a question I hadn't wanted to ask, but it was becoming more and more clear that I didn't have much of a choice. She knew more than I thought. I needed to know exactly what was going on.

She gave a small shrug, her nonchalance almost too practiced. "Funny story, actually..." She pursed her lips out, stubbing her cigarette out against the wall. "Liz was pretty upset today, after you left. She thought you were lying to her about going to work... she thought you were having an affair, or something."

My pulse quickened.

"...*and* she thought you were lying about staying with Malcolm last week, so, you know... I said I'd call him up to find out..."

My heartbeat pounded in my ears. It was deafening.

"I told her that you *did* stay with him," she continued, dropping the cigarette to the floor. Stamping it out for good measure. "Because, well... she's got enough to worry about right now, you know?"

My mind raced to figure out an answer to the question that she hadn't yet asked me. "Look, Vic, I-I haven't got time for this right now," I stammered, taking a small step backward. "I need to be with Allie—"

"She can wait a little longer."

"I—"

"I lied to your wife for you." Her eyes were black. Glazed over. "I lied to my *sister* for you. You can't give me five minutes of your time?"

She knew.

She didn't even need to say anything else. I'd known her for over 30 years, for Christ's sake. And she knew me just as well as I knew her.

"Where have you been, Frank?" she asked, and I had no fucking idea what I was supposed to say next. I couldn't think straight. "I mean, you haven't been to work... because, well, you haven't been back since Brooke went missing. I called them too. Obviously."

She fucking knew.

"I-I needed space." I regretted it the second it came out of my mouth. She scanned me up-and-down, as if she were dissecting my every gesture. The pressure mounted as I panicked, questioning what to tell her, if anything.

I thought about telling her about the money. About the note. But how could I tell her about the note?

How could I tell her I was with Lucy?

"*Space,*" she repeated, reminding me of the last word that I had said. "Is that what you'd call it?"

"Please, Vic, I need to see my daughter—"

"You *need* to tell me what's going on," she cut me off, her tone leaving no room for evasion. I stared at Vic's expectant face, searching for an escape route, but found none.

"Please—"

"What's her name?"

A pure, agonizing panic surged through my veins, the sudden, unfiltered question sending me into a spiral. It hung heavy in the air. My lack of response did me no favors as I watched Vic's initial questioning expression wash into one of shock. Her eyes began to widen, as if she hadn't originally believed what she was accusing me of. My shocked silence had given me away before I could even say anything.

I licked my lips in a desperate attempt to moisten my now entirely dried-up mouth. The realization hit me like a ton of bricks: there was no escaping this. There was no way out.

"Tell me her name, Frank."

I was still fighting hard to give off some sort of surprised expression, but I knew it wasn't working. She knew the truth. And she wasn't going to give up until I admitted it. "Vic—"

"Tell me her name, or I swear to God, Frank, I *will* tell my sister."

Game over.

I took a deep breath, reverting my gaze to the floor beneath me, entirely in disbelief that I was actually about to say it out loud.

"Lucy."

Her name lingered in the air for a moment.

It bounced off the walls surrounding us. The name felt like a lead weight in my chest as it echoed in the narrow space between us. It hung there, suspended in the air for what felt like a lifetime.

Vic didn't say a word for the longest time. She didn't have to; the silence that followed spoke volumes, pressing in on me with suffocating intensity. I couldn't bring myself to look up; the gravity of what I had just admitted crashed over me in waves.

Finally, after what felt like hours had passed, a loud, short laugh escaped her mouth. It burst out like a gunshot. "...you're kidding me, right?"

I closed my eyes.

"*...you... you have got to be FUCKING KIDDING ME—*"

"I'm sorry, alright—"

She shoved me hard, almost knocking me off my feet. Her eyes blazed with an intensity that scared the shit out of me. "You're *sorry*?!" she yelled as I quickly attempted to hush her, suddenly very aware of the reporters that were situated just a couple of feet away from us. "*You're SORRY*?!"

"Please, just keep it *down*—"

"*How could you DO this to her*?!"

Her words were like daggers, each one driving deeper into my chest. The panic and guilt swirling inside me made it even harder to breathe. All I could do was stand there, trying to find some semblance of a response amidst the storm of Vic's fury.

"I know," I tried to interject, attempting to get some words out as she continued to hiss at me. "I know, alright, I *know*—"

"How long has this been going on?!"

I shut my eyes again for a moment, bracing myself for what was coming next. There really was no way out of this. "Just over a year."

Vic's eyes widened further, and she took a step back, her face contorting into an expression of sheer disbelief. Her mouth worked silently for a few moments before shoving me again. Then hitting me. Hard.

"*Jesus*, Vic—"

"*A YEAR*?!" she repeated angrily as I tried to grab her wrists, attempting to restrain her. "No, no, *wait*... so, this isn't just a... a *fling*?! You're actually *seeing someone*?!"

"I'm *not* seeing anyone!" I argued, half telling the truth. "I... I *was*. Not anymore. It's over!"

"Were you going to stay with her tonight?!"

"What?! *No*..."

The lie came out so half-heartedly that even I didn't believe it.

Her eyes were wild as she took a step back, putting distance between us as if the very thought of being near me was now unbearable.

"*Christ*, Frank... I just... *ugh*..." She groaned, and for a moment, I felt like I was being scolded by my mother. "I mean... I-I mean, you know, if this had *just started*, maybe I would've got it a little... I-I mean, it wouldn't have been so bad because things have been rough recently, but... a *year*?! Before *any of this* even *started*?!"

"Are you going to tell her?"

She just stared at me for a couple of seconds, jaw hung over. Her lips twitched a little, as if she wanted to say something immediately but she didn't quite know how to word it. Jesus... her eyes were filling up a little.

She wasn't just mad. She was *devastated*.

"Well..." She straightened up a little, trying to cover it up. "Are *you* going to tell her?"

"Yes. But not until Brooke's home."

"You know she'd leave if you told her, right?"

"I know."

The silence that followed was heavy, charged with a tension that neither of us knew how to break.

Vic's expression shifted, her anger gradually giving way to something else—something more conflicted. I could see the wheels turning in her head, the inner turmoil that mirrored my own.

I had known Vic for so long. Liz and I had practically raised her throughout her teenage years. The idea of us breaking up... it wasn't just about me cheating anymore. It was about the potential destruction of something that had been a cornerstone of her life. Of *all* our lives.

As her face changed, I saw the 13-year-old that I'd met all those years ago—awkward and defiant. Seeing that same vulnerability flash across her face, it was like looking into the past.

All she knew was me and Liz.

Hell, it was all *I* knew.

"I just can't believe you'd do this to her," she said finally, her lip wobbling. "I just... I thought you were better." Those words cut deeper than any of her earlier accusations. "Are you going to leave her? Liz? Or were you just going to... let her decide?"

I didn't know what to say.

I guess I didn't know myself.

That night—the night before Brooke went missing—the plan was to just tell her the truth. I'd just told Lucy the truth, so it made sense to get it all out in the open, once and for all. At that time, being with Lucy wasn't an option anymore... but, now, things were almost back on with us. We hadn't slept together since that night I showed up at her apartment, but we'd seen each other a couple of times since. We'd barely so much as touched each other since that night, but somehow the situation felt more complicated than ever.

When it came down to it, I guess I wasn't really sure *what* I wanted.

It was clear me and Liz weren't working; we hadn't been working for a while. And it was clearer than ever that I still had feelings for Lucy, if not more than that. I just wasn't naïve enough to believe that anything substantial would come of it, even if Liz and I ended things.

"I mean… do you *like* this girl?" Vic asked, just before interrupting herself: "Well, of *course* you like her… Jesus, you've been with her long enough—"

"She's not a bad person, Vic."

"Oh, *please*—"

"She didn't know I was married when it started," I explained, my voice barely rising above a whisper. "This isn't her fault. None of it."

"Does she know *now*?" Her voice sliced through the air like a blade. I nodded slowly, my gaze dropping to the floor again. "*See*?! I'm sorry, but someone who's knowingly sleeping with a married man *is* a bad person in my eyes—"

"We're not sleeping together," I interrupted. "We're not… *together*. Not now. I told you, it's over."

"Does she know about the kids? About *Brooke*?!"

I folded my arms tightly, preparing myself for the inevitable fallout of what I was about to say. "She's one of the cops on her case."

Vic's eyes widened, and for a moment, the anger seemed to drain from her face, replaced by sheer disbelief. But it was only a moment before her expression contorted into something much darker.

There was no turning back now.

No more half-truths or evasions. I had to lay it all out, no matter how much it tore everything apart.

"Are you out of your *goddamn mind*?!" Vic's disbelief quickly morphed back into pure, unfiltered rage. "She's on the *case*?! *Brooke's* case?! She's a *fucking COP*?!"

"I know—"

"Oh, *hell* no," she cut me off, her words bursting from her mouth. "*Not* the blonde! *Not* the one Liz told me about—"

The idea that Liz had mentioned Lucy to Vic made me feel as if I'd been punched in the gut.

I knew Liz liked her; she had made that clear enough in the few conversations we'd had about the officers. But knowing that she'd actually talked about Lucy to Vic, probably with admiration—maybe even relief that someone so competent was on the case—my world crumbled a little more under the weight of that realization.

"The cop that's been in and out of your house for the past few weeks... the *kid*... you've been *screwing her* behind Liz's back?!"

"She's twenty-five," I murmured, realizing that this information was a comfort to neither of us. If anything, it sounded far worse than I'd expected it to. A dark laugh spluttered from Vic's throat.

"Twenty-five?!" she repeated, her voice laced with incredulity and disgust. "She's younger than *Mickey*?!"

I hadn't realized just how nauseating it would be to hear those words spoken out loud.

I remembered the moment I first calculated her age, realizing that, yes, she was younger than my eldest child. But until now, I'd never had to confront that fact with actual words. Hearing it now, in Vic's voice, made everything feel so much worse.

"You're old enough to be her *father*," Vic went on as my stomach churned. "What the *fuck* is wrong with you?!"

My mind raced, struggling to piece together any semblance of justification, but all I could manage were fragments of incoherent thoughts. No words were coming out.

All I could do was stand there and take it.

"...your daughter's *missing*... your other daughter's in the fucking *hospital*..." Her voice droned on, each word a relentless hammer striking at the fragile remnants of my resolve. "Where the hell is your head at, Frank?!"

"Vic—"

"You *were* going to see her tonight, weren't you?!" My expression must've given it away, because she immediately exploded again. "Oh, *congratulations*, Frank! Your daughter had the *shit beaten out of her*, all because you were too busy *fucking* some... some *child*—"

"*Jesus*, Vic, she's not a *child*," I hissed suddenly, becoming yet again aware of the reporters lingering within hearing distance. "And I'm not... I'm not *fucking* her—"

"So, what *were* you doing with her, Frank? *Huh*? Holding hands? Asking her to the fucking homecoming dance?!"

I groaned, covering my face with my hands.

"*...your daughter could've been killed today, and you weren't there for her because you were too busy with some girl half your* *age... that's a fucking PROBLEM, Frank!"*

The image of Allie, vulnerable and hurt, was etched into my mind, and Vic's anger only amplified the ache of my remorse.

"It's not what you think," I said finally, rubbing my eyes so hard that bright colors lit up through my eyelids. She laughed again.

"How could it *possibly*—"

"I'm being blackmailed, alright?!" I blurted out, the words escaping my lips in a desperate rush. I looked up, my eyes red and strained, meeting Vic's stunned expression. *"That's* where I was going today. I was trying to figure it out. I've been trying to handle this... this *mess*—"

"What are you talking about?!"

"Someone knows about us," I went on, pushing through the agony that I felt with each spoken word. "About Lucy. They want five grand or they're going to tell Liz.".

I could hardly believe I was giving Vic so much information. It felt like my sanity was unraveling in real-time. I was laying bare everything that I had been so desperate to keep hidden, and the absurdity of hearing it all out loud made me feel like I was losing my mind.

"I..." Vic paused, her eyes narrowing as the information settled. "I don't... how are they blackmailing you?"

"They took a picture."

"Of what?"

I hesitated, the words catching in my throat. "Of... us. Together."

Her face twisted into horror. Then disgust. Her face paled white, and for a moment I thought she was going to throw up. I quickly shook my head, putting my hands up.

"No, no, it's not..." I winced, beginning to wish I hadn't said anything at all. "We're just sat on her bed. Together."

"Right."

"But I... I'm kissing her. In the picture."

Her face didn't soften. If anything, it hardened. The weight of Vic's sudden disgust was almost unbearable.

"Liz can't see it." I rushed to get the words out before she could gather the courage to ask any further questions, realizing that any further investigation would make the whole situation worse. "I'm going to tell her everything—I *will*—but she can't find out like that. Not while Brooke's gone. Not while... *all of this* is happening. It's not fair."

Vic's eyes flashed wide, staring through me. Disbelief flickered across her face. "You're damn right this isn't fair," she said coldly. "How the hell could you do this to her?"

"I know—"

"No, you don't." Her eyes flared with a mix of disbelief and fury that made her look disturbingly like the teenager she once was, several lifetimes ago. "Clearly you *don't* know. She is... she is at *breaking* point. She is fighting *so fucking hard* to keep this family together—to keep *your* family together—and you're just... you're playing these *stupid games*?!"

I struggled to meet her gaze, my heart heavy with the weight of her words.

"When's the last time you even *talked* to her, huh? Your *wife*?! Do you have any idea how hard *all* of this is hitting her? She is hanging on by a *fucking thread*!" Vic started shouting again, jabbing a finger toward the entrance of the hospital. "And *you*... you are so busy with this... this... *Lucy*... that you can't even take *five seconds* to think about what *she* is going through—"

"*All of this* is happening because *all* I am thinking about is what she is going through!" I shot back, my voice low but fierce. "I'm doing *everything* I can to make sure she doesn't get hurt by this!"

"Well, maybe next time you could start by... *oh*, I don't know... *not hurting her in the first place*?!"

"I *know* I messed up," I hissed, my voice cracking as I tried to keep my emotions in check. "Trust me, I *know*... and I am *trying* to fix it. I am *trying* to stop this from going further. It is *all* I have been doing!"

"Do you even want to be with her anymore?!"

I paused for a moment, knowing that I probably shouldn't say the words out loud. I knew how bad it was going to sound before they even came out of my mouth. My mouth dried up. "...who?"

I may as well have murdered someone right in front of her.

"You're not serious," she said, her voice low and seething with rage. I swallowed hard, rushing to figure out what she meant.

"I—"

"*LIZ! Do you want to be with LIZ anymore*?!"

Again, I was lost for words.

"I..." I cleared my throat, trying so fucking hard to find the right words. "I just..."

"What?!"

"We haven't been good for a while, alright?!"

I'd only said it out loud less than two hours before—to Malcolm—but saying it to Vic was different.

She'd been a bridesmaid at our wedding. She'd lived with us when we first bought the house. She'd seen the good and the bad, the moments of joy and the arguments. She had been there from the very beginning, and now she was witnessing the collapse of something that had been a fundamental part of her existence.

Once again, I saw a flash of the younger Vic—my first child, long before Mick came along. She was now staring at me with a mix of rage and agony, an expression that shattered my heart into a million pieces.

Her voice broke as she continued, her anger giving way to an almost heartbreaking sadness. "I don't understand."

"We don't even talk anymore," I tried to explain, struggling to push through the anguish of my words. "Honestly, I can't believe we've lasted this long. It's not working. It hasn't been working for a long time."

"Do you still love her?"

Her question twisted in my gut like a knife. "I..." I nodded slightly, swallowing hard. "I'll *always* love her—"

"So, that's a no."

It wasn't.

Liz was the first person I ever truly fell in love with. For so many years, she had been the radiant center of my world. Her laughter, her touch, her unwavering support—they'd all made me feel alive in a way I hadn't felt since I lost my mother.

Even when I was on the road, traveling across the world and meeting countless women, none of them *ever* compared to her. We'd built a life together—a family, a home. She was all I ever thought about, and she was all I ever wanted to think about. It was more than love. It was more than anything I could've ever imagined to experience.

The breakdown of our marriage wasn't a sudden collapse, but

a slow erosion, so gradual that I barely noticed it at first. We fell into patterns. Routines. I couldn't pinpoint the exact moment when it started to slip away, only that it had.

But I *never* stopped caring about her.

I wouldn't have been fighting so hard to protect her from the fallout if I had.

"I don't want to hurt her," I finally said, only managing to get a small portion of my thoughts out. "She can't find out this way. Neither can the kids. It'll destroy the family—"

"Shame you didn't think about that sooner."

"When we find Brooke, I'll tell her everything," I continued, attempting to push past the harsh truth in her jab. "But not now. *Not* like this."

Vic folded her arms, her gaze unwavering. I honestly hadn't anticipated how difficult this would be—telling Vic. It drove home how much harder it would be when the others found out.

"Where are you going to get the money?" she asked finally, and a long exhale escaped my lungs. I shook my head slowly.

"I don't know."

She was quiet. Her eyes searched mine as if trying to find some hint of a plan or a solution that I wasn't revealing. Whatever affection or respect she once had for me had visibly vanished, leaving behind a void that felt both crushing and irreversible.

It was clearer than ever: the bond we'd spent decades building had been entirely shattered. And I wasn't sure I could ever fix it.

Vic pulled out another cigarette from the pack in her pocket, lighting it up with a practiced flick of her lighter. Moments passed like hours. I watched her silently, unsure of what to say next. Unsure of what was left to say.

"Do you need it in cash?"

The sudden words sent a ripple through my body, confusing the shit out of me. I stared at her, uncertain that I'd heard those words right. "What?"

"Cash or check?"

It didn't make sense.

My mind raced as I desperately searched for clarity in her expression. The anger and hurt that had been so vivid upon her face were now tempered by a strange, almost reluctant willingness to help. I didn't get it. "You're... you're serious?" I managed to stammer. She took a deep drag of her cigarette, now avoiding eye contact with me.

"She can't find out through a fucking photograph," she replied icily. "There's already enough shit in the papers about this family. I won't let you humiliate her like that."

A wave of conflicting emotions crashed over me—relief mingled with a heavy dose of guilt. Her anger was still there, but it was now overshadowed by a begrudging determination.

I had no idea what I was supposed to say. How I was supposed to thank her.

"I… *shit*, Vic…" The remaining air in my lungs escaped in a heavy cloud. "I'll pay you back, I promise—"

"Cash or check?"

The repetition of her words sent through me like a shock wave. The sudden realization that—at the *very* least—one of my problems had been solved felt like a temporary reprieve from the storm.

Thank God.

Thank *God*.

"Cash." The words finally made their way out. "Vic, I don't know what to say—"

"When this all comes out," she interrupted, looking me directly in the eye, "and it *will* come out… you do *not* tell her that I knew. And you do *not* tell her that I did this."

"Of course not—"

"And I'm doing this for her. Not you."

"I know."

"You…" She took a step forward, jabbing a finger in my face. "You are going to tell her *everything* the *second* this shit dies down. And when it all falls apart, it will be on *you*. *All* of it."

The familiar anger in her gaze had been replaced by a profound sadness that seemed to age her in an instant. Her eyes bore into mine, almost completely glazed over. They narrowed slightly, as if she suddenly saw something that she hadn't seen before.

"I don't even know who you are."

Those words hung in the air, more cutting than any accusation could have been.

My chest felt like it was imploding as I watched the love she once held for me diminish, fading from her gaze in real-time. The realization hit me with the force of a sledgehammer—this was not just about Liz, or Lucy, or the mess I had made. I was losing so much more than that.

And this was just the beginning.

She took another drag, half turning away from me. "Allie's still in the ER."

The mention of my daughter brought me back to the immediate crisis at hand. I nodded, unable to muster any more words. Vic finally turned away, continuing to smoke her cigarette at a rapid pace.

I turned toward the main entrance before she could say anything else. Each step felt like wading through thick mud, laden with the crushing realization and understanding of what had just been said and done. And now I had to face my family.

As I trudged forward, moving closer to the main entrance, I did all I could to focus all my energy on my daughter. *She needed me.* That was all that mattered.

That was all I could do for now.

18 DAYS AFTER THE DISAPPEARANCE OF
BROOKLYN NICHOLSON

FITZ | 7:19 PM

The *SOLD* sign outside the Turtin caught me off guard, even though I had been bracing for it. We'd all heard the rumors that the place was shutting down but seeing it in black and white made it all too real.

It hurt, seeing that it really was happening.

We'd spent so many nights here; me, Freddie, Joaquin, Hurley, the whole gang. It was our sanctuary; the only spot in town where we could hang out without needing an ID, even when we were still in school. I couldn't even remember how it started, but I guess at some point we'd gotten bored of sitting in the park after school and figured we'd try our luck at the dingy old bar right across the street. They served us right away, no questions asked, and from that point on, the Turtin became our place.

We'd head there straight after school on Friday, and we'd pretty much spend the whole weekend there—every weekend since sophomore year.

The group started splitting off after graduation, so we hadn't all been there together for a while. Al was the first to drop out, and then Mandy went off to college. And once I got Grandpa's house we started spending more time there than anywhere else.

It was only at that moment, as I looked up at the *SOLD* sign for the first time, that it hit me that there were only four of us left. Hurley and Mandy were gone forever, and I wasn't sure if I'd ever see Donnie again.

And until I got that phone call an hour ago, I didn't think I'd ever see Allie in the Turtin again.

When I finally pushed through the front doors, the familiar buzz of conversation and clinking glasses hit me like a nostalgic wave, but this time, it carried a strange undercurrent that made my chest tighten. As I made my way through the room, I couldn't shake the faint sense of unease that prickled at the edge of my awareness, making each step feel heavier than it should.

I tried to shake it off, focusing on the present—reminding myself that this could be my last time taking these steps. It was a short path that I'd walked along hundreds of times over the years, but now, the dim lights and familiar smells seemed oddly repressive, as if the place was closing in around me. Despite the tightness in my chest, a brief wave of sadness washed over me. I never thought I'd one day regret taking it for granted.

It was the dingiest, darkest joint in Mirrenville... but, well, it was home, you know?

It took a moment for my eyes to adjust to the dim light, but once they did, I spotted her right away. It wasn't that she stood out in any obvious way; at first glance, she just blended right into the crowd. But I knew what I was looking for. Even with the place packed, I could spot her messy, fiery hair from across the room; it was bigger than ever, like a bird's nest lit up in flames.

She already had a drink in her hand, and I wondered how long she'd been sitting there. The clock above the bar revealed that it was almost half seven, so I wasn't too late.

Maybe she'd only just gotten there, too.

As I made my way closer to her, the chatter around me—once

comforting—now seemed to close in, like the walls themselves were shifting. My breath caught in my throat, and I found myself struggling to push through the crowd, my pulse quickening for no apparent reason. The faces around me blurred together, and for a brief, disorienting moment, I felt like I was drowning in the noise and movement.

I focused on the bushy orange curls just ahead of me. I clung to its familiarity, allowing it to guide me through the crowd.

I finally reached the bar. Sliding onto the stool beside her, I let out a breath I hadn't realized I'd been holding.

"Hey."

She didn't respond immediately, and I wondered if she'd heard me over the crowd. It was getting pretty loud. It was as if she hadn't even noticed me, despite me sitting right next to her. My fingers drummed nervously on the bar, the rhythm shaky and uneven.

I forced myself to stop, gripping the edge of the counter instead, trying to steady the slight tremor that had taken hold of my hand. "Al?"

Her head spun toward me.

Seeing her face was like a lifeline tossed to a drowning man. The moment our eyes met, the chaotic noise of the bar seemed to recede, fading into a distant hum. She started smiling, and the tightness in my chest loosened just a little.

"*There* he is!" She grinned, wrapping her right arm around my shoulders. Her left arm was strung up in a sling, wrapped up in a light blue cast.

This was the first time I'd seen her since everything had happened.

It had been going through my mind constantly, the anxiety of this moment creeping in every time I thought about her. So much had changed since we last saw each other—so much had happened to her. To all of us. The broken arm was just a surface wound, and I had no idea what must've been going on inside her head.

Seeing her now, so close and real, I couldn't help but think I should've reached out to her instead of waiting for her to call me.

She looked different; her usual spark dimmed by something I couldn't quite place, though the empty glass in front of her and the way her words slurred together told me enough.

Her arm remained draped around my shoulders, pulling me in for a longer-than-anticipated hug. "Long time no see, my guy," she mumbled, giving me a kiss on the cheek before pulling back. I noticed the guy behind the bar watching her closely.

I quickly smiled back at her, squeezing her shoulder. "Started without me, huh?"

"*Psht...*" She put a finger to her lips, swaying slightly as she leaned closer. "You know how it is... just needed a *little* something to take the edge off. Before you got here."

"Yeah?"

"I was actually s-super scared about seeing you, actually."

"What?" I laughed slightly, briefly looking away as the guy behind the bar came over to us. I put one finger up toward him. "One beer? And maybe some water."

"*Water*," Allie repeated, her voice dragging on the word as she tried to keep her balance on the stool. The bartender nodded and walked off, leaving us with the hum of conversation and the clinking of glasses filling the space between us.

"Yeah, water," I replied, trying to keep my tone light. "For *you*."

She scoffed again before drinking the final few drops at the bottom of her glass. "Did you know they're selling the place?" she asked suddenly, her eyes lighting up. "Can you *believe* it? What the hell!"

"I know, right?" I replied, trying to match her enthusiasm, though my gaze kept drifting back to her face. There were deep purple-blue bruises surrounding both eyes; swelling had completely distorted her face. The right side of her cheek was a mottled mix of purples and greens, and a faint cut at the corner of her lip had scabbed over, giving her a grim, pained smile. The bruising extended all the way down her jawline.

The whiskey on her breath was sharp and foreign, and I struggled to push aside the unease it stirred in me.

Her smile faltered as she glanced around the bar, and I caught myself tensing. The hum of conversation seemed to grow louder, the clinks of glasses more pronounced. I shifted uncomfortably on my stool, trying to find a more stable position. "So, uh..." I hesitated, trying to figure out where to start. "How are you doing?"

That was probably the dumbest thing I could've asked her.

We hadn't spoken since the memorial, but I'd seen the papers. So much had happened, and I didn't even know where to start with it all. I didn't even know what I was supposed to say to her.

"*Oh*... not great," she admitted, still grinning. "Things are *pretty* weird around here..."

"Yeah. I heard."

"I'm basically a celebrity now." She shrugged, though the gesture was shaky. "It's like... people think they *know* me because of all the crap in the news... but, you know... not *all* of it is true..."

Her words tumbled out in a disjointed way. Her attempt to sound upbeat felt forced, and the alcohol wasn't helping her clarity. She was clearly going through it.

That made two of us.

"I'm sorry." The words came out before I could even think about it. Her eyes narrowed a little, turning her attention back toward the empty glass in front of her. A moment passed before she chuckled again.

"Why are you sorry?" she asked with a grin. "It's not like *you* knocked me up."

Jesus.

The grin on her face didn't quite match the sadness in her eyes, and it left me unsure of where to go next. In a way, there was a slight relief that came with that comment—at least she was jumping straight into it. No fucking around with small talk.

"You should've said something, you know," I went on, still attempting to keep my tone cheerful. "You could've told me."

"Why would I do that?"

"Because, you know..." I paused again, grabbing the beer and glass of water from the bar in front of me. "We're best friends, right?"

"Mm-hm... hey, anyway, how are things with *you*?" She jabbed me in the chest, smiling widely. "What's going on in *Bird World*?"

I laughed awkwardly, taking a sip from my beer. "Not a lot."

"Yeah..." She nodded, slowing down a little. "What a month, huh?"

"What a fuckin' month."

"It's been eighteen days since my sister went missing—you

know that?" she asked, and I shook my head somberly. "*Crazy*, huh?! And everything with, you know... the others... and *Melissa*..."

I took a long, hard gulp from the bottle, suddenly wishing I'd gotten something stronger.

"I-I didn't really know her *that* well... Melissa, I mean." Her voice lowered a little. "She... she was on the cheer squad w-with my sister—"

"Yeah."

"Brooke's *really* good. Like, really, *really* good. She can do all the... the... you know, all the *flips* and shit..."

"Yeah?"

She suddenly came to a halt, turning her head to stare at me through half-squinted eyes. It was as if I had something written on my forehead and she was trying to read it.

"Well..." She took my beer from my hand, taking a sip of her own. "*Apparently* she hung out with *all* you guys, so..."

Her whole demeanor had shifted in an instant.

The casualness, the forced cheerfulness, it all seemed to have evaporated within seconds. She continued to sway in her seat, her eyes narrowing with a hint of accusation. I cleared my throat, pulling the bottle back from her.

"*I* didn't know her," I replied, keeping my tone light but firm. "And I... I didn't know about Donnie. I swear."

I wondered if she believed me.

The silence that followed felt heavy, charged with unspoken questions. "*Hm...*" She lightly dunked a finger into the glass of water, flicking it a little. Water splashed across the bar.

"You know I would've said something," I added firmly. She nodded slightly, staring at the glass.

"Do you think he really did it?"

I stared at her, momentarily lost. She turned to me with an intense, almost pleading gaze, and I knew—at that moment—that I had to start thinking very carefully about what I said to her from that point onward.

Something told me that it would be too easy to tip her over the edge, without even realizing it.

"I-I thought they had evidence," I replied carefully, scanning her face. "I thought they it on tape, or whatever..."

Confusion lit up her face for a brief moment before clarity returned. She quickly shook her head, almost laughing again. I wasn't sure whether I was supposed to laugh back. "*No*, no… that's not…" She stopped, attempting to compose herself. "Do you think he *killed* them? Like… *Mandy*, and *Hurley*… and *Melissa*…"

I sat very still, suddenly extremely conscious of who could've been listening to our conversation.

She'd said it herself: her whole family was practically famous at this point. I'd seen the pictures of her family at the hospital a couple of days ago; the reporters had been camping outside and everything. It was fucking *insane*.

She began swaying even more as she tried to pull something out of her jacket pocket. A cigarette.

As she continued to pat herself down—looking for a lighter, I figured—I wondered if this was even a good idea. Her being so drunk and talking so loudly about this kind of thing, I mean.

"Honestly, I… I don't know," I admitted, watching as she lit up her smoke. "I mean… yeah, he's pretty fucked up… but I don't know if he could… *you know*. I just don't think he could do something like that and keep it to himself."

"He raped my sister and kept it to himself."

Jesus.

It was as if she wasn't actually hearing the words that were coming out of her mouth. And this just wasn't *like* her. Sure, she was drunk out of her mind, but this was a completely different person.

"I'm sorry," I repeated, not sure what else I could say.

She shook her head again, pulling the whole pack of cigarettes out of her pocket and offering them to me. "Want one?"

I took one without saying a word, picking the lighter up from the bar. The spirits on the shelf ahead of us were becoming more and more appealing, but something was telling me that I had to stay sober for the rest of this conversation. One of us had to.

"I need to tell you something," she announced suddenly, and for some reason, the words sent a shiver down my spine. I had a feeling that whatever she was about to say couldn't be good. Or reasonable.

"What's up?"

She blew a cloud of smoke into the air, watching it curl into shapes in the small space between us. She stayed quiet for a moment, clearly thinking hard… or, at least, as much as she could.

"Look…" She tapped her fingers against the bar, becoming visibly agitated. "I-I need you to listen to everything that I'm about to say, okay? You can't interrupt or anything. You just… you've got to listen."

I straightened up, my attention fully on her. I nodded, signaling that I was ready.

She seemed to appreciate the silence, her expression becoming more focused as she prepared to speak. A strange, distant look settled over her eyes. "You know someone tried to kill me last week, right?"

I wanted to say "sorry" again, but I figured that it would've been pointless. And, besides—she'd told me I couldn't speak.

So, I just nodded.

"They came up to my front door, and they had a knife," she went on, speaking so nonchalantly that I thought I'd misheard her for a second. "Swung at me with the knife… caught me a couple of times. I wasn't *stabbed*-stabbed, you know… I mean, I wasn't bleeding out, or anything. I just started running, and I guess I got away before they could, you know… actually *kill* me, or whatever."

I kept nodding, overly aware that my eyes were widening with every word she said.

"Anyway, *whatever*… the point is… *ugh*…" She stopped, covering her face with her hands. "Dude, I don't even know where to *start*…"

"Just take your time—"

"*Shh.*"

She held her hand up, halting me. I closed my mouth again, waiting for her to speak. "Okay… okay, so…" She shut her eyes, clearly struggling to get the words out. "I saw *Mandy*. At the memorial."

For some reason, hearing Mandy's name cut deeper than I expected. Maybe it was because she was the last to go, or maybe it was the fact that I'd known her the longest.

Either way, it felt like a wound opening back up every time I heard her name.

"She dragged me into the alleyway—the one here, next to the bar—and she just... she started telling me all this... *shit*..." Al's voice cracked, and she took a shaky breath. "She told me that, you know, she was going to be the next one to die, and then *I* was next, and—"

"What?"

"I probably shouldn't even be *telling* you this..." She groaned, laughing a little. "Because, you know... *some people* think *you're* the killer..."

I froze up, staring at her. She just kept laughing, like it was all somehow hilarious. "What are you—"

"No, hey, *I* don't think you did it," she chuckled, putting a hand on my shoulder. "But, you know... *Mandy* said I shouldn't tell *anyone* about this... but I guess I don't really know how I'm supposed to go forward *without* telling you, so—"

"What are you talking about?"

"At the party—*your* party—there were a couple of us sat out the back. Near the forest. I think it was me, Mandy, Hurley, Melissa—"

"I thought you couldn't remember anything from the party."

"I *can't*, but *Mandy* told me!" she moaned, clearly getting agitated with me trying to talk over her. "Just... *listen*, alright?! So, Mandy saw someone putting a body in a car and driving away—"

"What?!"

"*But* she couldn't see who it was... *BUT* she said that *they* saw *us*!" She began pointing at herself with an overly exaggerated gesture. "So *whoever that was... THEY wanted to kill US*! To keep us *quiet*, you know?"

Her casual delivery of such horrifying information made my head spin. I *had* to have not heard her right.

"And, so, then, they wrote these letters—"

"Letters?"

"*Letters*," she repeated, lingering on the word a millisecond too long. "Well, *poems*, actually... they were these poems that were... *threatening* us, I guess? I had mine the day before I got attacked, and *Mandy* had hers the day before *she* died, and *Hurley* got one the day before *he*—"

"Al, just stop for a sec—"

"No." She held a finger up to my face, glaring at me. "I'm *not* done. So, they were these super cryptic poems that said, basically, that if we talked to the cops, they'd kill our families or whatever... like, *real* weird shit..."

Her words became more slurred as the sentences ran into each other, and I had to question not just the validity of what she was saying, but also the reasoning behind it.

I mean... bodies, alleyways, *poems*... none of it was making any sense.

"Is this supposed to be a joke or something?" I asked, torn between wanting to laugh and feeling the need to take her seriously. "I don't understand what—"

"Am I *laughing*?!"

But the thing was, she *was* laughing. She had this big, almost eerie grin that only made everything more confusing. "I'm being *so* serious right now... and I need *you* to find Melissa's letter!"

"So... wait..." I stared at her blankly, my brain scrambling to keep up. "Rewind a second... you saw someone putting a *body* in a *car*? At the party? *My* party?"

"Mm-hm."

"Well... who was it?"

"I guess it was my sister."

I blinked, trying to process what she'd just said. "You think... you think you saw your sister being... like... *kidnapped*, or something?"

She leaned back, letting out a frustrated sigh as if *I* was the one not getting it. "That's what *Mandy* told me, okay? *She* said *she* saw someone by the forest, putting someone in a *car*... and, I mean, who else could it be, right? It *had* to be Brooke. No one else went missing that night..."

The noise of the bar faded into a dull roar in the background.

A bead of sweat formed at my temple as my breathing got a little quicker, a little shallower.

"I don't..." My voice trailed off as I tried to grasp onto something solid in this mess of a conversation. The tightness in my chest was growing worse by the second, and Allie was just talking in circles.

Everything just felt too loud.

Too close.

"What does this even mean? Why are you—"

I stopped again, realizing I didn't even know what I was trying to ask. Allie was way past her limit, and I was starting to feel like I was reaching mine, too. My thoughts were scattered, my hands trembling slightly as I took a drag from my cigarette, hoping it would calm me down. But it didn't.

"You *need* to find Melissa's letter," she repeated, her voice insistent—like this was the key to everything. Like this was the one thing that would make it all make sense.

I let out a shaky laugh, trying to play it off, trying to keep it together. But the laugh sounded hollow, even to me. The panic was creeping up on me, tightening around my throat.

I wasn't even sure why this was happening, but I just knew I felt it—this overwhelming sense of dread.

"Okay, Al, just—"

"No, you're *NOT listening to me!*"

Her hand hit the bar with a loud thud, and I flinched. The suddenness of it sent a jolt through me, like someone had just flipped a switch, turning the panic up to full volume.

"*Don't you get it*?! Someone tried to *kill* me! The *same person* that killed *your girlfriend*—"

"Al, stop—"

My voice was being swallowed by the chaos around us.

The lights felt too bright, the sounds too sharp. Every nerve in my body was on edge, like I was being pulled apart from the inside.

"—the *same* person that killed our *friends*—"

"*Al.*" Her name slipped out like a blade, sharp and edged with something I didn't want to acknowledge. The dread had turned into fire, burning in my chest.

But she didn't stop.

"They're *dead*, Fitz!" She leaned in so close that all I could smell was the alcohol hot on her breath. My fists clenched instinctively.

"*Yeah*, they're *dead*, Al!" I spat back, not entirely sure where the sudden anger came from. "I was *there*! I-I watched Hurley *die*, and he didn't say *shit* about a… a *fucking letter*—"

"*Because the letter said for him NOT TO SAY ANYTHING!*" She threw her arms out, getting louder with each word. "*WHY

AREN'T YOU LISTENING TO ME?!"

"God... god*damn* it, Al..."

I tried so fucking hard to keep it together.

All the noises of the bar together were swelling, filling every space in my head until I couldn't think, couldn't breathe.

"I'm trying to help you, alright?! But you can't... you *can't* just... just say shit like this! You sound *insane*—"

"*I'M NOT INSANE*!"

I was losing it.

I knew I was losing it, but I couldn't stop it.

The anger, the fear, the panic—they were all tangled together, and I couldn't separate one from the other. My fists were still clenched, trembling with the effort to keep myself from completely snapping.

"Look... I know more than *anyone* how hard this is," I said, trying really hard to keep my voice low and cool. "Trust me—I *know*. A lot of... of *traumatic shit* has happened, and we've lost a *lot* of people, and—"

"That's not what this is—"

"—you can't just... y-you can't just..." It was suffocating. *I* was suffocating. "I-I mean... we haven't seen each other properly in *months*, and you're just pulling this shit out of *nowhere*—"

"*How is it out of nowhere*?! This is happening *now*! *Don't you get it*?! *WHY DON'T YOU BELIEVE ME*?!"

"Because you're *drunk*," I snapped back, my own voice rising. "Because you're *fucked up*, and you're not thinking straight, and I—"

"I'm fucking *scared*, Fitz—"

"*YOU THINK I'M NOT*?!" The words flew out of my mouth before I could stop them. "You think *I'm* not going through it?! You think *I* haven't been reliving it *every fucking day*?!" I jabbed the side of my head angrily, watching as she scrambled to pull something out of her pockets. She threw a bunch of crumpled papers onto the bar in front of me, practically shoving them into my arms.

"Read them." She was pleading now. "*Read* them, Fitz—"

"Stop—"

"Mandy, Hurley, *and* Melissa were killed by the *same person*," Allie shouted, her voice raw with anguish. "*Mandy* and

Hurley had letters, *I* had a letter, *they're all right here—*"

"*Al—*"

"I *need* to see Melissa's! You *have* to find it, Fitz—*you HAVE to*! I *know* she had one, *she was the first to die—*"

"*AL!*"

"I'm *not* fucking around, Fitz—"

"They're *fucking DEAD!*" I growled, the words escaping before I could stop them. "They're *gone*! It happened! This isn't some... some *goddamn murder mystery*!"

Her whole demeanor—her every action—was triggering something deep inside me, a raw, gnawing sense of dread that I couldn't shake off.

"Look, I... I *know* things have been rough for you," I said, my voice shaking with rage. "With your *sister*, and everything, but—"

"*All* I'm asking you to do is *find Melissa's letter—*"

"No."

"Why not?!"

I couldn't.

I saw it all again—the flashing police lights, the tape cordoning off the scene, the oppressive silence that swallowed everything.

Mel's bloody sweatshirt.

Hurley's face.

"Fitz, *please—*"

Each breath came in harder and faster.

Her continuous words felt like a relentless assault, chipping away at whatever I had left to hold onto.

She kept saying that I didn't get it, but *she* didn't get it.

She didn't fucking get it.

"Fitz, just *listen* to me—"

I grabbed onto the bar, dragging myself up.

Allie's voice faded into a distant roar as I pushed through the throng of people. Faces blurred—laughter and conversation blended into a chaotic mess of sound that pressed in on me from all sides.

"*—FITZ—*"

Her voice cut through, sharp and frantic.

I kept moving.

I shoved open the bar's door, the cold night air hitting me like a slap to the face. I staggered outside, gasping for breath. The street was a blur of flashing lights and shadowy figures that I couldn't make sense of.

I *knew* she wasn't thinking straight. I *knew* she wasn't in a good place. But she couldn't keep doing this.

She didn't know Mel.

She barely knew Hurley or Mandy in the end.

She was just another person caught up in their own twisted fantasies about the murders, adding to the endless fucking chaos.

I didn't want to think about *any of it*.

They weren't coming back. They were gone, and nothing was going to change that. I wanted to scream at the world to just *stop*, to stop dragging up the past like it was some kind of sick game.

I just wanted to forget.

LUCY | 9:02 PM

"...I just don't understand," I mumbled, placing my empty glass down on the bar. "How did she even find out?"

Frank finished off his beer with a long, drawn-out gulp, the sound of the glass meeting the bar punctuating the uneasy silence between us. He didn't meet my gaze, staring off into the middle distance as if searching for something to fixate on. He'd barely looked me in the eye since we'd gotten there, and it had only gotten worse since the clock had struck nine.

"I said I stayed with my friend the other night, when I came to see you," he finally said, his voice barely audible over the ambient noise. "Liz didn't believe me, so Vic called him."

"And she didn't tell her?"

He shook his head, the gesture slow and deliberate. Panic rose inside my chest at the very thought of it.

Knowing that someone so close to Frank—so close to Liz—

was now aware of what had happened made everything feel so much more real. Up until now, it had stayed between us.

"But she knows that nothing is going on now, right?" I pushed, suddenly desperate to cling onto the one piece of dignity and self-righteousness that I had left. "And that I didn't know when it started—"

"I told her," Frank cut me off, his voice heavy with frustration. "I said you're not a bad person."

I thought those words would've given me some comfort; after all, it was all that I had been telling myself for weeks. I'd believed those words for so long, and I thought I would feel some reassurance hearing it from someone else for once.

But it wasn't true. Not really.

I knew this because as we sat there at that bar—the same bar where we met, the same bar we met up at several times a week for almost a year—my heart ached for what had once been normal to us; or, at least, normal to me. A deep pang of loss spread through my chest as I craved the time when everything felt right, or at least manageable.

I watched Frank carefully, trying to decipher whether or not he felt the same way. Part of me hoped he didn't.

It would've been easier if he didn't.

His eyes kept wandering toward the door, toward the tiny window next to it. We'd strapped the cash to the tire of his car and walked away, figuring whoever it was wasn't going to show their face if they knew we were there. If they were smart, they wouldn't have shown their face in the bar.

I'd suggested hiding nearby, just close enough that we could see who it was. Now that Liz's sister knew about the affair, it made sense for us to at least know who the other person was. The more we knew, the easier it would be to control the inevitable fallout.

I knew, more than anything, that we were on borrowed time. Now that two people knew, it was only a matter of time before there was a third. And a fourth. And then, everyone would know.

Everyone would hate me. I was the "other woman", and I already knew that the scrutiny would be relentless. But Frank would be fine. Despite everything, he would maintain his status as the grieving father of the most talked-about missing child on the West Coast. People would find reasons to forgive him. How could they not?

All I could do was prepare myself for the foreseeable.

"It was good of her to give you the money," I said finally, waving toward the bartender to bring us another round of drinks. "Victoria. She didn't have to do that."

Frank stared into his glass, his face shadowed by the dim bar lighting. He broke his silence with a sigh, his voice heavy with resignation. "Yeah, it was good of her. I didn't think she'd come through like that."

"I don't think I would have."

"She's got a big heart." He reached over, picking up his new drink. "Always has. Especially when it comes to family. Bottom line is that she didn't want Liz to get humiliated. She was looking out for her."

I could see the internal battle waging within him—regret, guilt, and a faint glimmer of gratitude. It was a messy cocktail of emotions, one that had become all too familiar over the past few weeks.

"Do you know the worst part?" he asked suddenly. I shook my head slightly. "Liz had told her about you. About how much she likes you."

My chest tightened with a crushing sense of guilt and dread.

He wasn't saying anything I didn't already know; I'd been showered with enough "*thank yous*" and "*how can I ever repay yous*" to know what she thought of me. And it killed me. Every time.

"I like her too." The words slipped out. "She's a good mom. A good person. Makes a killer chai tea."

He actually chuckled slightly. "You should try her hot cocoa," he replied, his voice softening a touch. "She puts a little cinnamon in it, sprinkles a little chocolate over the top and it's... it's perfect."

The sudden warmth of his tone caught me off guard. This was the first time I'd heard Frank speak about Liz with such genuine affection, untainted by the bitterness or frustration that had colored so many of our conversations. There was something tender and nostalgic in his voice, something I had never heard before when he spoke about his wife.

I'd almost forgotten that this wasn't just some person that he knew; this was someone that he'd shared a life with for 30 years.

The oddest thing was that, even after just a brief moment of vulnerability—even if he was just talking about hot chocolate—part of me hoped that they would make it. Maybe she could forgive him and move past it. They had a family. They had a whole life together.

But an even bigger part of me felt crushed, and I didn't know how to ignore it.

Watching him reminisce about a life with another woman stung more than anything; a sharp, relentless reminder of what *I'd* lost. Or, more realistically, what I'd never had. What could never be mine.

And I hated myself for even thinking it.

"Do you think you'll work things out?" I asked softly, my voice trembling. I wasn't sure if I was asking because I genuinely wanted to know, or if I was just seeking some form of comfort for myself. But he shook his head almost immediately.

"I don't think she'd give me another chance, even if I wanted it," he said emotionlessly. "And I don't think I do."

"Are you sure about that?"

Again, the question came out before I could fully think about what I was saying.

The words hung in the air, awkward and heavy. Frank's eyes met mine, and although subtle, I saw a flicker of doubt. There are no words to describe the self-hatred I felt as the jealousy surged up inside me at the sight of it. It was raw and relentless, an unwelcome reminder of the emotions I'd been fighting so hard to suppress. It wasn't fair of me to feel that way. He wasn't mine to lose. He never had been.

"I just think... well, it must be worth a try," I added, picking up my own drink. "Cam's just a kid. He shouldn't have to watch his parents go through a divorce. Trust me—it sucks."

"Wouldn't it be worse than him growing up, knowing his parents don't love each other?"

A pang of relief washed over me, almost immediately followed by a flash of guilt and self-loathing. I pursed my lips out, trying not to let it show. Not wanting him to see it.

"Maybe it's not about love," I offered, the word getting caught in my throat. "Maybe it's about just... doing what's right. For a family."

Frank shook his head, taking another sip from his glass. "My mother loved my father," he said, his voice thick with an emotion I couldn't quite place. "*Worshipped* him. She only ever made his favorite food; rubbed his feet when he got home from work. She never said a bad word about him—not to me, not to anyone."

He paused suddenly, his eyes darkening as if the memories were physically painful.

"She got cancer," he went on, barely even glancing in my direction. "Ovarian. I mean, it started there, and it spread to her bones, and... anyway, I sat with her the night she died. Didn't leave her side 'til she was gone. I went downstairs to tell my father, and he was sat on the couch with our neighbor. Three days after the funeral, he married her."

I sat in complete silence, just watching him. His face was a mask of controlled emotion, but I could see the cracks forming. The pain of that memory was etched into every line of his expression.

"She never knew, you know?" His eyes wandered over to my direction, barely rising. "She loved him. She really did. And, well... he was just waiting for her to go."

"I'm so sorry, Frank."

"I never forgave him," he continued with a sad smile, raising his glass. "And I told myself that—no matter what happened—I could *never* do that to Liz. I couldn't do that to my family."

Frank took another long sip from his glass, lost in thoughts that seemed to be pulling him apart. I had frozen into position, realizing what he was saying. Wishing that I could save him from his own thoughts in that moment.

"You spend enough time hating someone, berating them for what they did," he added, "and before you know it, you go from judging them to understanding them. And then, you know... all that hatred you once had for them turns inward. Because now, you know *why* they did it. *You get it.* Somewhere along the road, I had to stop hating him, because... because I *was* him."

His confession hung in the air, heavy and suffocating, as I absorbed the shock of realizing he had just peeled back a layer of himself that I wasn't sure he'd ever revealed to anyone before this moment. A new wave of emotions came crashing over me—grief for him, anger at his father, and something else I couldn't quite name.

Maybe it was fear. Regret. A deep, aching sadness that there was no fixing any of it.

Frank finally looked at me, and I watched the war raging in his mind. I wanted him to find the strength to fight for his family. I truly wanted that more than anything.

But another part—the selfish part I hated—wanted him to choose me, to let everything else fall away.

And that was when it hit me: I couldn't comfort him. I couldn't tell him that he was wrong, because he wasn't. He wasn't a good person, but neither was I.

And if I couldn't find comfort in that, where could I?

"What do *you* want?"

He looked up at me, seemingly confused that I'd broken my silence after so long. His eyes bore into mine with a sad yet cold darkness.

"What do I want?" he repeated, and I nodded slowly.

"Forget about the fact that you and Liz have... drifted," I said, thinking a little while about what word was best to use. "And that your number one priority is the kids, because, well... that's a given. But if everything could be perfect *right now*, and there were no repercussions for your actions, and you could make *anything* happen... what would you want?"

He stared at me for a long moment, his expression unreadable, but for a second, I truly felt that I could read his mind.

He wanted the simplicity of the earlier years of his marriage when they were happy. When they were in love. He wanted the life he had lost; the life that included Liz, his children, and all the happiness they had all once shared. I knew it, deep in my heart, because that was what made sense. That was what was *right*.

His eyes eventually dropped to the table, his fingers tracing patterns on the edge of his glass. "It doesn't matter," he replied finally, and I shook my head.

"That's bullshit. Of course it matters."

For the first time, I saw a flicker of something different in his eyes. It was a raw, vulnerable honesty that caught me off guard.

He leaned forward, his gaze locking onto mine with a fierceness that made my breath catch. Slowly, almost hesitantly, he reached out, his hand closing over mine.

The contact was warm and intense, yet it sent a shiver through me. His fingers tightened around mine, and I looked into his eyes, seeing not just his choice but my own reflected back at me. For a moment—just a brief moment—I found myself drawn to the clarity of his decision; the way it offered a glimpse into a future that felt, if not right, then at least undeniably real. I hadn't expected it, not for one second, but there was no doubt that this was what I had wanted all along. There was no way of denying that truth.

He stared deep into my eyes as he finally placed his other hand on top of ours, softly stroking the back of my hand with his thumb. The sadness returned to his gaze as he repeated those words: "It doesn't matter."

We pulled our hands back almost in unison, the abrupt separation leaving a cold emptiness in its wake.

I was so mad at myself.

I was so mad at *him*.

I didn't want him to want me—I wanted him to do the right thing. Because if *he* wanted the right thing, then *I* could want the right thing too. Then *I* could let it go.

He was right. It didn't matter.

It couldn't.

As I attempted to shake away the overwhelming emotions that were now flooding my system, I watched as Frank waved toward the bartender, asking to pay. I instinctively downed what was remaining of my drink before sliding my arms into my coat. Every action felt forced but necessary.

We had to get out of there.

As we stepped out of the bar into the cold night air, I pulled my coat tighter around me, attempting to ward off the chill that seemed to seep into my bones. The dim glow of passing headlights illuminated the way to our cars; they were the only vehicles left in the lot, parked on opposite sides, far enough apart that any passersby wouldn't see any connection between them.

As we reached the midpoint between our cars and were about to go our separate ways, I saw Frank's posture tighten as he glanced over at his vehicle. It was only then that I remembered why we were there.

Despite the dim lighting, I noticed that the envelope of cash had disappeared. The transaction had been completed.

I turned back to Frank, and he met my gaze. In that moment, a profound sense of finality settled over us. This was it: the end of something we had both been needlessly holding onto for too long. The cold, empty space between our cars felt almost symbolic as we prepared to move our separate ways.

Aside from brushing past each other at the police station, or at the occasional visit to their house, we weren't going to see each other again. At least, not like this.

I swallowed hard, trying to choke back the surge of emotion that was hastily rising within me as I realized it was all over. I blinked rapidly, trying to clear my vision, hoping the darkness would hide the sheen in my eyes. The tears pooled at the corners of my eyes, dangerously close to overflowing.

I turned slightly, angling myself away from him, but he wasn't oblivious. Even in the dim light, I noticed his posture shift.

"*Luce...*"

I shook my head, taking a step back. Swallowing it down. With a deep breath, I found the courage to face him one last time. "I hope you work it out with Liz," I said finally, the crack in my voice giving me away. "I really do... I-I want you to be *happy*..."

I had barely gotten the words out when he closed the distance between us in a few quick steps, pulling me into a firm, unexpected embrace.

His arms tightened around me, and the dam broke. My hands found their way to his back, clutching at his jacket as if it were the only thing keeping me grounded. I buried my face in his chest, the tears finally spilling over as I let out a shuddering breath.

Frank didn't say anything. He just held me, his hand gently stroking the back of my head.

"I'm sorry," I whispered into his chest, my voice barely audible.

I wasn't even sure what I was apologizing for. Maybe for crying. Or for letting things go as far as they did.

For wishing that this moment didn't have to end.

"*...I'm sorry too...*"

Frank's hand continued its slow, soothing motion, and I felt his breath against my hair. We just stood there for a moment, holding each other.

After what felt like both an eternity and a heartbeat, I pulled back, wiping my cheeks with the back of my hand. The cold night air rushed in as the warmth of his embrace faded, leaving me feeling more vulnerable and lost than ever. The light from the bar cast upon his face just enough that I could make it out. I took it in, memorizing it—reminding myself that this was the last time we could do this.

His hands found their way to my face once more, and before I could process it, his lips found mine. I immediately leaned into it, allowing it to happen. My hands found their way to his chest, resting there as I felt the quickening beat of his heart beneath my fingertips. The kiss was slow, unhurried, as if we were both trying to savor every second.

When Frank finally pulled back, his forehead rested against mine, our breaths mingling in the cold night air. I closed my eyes.

"I love you."

It was the first time I had ever said those words out loud to him.

For the longest time, I had wondered if I even felt that way. There was no doubt that I cared for him, that I was drawn to him in ways I couldn't fully explain. It was just all so complicated. And it didn't feel right to love him.

Yet, as the silence stretched between us, the weight of what I had said settled into the space, and I realized with a startling clarity that I really did mean it.

I loved him.

Frank's expression shifted, something softening in his eyes as if the words had somehow startled him, but at the same time, they hadn't surprised him in the slightest. My heart prematurely shattered as the seconds passed without him saying a word.

I shouldn't have said it.

I should *never* have said it.

His thumb gently brushed against my cheek, wiping away a tear I hadn't realized had fallen. "*I love you.*"

If he hadn't said it back, I could have walked away with some semblance of closure.

I could've convinced myself that this had been one-sided— that I was alone in this impossible situation. At least I could've moved past it. I could've moved on.

Hearing those words from him—the words I'd longed to hear for so long—should have filled me with joy. Relief. Maybe even hope. Instead, they shattered what was left of me.

I wished he hadn't said it back.

His lips brushed against mine once more; a small, gentle kiss that only deepened the ache inside me. I wasn't sure how I was going to move on from this. I wasn't sure how I ever could.

We pulled away for the final time. The warmth of his embrace, the tenderness of his kiss—all of it seemed to evaporate into the frigid night air. A painful silence stretched between us, filled with the echoes of what could have been. There was nothing left to say. In so many ways, it all felt too perfect a goodbye.

Frank was the first to turn away. He turned his back to me, taking a few steps before abruptly halting to a stop.

He just froze.

The sudden shift in the atmosphere was like a physical blow. I watched in horror as Frank's entire body went rigid, his shoulders tensing with a focus so intense it was almost palpable. My heart raced as I followed his line of sight, squinting into the darkness.

He stumbled forward, his movements slow and deliberate. My vision struggled to adjust. The scene before me came into sharp, horrifying focus. Terror gripped me when I saw the shadowy figure standing right next to Frank's car.

The world around us seemed to crumble as Frank's voice broke through the silence.

"...Al?"

Her name hung in the cold air.

My heart raced as my eyes adjusted to the dim light, locking onto her face. Her eyes were on Frank. Only Frank.

The light from the parking lot cast eerie shadows on her face, making the uncertainty in her eyes all the more intense. Jaw open. Eyebrows knotted. She was frozen in place—mirroring her father—unable to process the scene before her. I wondered what she'd seen. In my heart, I knew she'd seen all of it. I saw it on her face.

She'd seen *everything*.

Her breaths came in shallow, uneven gasps, as if every inhale was a struggle against the overwhelming flood of emotions. I watched helplessly as her shoulders began to shake. Her eyes were locked on her father.

But then they flickered to me.

Our eyes locked in a brief, electric moment. Her eyes, wide and tear-filled, seemed to ask an unspoken question that I couldn't answer. She recognized me; there was no doubting that. Her eyes moved back to Frank, then back to me. Then back to him again. The shocked expression slowly but suddenly melted into something more.

Rage.

"Al..." Frank's voice finally broke through the seemingly endless silence. He slowly began staggering toward her. "*Al...*"

I couldn't move.

I stood there, watching them. Watching as he moved closer. Her eyes were once again on me. Locked in. The intensity of her gaze felt like a physical force. I could barely breathe under its weight.

The darkness around us seemed to close in.

A cold sweat broke out on my forehead, my heart pounding so loudly it was almost deafening. Every second felt like an eternity as I watched the scene unfold, paralyzed by horror and helplessness.

I watched as Frank tried to reach his daughter.

"...Al, *please...*"

Allie's figure continued to tremble in the dense light, her gaze still fixed on me. I was unable to move, to speak, to intervene. The whole world seemed to have narrowed to this single, heart-stopping moment.

I couldn't do anything.

As Frank's figure faded into the darkness, I began to imagine what would happen next. How it would happen. How quickly it would happen.

The situation had always been a house of cards: precariously balanced and destined to collapse. But I thought we had more time. I thought I could prepare for it.

I watched as Frank ran to his daughter.

I imagined the thoughts running through his head. He thought he could fix it. He thought he could stop it.

I knew it was futile. I also knew I couldn't stop him.

It was over.

LIZ | 9:19 PM

"It sounds like a good idea, Liz," I heard my sister saying across the counter. "I think you should go for it."

My hands trembled as I linked my fingers together, piecing it all together in my mind. My mother's voice crackled through the speaker, warm and familiar, despite the static: "...*we would love to have him here, Lizzie—*"

"He belongs *here*," I interrupted firmly, barely lifting my head enough to make eye contact with Vic. "He's going through enough as it is. The last thing he needs is for his life to get even more chaotic."

"But that's the *whole point*!" Vic threw her arms out, entirely exasperated. "His sister is missing, his *other* sister has been beaten up more than Evander Holyfield over the past two weeks—"

"*Vic*," I heard Dad's warning tone over the phone.

She began tripping over her words, almost too excited to get them out. "His dad's *continuously* MIA," she went on, striking a chord in my chest. "And *you* are struggling! This isn't fair on anyone, Liz, and *especially* not Cam. And you *know* it."

A lump formed in my throat.

It felt like an ambush. The last people I'd expected to call at this time of night were my parents, and despite the brief comfort I felt in hearing their voices, I couldn't grasp what they were trying to say.

They wanted to take Cam.

"He is *my* son." The words shot out like venom. "This is *my* family, and they *all* belong *here*—"

"*Of course he does, sweetie,*" Mom said calmly, her voice

337

crackling through the phone. *"But we're just thinking about you and Frank... AND the kids..."*

"Allie and Cam both need a lot of support right now," Dad added. *"And you're going to end up tearing yourself apart if you're doing it all alone!"* Vic was nodding along to his every word, gesturing toward the phone. I wanted to hit her.

I felt like I was losing control of everything. All of it. I couldn't understand how they could all act like this was such a good thing.

"I am *not* alone," I replied angrily, staring at Vic. "I've got *you*! And I've got Frank!"

Her face hardened. "So where is he right now?"

I sighed, rubbing my eyes hard. Her gaze was sharp, and there was a flicker of something I couldn't quite place.

She'd been off with Frank ever since we'd gotten back from the hospital with Allie. She wasn't happy that he was working a lot. It was nice to have her support, but now wasn't the time or place.

In all honesty, I didn't care where Frank was at that moment.

"We've already spoken to the school," Mom went on. *"They said there'd be no issue getting Cam a temporary place for as long as we need—"*

"You've already spoken to the school?!" My voice got louder as anger built up inside me. "Mom, I'm *not* doing this! It's *insane!*"

"Liz, Liz, listen..." Vic took both my hands in hers. "The holidays are coming up... Halloween, Thanksgiving, Christmas, Cam's *birthday*—"

"It's *October!*"

"But it's all going to come around pretty fast, just like it does every year," she pointed out, giving me a look. "And what if Brooke's not home by then? Are *you* going to be taking Cam out trick-or-treating at the end of the month?"

"I was hoping you would do it," I mumbled.

Vic's eyes softened, and she squeezed my hands gently. "You know I would, in a heartbeat," she said, her voice full of warmth. "But... come *on*, Liz. Cam is a little kid. He needs stability, and it's not just about the holidays. His life is *so* far from normal right now."

"We'll take him to the pumpkin patch!" Mom jumped in

suddenly, her tone bursting with excitement. *"The one we used to take you three to when you were kids! I'll make him my pumpkin soup—"*

"Can I come stay with him?" Vic asked jokingly, gently nudging me. I didn't budge.

It wasn't working.

"I can take him fishing with me on Sundays." There was a hint of enthusiasm in Dad's voice that I hadn't heard in a long time. *"He'll love it—just like his brother did!"*

My heart almost warmed at the memory of my father taking Mickey out on the boat, the two of them floating out into the distance together.

After raising three daughters, I had never seen Dad happier than when he held my firstborn for the first time, and that joy was repeated when my youngest was born. He loved the girls too—of course he did—but nothing made him happier than spending time with his grandsons.

I *knew* they would take care of Cam. Of course they would. And I knew he would love being with them.

But I couldn't lose him.

"Cam hasn't been to Portland since he was a baby," I reminded them all, shaking my head. "He's... he's *sensitive*. He'd get homesick!"

Mom's voice softened further, filled with a gentle conviction. *"Of course he'll miss you, Lizzie... but that's why it's important to give him a stable environment right now. It's not about taking him away from you—it's about providing a safe space where he can be happy!"*

My eyes began to fill up dangerously quickly. I quickly shook my head again, trying to push it back. "I don't even know what Frank would say," I added shakily. "I-I don't think he would want this—"

"Oh, who *cares* what Frank thinks?!"

"Vic." Dad's voice crackled through the speaker again, firmer this time; it was the same tone he'd used when we were little kids. Vic began laughing, staring at me with wide eyes.

"Look *around*, Liz!" She waved her arms out. "He's not here! He's *never* here! He wouldn't even *notice* if Cam left—"

"What's your problem?" I suddenly snapped. "There's enough

sh—c-crap going on right now without you having an issue with my husband!"

"My "issue" with your husband is exactly *this*!" She slammed a hand onto the counter. "This family is falling apart, and every time—*every* time—it's on *you* to fix it! How is that *fair*?!"

"*Now's not the time, Vicky*," Mom tried to intervene, but it was too late. Vic had already started.

"You don't know what it's like, Mom," she huffed, crossing her arms against her chest. "I've been back, what, a *week*? And he's *never here*! Liz has to do *everything* around here, and he just *waltzes* back in whenever he feels like—"

"He's *working*," I said through gritted teeth. "If he doesn't work, there's no food for *you* to eat out the fridge. There's no *house* for you to wander into whenever you—"

"Are you kidding me right now?!"

"*Girls*," Dad's voice rose in authority, cutting through the argument. "*Let's take a step back, alright?*"

"*This isn't helping anything*," Mom added.

"*None* of this is helping *anything*!" I suddenly exploded, grasping my hair in handfuls. "*I'm DROWNING!* My daughter has been *missing* for *eighteen days*, and *you think the solution is to take ANOTHER one of my kids away from m*e?! *You think taking my SON away from me will HELP*?!"

The room fell silent, the intensity of my outburst hanging in the air. My chest heaved as I tried to catch my breath, the weight of all that had happened—all that was *happening*—crashing down on me.

I couldn't fucking *breathe*.

"You think I haven't got *enough* going on right now?!" I kept shouting, pulling myself onto my feet. "I-I'm sorry, Mom, but *I*... mother of *God*... Allie was *pregnant*! And I-I'm trying to live with *her* right now, knowing that *she* might have something to do with *all of this*—"

"Oh, *here* we go..." Vic chuckled humorlessly, shaking her head with blatant judgment. "Yeah, let's blame it *all* on Allie—"

"*Screw you!*" I jabbed a finger in her face before turning back toward the phone. "If you're going to take one of my kids, *take her*! *Take HER!*"

A sudden scuffle came from the hallway. Both mine and Vic's

head span toward the door.

There were whispers. Movements.

Before I could react, the door burst open.

Cam ran in, his small face flushed and red. I stared at him, speechless, trying to process the scene unfolding before me.

"*Stop* being mean to Allie!" he started shouting, throwing his arms out at me. "It's not *fair!*"

"*Cameron?*" My mother's voice crackled faintly through the phone, but it felt distant, barely breaking through the haze of confusion I had fallen into.

"I don't *want* her to go!" he kept yelling, glaring at me through glassy eyes. "And *I* don't want to go! *We're not going ANYWHERE!*"

"Cam—"

Before I could finish my sentence, he ran back out of the room.

I caught a glimpse of Vic's face; she appeared anguished, her usual resolve softened by the scene unfolding before her. She turned to me in shock. I had frozen up. I couldn't move a muscle.

My mind scrambled to figure out exactly what I'd said.

What he had heard.

Shit.

My legs began moving before my brain could catch up.

I started running toward the door, hearing Vic saying something to the phone as I left.

I swung the door open, bursting into the hallway. My heart ached, realizing what I had said. Realizing what he'd heard.

But I couldn't think about it, not at that moment.

I just had to fix it.

Cam was sitting on the stairs, his eyes all red and puffy. As I moved toward him, he stood up angrily, turning to run up the stairs.

"Allie's not going *anywhere*—"

"Baby, please," I reached out and grabbed his arm. "I didn't mean what I said. Mommy was just… I was *angry*, okay? I shouldn't have said that about your sister, and I'm *sor*—"

"This isn't *her* fault!" he shouted, trying to yank away from me. "This is *your* fault!"

My hand loosened around his wrist. "What?"

"*You hit her!*"

My grasp loosened.

His arm fell from my grip, and he yanked it away, stepping back as if he couldn't stand to be near me.

"*You hit Brooke!*" he shouted, the anger and hurt in his voice cutting deeper than anything I'd felt before. His small chest heaved as he glared up at me. His face twisted in a way that didn't belong to a child. "I *saw* it! *I saw YOU!*"

I stared at him, dumbfounded.

My heart pounded in my ears, my vision blurring. "Cam…" I tried to speak, but my throat tightened, choking on the words. "I-I didn't—"

"*You* made her leave!" he screamed, tears pouring down his face now, his tiny fists clenched at his sides. "She's gone because of *you*! You hurt her, and now she's *gone*, and *it's all YOUR fault!*"

He began running up the stairs, leaving me standing there, frozen at the bottom of the stairs, my hand hovering in mid-air. I watched as he stomped up each step, screaming, "*I'M NOT GOING!*" as he moved.

I heard his bedroom door slam shut. Tears blurred my vision. My jaw hung half open.

He saw it.

Slowly, I turned, feeling a presence behind me. Vic was standing in the doorway, her face pale, eyes wide, taking in the scene. For a moment, neither of us said anything.

I wasn't sure what to say. Or how to say it.

"…*Lizzie?*"

Mom's voice rang through the kitchen, barely audible. I couldn't move. I just couldn't move.

Vic's eyes remained locked on me. She shook her head, stepping forward, her eyes searching mine as if trying to find the right words, but nothing came. There was no way to fix this.

"I-I didn't…" The words came out in short bursts. "I *didn't*…"

But I did.

Silence rang through the house. I stared back up the stairs, retracing the steps my youngest child had just taken. I thought back to that night. I could still feel the anger. The resentment.

"What the hell did you do?" I heard Vic finally ask, her voice barely a whisper. I swallowed hard, trying to push it away. Trying to forget. It was all I had done for the past 18 days.

I could still see her face. The way she looked at me.

The last time she ever looked at me.

ALLIE | 9:24 PM

The world outside the car was a spinning haze of neon lights and shadowy blurs, every flicker and flash taunting me with its disorienting chaos.

I slumped against the seat, fighting the intense urge to throw up, my head throbbing. It was *insanely* hot in there. It was like all the air had been sucked from the car, amplifying the sickness that churned violently in my stomach.

I had no idea where we were going, and honestly, I didn't care.

Neither of us had said a word since we'd gotten in the car; not a *"let's go"* or a *"we need to talk"*. Nothing. We were moving way too fast; the speed made the car feel like it was on the edge of spinning out of control, just like everything else.

And do you know the weird thing?

On top of everything else that had happened—what I had just seen—I just kept thinking about Fitz.

His face kept flashing through my mind; the way his face changed when I said...whatever stupid thing I said. God, what *had* I even said? The whole stupid night seemed to merge into one, becoming one big tangled mess. Strands of the night flashed through my brain like a clip show from a bad sitcom. None of it was processing. None of it made any sense, not even a little bit.

And now, here I was, stuck in Dad's car, speeding through the night like we were running from something. I just needed the world to stop spinning, just for a second.

I was lost in it. Drowning.

I needed it to stop.

"...stop the car..."

I don't know how long we'd been driving at this point.

It could've been hours. Seconds. The world span at a speed I couldn't adjust to, the lights outside blurring into a dizzying mess. Liquid whirled in my stomach. Pain blistered through my abdomen.

"Dad, *st*—"

My hand flew to my mouth before I could finish my sentence.

Sour fluid rushed from my throat, filling my mouth. My cheeks inflated, almost bursting.

I felt the car pulling to the side of the road in a swift motion. Too swift. Too fast. Vomit burst through my lips, spluttering all across the dashboard. "*Shit*—"

The door swung open.

Next thing I knew I was on my knees; cold, wet concrete beneath my bare legs. There was a hand on my back. Under my arms. Trying to pull me up.

"*...you're okay...*"

Vomit sprayed through my nose, streaming from my throat.

I heard myself roaring like a fucking werewolf. Tears streamed down my face, my body convulsing uncontrollably.

"*...you're okay... you're okay...*"

He kept repeating it, over and over.

His voice felt distant, like I was underwater.

I retched until nothing else came up, my stomach twisting in dry, painful spasms. Even then, my throat rumbled with the effort, like my body was trying to purge itself of *everything*—the whiskey, the repulsion, *all* of it—until there was nothing left.

My hands pressed into the concrete, trembling with the force of the convulsions.

My whole body *burned* as I choked on my own swollen throat.

"*...you've got it...*"

Suddenly the sound of his voice switched something inside of me.

Up until this point, I'd leaned into it—the voice that was more familiar to me than anyone's. The voice that always seemed to be there whenever I threw up uncontrollably, stretching back to when I was a little kid. It was the one and only comfort in that moment.

Then it all came back to me.

Then I remembered.

"…g-g-get *off* me…"

I shoved him away with the little strength I had left in me.

He didn't fight it. I watched through my blurry vision as he recoiled, slumping onto the sidewalk. I tried to wipe my face, smearing tears and vomit across my cheeks.

The air between us was heavy, suffocating. And I couldn't stand it. I couldn't stand *him*.

I hated him.

He was quiet now. I pulled myself together, dragging myself upright with my one arm, the dampness of the concrete soaking into my jeans and cast. It took me a moment to catch my breath.

My *whole body* ached.

As I lifted my head, everything around me seemed to wobble. I wasn't entirely sure what was real. I couldn't make it out.

If he hadn't been sat there on the sidewalk, distancing himself, maybe I could've convinced myself that none of it had been real. I was *so fucking drunk*. I could've made it up. I could've seen it wrong.

But the way he sat there—knees to his chest like a little kid—told me all I needed to know. The look on his face told me everything.

He was *fucking terrified*.

"…I-I need M-*Mom*…" The words stumbled out of me, slurred and shaky, but it was the truest thing I'd said in a long time.

It felt weird, foreign, like those words didn't belong in my mouth. It'd been a long fucking time since I'd said those words out loud. I wondered if I'd ever said them before this moment.

Despite everything, I needed her.

Not just because I felt like I was going to die, but because she needed to know.

She needed to know.

"Hey, come on…" His voice got closer and closer. "Let's just get you home, alright? You've got *me*—"

"I don't *w-want* you…"

He moved closer again, reaching out like he wanted to guide me back to the car. But I could see it in his eyes—the desperation, the fear. Maybe he thought I was too drunk to notice. "*Come on, honey*—"

"I need to t-talk to *Mom*—"

"It's late."

His voice suddenly became firm. Hard. It jolted me, cutting through the haze of alcohol clouding my mind.

For a moment, the nausea, the dizziness, all of it faded into the background as I turned to face him fully. His eyes met mine. The rage that had been simmering inside me, pushed down by the overwhelming sickness, started to bubble back up, hotter and more intense than before.

"You…" I stretched a finger out toward his face, practically poking him. "*You…* are f-fucking *insane…* if you think I'm not t-telling her—"

"You're drunk, Al—"

"*No,*" I began to shout, glaring at him through the tears. "*Don't* do that! I *saw* you!"

His eyes darted around, clearly searching for an escape route. The desperation was clear now. "Al, you need to calm down," he said, his tone now a mix of irritation and pleading. "We'll talk about it in the morning, alright?"

"Well, *I*-I think we need to talk about it *now*—"

"There's nothing to talk about."

The stench of vomit was overpowering. It filled the air around us.

It soaked into my clothes, my hair, even into my cast and sling. I could barely *breathe*, the sour smell mixing with the burning in my throat. The nauseating combination only fueled my anger.

"How… how *old* is she?" I asked suddenly, watching as his face fell. "Officer H-*Hardie*—"

"I don't know what you're talking about."

"No, no… it's just…" A laugh slipped out. "*She…* she can't be much older than *me*, right?"

His eyes flicked nervously toward the road, and I wondered if he knew how much his face was giving away at that moment. And his sudden silence was deafening. The realization that I was more coherent than he'd hoped clearly scared the shit out of him.

A heavy rumble of laughter burst out of me. Once it started, I couldn't stop. It echoed around us as my father's face washed pale white, his eyes widening until they almost popped out of their sockets.

"…you *asshole…*" I hollered, tears streaming down my face.

"…you *fucking ASSHOLE*—"

"I don't know what you think you saw, but—"

"Oh, I *know* what I saw!" I cut him off, grinning manically. "I saw *you* and that… that *slut*—"

"*Don't.*"

It came out so harsh, so cold, that it cut me off immediately.

The laughter died on my lips, replaced by a stunned silence. His command hung in the air. I stared at him, eyes wide with fear and defiance, waiting for the next move in this twisted game.

He shook his head ever so slightly, as if he'd realized what he'd done. He just kept shaking his head, immediately trying to backtrack. "It's not…" he started, his voice faltering as he searched for the right words. His eyes darted around, as if hoping the right explanation would magically appear before him.

Then, a short, sharp sigh escaped his lips; a sound filled with defeat.

"…it's not her fault."

It was weird, because even though I *knew*—more than *anything* in this world—what I saw, I couldn't have anticipated the shock I felt, hearing him actually admit it. Watching him give up.

I thought he would've fought a little longer. I really did.

But there was no denying it now.

This was happening.

"She didn't know, alright?" He just sounded utterly defeated. "She didn't know… that I was married—"

"What the *fuck* are you talking about?!"

"I didn't tell her."

"She's at our house *every day*," I argued, so entirely confused by his words. "How could she *not know* you were married?!"

"She didn't know when it first started."

I just sat there, processing that last sentence.

Trying to make it make sense.

I tried so desperately to piece together the fragments of what he was saying, but it felt like trying to grasp smoke.

"You…" I hesitated, squinting against my thoughts. "*Wait…* this… this started *before*…"

The pale light from the street lamps cast harsh shadows onto his face, making him look even smaller, even more broken. I could see it now: the way his shoulders slumped and his gaze dropped to the pavement, unable to meet mine.

I hated him more than I ever thought I could.

"I didn't want you to find out like this…" I heard him saying, and I started laughing again. I wasn't sure why. There was nothing funny about this—not a goddamn thing.

"Yeah, no *shit*," I spat out, the words laced with venom. "As if there's not enough… enough *shit* going on right now without you shacking up with *D-Detective B-Barbie*—"

"It's not her fault," he repeated, as if that would, somehow, make everything all good. *Unbelievable*.

"Yeah, well, *Mom* can be the judge of that—"

"You can't tell her." The words shot out like bullets. He somehow found the nerve to glare at me, like *I* was the problem here. Like *I* was the one that had fucked up. "Y-you can't tell her—"

"Oh, *can't I*?!"

The realization hit me like a jolt of electricity. For the first time in what felt like forever, *I* had control. All the chaos, all the lies, all the secrets—*none* of it had been in my hands until now. And I didn't want it. I didn't want any of this, but there was a small part of me that felt fucking *good* knowing that for once—for *one goddamn time*—I wasn't the one who'd fucked up.

"It's over!" He began scrambling over his words, his voice shaking as he tried to piece together something, anything, that might stop me. "It's been over for a long time—"

"*THAT* was *over*?!" I screeched, my voice reaching an octave that I hadn't known I could reach before. "*That* did *not* look "*over*"!"

He groaned, covering his face with his hands.

"*That* shouldn't have happened," he continued, frustration bubbling over. "And I'm *sorry*… I'm so, *so* sorry that you saw it, and I'm *so* sorry that it happened. It *is* over."

"When did it *start*?!"

Dad hesitated, his hands trembling as they rubbed his temples. Summoning the courage to say what we both knew would only blow the situation so much wider. "Last summer," he said finally, causing my jaw to drop. "Last August—"

"*Last AUGUST*?!"

Over a year.

He'd been fucking the badge-wearing bimbo for over a *year*.

"But it's *over*," he repeated once more, but the word was slowly losing all meaning. "It's been over for a... a while—"

"Since *when*?!"

"Since..." He stopped, shaking his head. "Look, we can talk about this another time, alright? Can we please—"

"*Oh*, no—we're talking about it *now*!"

"Please just get in the car—"

"*When did you end it*?!"

His hands were still trembling, and the look in his eyes was one I'd never seen before—defeated, desperate, like he was standing on the edge of a cliff. There was no way out of it, and he knew it.

His lips quivered as he fought to find the words. "...the night before..."

I barely heard him.

His voice was so low I could barely make it out.

"...the... *the night before Brooke went missing*..."

My brain flipped a hundred times over before I could make sense of that sentence.

Between the drinking and the shock, I just couldn't work it out right away. It didn't make sense. It wasn't clicking. My eyebrows fused together as I went through it in my head, over and over.

"You..." The word hung in the air as my mind raced to catch up. The pieces were there, scattered and jagged, but fitting them together felt impossible. "...but... I don't understand—"

"Please can we just—"

"How were you with her that night? You were home... you were with Brooke, in the house," I said, running through what I thought I already knew in my mind. "Did you bring *her* to the house? While Mom was out? Was *she* in *our* house?!"

He shook his head, confusing me further.

"But... you were with *Brooke*, in the house," I repeated, staring at him as he shifted uncomfortably. "You were *home* that night. You... you were with *Brooke*."

He barely lifted his head. "I was gone less than four hours."

The penny dropped.

A cold, heavy dread began to unfurl in the pit of my belly. It started as a small, gnawing discomfort, a sensation that made it hard to breathe. As the full weight of his admission settled in, that gnawing twisted into something far more intense.

It spread through my core, igniting with each breath I took, the heat pooling and swelling inside me.

It wasn't just anger.

It was *so much more* than anger.

"You *left* her?" The words spilled from my lips as the flames in my gut grew wilder. "You… you *lied*? You *weren't THERE*?!"

Dad's reaction was immediate and complete. His face drained of color, his features slackening into a mask of numbness.

"You left her in the house alone so you could go…" My words broke into gasps. "…go and see *her*?! *You left Brooke to be with HER*?!"

"I was gone less than four hou—"

"*FUCK YOU*!" The words ripped from my throat with a raw, guttural intensity. "*FUCK YOU—*"

"*Stop* yelling," he snapped suddenly, his voice cutting through the air like a blade. The command was almost absurd in its detachment, as if he could still assert some semblance of control despite what he had just said. What he had just admitted.

"You have *no idea* what happened to her, do you?!" I yelled. "You have *no idea* because *you WEREN'T THERE*!"

"She was *in the house*," he started shouting back, his voice rising in panic. "She was *fine*! I left her alone for *four hours*… sh-she's *fifteen*!"

"*Someone could've TAKEN her*! *Someone could've done something to her, and YOU WEREN'T THERE—*"

"*YOU THINK I DON'T KNOW THAT*?!"

The sudden eruption in his voice caught me off guard. The volume, the intensity—it wasn't like anything I had ever heard from him in my entire life. For a moment, I was paralyzed; the deep, raw anger in his voice was so foreign. It was a depth of rage I had never known existed within him.

But then something came to me.

It hit me, paralyzing me further.

"Did she know?"

His face very quickly softened over the seconds that passed, even before I'd asked that question. It was as if he was attempting to cool the flames before they spread further.

When I asked him that, a slight glint appeared in his eyes. It was like something lit up inside his brain.

"What?" His voice dropped to a confused whisper.

"Did *Brooke* know? About... *this*? About..." The words trailed off, but there was no doubt that he knew what I meant.

He knew what I was saying.

His eyes flickered manically. He hadn't said a word, yet somehow, I already knew his answer. My heart stopped as I worked it out.

"She fucking *knew*..."

The words came out in a sharp, incredulous whisper. Somehow, this information cut deeper than *anything* I'd felt before.

If I hadn't known what betrayal felt like before that moment, I knew then. I knew better than ever.

Dad's face was a mask of despair now. "Al, please—"

"When did she find out?"

The thought of her knowing sent shockwaves throughout my entire body. The thought of her lying to me, lying to *Mom*— covering up Dad's dirty little secret and not saying a fucking word to *anyone*.

How *dare* she?

"She was grounded... Mom was away..." I pieced it together, speaking my thought process out loud. "You wanted to see... *her*... so, what, did you make some sort of pact, or whatever? So Brooke could go to the party, and you could see your fucking *girlfriend*—"

"She never said anything about a party—"

"*ANSWER THE FUCKING QUESTION!*"

"She found out a while back, alright?!" His words were laced with frustration. "I can't remember when, but... I-I didn't tell her where I was going that night. I *didn't*. But I... I think she knew. I don't know, Al."

It had been so long since I'd thought of Brooke without an overwhelming sense of sadness and grief.

All of that torment had dissolved within an instant, replaced by a searing bitterness. She was in on it the *whole goddamn time*. I couldn't believe she did it. I couldn't believe she *could* do it.

She didn't say a fucking word.

"It's not her fault, Al," Dad said suddenly, clearly aware of my thought process. I scoffed loudly.

"Well, I guess it's no one's fault!" I spat, my voice dripping with sarcasm. "Not *hers*, not *Nancy Drew's*—everyone gets a free fucking pass, right?!"

"It's *my* fault. This is on *me*."

"Yeah, well, I can't blame you for telling Brooke," I chuckled, the bitterness spilling over every word. "I mean, if *anyone* can keep a secret—"

"I made her promise not to say anything," he interrupted, getting all defensive all of a sudden. "And I *shouldn't* have. It wasn't fair of me to do that to her—"

"And what about *me*, huh?!" I demanded, the anger boiling over into a raw, accusing yell. "You gonna feel bad about making *me* lie to Mom too?!"

"That's different—"

"You're *damn straight* it's different!" The pure, unfiltered rage in my voice cut straight through the air. "Because I'm *not* Brooke! *God*... just... who would've *ever* thought that the perfect goddamn *golden child* would turn out to be such a good *goddamn LIAR*?! But, hey—*I'm* the screw-up! *I'm* the *fucking disappointment*!"

Dad's face twisted in confusion.

"You're not a disappointment," he began to say but I wasn't interested in his sudden words of compassion.

These thoughts had been simmering in my mind for too long, and now they were pouring out uncontrollably.

"She's a *dirty fucking liar*, just like *you*!" I shouted. "And I can guarantee that *no matter what—some-FUCKING-how*—even *THIS* will get turned on *me*! I *guarantee* this will *somehow, some* way, *become MY PROBLEM*! *Just like EVERYTHING ELSE*!"

Dad's eyes widened in devastation, but I couldn't stop.

The floodgates had opened.

"Look at my fucking *arm*," I yelled, thrusting my casted wrist in front of his face. "My *face*, my *skin*—people want *me DEAD*! No matter what *she* does, it's *always MY fault*, right?! *Donnie* gets arrested, *you* have an affair—Brooke lies about *everything*—and *I take the hits*! *I PAY THE PRICE—EVERY FUCKING TIME*!"

My breaths came out in ragged sobs. Tears streamed down my face, hot and relentless.

I instantly knocked Dad's hand away the second it touched my shoulder. Despite his attempts to reach out, his words caught in his throat. He didn't say a word.

"I-I'm *done*," I said, my voice trembling but firm. "I'm *done—*"

"Al—"

"*I want to go home.*"

With that, I began pulling myself up, gripping the car door with my unbroken arm. A gasp escaped as pain flashed through my ribs, momentarily winding me.

Dad began moving behind me, reaching out to help me up. I shoved him away again.

I didn't want him *anywhere* near me.

His keys jingled as he shakily rummaged through his pockets, watching me climb back into the car. I slammed the door shut with a force that left my hand throbbing. Everything stunk of vomit. The wetness seeped into my clothes as I slouched back into position, staring straight through the windscreen.

It took him a couple of seconds to make his way to the other side of the car, climbing into the driver's side. As his door shut, we were plunged into complete darkness once again.

He didn't put the keys into the ignition right away.

"*...please don't tell your mother...*"

A jagged guffaw escaped me, the sound harsh and raw. But I didn't have the energy to fight anymore.

I couldn't bring myself to say anything else.

Dad's silence was his only response; a painful acknowledgment of how deep his desperation ran. I could sense the cold, hollow emptiness of his regret, but it was too little, too late. I couldn't feel anything anymore.

And then, out of the darkness, his voice came again, soft but insistent: "*...you're not a disappointment.*"

Despite the numbness that had flooded my whole body, a final tear slid down my cheek.

He jammed the keys into the ignition. The engine roared.

We drove home in stifling silence; the only sounds were the steady hum of the engine and the occasional *whoosh* of passing traffic. I stared out into the black space. In the window's reflection, I watched as the streetlights cast fleeting shadows across my father's face, highlighting deep lines and a rigid jaw.

I thought about Brooke. I wondered if she'd thought his face had changed too, when she found out.

I didn't want to hate her. Really. I didn't.

It was just getting harder not to.

19 DAYS AFTER THE DISAPPEARANCE OF
BROOKLYN NICHOLSON

FITZ | 4:51 PM

I pulled up just outside the house, just as I had done hundreds of times before. Thousands of times, even. My usual spot was still empty as if it had been kept open for me.

I pulled up, switched the engine off, and my eyes were immediately drawn to the Benz, still sitting in the driveway like a ghost. The white paint gleamed faintly under the pale autumn sunlight. I figured it hadn't been touched in around three weeks. It surprised me somehow, seeing it. I guess part of me figured they would've moved it.

Just seeing it there—parked up in the driveway, like nothing had changed—made it feel like she was home.

My fingers rasped against my steering wheel as I tried to pull myself together. The air felt thicker than usual, heavy with the kind of silence that wraps around you and makes it hard to breathe. Nothing about this felt right. None of it.

I had to force myself to move. If I'd thought about it any longer, I would've ended up driving away.

I stepped out, the crunch of gravel underfoot sounding louder than it should have. I could almost hear her voice in the back of my mind, as if she might appear around the corner. I'd half expected it. I'd never made it this far up the driveway before without her opening the door for me, calling me in.

I had to keep reminding myself that we had broken up.

It was as if I'd created this whole scenario in my head that we had been together when she died, and we were happy.

But we weren't.

I hesitated before the door, my hand hovering over the handle. The house looked the same as I remembered: white siding, neat garden, everything in its place. But it was wrong. All wrong. I felt that strange but all-too-familiar knot in my chest as I stared at the door in front of me.

I forced myself to rasp my knuckles against the door. Every fiber of my being wanted to bolt immediately. I did *not* want to be there.

Too late.

There was a rustling on the other side of the door. My heart picked up speed, following the repeated sounds of movement coming from inside the house. It just all felt so absurdly formal. I'd *never* knocked before. I'd never had to.

The door opened up. Tanya MacKenzie was standing there, and the whole world seemed to whirl around us.

I hadn't seen her since the funeral.

Her face remained hard at first, as if I was a complete stranger. Then, within milliseconds, a smile stretched across her face. A *real* one. I'd anticipated a hundred different reactions from her, and this hadn't been one of them.

"Fitz?!" She immediately pulled me in for a hug, her huge jugs squishing against my chest. The brief distraction was more than welcomed. "Oh, my *goodness...*"

Her embrace was warm, but it felt like it belonged to someone else. I hadn't expected this, and I wasn't entirely sure how to react.

I just stood there, momentarily frozen, trying to reconcile the image of Tanya MacKenzie I'd held in my mind with the reality of her standing before me.

I couldn't remember the last time I'd seen her not crying.

When she finally pulled back, her eyes were full of sadness and relief, like she had been waiting for someone to come by but hadn't expected it to be me. Her hands lingered on my shoulders. "How are you?!" she asked.

I laughed awkwardly, sliding my hands into my pockets. Using all my strength not to freak out. "Ah, you know…" My voice wandered off as I struggled to find the words. "I'm, uh… I'm… it's good to see you, Tanya."

She smiled, widening the door. "Come on in!"

I *really* didn't want to.

She practically pulled me inside. The second my shoes touched the cream carpet beneath me, I felt the world crumble around me. My gaze immediately shot toward the staircase. I couldn't help it. It was automatic.

I stared at the staircase, unable to break away from it.

"I've made some cookies," I heard her saying, but her voice was all distorted. "Come, have some…"

I finally managed to pull myself out of it, just enough to bring myself back to reality. I followed her through the house, feeling as if I was walking on the moon. Nothing felt real. Everything was moving.

And there were so many flowers.

So many flowers.

They filled up every available surface; vases overflowing, bouquets in every corner. The hallway was awash in a sea of colors and scents. The whole fucking house had become a shrine. A memorial.

"…I've been baking a lot," Tanya continued. I was unsure how much of the conversation I'd missed while scanning my surroundings. "You know, just… keeping myself busy… I made some apple pie yesterday…"

Suddenly, we were in the kitchen, and there was a plate of chocolate chip cookies under my nose. She held the plate with both hands, waving it into my face.

I wasn't hungry. I didn't want one.

I took one anyway.

"They look amazing," I forced myself to say as I broke it into two. I took a small nibble, unable to taste it. Crumbs fell all over my shirt.

"I was hoping you'd come over," she said, placing the plate down on the counter. "It's been weird, not seeing you around the house anymore. I've missed having you around."

It suddenly hit me—now that I was seeing her properly—how good she looked. She looked fucking amazing.

I mean, Tanya MacKenzie *always* looked amazing.

I never would've told Mel, obviously, but I'd find myself staring at her mother for *hours* whenever I stayed over. She was just like Mel... but with curves. And they were *all* in the right places. Even now, she was wearing this tight little dress that clung to her body.

She looked fucking *awesome*.

"Yeah, I-I've missed being here," I mumbled, turning my attention elsewhere. "Sorry I didn't come over sooner."

"Oh, *sweetie*..." She came back over, giving me another tight hug. For the first time in two weeks, I forced myself to think about Mel. When that didn't work, I thought about my grandma. "I don't blame you at *all*. This must be *so hard* for you."

"Yeah."

As Tanya stepped back, she looked at me with concern. "How have you been holding up? And don't give me any of that "*I'm fine*" crap..." I chuckled slightly, looking down at the floor. My heartbeat picked up speed as I remembered where I was. And why I was there.

"I'm getting through it," I said semi-truthfully. "It's been a weird couple weeks, you know?"

"You could say that."

The cookie began to melt in my hand. Brown goo spread across my fingers. I quickly slid both halves into the trash when she was looking away, wiping the melted chocolate and crumbs against my jeans. She leaned against the counter, turning back toward me. Her smile was slowly disappearing.

"I'm so sorry about everything that happened with the police," she said finally, shaking her head. "I told them you wouldn't have... you know..." She paused, taking a breath. "...I *know* you wouldn't have done that to her."

I cleared my throat, looking away. "They were just doing their job."

Her face hardened suddenly, as if she'd remembered something. "Well, at least they've got him now," she said coldly. "Donnie Booker."

I knew better than to say what I wanted to say.

"And what he did to your friends..." she went on, her voice tightening with anger and sadness. "I can't even *begin* to understand how someone could do that. *Any* of it."

I wanted to ask her what really happened.

It had been playing on my mind for three weeks. I kept telling myself that I didn't want to know the details, but at this point, I knew whatever had gone down couldn't be any worse than the shit I was conjuring up in my head. And there were so many rumors. So many *fucked up* rumors.

I thought about asking her. Figured it would've given me some sort of comfort to know exactly how it happened.

But I knew I couldn't. It wasn't fair.

"Are you still close with Allie Nicholson?" she asked suddenly, catching me off guard. The question made me flinch, and more images flashed through my mind—Allie at the bar, screaming at me, her eyes wild with anger.

"Uh, yeah," I said quietly, rubbing my neck. "I saw her yesterday, actually."

Tanya's face softened a little, but there was a lingering sadness in her eyes. "I can't imagine what her family is going through," she said. "It's been hard enough for us, but, well... I *know* where my daughter is. It must be unbearable... and Allie, with everything she's been through. It's just awful. *Disgusting.*"

I wondered if she knew how much Mel had hated Allie.

I wasn't even sure *why* she hated her so much, but Allie didn't like her either. They had serious issues with each other, and it always made things super awkward whenever I brought Mel to hang out.

And it was weird because Mel had *never* had an issue with Mandy... who was, you know, technically my ex. Maybe she never saw Mandy as a threat because she was always with Hurley.

But she had *always* seen Allie as a threat, from day one.

It was so weird.

"It's crazy," I said, unsure of what else I was supposed to say. It didn't feel right, talking to Mel's mother about someone that Mel didn't like. She couldn't have known anything about it—she wouldn't have brought her up otherwise, surely.

"I remember her sister," she went on, smiling slightly. "Brooklyn. Such a small, *skinny* little thing... she didn't look old enough to be a Meteorite."

"Mm-hm."

Tanya sighed and glanced around the kitchen, her gaze landing on a framed photo of Mel up on the wall. I hadn't noticed it before this moment, but now it was staring me right in the face. I locked eyes with her. My stomach turned. "It's been hard to keep up with everything that's happening," she said as I struggled to break eye contact with Mel's photograph. "I've tried to stay strong for the sake of... well, everyone. But it's not easy. Sometimes, it feels like we're just going through the motions."

"I get that," I said softly, crossing my arms awkwardly. "It's hard to know what to do or say when everything's so... messed up."

There was a pause. Tanya turned to me, her expression laced with a hint of curiosity. "How come you decided to come here today?" she asked. My blood ran cold. "Surely you didn't want to waste your day talking to an old lady..."

"*Old?*"

I laughed loudly, quickly trying to reel it back in. She knew *exactly* what she was doing; she'd pulled her arms together slightly over her chest, emphasizing her cleavage.

Her *perfect* fucking cleavage.

I quickly glanced back to Mel's photograph. It was as if her frozen smile had slipped into a slight grimace.

"No, I, uh..." I paused, wishing I didn't have to say it. Wishing I didn't have to do it. "I don't know if this is weird, or whatever, but... I-I was wondering if I could go up and see her room, maybe? If that's okay."

Tanya's face softened. She took a deep breath and nodded, though a trace of sadness lingered in her eyes. "Of course you can, Fitz."

Part of me wished she would've said that I couldn't.

I genuinely wished, more than anything, that I didn't have to go in there. The thought of it made me want to throw up. My pulse quickened further as I realized that there was no backing out now.

"Great," I said, forcing a smile despite the rising tension in my chest. "Uh... thank you, Tanya."

She gave a small, encouraging nod before leaning forward and squeezing my shoulder. "I'll be in here if you need anything," she said, her voice gentle. "You take your time."

No backing out.

She gestured toward the door, and I walked out.

Each and every footstep felt like it echoed through the house, amplifying the unease that was growing inside me. I didn't want to do it. I did *not* want to do it.

More than anything, I didn't want to see the staircase.

As I made my way around the corner—my senses flooded with overpoweringly floral scents—I locked onto the stairs. As I got closer, it hit me that the cream carpet covered not just the hallway floor, but it covered the staircase too. It went all the way up.

See, the only thing I knew for certain about Mel's murder was that it happened on the staircase. That was the only thing I knew.

And it was all I could think about.

I forced one foot onto the first step. Then the other. The carpet beneath my feet felt unnervingly soft, muffling my footsteps but doing nothing to ease the pounding in my chest. My breaths came in shallow bursts as a disordered churn of fragmented images flooded my thoughts. The stairs seemed to stretch infinitely, each step feeling heavier than the last.

I gripped the wooden railing, my knuckles turning white as I pulled myself up.

When I reached the top steps, I froze. A strong scent of bleach filled my nostrils, and at first, I didn't see it. Maybe I wouldn't have seen it if I hadn't been looking for it.

There was a light pink stain across the final three steps.

It was faint—mostly bleached away—but unmistakably there.

I almost stumbled backward at the sight of it, losing my footing on the fourth-from-last step.

I could see Tanya MacKenzie on her hands and knees, scrubbing away the final remnants of her daughter. But she couldn't get rid of all of it. Mel's final moments clung to the fibers of the carpet, refusing to be erased, as if they were embedded in the very fabric of the house.

My hand gripped the banister tightly, knuckles white as I tried to steady myself.

I couldn't turn back.

I *couldn't*.

My right foot found its way onto the third-from-last step, stepping directly onto the pink stain. I pulled my left foot up onto the second-from-last step.

With one final push, I made it to the top.

The door to Mel's room loomed ahead, a dark silhouette against the pale walls of the hallway. I stood there for a moment, my chest heaving. I took a step forward, each movement still feeling like a struggle against an invisible force.

My hand trembled slightly as I reached for the door handle, the cool metal sending a shiver up my spine. I hesitated again, my mind racing with what-ifs and dark thoughts. The fear was fucking paralyzing.

I turned the handle.

The door slowly swung open, revealing a space that I had long become familiar with over the past year.

The room itself was dimly lit—the curtains drawn tight against the sunlight. I shakily switched the light on, watching as the room lit up into pink and white. Her bed was neatly made, adorned with a quilt patterned in pastel shades. A small, stuffed teddy bear sat perched on one of the pillows, its button eyes staring blankly out at the room. Her New Kids on the Block poster was still hanging on the wall, its edges frayed and curling slightly.

There were all these tiny details that I'd never cared to notice before, but now they seemed to pulse with a haunting familiarity.

I slowly waded over to her bed, picking up the picture frame on the bedside table; it was the one of us at prom. I'd hated it at that time… and, being honest, I still wasn't a fan of the picture; I looked like a fucking idiot, covered in blue frills to match her dress. The guys didn't let it go for *weeks*. It wasn't even Mel's prom—I had to sneak her in, with her being a junior from St. Mary's and all—but she still made damn sure I was wearing what she wanted me to wear.

I looked like a fucking *pompom*.

And she made me take off my Prom King crown for the picture. I still couldn't figure out how I'd won, you know—I still figured it was a prank gone wrong. Freddie must've rigged the votes, or something. All I could see, on that stage, was Mel's face in the crowd, absolutely *livid* that I had to stand there and take pictures with Michelle Taylor.

A sudden wave of guilt came crashing over me. I should've been thinking about all the good times. But instead, all I could focus on were the awkward photos and the fights we'd had over the dumbest things.

I tried to remember the good times.

For a moment, I wasn't sure we'd even had any.

I suppose it was good in the beginning. When we first met, I mean. The first time she came over to talk to me, I thought it was a prank—she was a fucking cheerleader, you know? We didn't hang with those crowds.

It was the first Friday of senior year, just after Grandpa had installed the home gym and I'd lost all my puppy weight over the summer. It was the first game of the season—M. High versus St. Mary's—and me and the guys were under the bleachers, not giving a shit about the score.

When Melissa MacKenzie, of all people, came skipping over to us at half-time, it felt like a fucking setup. She just stood there, twirling her ponytail and pompoms, acting like hanging out with the "bad kids" was normal for her.

I said I'd take her out, and she said she wanted to go see a movie. I picked her up the next day. She made me watch *Sleepless in Seattle.*

We got along back then, you know? And this was before we even started sleeping together. We just used to go for rides in my car, picking up food from the drive-thru. We laughed a lot, in the beginning. We had fun together.

I lay back on her bed, putting the photo frame back on the table.

I stared up at the ceiling, remembering every night I'd slept there. I remembered the sound of her laughter, the way she'd curl up against me under the covers, the warmth of her body on mine.

Tears blurred my vision as I thought about how I'd fucked her over. She could be a world-class bitch at times—99% of the time—but I shouldn't have done what I did, either. I'd slept with half the Meteorites before winter break, for Christ's sake. I could've just ended things with her. I could've just admitted that we weren't working out instead of letting it drag on as long as it did. She'd wasted the last few months of her life with me.

The last time I saw her, she asked if I loved her. And I couldn't even say it.

She didn't deserve that.

As the weight of the guilt pressed down on me, the tears came harder. But it wasn't just Mel. Hurley and Mandy's faces flooded my mind, and I could barely breathe through the sobs.

Mandy was my first girlfriend. She was the first girl I ever loved... or, at least, whatever I thought "love" was in the eighth grade. And then she was my friend. A *good* friend. She'd been there for me throughout everything, no matter what stupid shit I did.

And Hurley was my boy. I'd never known life without him, not until now. I was the last face he ever saw, and I couldn't save him. I couldn't stop it.

I couldn't stop it.

Just like that, I was drowning. My chest heaved with each sob, my body shaking with the intensity of my emotions.

And then I thought about Allie.

My best friend.

She was the one person I cared about more than *anything*. She almost didn't make it, and I could not bring myself to think about how it would've felt to lose her. I *hated* that we didn't see each other anymore. I hated that I'd walked out on her at the bar.

I hated that I was lying in Mel's bed, suddenly sobbing uncontrollably over *Allie*... mostly because, well, I knew she would've hated that too. Mel, I mean.

I just lay there for a while, feeling the full force of the grief that had been building inside me, knowing that no matter how hard I cried, it wouldn't change what had happened. *It wouldn't bring them back*. It wouldn't make *any* of it right.

That was when I felt it.

I sat up slowly, patting down the pillowcase that I had been lying on. It made a crinkling sound as I touched it. I pulled the pillow from beneath me, sliding my hand inside the fabric.

There was something in there. Paper.

I hesitated, telling myself that there was no way it could be what I thought it was.

I pulled it out.

I stared at it for a moment, unable to fully comprehend what I was seeing. Not believing it.

It was an envelope.

Mel's name was scribbled on the front. I shakily turned it over; there was a small drawing of an apple on the crease. It had been torn open. The letter was still inside. I shakily pulled it out as Allie's face once again flooded my thoughts.

The paper was slightly wrinkled. I unfolded it, mouthing the words as I read each line:

Melissa, Melissa; Mirrenville's heir.
A princess in pink with flowing blonde hair.
Beneath the stars, where whispers creep,
Our whispers should lie in shadows deep.

I paused, almost too scared to continue. My hands began to shake so hard that the letter almost fell out of them.

But I kept going.

So take this warning, softly spoken:
Promise your silence will never be broken.

The weight of the letter in my hand felt heavier as I reached the final lines:

Hold the truth from those who pry,
Or hold your silence up in the sky.

She was right.

Al was right.

The realization hit me like a punch to the gut. If she was right about this, she had to be right about everything else. They saw something at the party—Allie, Hurley, Mandy, *Mel.*

Allie was fucking right.

I remembered the last time I saw Mel. In the garage, after the party. She said she was going to the police station.

She was going to tell them about what she saw.

She was going to tell them about the letter.

I clutched the paper tightly as fear and determination surged through my veins, burning like fire. I had to move. I had to see her. Allie. I *had* to see her.

I had to show her the letter.

Everything moved fast after that. I jumped from the bed, running out of the room. Running down the stairs. I ran to the kitchen, quickly crumpling the letter into my pocket before I got there.

I stopped outside the door, smoothing down my shirt. Wiping my face. Taking a deep breath.

I pushed the door open and ran in, preparing myself to calmly say goodbye before speeding to Al's place. Tanya was turned away from me, facing the corner of the room. I couldn't see her face at first.

"Tanya…"

As I moved closer, I realized what she was doing. I could hear it. She was staring at the radio. It was turned on, but it wasn't playing music.

"What's up?" I asked, but she held a hand up, silencing me. She slowly turned to face me with wide, glassy eyes. The look on her face scared the shit out of me. "Tanya, what—"

"*…has been rushed to the hospital… suicide attempt…*" a voice on the radio announced. I could barely make it out through the speakers. "*…close sources have confirmed that she… critical condition and fighting for… life…*"

A muffled gasp came from Tanya's mouth.

I followed her gaze toward the radio, confused. Trying to figure out what celebrity they were talking about this time.

"*…details are still emerging… sources indicate that… unresponsive… earlier today…*"

"Who are they talking about?" I asked, half-intrigued. The last time I'd heard anything like this was when the news broke about Kurt Cobain earlier in the year.

My mind was still on the letter, though, so I wasn't keen on wasting too much time on whatever this was. I had to get going.

The radio kept playing.

"*...our thoughts are... Frankie Fl... Elizabeth Nichol... at this time...*"

I froze.

"*...losing... two daughters...*"

No.

I stared at the radio.

The news anchor's voice continued, droning on about the details that now seemed irrelevant. But I barely heard any of it. All the words were now blurring into one.

Tanya reached out, putting a hand on my shoulder. "Fitz," I barely heard her saying, "I can't—"

I didn't wait for her to finish.

Suddenly I was out in the front yard, running to my car. My hands fumbled for my keys as I moved. I dropped them twice.

I couldn't get them in the door.

Couldn't get the goddamn keys to *work*.

Then I was in the car. I gunned it out of the driveway, tires screeching against the pavement. The world outside the windshield became a blur of streetlights and passing cars.

Sweat glided between my palms and the steering wheel. All I could do was drive.

I wasn't even sure where I was going.

I couldn't think.

I just

I couldn't lose her too.

ADJACENT

22 DAYS AFTER THE DISAPPEARANCE OF
BROOKLYN NICHOLSON

FRANK | 7:58 AM

We hadn't spoken in days. Me and Vic.

It'd been just the three of us for almost 72 hours: me, Vic, and Liz. Liz had done most of the talking, and even she had barely said a word during that period. Whenever we sat together—in the waiting room, in the cafeteria, in the hospital room—Liz made sure she sat between us, taking turns to make conversation with me and her sister individually. She'd tried to open the conversations up, getting us all to talk together, but it wasn't working. Mainly due to Vic.

She couldn't even bring herself to look at me. It'd been almost a week, and nothing had changed.

When Liz left to pick up some coffee, it was the first time that we'd been left alone together. I'd offered to go get the coffee, as I had every other time, but Liz insisted that she wanted to do it. She'd been there the longest out of the three of us; just sitting around, waiting for news, staring at the same gray walls for almost three days straight. Aside from bathroom breaks, she'd only left twice during this time, and both times she came back smelling of cigarette smoke. She hadn't smoked since 1968. I figured Vic had been giving them to her.

I'd thought about asking for one myself, but something told me that Vic wasn't about to go out of her way to do me any more favors.

This time, when Liz left to get coffee, the silence between me and Vic seemed to stretch on into eternity. We barely even glanced in each other's direction, despite sitting directly opposite each other. In the tiny, borderline claustrophobic waiting room, it felt like all we could do was breathe each other's air. The only sounds were the distant hum of hospital machines and the occasional footsteps out in the hallway.

I could feel Vic's eyes on me sometimes; quick, sharp glances that lasted less than a second. I pretended not to notice. It was easier that way.

The tension was unbearable. I wanted to say something, anything, just to break the suffocating quiet between us. I was on the verge of opening my mouth, about to mutter something about needing the bathroom, when the waiting room door swung open.

But it wasn't Liz. It was Dr. Longden.

We both immediately straightened up, pulling ourselves out of the slumped, practically vertical positions that we had gradually collapsed into over time. Dr. Longden stepped into the room, clipboard in hand, shutting the door behind him.

I licked my lips, attempting to create some form of moisture in my dry, cracked mouth. "Liz just went to get coffee." My voice cracked as I said my first words in almost five hours. "She'll be back—"

"It's no problem, Mr. Nicholson." Dr. Longden's voice was calm, yet there was an underlying tension in his demeanor. He glanced at the clipboard, then came back at us with a practiced, reassuring smile. "I just wanted to let you know that visiting hours will be starting soon. Have you been waiting here all night?"

For the first 24 hours, we'd spent almost every second in the room with her. Neither me nor Liz left her side the entire time, minus bathroom breaks. Vic came and went frequently, switching shifts with Malcolm every few hours to take care of Cam. Liz's parents were en route from Portland. They were expected to arrive in Mirrenville at any moment.

Despite now being unable to see our daughter outside of visiting hours, we never left the hospital.

We'd set up camp in the waiting room, creating make-shift beds out of pushed-together chairs and our own coats. I had become too familiar with the building itself at this point—after all, this was the third time my daughter had been admitted in 3 weeks.

But this time was different.

In my sleep-deprived state, I was strung up on the thought of my in-laws taking Cam without bringing him to say goodbye. I knew they wouldn't, but it was on my mind. We hadn't seen him in days. I had to see him before he left. I wasn't sure when we'd get to see him next.

But I knew it was the right decision, no matter how much it hurt.

No matter how much I didn't want him to leave.

"How is she doing?" I heard Vic asking, breaking her silence. Dr. Longden sat on a chair just across from us, placing his clipboard on his lap. I hated the way that these doctors would just sit down without saying a word. Every second of silence felt like an eternity.

And every time, it felt like bad news was coming.

Every time.

"She's been stable throughout the night," he finally revealed. A long exhale burst from my lungs. "The immediate danger has passed, but we're concerned about her liver and kidneys. The treatment has helped stabilize her, but we need to monitor her closely for any signs of further complications."

"Is she awake?" I asked, each word tinged with both hope and anxiety. He nodded slowly.

"Yes, but she is very weak," he added. "And disorientated. She's not out of the woods yet."

But for me, those words barely registered.

She was awake.

Relief washed over me in a cool, fresh wave. The whole room seemed to brighten with his words. I cannot describe the pure, unfiltered euphoria I experienced in that moment.

Dr. Longden continued, sensing our need for further clarity. "When a patient comes out of a medically induced coma, their body needs to adjust to the transition. It's a gradual process... like waking up from a deep, deep sleep. She's going to need a lot of rest to recover."

"Can we see her?" My voice was filled with urgency. Desperation. I watched as Vic sat forward slightly, equally anticipating his answer. When he nodded, my heart exploded.

"Keep the visit brief," he replied in a warning tone. "And do *not* overwhelm her. Be gentle. Calm."

I wanted, more than anything, to replace the image of the last time I saw her in my mind.

For the past 72 hours she had been hooked up to a labyrinth of tubes and wires; a thick, long breathing tube had been shoved down her throat, assisting her labored breaths. She was so pale. So small. It was a mental image that I wasn't sure I'd ever be able to shake.

I just needed to see her awake.

I needed to see her eyes open.

"What did you say about her liver? And kidneys?" Vic continued to ask as I began collecting my belongings from the seat next to me. "What does that mean?"

"Her kidneys have taken a significant hit," Dr. Longden began, trying to explain clearly. "When they're damaged, they can't do their job, leading to possible fluid buildup and waste accumulation... if they don't improve, we may have to consider dialysis—"

The technical details, the medical jargon—they all blurred into the background.

I tried to absorb the information. I really did. But my thoughts kept circling back to what he had said just before that. She was *awake*. She was *okay*.

I needed to see her, to be by her side. The urgency of that need overshadowed everything else in the moment.

I just had to see her.

Before I knew what I was doing, I was pulling myself out of my seat. I made my way toward the door, opening it up.

The ward seemed just a little brighter than it had a few hours prior. My head spun left, facing the direction of her room. I could see the doorway from where I stood. As I began picking up my pace, I noticed Liz standing by the nurses' station, a cardboard tray of coffee in her hands. She was smiling.

They must've already told her.

I began walking faster, my steps quickening with each beat of my heart. My excitement was overwhelming; a tidal wave of relief and joy jolted me forward. I needed to share this moment with Liz.

I wanted *nothing* more than to share this with her—the only other person in this world who felt what I felt.

But as I got closer, my steps slowed.

I saw the blue uniforms first. Then the backs of their heads; one bald, one short and blonde. I recognized the second head almost instantly.

My whole body froze.

"Frank!"

Liz's eyes locked onto mine. She began beckoning me over, smiling genuinely for the first time in forever. My feet had sunk into the floor, holding me in place.

Both officers turned to face me, and I sunk even further. Lucy's eyes met mine.

"Have you heard?" Liz asked as she ran over to me, wrapping her arms around me. I loosely hugged her back. "She's *awake!*"

I couldn't pull my eyes off Lucy.

"She's *awake*, Frank…" Liz pulled back, placing her hands on my cheeks. I forced a smile back. I could feel the tremor in her touch, the palpable relief that mirrored my own. I just wished I could fully lose myself in it.

Frustration built up inside me as the moment—what should've been one of the happiest moments of my life—was instantly tainted.

Liz's arms wrapped around my neck once more, and I pulled her in, trying to let myself take it in. Trying to embrace it. As I glanced back to Lucy, her gaze had dropped. Her whole demeanor switched as she began to shrink in size, almost cowering. I initially assumed it was the awkwardness of seeing me and Liz together.

But then I felt another presence looming behind me.

I turned to see Vic, her face a mask of tense frustration. Liz had just pulled away, rushing into her sister's arms, but Vic's eyes were locked onto Lucy with a cold, piercing stare.

Liz, entirely oblivious to the situation unfolding before her, clung to her sister. "...*she's awake*..." I heard her mumbling.

Vic continued to stare daggers into Lucy, who was desperately attempting to look anywhere else. Her face darkened with each passing second. A knot tightened in my stomach. *Not now*, I thought desperately.

Please, not now.

"This is my little sister," Liz said to the officers, still holding onto Vic. "Vic, this is Officer Anderson and Officer Hardie. They've been working on Brooke's case."

Time seemed to stand still as Liz's eyes moved from Vic to Lucy, seemingly unaware of the mounting tension. At that moment, I noticed Anderson's gaze mirroring Liz's. There was something in his expression that was missing from Liz's—a sudden alertness.

"Is everything okay, officers?" Vic asked suddenly, the palpable strain in her voice slicing through the room.

I nervously glanced back at Lucy. She was holding her own, but barely. As my eyes flickered back to Anderson, I noticed his eyes were already locked onto me. His face was hardening with an emotion I couldn't quite place.

The four of us—me, Lucy, Anderson, Vic—seemed to share a moment, an understanding, while Liz remained none the wiser.

Thank God.

"We just wanted to check in," Anderson said, his voice steady but carrying a hint of reluctance. "We're glad to hear Allie's recovering. Can't imagine what you've gone through these past few days."

Liz, still holding Vic's hand, beamed at Anderson's words. "Thank you," she said, her voice trembling slightly. "It means a lot to us."

Lucy shifted awkwardly beside Anderson, casting a quick, almost apologetic glance toward me. Her attempts to maintain composure were faltering. I just wished she would say something. *Anything*. Her ongoing silence was somehow drawing more attention toward her.

"Keep us updated," Anderson added. I forced myself to nod firmly.

"We will," I replied, and his head snapped back toward me. "Thank you, officers."

His gaze lingered on me for a second longer than expected. He appeared conflicted. Uncomfortable. I noticed his eyes flicker, very quickly, toward Lucy, and then back to Liz. Then he began moving.

Lucy followed closely, not saying a single word. Not even looking back at us.

"...her liver and kidneys are in bad shape," I heard Liz saying to Vic. "They said that they're going to have to keep pumping her with all these... *fluids*—"

"Yeah, I heard."

Liz linked arms with me, pulling herself closer. This was the most we'd touched each other in a long time. The strangest part was that it actually felt natural to do so.

"We should go in first," she said, turning to me. "We don't want to overwhelm her. It should just be us."

Vic's face soured once more. For a moment, I thought she was going to fight it. She looked ready to explode. I'm still not sure how we all made it out of that situation unscathed. I had been so sure that it was all going to come crashing down, there and then.

Now that it was over, all I could feel was relief. Relief for Allie. Relief for my family.

Maybe it was all going to be okay.

"I'll leave you two to it," Vic replied, stepping past us. Her hand brushed against Liz's shoulder as she walked away.

When we were alone, Liz pulled me back in for another hug. I wrapped my arms around her, holding her tightly. I closed my eyes, finally allowing myself to fully sink into her embrace. It felt like coming home after a long journey, a rare sense of peace settling over me. Nothing had felt this right in a very long time.

For the first time in what felt like an eternity, there was a glimmer of something to hold onto.

As we pulled away, our eyes met with a shared understanding of the gravity of the situation, but also with a renewed resolve. I saw something in her eyes that I hadn't seen in a long time—a flicker of the woman I fell in love with.

It had been so long since we'd felt like a team. And it felt good. Better than good.

I took her hand in mine, and together, we made our way toward our daughter's hospital room.

23 DAYS AFTER THE DISAPPEARANCE OF
BROOKLYN NICHOLSON

FITZ | 6:12 PM

The corridor seemed to stretch on forever.

Each step I took felt heavier than the last, and the sterile, faintly chemical smell of the hospital clung to everything in my path. The hum of fluorescent lights overhead buzzed; a constant, dull noise that somehow made the silence feel even louder.

I shoved my hands deeper into my jacket pockets, trying to keep the tremor in my fingers under control.

"...dude, what if they don't even let us in?" Freddie chimed, skipping goofily at the side of me. "We don't even know if she's awake... or, well... *alive*, even—"

Joaquin shoved him hard, almost knocking me over in the process. "Can't you just shut the fuck up for five seconds?!"

"Am I *wrong*? I'm just saying—what's the point in coming all the way over here if she's not even gonna know we're *there*?!"

A couple of nurses passed us as we moved closer to the ICU. I could've sworn they gave us dirty looks… well, Freddie, at least. He kept bouncing along, acting like a fucking kid. I wished I'd never asked them to come.

I should've just done this by myself.

"*Do* you think they'll let us in?" Joaquin asked suddenly, lowering his voice as Freddie bounced down the corridor. "They have to, right?"

"They have to," I repeated, suddenly feeling less sure of my answer.

I hadn't seen Allie's parents since we were little kids. I wasn't even sure I'd ever been inside her house; I only remembered ever playing in her front yard a couple times, and out on her street.

She'd always been weirdly secretive about her family. She *hated* anyone bringing up her dad. Maybe it embarrassed her. I mean, I couldn't imagine *my* dad being some washed-up rockstar, now working in an office in a shitty small town. It was pretty tragic.

He seemed like a cool guy, all in all. And I never got the feeling that Allie didn't like her dad—if anything, they seemed pretty close. I guess it was just weird for her, knowing who he used to be. Maybe that's why she never wanted to talk about him. Maybe it was easier to just downplay it all, pretending her family was as boring and normal as everyone else's.

I suddenly wondered if he'd know who I was. Or her mom.

I only remembered what their faces looked like after seeing them on the news so much. Allie looked a *lot* like her mom; they had the same red hair and freckles. Her sister looked more like their dad, with darker skin and hair. Their dad was Italian or something, and their mom was Irish. And based on the pictures on the news, it was pretty obvious which sister got which genes.

"It's over here," Joaquin said suddenly, running ahead. He was heading toward the big sign that said *Intensive Care Unit*.

Freddie started running after him; their footsteps thudded against the shiny, polished floor. I followed behind, my pace slowing as we got closer.

The ICU felt like a whole different world from the rest of the hospital. It was quieter. Had more of a serious vibe. The faint beep of machines and the low murmur of nurses talking in hushed tones echoed through the corridors, filling me with dread.

Joaquin had stopped just ahead, waiting for me to catch up. Freddie, on the other hand, was already halfway inside, barely registering the evident tension in the air.

"You good?" Joaquin asked as I finally got to him. I nodded without saying a word, and he squeezed my shoulder as we moved forward together.

The room on the other side smelled of antiseptic, and the machines beeped in a steady rhythm, filling the otherwise silent aura. The ICU itself was stark, with white floors so polished that they reflected the fluorescent lights overhead. Glass-fronted rooms lined either side of the hallway, each filled with blinking lights, tubes, and patients who looked more machine than human. I didn't want to look at them for too long. It didn't feel right.

"*Yo!*" Freddie's voice echoed down the corridor. "Mrs. Nichy!"

My gaze glazed over to where Freddie was heading. He swaggered over to a tallish lady with red hair, standing outside one of the rooms, talking to a nurse in light blue scrubs.

It was her. Allie's mom.

There was something so weird about seeing her in the flesh after seeing her on TV so much over the past few weeks. It was like seeing a famous person in public. She glanced up at the sound of Freddie's voice, and for a moment, her eyes widened in surprise. A dozen nurses and doctors turned to stare at him, and I wanted to bolt out of there as quickly as we'd entered.

To my surprise, a small smile stretched across Liz Nicholson's face. She actually looked happy to see him. "Freddie Kaminski," she said, her tone warm.

I just couldn't believe it.

The same guy who'd just been cracking jokes about whether Allie was even *alive* had managed to get a smile out of her mother.

"Long time no see," he grinned, striding over like he owned the place, all nonchalant. Joaquin and I followed, but I kept my head down, trying to blend into the background.

"My *goodness*, you've gotten tall..." Allie's mom leaned in for a hug, barely reaching his height. "When did you get all grown up?"

It never failed to surprise me how good Freddie was with mothers. Or just women, in general. My mom fucking *loved* him. He was like some kind of snake charmer, but for women in their fifties. And here it was again: Mrs. Nicholson, whose daughter was lying in a hospital bed in God-knows-what condition, smiling at him like he was the golden child coming home.

Freddie, of course, played into it perfectly. He flashed that wide, easy grin of his, like nothing in the world was wrong. "Just trying to keep up," he said smoothly, running a hand through his thick curls.

Liz pulled away from him, turning to Joaquin next. A slight uncertainty crossed her face as she tried to place him.

"Joaquin Garcia," he introduced himself with a polite smile. "I'm friends with Allie. I don't think we've met."

Liz's expression cleared with a touch of recognition. "I think I know your mother... *Elena* Garcia? From the salon on the square?" Joaquin nodded, and Liz smiled. "Well, it's nice to meet you, *Whacking*."

He didn't bother correcting her. None of us did. I guess we all figured there were bigger things going on at that moment.

With that, she turned to me.

At first, I wasn't sure if she knew who I was—granted, it'd been a while since I'd seen her in person. The last time she'd seen me I was 50 pounds heavier and had barely hit puberty. A slow realization set in as she scanned my face. Her eyes glistened as she looked me up and down, fully taking it in, and her realization quickly faded into confusion. Then shock. Her eyes widened. "Fitz?!"

I nodded with an awkward smile, feeling a little self-conscious under her intense scrutiny. "It's good to see you, Mrs. Nicholson."

She wasn't even attempting to cover up her surprise. I'd gotten used to it; when you grew up as the fat kid, people loved to gawk at you when you finally shed the weight.

Her eyes lingered on me a little longer than anticipated, slipping past my face, down to my torso. "Oh, my..." Her face flushed. "I almost didn't recognize you." I laughed clumsily, rubbing the back of my neck.

"Yeah... I, uh, cut out the Twinkies."

A slight giggle slipped out as she continued to stare at my body. It was so fucking weird. I mean, it was a compliment, sure—I just couldn't help but imagine Allie's reaction. Suddenly, the whole scenario became fucking hilarious.

Part of me couldn't wait to tell her.

Liz seemed momentarily lost in thought. She shook her head, a small, somewhat embarrassed smile playing at her lips. "You look… great," she said, the words almost slipping out in a wistful tone. My cheeks began burning. "Keep doing whatever you're doing!"

Freddie shoved me playfully, and my fist clenched instinctively. I quickly shook my head, turning back to the matter at hand. I turned my gaze to the door behind Liz, remembering what was behind it. *Who* was behind it.

"So, where is she?" Freddie asked suddenly, jumping straight in before I got the chance to change the subject. "We figured we'd try and cheer her up, you know? Snap her out of it."

I wanted to hit him so fucking bad.

Liz seemed to snap out of her reverie, her face regaining its serious, focused expression. She gestured toward the door behind her. "She's resting…" she began before pausing, hesitating. "She only woke up yesterday. She's… *fragile.*"

A knot tightened in my stomach.

Images flashed through my mind once again as I imagined the worst. I remembered how Grandpa looked just before he died; tubes coming out of every vein, the sallowness of his skin, the unnerving stillness. The noises he made when he breathed.

Images of Hurley flooded my brain.

The blood.

"I, um…" Liz paused again. Her face suddenly hardened, as if she'd just remembered something that had completely thrown her. "I'm not entirely sure she'd want to see you."

"What do you mean?" Freddie asked, as brazen and insensitive as ever. But I'd already put the pieces together. Somehow, I'd already figured it out.

She was talking about Donnie.

"I don't know how much you knew," she went on, crossing her arms loosely, "about what… what your *friend* did, but—"

I immediately stepped forward, holding a hand up and shaking it. "Mrs. Nicholson, we had no idea. We swear."

"About what?" Freddie asked before suddenly clicking on. He then began shaking his head, pulling a face. "Oh, shit—you mean Donnie? Yeah, we never liked him anyway." He rested an arm atop my shoulder, leaning against me. "Trust us—he was *always* an asshole."

I shoved him away from me, shooting him a warning look. Liz's eyes widened slightly at the interruption, but she kept her focus on me. "She's been through a lot recently," she went on, gesturing toward the door behind her. "I mean, we *all* have... but, well, she's... she's struggling."

I nodded silently. I knew more than she thought I knew. Something told me she didn't know about me meeting Allie at the bar, and I figured now wasn't the time to bring it up.

It didn't matter anymore.

"Mrs. Nichy..." Freddie began, and all I could do was brace myself for whatever bullshit was about to come out of his mouth. "I know you probably think we're just a bunch of idiots, but... look... we *really* care about her. I get it—you don't want to stress her out—but we're not going to do anything stupid. We just wanna see her. We're worried about her, you know?"

I stared at him, stunned.

Joaquin caught my eye; he looked just as surprised as I felt. It was the most serious I'd seen Fred in a long time. Maybe *ever*. I didn't think he had it in him.

And, hell—it was working.

"Please, Mrs. N," he continued, breaking out the puppy dog eyes. "We'll be ten minutes tops. *Pinky* swear." He held out his pinky finger, but she looked at it with confusion. It was a moment of awkward silence, the sincerity of Freddie's request clashing with the unfamiliarity of his gesture.

Liz's eyes flickered between the three of us before she finally—hesitantly—linked her little finger with his. "Ten minutes," she repeated, giving Freddie a serious look. "Tops."

He saluted her jokingly before shuffling toward the door, opening it up and wandering inside without a second thought. Joaquin followed, leaving me on my own. I looked back at Liz; she looked a little confused, waiting for me to follow the others. "Thank you," I said quietly, and she gave me a tight smile.

"Be careful with her."

I nodded again. Then, I began moving. I forced myself through the door, into the darkness.

The room on the other side was dimly lit, the main light coming from a single, muted lamp near the bed. The air was filled with the soft hum of medical machines.

An abrupt beeping sound kept repeating, over and over.

"...*there* she is!"

I followed Freddie's voice, watching as the two of them made themselves comfortable around the bed. Joaquin sat down on the chair at the side, and Freddie wasted no time planting himself on the edge of the bed, bouncing with the force. I slowly moved forward, searching for her face in the dim lighting.

There she was.

The oxygen mask covered part of her face; its straps were snugly fitted, tight enough that they left visible marks on her skin. Her lips, dry and cracked, were barely visible beneath the mask. Her orange hair was a tangled mess, some strands sticking to her forehead with sweat, while others splayed out chaotically on the pillow. IV lines snaked in and out of her arms.

She didn't look quite as bad as I'd expected her to. The horrific images in my mind slowly faded as I finally saw her in the flesh. Her skin didn't appear any paler than usual. Her eyes looked a little darker, though.

Seeing her like this, so small and vulnerable in the hospital bed, brought a lump to my throat.

"Shit... who let *you* in?" Her voice was a little croaky. But, again, it was nowhere near as bad as I'd expected.

Fred took hold of her hand, grinning madly. "We're here to cheer you up, you depressed bastard." As he held her arm up, ever so slightly, I noticed the bandages; her left arm was still tied up in a sling, but it was the right arm that caught my attention and twisted my gut. The fresh bandages were thick and tightly wrapped, spotted with dried blood.

Just as the room began to spin around me, I noticed her face change. She'd spotted me.

The second she saw me, her whole demeanor switched up. Her expression softened. The wide grin that Freddie had just painted onto her face slowly faded, and I wanted nothing more than to run out of there.

Suddenly, she began pulling herself up. Joaquin rushed to her side, steadying her. "*Whoa*, Al... don't hurt yourself—"

She was wincing as she moved, but she wouldn't stop.

That was when I remembered that she'd broken her ribs, too, when they attacked her in the street. I was completely frozen for a moment, trying to figure out if there was any part of her that hadn't been broken over the past few weeks.

She kept struggling. It only occurred to me, as her eyes locked onto mine, that she was trying to see me better.

She was moving for *me*.

I ran over to her, positioning myself on the bed on her left side. She grabbed my hand right away. Through the haze of pain and exhaustion, she smiled; it was barely visible through her mask, but I saw it.

It was the most beautiful and heart-wrenching thing I'd ever seen.

"*Hey*," I heard her croak.

I squeezed her hand slightly, trembling as I finally got to examine her up close. "Hey."

Her hand was warm. Blood was still pumping. I thought about how her hand would've felt if they hadn't found her when they did.

More images of Hurley flashed before my eyes.

"I can't believe my mom let you in here..." she mumbled, looking around at all three of us. "She's like a fucking SS commander."

"Thank Fitz." Freddie poked me in the arm, smirking. "Worked his charm. She practically grabbed him by the dick." I shoved him back, making him laugh even harder. Al's face twisted in disgust.

"What the *hell*?"

"Oh, I wish I was kidding," Freddie protested with a grin, rubbing her shoulder. "Seriously. Your mom's about to marry a rich man."

"Not if I get there first." Her voice came out as a forced whisper, but there was a mischievous glint in her eye.

I forced a laugh, struggling to keep up with them. "In your dreams."

I was trying.

Really, I was.

Fred and Al had fallen into their regular back-and-forth banter without breaking a sweat, and even Joaquin was cracking up, rolling with laughter in his chair. It just felt like a strange, dissonant scene: the laughter and teasing clashing sharply with the reality of the situation. Each sound, each beep, seemed to echo louder in my mind.

I shifted in my seat, glancing at the IV drip, the heart monitor, and the shaky rise and fall of Allie's chest with every breath. Her attempt to joke felt almost like a desperate grasp of normalcy, and it tore at me.

It was as if I was the only one that could see the strain in her eyes as she laughed. The sheer effort it took to even muster up a smile.

She was barely alive.

The guys continued cracking jokes as I just sat there, counting the tubes streaming from her arms. Freddie's loudness was a jarring distraction, but it felt distant, like it was coming from another room. Their laughter seemed to bounce off the walls, ringing through my ears. I wanted to say something—to break the facade of normalcy they were trying to uphold. I just wanted them to stop, just for a second.

But the words wouldn't come.

Instead, I found myself running my fingers across the back of Allie's hand, tracing the clear tube that poked through one of her veins.

"…you could've at least brought some flowers," I heard Allie mumble, barely able to catch her breath. "Or a Get Well Soon card—"

"Oh, our *deepest* apologies!" Freddie exclaimed, his voice dripping with sarcasm. "You know, maybe next time you can schedule your suicide attempt closer to payday."

My whole body tensed up.

A surge of anger roared through me, hot and sharp. Allie's hand dropped from mine as I lost my grip.

I couldn't look at him.

I couldn't even bring myself to look up.

"…what about you, huh?" It took me a second to realize Allie was talking to me now. I couldn't look at her either. I didn't want to. "Did *you* bring me anything?" When I didn't reply, she tried to hold my hand again. I clenched my fist, stopping her.

There was a brief silence, and I could only imagine their reactions around me. Even Freddie remained quiet for longer than five seconds. I just sat there, staring down at the bed. Seething.

It felt like hours passed before anyone said another word.

It was Allie that eventually broke the silence. "Make it up to me," she said suddenly, leaning over to grab something from the table at the side of her. There was a light jingling sound. "Grab me a Coke from the machine, would ya?"

"Seriously?" Freddie asked, and there was another silence. This time it was more than clear that she had shot him a look, because within seconds he was scrambling to his feet. Joaquin got up at the same time. They both began moving toward the door, but I still couldn't bring myself to look up.

"Get me a Snickers too," she added as they walked away. "I'm starving away in here—"

"Yeah, yeah," Freddie grumbled, half-joking, as the two of them slipped out of the room. The door swung shut behind them, sending us into another deep silence.

The beeping sound was getting faster and faster. I glanced up slightly, trying to figure out which of the machines it was coming from.

"Just say it."

I leaned away from her a little, pursing my lips. "I don't know what you're—"

"You're mad," she cut me off. "Why are you mad?"

I finally looked up, looking her dead in the eye. She seemed confused. Upset, even. The brazen, happy-go-lucky front that she'd been showing off in front of the guys had completely faded.

I wished I could've lied to her. I wished I could pretend that everything was okay, just so I could make her smile again.

I just couldn't do it.

"Why am I mad?" I repeated. "You tried to kill yourself. Of course I'm fucking mad."

The words shot out like bullets.

Allie flinched a little. It was as if I'd physically hurt her.

"Hurley's dead," I continued, unsure of why I thought now

was the right time to do this. It was *not* the right time. But I couldn't stop. "Mandy's dead. *Mel's* dead."

"Fitz—"

"*No*... no... *they* didn't make that choice," I interrupted, barely able to mask my mounting anger. "*They* didn't want to die. But *you* did. You *chose* this."

Her lips moved, but no sound came out. I wished I could've stopped there. But I couldn't.

I guess I didn't want to.

"I've lost so many people, Al." I kept going, driving the knife even further. "I've lost my grandpa, my friends, my girlfriend... I've lost *so many fucking people*. What the *fuck* were you thinking?"

"I wasn't thinking about that," she said, her voice soft. "I'm sorry—"

"*Fuck that.*" I pulled my hand from her, making her jump. "Do you have *any* idea what would've happened if you didn't make it?! What it would've done to *me*?! To your *family*?!"

"I wasn't *thinking* about that—"

"Then, what the fuck *were* you thinking?!"

Her face twisted in frustration, her weakness barely masking the fire that ignited in her eyes. "You have no idea."

"What—"

"No, Fitz." Her voice got louder. Stronger. "You have *no* idea. You have *no fucking idea.*"

"What are you—"

"Didn't you see the news?!" Her voice cracked. She tried prying her mask off, trying to make me hear her clearer, but I grabbed her hands to pull them away. "*No*... they *filmed* me coming out of my house... as they put me in that... that *fucking* ambulance—"

"Al—"

"*Didn't you HEAR them*?! They were *cheering*! The *whole* street! *They WANTED me dead*!"

Of course I'd seen it.

I watched as they paraded the footage on TV—live footage of her being carried out on a stretcher as a crowd grew around her front yard. The street was packed with reporters and onlookers.

The camera had zoomed in on the crowd, capturing their

reactions as the paramedics loaded her into the back of the ambulance. It was like watching a public execution. They'd turned this horrific moment into a grotesque spectacle. And I had never felt anger like that in my entire life.

I wanted to beat the life out of every last one of them; the men, the women, the children. The anger was raw and unrelenting—a fierce, uncontrollable fire. The realization that *this* was how they had chosen to remember her—to exploit her darkest moment, and potentially the final moments of her life—fueled a rage that I could barely contain.

I wanted *them* dead.

"I mean... what's the *point*?!" She kept trying to shout but her voice was too weak. "They *want* me to die... I can't even walk down the street without someone trying to kill me... so, I-I figured, *why not*?! If *they* can't do it right, *I* should do it... save everyone a *whole* lot of trouble..."

The fire that had sparked in her eyes flickered out, replaced by a hollow resignation as she slumped back on her pillow, unable to fight it any longer. Her breathing became shallower. Raspier. I carefully took hold of her mask, sliding it back over her face.

"...*I don't want to be here anymore...*"

My fingers locked up. The words had come out in a hoarse whisper, but I heard it clearer than anything.

"...I know you don't want to hear it," she went on, trying to turn her face away from mine. "And I'm *sorry* that you've lost so much already, but... *I'm so fucking tired*, Fitz. This is how it has to be. I've *got* to do this. I *have* to—"

"What the hell does that mean?"

"I'm gonna do it right next time."

My heart slammed in my chest. Before I could stop myself, I was on my feet. "You shut the *fuck up*, Al—"

"You can't stop me—"

"Oh, *yeah*?!" I yelled, cutting her off. Jabbing a finger in her face. "*You wanna bet*?! 'Cause I'll follow you around *every second of the fucking day* if I have to! I'll watch you fucking *sleep*! If you think for *one second* that I'm going to let that happen, *you're fucking INSANE*!"

She stared at me with wide eyes.

But I couldn't stop.

"*Jesus*, Al… *h-how could you be so fucking SELFISH*?!"

Something changed in her eyes. Her lips quivered. A hot wave of regret hit me as I saw her face crumple, just slightly.

I took a step back. My heart pounded in my chest as I tried to shake off the anger, but the sight of her crumbling under the weight of my words made it almost unbearable. I ran a hand through my hair, pacing.

I had to calm down.

I had to be *better*.

I slowly turned back to her, fully preparing to apologize; not for what I'd said, but how I'd said it. I'd meant every word.

But I hadn't expected to see her eyes flashing with anger, her lips tightening into a grimace. That brief flicker of vulnerability had diminished as quickly as it had appeared, and the fire returned tenfold. "How *dare* you?!" she tried to shout back, attempting to pull herself up again. "How *dare* y—"

What about your parents, huh?!" I took another deep breath, attempting to steady myself. Fighting *so hard* to keep it cool. "What about your little brother?! He's just a *fucking kid*, Al! What the *hell* do you think this would do to them?!"

"They'll be fine once Brooke comes back—"

"And what if she *doesn't* come back?! What if she…" The words trailed off as I realized what I was saying. Her eyes glazed over. "You just… you *can't* talk like this, Al. You *can't* do it to them."

"They'll be fine."

"*I* won't." My voice cracked. The anger drained from my face, leaving behind only raw desperation. "I… I-I couldn't get through that. I'm barely getting through *any* of this, and if *you*…"

I let the sentence trail off as I realized I couldn't say it.

Images just kept flashing through my head—flashes of all of it, all that had happened. And I couldn't take it anymore. I *couldn't*.

"I'll stay with you." The words came flying out senselessly. "I-I'll sleep on your parents' couch, or whatever, and I… I'll walk with you, *everywhere*… and if I hear *anything*… if I hear *anyone* saying *anything* to you…"

I pictured what I'd do if I heard anyone saying that to her— what they'd said on the news. The cheering. The celebrating.

I imagined how it would feel to grab hold of them, *every single* one of them. My knuckles paled white as my fingers curled into my palms, my nails digging into my skin.

"There's too many of them." A brief, humorless laugh slipped past her lips, and I watched as her eyes got glassier by the second. Mine had begun to follow suit. The anger had slipped from both of us, leaving behind a hollow sort of exhaustion.

It was as if the fight had been drained out of us, replaced by nothing but the weight of everything we couldn't control.

"I don't care," I muttered, sitting back down on the bed. I took her hand back in mine. "I wouldn't stop. I'd *never* stop."

I looked at her right arm again, examining it up close. The bandages wrapped around her entire forearm—starting at her wrists, reaching her elbow. I absent-mindedly rubbed my thumb against hers, attempting to comfort her. Or maybe I was trying to comfort myself.

"I'm sorry," I said finally, unable to reach her gaze. "About last week."

"Don't be—"

"No, I shouldn't have walked out on you like that," I cut her off. "And I'm sorry I didn't believe you."

She squeezed my hand weakly. "I was acting crazy."

"You *are* crazy," I replied, wincing at my half-assed attempt at lightening the mood. But it worked; she laughed quietly, just a small sound, but enough to make me feel like maybe, for a second, we were okay again. "But I shouldn't have... you know... I shouldn't have just left. It could've been the last time I saw you."

She shrugged a little, and I heard a slight sniff. It was unnerving—seeing her cry—even if she was doing everything she could to cover it up. "Well... it *wasn't*... so..."

I put both hands around hers, rubbing them together to warm hers up. Her skin was so cold. Freezing.

"I won't do it again," I added. "I'm not going anywhere... and... neither are you, alright?"

She didn't say anything for a moment. She just stared down at our intertwined hands, her lip trembling slightly.

"Al," I pressed, desperation flooding my tone. "*Please*. Just... promise me."

But to my brief annoyance, she didn't say another word.

Instead, she put her arms around my neck, pulling me in. I hadn't expected the strength of her hug. I put my arms around her, holding her even tighter. Her shaky breath was warm against my shoulder.

The smell of antiseptic, the beeping machines, the sterile air—none of it mattered. All I could feel was her clinging to me, as if letting go would mean losing everything.

I closed my eyes, and for the first time in a long time, the images in my head stopped. Everything went black. Silent.

Suddenly, the door swung back open with a force that made both of us flinch. Our heads turned simultaneously, watching Freddie swagger back into the room with a Snickers in his hand and a wide smug grin plastered on his face.

"Shit... should I have knocked?"

The smirk grew wider as he took in the sight of us, still close, but now awkwardly pulling away from each other. My face heated up instantly, a combination of embarrassment and raw irritation swirling in my chest.

But Allie answered before I could: "Don't get too jealous, asshole."

"Jealous? Of *this* fucker?" He tossed the candy bar onto her lap as Joaquin wandered in behind him, juggling four Coke cans in his arms. "Trust me, sweetheart—been there, done that. Got the herpes to prove it."

My chest tightened again, but Allie burst out laughing. It was as if she'd completely switched personalities within a moment's notice. "Could be worse," she shot back, almost completely turned away from me at this point. "Could've knocked me up."

Jesus fucking Christ.

Even Fred was taken aback by that one. His eyes widened before he started laughing again, staring at her in disbelief.

"And, *hey,* you've *got* to stop telling people that," she added, her tone becoming slightly more serious as she unwrapped her Snickers. "There's already enough rumors about me going 'round—"

"Who said it's a rumor?" he shot back, sitting back down on the other side of the bed. She shoved him playfully.

I glanced between the two of them, reeling at the way they could, somehow, always find humor in the darkest, most twisted shit. I just couldn't get how they could do it. In so many ways, they were the perfect match—it was like they were made for each other. There was no one else in the world that could ever handle them, myself included.

"Hey, Nichy," Joaquin cracked open one of the cans, carefully handing it over to her. "Your mom said our time's up. We've got to get out of here."

"What, *already*?" She groaned, taking a sip before turning back toward me. Her eyes softened slightly. "I don't want you to go."

I quickly squeezed her hand again when I knew Freddie wasn't looking; I didn't want to give him any more ammo than he already had. "I'll come back tomorrow… if you want, I mean."

She nodded with a small smile. "Yeah."

Joaquin moved past me, giving Allie a quick hug. Then Freddie extended a fist to her; she bumped it. "Get well soon, freakshow," he said, half-earnestly. She stuck her middle finger up at him.

"Get out of here."

As the guys pulled away from the bed, I slipped my hand into my pocket, pulling the envelope out. I slid it onto her lap as I stood up, moving it toward her fingers. She looked down at it, confused for a moment. I kept moving toward the door, not wanting to draw attention to it. The guys said their goodbyes, making their way back into the hallway.

I stood in the doorway for a final moment, watching her as she opened up the envelope. It took her a second to work it out. She began mouthing the first line.

Her head snapped up. Our eyes met.

"*…Fitz? You comin'?*"

I gave her a reassuring nod, trying to convey all the words I couldn't quite find. Her wide, glassy eyes were filled with something: gratitude, I figured. Hope, even.

I slowly shut the door behind me, catching one last glimpse of her turning her attention back to the letter, using her finger to trace each line. I let go of the handle, making my way over to the guys; they were waiting at the entrance of the ICU. Freddie was talking to Allie's mom again.

I had no idea what she was even going to do with that letter. I didn't want to ask. I wasn't even sure I wanted to know.

I just hoped it meant something.

LIZ | 6:36 PM

"…so the tall one, with all the hair," Vic went on, pushing her own hair back to replicate the hairstyle she had just witnessed; "*that's* that rich guy's grandson? The one with the mansion?"

"Yes, Vic."

She'd been asking a million and one questions ever since she'd caught Allie's friends leaving her room, and it'd been almost an hour since.

I took another sip of my coffee, trying to ward off the exhaustion that had been settling into my bones for days. My attention drifted back and forth between my lukewarm espresso and my sister, who was practically glowing with excitement. "So… how old is he?" she asked slowly, with a slight hesitation to her tone. I shot her a look.

"He's nineteen," I muttered. Her face lit up with joy. "They're *all* Allie's age. Eighteen, nineteen—"

"I've *never* seen a boy like him before…" she cut me off, almost falling into a dreamlike state as she clearly lost herself in her own imagination. "I mean… that *bone structure…*"

"He's half your age, you witch."

Just an hour ago, I had caught myself blushing when Fitz Bird smiled my way, his charisma undeniable. But I wasn't going to give Vic the satisfaction of knowing that.

She certainly wasn't wrong—the boy had the face of an angel.

And it had come as the biggest surprise, considering what he looked like as a kid. He'd always been this… well, a *chubby* little thing. A pudgy boy with a round flushed face. But *now*, looking at him—lean and muscular, with a striking jawline and a confidence that seemed to command attention—it was almost like witnessing a complete transformation. I'd barely recognized the boy.

"Imagine looking like that *and* having the money behind you," Vic continued hazily, practically radiating with lust. "Allie's a fool. I would've climbed him like a jungle gym at her age."

I pinched her arm hard. She shoved me away before quickly composing herself as two doctors walked past us, making their way to the other side of the corridor. Vic's eyes followed them intently, her gaze lingering on their backs. My eyes practically rolled back into my skull.

"You really need to start thinking about settling down," I told her firmly. She barely even registered that I was speaking to her, clearly distracted by the doctors. They weren't even *that* attractive. "With someone your *own age*, may I add—"

"What do I look like to you, a child bride?"

"You're forty-four!"

"Yeah, well…" Her gaze flickered back to me, though it was clear her mind was elsewhere. She pursed her lips, clearly gearing up to say something that would hit a nerve. "It's not like you've been exactly selling the idea of marriage lately."

I straightened up, staring straight ahead. "Screw you."

She scoffed loudly, leaning against the wall at the side of me. We both stared down the corridor, returning to silence.

Behind us, through the door, I could hear muffled laughter. I zoned in on it, listening to my children joking around in there. It was almost as if everything was back to normal, albeit temporarily. The sound of Cam's giggles dragged me right back to the moment we had found ourselves settled in, and my chest tightened as I remembered what was about to happen.

"This is going to be good for him," Vic said suddenly, as if she could read my mind. "You'll see. He's going to have the best time."

"Mm-hm."

"You know they'll look after him… and he doesn't deserve to be around this, Liz. It's not fair."

I kept nodding, my lips tightening into a grimace. But she was right. Cam hadn't deserved to have walked into his sister's room and seen what he saw.

He hadn't deserved to be the one to find her.

He'd called for an ambulance before he even told us. Somehow, he knew exactly what to say to the 911 operator. He was so calm. So focused. I couldn't shake the image of him running to the top of the stairs, calling for us, gripping the empty pill bottle in his tiny fist.

Just moments before, I had fought against the idea of him moving to Portland. Just *seconds* before it all broke loose, I had been sat there, still convinced that I had everything under control.

I couldn't fight it anymore. It wasn't fair on any of us, and it certainly wasn't fair on Cam. He was *10 years old.*

God only knew how this would all impact him once he got older.

"Is he talking to you yet?" Vic asked suddenly, breaking me out of my daze. "I mean… did you explain—"

"He's fine," I interrupted, not wanting to talk about it again. "Cam's fine. He knows all he needs to know."

"Hey, don't get all crabby with me." She paused, clearly deep in thought about something. I just wished she'd drop it. "I mean… I get it, you know? It's not as if Mom wouldn't have done that to us if—"

"Liz Nicholson?"

We both looked up at the sound of my name.

A lady in scrubs stood by the nurses' station, gesturing toward me. Her tone was polite but firm, a kind of practiced efficiency that came from handling patients and families all day long. I half recognized her, and I wondered if we'd ever worked together.

It'd felt like a lifetime since I'd last worked a shift at that hospital. I'd spent over 30 years at that reception desk, and this was the longest I'd ever been out of work.

It all felt so surreal, spending so much time in my place of work but being on the other side of it now. I had become so used to sitting behind that desk, answering phones, directing families, organizing the chaos of the hospital floor. I'd always been the one offering reassurance or giving directions, but now, here I was— just another worried face lingering in the waiting area.

I left Vic behind, making my way to the nurses' station. The lady in green held something out to me. A piece of paper. "We found this on the desk over here," she said as I examined it closely. "Is it yours?"

It was a white envelope with *LIZ* scrawled across it. I didn't recognize the handwriting, and I wasn't entirely sure it was even meant for me. There had to be hundreds of Lizs passing through the hospital that day, so there was no real way of knowing if this was mine.

"Are there any other Lizs here?" I asked, and the lady shook her head. "No Elizabeths?"

"Just you, ma'am."

"Hm…" I turned the envelope over, noticing a tiny sketch of an apple on the other side. "Maybe it *is* for me—"

"Is everything okay?"

I spun around, suddenly realizing that Frank was right behind me. I quickly nodded, reassuring him as I carefully tore open the envelope. "Yeah, yeah… Cam's still in there with Allie," I said as I stuck my hand inside, pulling out a piece of paper. "No updates so far—"

"What's that?"

He suddenly reached for the envelope, trying to snatch it out of my hand. I tugged it back from him. "What's wrong with you? It's mine," I said, watching him with confusion. His eyes were wild, darting between the envelope and my face as if I were holding a ticking bomb.

"Let me see it," he demanded, his hand outstretched, fingers twitching. The intensity in his voice caught me off guard, and for a split second, I almost handed it over.

But then my confusion turned into irritation. He lunged again, more desperate this time, and I yanked the letter back with even more force. "It's *mine*," I repeated, trying to keep my voice low.

I just couldn't understand why he was acting like this. His face had drained of all color, beads of sweat forming on his brow.

"Liz—"

I pulled the paper from the envelope, quickly unfolding it before he could stop me.

In just a brief moment, I had gone from not caring about the mystery envelope at all to feeling an overwhelming sense of urgency. Frank's panic had transferred to me, and now I *had* to know what was inside.

I unfolded the paper, scanning it with mounting dread. Frank's presence loomed as he leaned over my shoulder.

The first word immediately caught my attention.

Mom.

My thoughts instantly rushed to Mick.

I knew my other children's handwriting—I could've recognized theirs anywhere. And, besides, it didn't make sense for Cam or Allie to have left a note for me when they were just in the next room over.

I couldn't remember what Mick's handwriting looked like. It had been too long since I'd seen it.

Frank began to tense up at the side of me, and I realized that I should've told him about Mick getting into contact with Vic. Between everything that had happened—and the fact that Mick had told Vic that he still didn't want anything to do with us—I hadn't said a word.

Maybe this letter was the start of something.

This was it. He'd decided he wanted to see us again. He wanted to forget the past and start anew.

But why would he leave me a note? And why would he leave it in the hospital, of all places?

Was he *there*? At the hospital?

I kept reading:

I'm so sorry for everything that's happened. I'm sorry I left. I'm sorry that I didn't say anything. More than anything I just want you to know that none of this is your fault. I forgive you.

My chest tightened as I remembered that night. The last time I ever saw him. The look on his face before he left. I'd thought, at that moment, that he would hate me forever.

I hadn't realized how much I'd needed to read that.

Tell Dad that I forgive him too. I know he never meant to hurt any of us, and that he never meant to hurt me. I want him to know that I get it.

Frank's breath got faster, burning against my neck. My eyes scanned the following words quicker than I'd ever thought I could read:

Thank you for the money. I'll pay you back—I promise. Every last cent.

We hadn't found out until after he'd left that he'd emptied our savings. I still had no idea how he'd gotten into those accounts. Frank had never let go of that. I was angry too, at first, but as time went on, all I cared about was where he was.

Knowing that he had the money gave me a small amount of comfort, knowing that he had enough to get him by, wherever he was.

And tell Allie that I love her and I'm so sorry she's had to go through all of this. Please take it easy on her Mom. She didn't mean it. She didn't even know. I kept it all to myself, and I hate the thought of everyone turning against her.

Its <u>not</u> her fault.

It was at this point that I paused.

Allie was just a kid when Mick left; just a little younger than Cam. As far as I had been aware, she hadn't known anything about him leaving. She didn't even know why he'd left; we'd never told her. We didn't want her to know.

"Allie knew?" I asked out loud, more to myself than to Frank. "She... she knew he was going to leave?"

A brief surge of anger rose inside me when I realized what he was saying. I just couldn't understand it. Did *he* tell her? Why wouldn't she tell us if she'd known all this time?

I kept going:

Please look after each other.

I love all of you, no matter what. We've all made mistakes, and I just hope I can make mine up to you sometime. I don't know when I'll be back. I need to stay away a little while longer. I hope you understand.

I am safe. I'm happy. Just focus on Allie and Cam and make sure their happy until I come home.

I had been so sure I'd recognized Mickey's voice in that letter.

I'd read the whole thing in his voice, hearing it so vividly. I had wholly convinced myself that this was my eldest child.

This *was* my son.

And one more thing… make sure <u>he</u> stays in prison. Make him <u>ROT</u> for what <u>he</u> did.

As I read those last lines, it struck me like a cold wave—the sudden realization that I had read it all wrong.

The tone of the letter shifted as I began to read it differently.

My knees buckled.

All my love,

The letter fell from my hands.

My vision blurred, the edges of reality beginning to warp.

Frank said something. I couldn't hear it. The letter fluttered to the floor, and I watched.

It caught in my throat. The name.

It stuck in my throat like a jagged shard of glass.

Frank's voice was distant—a muffled, panicked murmur as he tried to reach me. I heard his footsteps, felt his hands gripping my shoulders, but they seemed far away, like I was underwater.

My eyes locked on the letter, now fallen at my feet. It had fallen upright; the writing was clearly visible.

The name was there.

It was right there.

Brooke.

Brooke.

Brooke.

Frank kneeled before me. He picked up the letter. The envelope.

He stayed there, on his knees, staring at the envelope, the seconds stretching into what felt like hours.

Someone was behind me. They touched my shoulder.

"...*Liz*..."

Everything felt so distant. So far away.

"Brooke." Her name slipped from my mouth.

A figure moved into my line of sight. Vic. Her lips were moving but no sound was coming out. Everything had halted to a standstill. Time had stopped. Everything was frozen.

Everything had stopped.

"...*Liz*..." Vic's voice came out slow, drawn out, as if in slow motion. I just stared at her. I couldn't do anything else.

I couldn't move.

"She's alive." The words came out slowly, painfully. I barely recognized my own voice.

Brooke.

Frank's face swam into view, his eyes wide with concern. His presence felt distant, like he was in another world.

A hand gripped my arm. I couldn't answer.

Her name echoed louder and louder.

Brooke.

The world felt like it was collapsing in on itself. The realization set in. I worked it out. Pieced it together. My eyes locked onto the letter.

She'd written that letter. She left it there for me.

She was in the hospital.

"...sh-she's here..."

She was in the hospital.

My body unlocked. I began running. I didn't know where I was going, but I kept moving. I had to find her.

My sister shouted after me.

I barely heard her.

Corridors blurred into streaks of sterile white. The hum of fluorescent lights was a distant buzz. I pushed past anyone in my way. I couldn't see them. I couldn't see anything but white light.

I began calling her name.

I *screamed* her name.

A haze of blue scrubs approached me as I kept pushing forward; some of them were touching me. Holding onto me. I pushed through them. My legs kept moving. I couldn't stop myself.

Then I saw her.

At first, I completely froze. I stared at the long dark hair spilling down my daughter's back, tied into braids. My heart leaped into my throat. Before I could fully process it I was running toward her, my body moving faster than my mind could process.

"*...baby...*"

I reached her in seconds, grabbing her shoulder and spinning her around. The world slowed down as I looked into her face.

The girl's wide eyes stared back at me—confused, scared.

Her lips trembled, but it wasn't Brooke's face.

My hands fell from her shoulders, my breath catching in my throat. Everything crashed down around me at once. The girl's mother appeared from behind, furious. "What the hell are you doing? Get your hands off my daughter!"

Suddenly, there were hands on *my* shoulders.

There was a voice behind me as they pulled me back. "I'm so sorry," I heard Frank saying as the woman soldiered away, dragging the little girl with her.

He tried spinning me toward him but I pulled away.

I was about to start running again—continuing my search—when he dragged me backward, gripping my arms. His face was inches from mine.

I spoke before he could: "She's here, Frank... *we've got to find her...*"

His expression was completely unreadable.

He just stood there, frozen, his eyes flicking back and forth between mine. His lips parted as if he wanted to speak, but no words came out.

"Frank, we've *got* to find her," I repeated, struggling against his grip. "She's *here*! Brooke's here... we've *got* to—"

He started mumbling something.

I couldn't quite hear it. His words were so low, so quiet that I could barely make it out.

I could just make out the words, "*...can't be...*"

"*...why would she...*"

I began spinning around, moving in a perfect circle as my feet barely budged against the floor. Attempting to scan my surroundings. Trying to catch a glimpse of her dark braids.

"...*she wouldn't...*"

The letter was in his hand.

I snatched it from him, quickly re-reading the entire thing; scanning the words so quickly that I couldn't make sense of them. It was all a blur.

"We need to call the police," I stammered as the paper crumpled under my grip. "Officer Anderson... and Hardie... *we need to call them—*"

Frank kept trying to grab me as I continued to spin, frantic and disoriented.

My thoughts were a tangled mess. Frank's voice blended with the chaotic rush of noise in my head, barely audible over the pounding of my heartbeat. I couldn't see him. I couldn't see anything through my blurry vision.

I stumbled, my knees hitting the hard floor.

The letter slipped from my hands, fluttering down beside me like a fallen leaf. I was on the ground now, gasping, sobbing—desperate.

"*Brooke...*"

Her name left my lips in a whisper now, barely audible over my own ragged breathing.

"I-I've *got* to find her..."

Frank knelt beside me, his hands gentle now. He was saying something, but I couldn't hear it. I was in my own bubble, barely touching the outside world.

My mind was fraying, but I clung to the one thought I could hold onto—my baby girl.

She was here, somewhere. Maybe just around the corner, waiting for me to find her.

I didn't care who heard me. I didn't care how crazy I looked.

We stayed there, kneeling on the cold hospital floor, surrounded by the sterile lights and distant murmurs of the world continuing on and on around us.

But for me, time had stopped.

Because my daughter was here. She was still here, somewhere.

And I would *never* stop looking for her.

ADJACENT

29 DAYS AFTER THE DISAPPEARANCE OF
BROOKLYN NICHOLSON

ALLIE | 6:57 PM

"Who was that on the phone?" I heard Mom asking as Dad wandered back into the dining room, carrying two pizza boxes. He shook his head a little, seemingly confused.

"I couldn't hear anyone. Line went dead."

As I reached over to the box nearest to me—pulling out the *fattest* pepperoni slice, smothered in bubbling, gooey mozzarella—Mom came rushing back into the room. She almost dropped the plates in her hands.

"What if it was her?" she asked, her eyes widening. "Was it Brooke? Did it sound like Brooke?!"

My whole body tensed up. I forced myself to focus on my fingers as I carefully dissected my pizza slice, plucking black olives out of the cheese with my free hand.

I barely glanced up as Dad pulled the chair out opposite me, sitting down in his usual seat. "I didn't hear anyone," he replied, sounding as tense as I felt. "Like I said—line went dead."

Mom came back into the room with three glasses and a big bottle of Coke. She set it all down on the already-filled table before sitting down in *her* usual seat at the end.

It was funny, you know, how we'd all claimed our own places at the table over the years.

And even though they weren't there, no one dared sit in Cam and Brooke's chairs—even if that meant that me, Mom, and Dad were sat miles away from each other, my siblings' empty chairs filling the gaps between us.

"Maybe she heard your voice and got scared," Mom went on, passing a plate each to me and Dad. "Maybe she panicked."

I watched Dad's face fall slightly, just as it always did nowadays, whenever someone mentioned Brooke's name. I wondered if my face was giving me away as much as his was.

He'd told me about the letter—his letter.

Someone had blackmailed him into giving them money to keep their mouths shut about him and that cop, and the envelope had a drawing of an apple on it. Just like my letter, and the others.

Just like the letter Mom got from Brooke.

I hadn't told him about my letter, or the letters that the others had; I knew better than to do that, even if it seemed pretty clear, at this point, that it had been Donnie the whole time. No one had died since he'd been arrested. Everything had just kinda come to a standstill. For the first time, I began to accept the fact that, maybe, there wasn't a "bigger picture". Sometimes an apple *is* just an apple.

But what didn't make sense was why Brooke's letter to Mom had the same apple drawing as my letters. Or the same handwriting.

And it didn't make sense that Dad had been blackmailed by the same person. I mean, why would Donnie blackmail my dad?

He didn't even *know* him.

And I really didn't want to accept the alternative… which, you know, would explain *why* Mom's letter was so similar to mine. And Hurley's. Mandy's. Melissa's.

But Brooke wouldn't have hurt me.

And she certainly wasn't capable of murder.

The part that confused me the most was that, in *Mom's* letter, Brooke mentioned the money—the money that Dad had given to the "blackmailer". That information alone suggested that the person behind *Mom's* letter was the same person who had blackmailed Dad—and apparently, that person was Brooke. So, by that logic, Brooke had blackmailed Dad.

Of course, I'd considered the other alternative: that Brooke hadn't written any of the letters at all.

After all, it wasn't her handwriting. I *knew* her handwriting, and it didn't look like that at all. I hadn't seen Dad's letter—I didn't want to see it, *or* the photograph—but Mom's letter and my letter, plus the letters for the others were all written in handwriting I did not recognize.

In my heart, I knew the truth. I knew Mom's optimism, along with Dad's feelings of guilt and betrayal, were all in vain.

But I didn't want to think about that.

Not yet.

"Put that *down*," Mom scolded Dad, slapping his third slice of pizza out of his hand. She then took hold of his hand, reaching across to grab mine with her other. Dad took mine. "Bless us, O Lord, and these Thy gifts, which we are about to receive…"

So much had already happened, and for the first time in forever, there seemed to be some kind of peace in our house.

Mom was the happiest she'd been in weeks, and even Dad was spending more time with us. For the first time since Brooke had gone missing—for the first time in almost a month—things were settling. Even I felt a little more at ease. It was as if the whirlwind that we had been living for the past 29 days was finally letting up, allowing us to breathe for just a second. And God knew we needed it.

I just wanted to cling to this fragile sense of normalcy before the next big thing happened.

I wasn't stupid—I knew this wasn't over.

I just needed to catch my breath.

"Make sure you're eating enough," Mom said suddenly, piling slices onto my plate. "You're losing weight too quickly… you need to get your strength back up. You don't want to get too skinny."

"I liked the IV diet," I replied, turning my attention to my father, who needed no help filling his plate. "You should try it, Dad."

He shot me a look. "And what's *that* supposed to mean?" he asked, his mouth half-stuffed with food. Mom chuckled, pouring some water into her empty glass.

"It means you should probably look into that gym membership that we've been wasting money on all year," she joined in, leaning over to poke Dad's arm. He scoffed, wiping the grease from his mouth as Mom and I exchanged laughter.

"Wait a minute—since when did you two become the new Laurel and Hardy?" he asked, barely hiding his smile as he shook his head. "I don't like it… go back to yelling at each other, *please—*"

"Who the hell's Laurel and Hardy?"

Mom leaned over, poking *me* in the arm. "Watch your language around the dinner table."

"*There* it is," Dad snickered, stuffing his third slice into his mouth. I rolled my eyes a little, still smiling. Mom was too.

It felt almost unnatural. Unnerving, even.

I hadn't forgotten anything, and I wasn't planning on doing so. As much as things felt a lot calmer recently, I still couldn't bring myself to spend too much time with my father. He'd been around more these past few days, which reassured me that he really had ended things with that cop. But my anger was still simmering beneath the surface.

The mental image of them together, making out outside that bar like fucking teenagers, still made me want to throw up. And I knew I'd have to tell Mom at some point. There was no way it could stay hidden forever.

But for now, things were going well. *Too* well, even. I honestly couldn't remember the last time I'd seen my parents laugh together; it'd been a long time, long before Brooke even went missing. Again, I didn't want to ruin that just yet.

We could wait a little longer.

On another positive note, I was no longer public enemy number one, thanks to Brooke's letter.

She'd written down that none of this was my fault, and

apparently, that was all it took—suddenly, I was being treated like a fucking saint. Everyone that had once hated me now loved me. Our street was packed when I got home from the hospital, filled with people cheering and applauding. The same people who had wanted me dead just a week before were now acting as if I was the new Princess Diana, celebrating my return home. It was crazy, how quickly everything had switched. I wanted to be grateful. I really did.

But even now, sitting around the table with my family, the warmth in the room felt hollow. The jokes and laughter were a temporary balm, and I couldn't shake the feeling that this fragile peace might shatter at any given moment.

There were too many unanswered questions. And if we were being real about it, the whole "loving family routine"—none of it was real. It was never going to last.

But we could pretend.

Just for now.

Mom had begun cutting up my slices with a knife and fork, just as she had done with every meal I'd eaten since I'd woken up in hospital. I glanced down at my cast, trying to remember how much longer I had until I could get it sawed off.

At this point, I couldn't remember what my body looked like without cuts and bruises, inside or out.

"Where's Vic?" Dad asked suddenly, picking up a single leaf of lettuce and flinging it to the side of his plate. "Is she coming over?"

"I gave her the night off," Mom replied jokingly, setting the knife and fork down on my plate. "She said she'll come around sometime tomorrow."

"Did you hear about her and Malcolm?"

"*I* haven't." I looked up, watching the confusion wash over Mom's face. I figured she hadn't heard either. Dad chuckled as he poured himself a glass of Coke. "What are you talking about?"

"He's taking her out tomorrow night. To the movies."

I pulled a face, trying to figure out if I'd heard him right. Despite everything, *that* had to be the grossest thing I'd heard in a very long time. "You're kidding, right?"

"She didn't say anything," Mom added, barely masking her own disgust. "How do you know?"

"He told me," Dad replied, shrugging it off. "He's taking her to see that prison movie. The one with the guy from *Driving Miss Daisy*."

Mom began pushing her food around with her fork, something she would've yelled at Cam for doing. Playing with her food. It was like she was deep in thought about the whole scenario.

I mean, I got it. Entirely. Vic and Malcolm—it was truly nauseating to think about.

"It didn't work out the first time," Mom muttered finally, barely lifting her eyes. "What makes them think it's going to be any different now?"

"*Oh*, leave them to it," Dad grinned, leaning across to squeeze her shoulder. She barely budged. "Malcolm's a grown boy—he can take care of himself. And it's about time Vic settled down."

"Yeah, but with *Malcolm*?" My face scrunched up like I'd just licked a lemon. "That's too weird."

Suddenly, Dad reached back over and took hold of Mom's hand. The sight of that was even weirder. She finally looked up, her expression tight, as if she'd just been caught in the middle of something. "We'll have to ask them if the movie's any good," he said, shooting her a smile. "Maybe *we* could go see it next week."

Mom's face softened ever so slightly. Then she let out a small, almost reluctant laugh. "Sure. Why not?"

It was honestly as if I was watching two complete strangers interacting in front of me.

My parents hadn't been this... *normal* in years. I mean, planning a date? Holding hands? Part of me wanted to puke. The other part of me felt a small, warming sensation in my chest; a flicker of an emotion that I barely even recognized. I wasn't used to this version of them, the version that laughed together and talked about movies.

For a moment—just a moment—we were a regular family, eating takeout around the table.

"Hey, Al, maybe you could go see it with that boy," Dad added, catching me off guard. "The Bird kid."

I glared at him. "Shut *up*, Dad—"

"What's wrong with that? He clearly likes you," he commented, grabbing another slice from the nearing-empty box. "He's come to see you every day. He got you flowers, for Christ's sake!"

"*Ugh*, don't make it weird..." I groaned a little, sinking back into my chair. "It's *not* like that."

"I'm just saying..." He paused, chewing on the pizza. Shrugging. "You could do worse than a kid with a million-dollar mansion. It'd certainly help *us* out, you know—"

"Shut *up!*"

I watched as Mom shot him a warning look, but he just kept laughing. I rolled my eyes, hating him at that moment.

I didn't say it out loud, but it actually sounded like a pretty good idea—going to the movies with Fitz. Freddie and Joaquin, too. I couldn't remember the last time I'd done something as simple and carefree as going to the movies. It actually sounded pretty fun.

I decided I'd ask him the next day. He said he was going to come to see me once I'd settled in, and I had no reason not to believe him. He'd seen me every single day that I was in hospital.

He'd stuck to his word.

KNOCK-KNOCK-KNOCK.

We all paused, glancing toward the door. I looked back up at the clock above Dad's head: it was just past seven. And it was Sunday.

Mom and Dad exchanged a quick look, and Dad reluctantly got up from his seat. "I'll get it..." he said, wiping his hands on a napkin before heading toward the door.

"Maybe it *is* Vic," Mom commented as he left the room. "I could've sworn she said she wasn't coming around tonight..."

I strained to listen as the front door opened. I could make out some whispering and hushed voices, but it wasn't until I heard the unmistakable pitch of a somewhat familiar voice that I realized it wasn't Vic. But I knew that voice. I just couldn't place it at first.

Mom's face paled as she worked it out, just seconds before I could catch up. "Is that Officer Hardie?"

It hit me like a punch to the gut.

Before I could process it, I pulled myself out of my chair and rushed out of the room. Mom was calling after me, but I barely heard her.

I bolted through the hallway, toward the front door. Mom was right. It really was her. She was hunched over in the doorway, somehow making her frame appear even smaller than it already was. Dad had his back to me, but I could hear the low murmur of their conversation. A knot tightened in my stomach, just seeing them together.

I could barely make out what she was saying. She said something about a note.

A picture.

"*...they sent it to the station...*"

Officer Hardie's eyes widened as she noticed me approaching, and Dad spun around, confusion evident on his face. He looked between me and Lucy, clearly trying to make sense of the situation. He looked just as surprised to see her there as I felt.

"What the hell is this?" I asked slowly, attempting to keep my voice low. They both just stood there like a pair of deer in headlights.

Behind me, I could hear Mom approaching us. My pulse got faster as I watched the panic rise on Dad's face. Hardie's mouth opened as if she was about to speak, but before she could get a word out, the sound of a car door slamming shut cut her off.

All three of us turned toward the sudden noise.

There were footsteps behind Hardie, making their way closer to the door. Dad saw who it was before I did. His visible confusion grew as he clearly recognized who it was, but couldn't figure out what they were doing there.

Then I heard their voice:

"*Hardie? What are you doing here?*"

It was Officer Anderson.

His face was set in a grim expression as he stepped into the doorway, his gaze locked onto Dad. The weight of his stare was heavy, and it felt like the air around us grew thicker. I watched as Hardie's eyes darted between Anderson and Dad. A wave of nausea settled over me as it became clearer that something was wrong.

Something was seriously wrong.

"Frank Nicholson," Anderson stepped forward, his face remaining stone-cold. "You're under arrest for obstruction of justice and conspiracy to conceal evidence—"

No.

"—you have the right to remain silent; anything you say can and will be used against you in a court of law—"

"What is this?" Mom's voice echoed behind me, breaking through the commotion. "Frank?!"

Dad's face twisted with a mix of anger and fear. "What the hell is this?!" he began shouting, pulling away from Anderson. "What are you doing—"

I watched as Anderson began wrestling Dad's arms behind his back, gripping him so tightly that he couldn't move.

My legs felt like lead, rooted to the spot. Mom's sobs filled the room, mingling with Dad's yells. The sound of the handcuffs clicking broke through the commotion.

No.

No.

"You have the *right* to remain silent," Anderson repeated forcefully, dragging Dad so hard that he tumbled to his knees. "Anything you say can and will be used against you in a court of law... *do you understand these rights*?!"

"I haven't done anything!" Dad shouted back.

Mom stepped forward, visibly shaking. I didn't know what to do. I didn't know who to turn to, or who to focus my attention on.

My thoughts raced back to that night in the car.

The night Dad told me everything.

"There was a note." Words began spilling out of Hardie's mouth, despite Anderson glaring at her. "And the picture—"

"Hardie," Anderson's voice cut through sharply, his frustration evident. "*Stop—*"

"*They know you weren't here—*"

"*HARDIE!*"

The picture.

The one of Dad and Hardie.

I watched as the scene unfolded before me, piecing it together. Scrambling to gather my thoughts.

Obstruction of justice.

Conspiracy to conceal evidence.

They knew he lied about his alibi. They knew he was with her that night. And that was why Anderson was so confused about her showing up here first.

She was trying to *warn* him.

"What are you talking about?!" Mom's voice cut through the chaos, her desperation growing. "What *is* this?! Frank, what the—"

A cold wave of panic washed over me.

My mind raced to piece together the fragments. The memory of Dad's confession, the details he had shared about the night Brooke went missing, and the image of him and Officer Hardie together—it all came crashing down on me.

The handcuffs were now securely fastened. Anderson began to lead Dad out the door. I stepped forward.

"Stop," I said shakily, barely able to get the words out. "Y-you can't do this—"

They weren't listening.

"He didn't do anything..." My voice grew louder, desperation seeping through every word. "He... he didn't—"

They kept moving.

Mom kept yelling, pushing past me to catch up with them. My eyes locked onto Hardie's; she was staring at me with wide eyes, mouth half open. It was as if she was telling me, without using words, to say something.

She wanted me to say it.

"...please stop," Mom sobbed, trying to pull Dad back. *"Please..."*

The intensity of the moment swelled within me, pushing me to the brink. It built up until I couldn't take it anymore. I couldn't hold it back. *I couldn't stop it.*

I ran through the door.

"He didn't do anything!" I shouted, causing Anderson to actually stop for a moment. "He wasn't with Brooke—"

"Allie—"

"He was with HER!" My finger shot out, pointing shakily at Hardie. The ground seemed to collapse beneath me as my accusation hung in the air.

Everyone stopped.

Everyone stared at me.

"They were having an affair!" I screamed, my voice breaking under the strain. "He's been... he's been w-with her for *over a year*! *He lied about his alibi to cover it up! HE WAS WITH HER!"*

My breath came in ragged gasps, my vision blurring at the edges as the enormity of what I had just said—what I'd *done*—sank in.

All eyes were on me, and for a moment, no one moved. No one breathed. All I could hear was my own heartbeat in my ears. Everything ground to a complete halt as my words echoed around us, stretching outward.

I locked eyes with Anderson. His stance, once firm and authoritative, now carried a trace of uncertainty. He looked into my eyes with a fleeting expression of empathy. Shame, even.

But not surprise.

I began to wonder what he already knew. If he'd seen the photograph, he would've already known about them. Maybe he already knew that Dad had been with her that night. Maybe my declaration had been wasted. I hadn't needed to say anything. I *shouldn't* have said anything.

Mom's unsteady breaths brought me back to the present.

I'd forgotten she was there.

"What are you talking about?" Her words came out sharp. Barely audible. "What do you... *what*..."

I watched as she turned toward Dad.

Her face was completely blank. Emotionless. I tried telling myself that maybe she hadn't heard me, but I knew that was bullshit. I'd shouted it so loud that the whole street would've heard it.

She'd heard me. She knew.

I thought that, maybe, Dad would've fought it. I thought he would've at least attempted to deny it.

But he didn't.

His face immediately flushed with a deep, agonizing shade of red, his eyes darting away from Mom's penetrating gaze. The defeat in his posture was palpable. He wasn't even trying to fight it. It was almost as if he didn't want to. Mom's eyes remained wide and dark, unable to move from him. I watched as she tried to find some sort of sign that I was wrong. She wanted him to deny it.

But he *didn't*.

Finally, my eyes flickered to Hardie. Out of the three of them, *she* was the one that was barely holding it together. She was just staring at the ground. Mom slowly turned to her, still searching for answers. As she locked her gaze onto Hardie, her face slowly began to harden. The lines on her face danced as she struggled to decide what she was feeling at that moment.

Confusion.

Betrayal.

Rage.

Anderson was the first to break the silence. "Hardie, get in the car."

Hardie flinched slightly, a mix of guilt and shame etched into her features. Before she made her way toward the police car parked up out front, she turned to look at my father.

It was this final gesture that tipped my mother over the edge.

"You..." Mom's voice broke through the stillness, a thin whisper of disbelief that grew louder with each word. "*You...*"

Hardie shuffled toward the car, jumping into the passenger seat before Mom could reach her peak. As the car door slammed shut, Anderson continued to drag Dad up the path, following her. Dad—stupidly—kept glancing over at the car; at Hardie.

And this only drove Mom further into emotional turmoil.

"...*you BITCH*!" She began screaming, throwing her arms toward the car. "*YOU... Y-YOU FUCKING BITCH*!"

It was like a dam breaking.

The rage poured out uncontrollably, her hands suddenly gesticulating wildly as she dove toward Dad. She tried to grab at him but Anderson was too fast. "Liz, I'm sorry," he said through gritted teeth, holding her back with just one hand as he led Dad forward with the other. "Please, you need to just let me—"

"*Take him,*" she spat suddenly, shoving Anderson further up the path. "*Lock him up*! *Throw away the f-fucking key*—"

Dad's face, already pale, turned ghostly white as he struggled to keep his composure. The pure agony was visible on his face, and he'd remained silent until now. "Liz," he finally broke his silence, his voice strained but firm; "Liz, I—"

"Stop talking," Anderson cut him off, shoving him toward the car.

My feet had sunk into the ground, my body rooted in place as I watched the scene unfold. Mom's screams continued to pierce the air, but their intensity was starting to dull, becoming a distant hum as my mind focused on Dad's pained expression.

He couldn't even bring himself to look at me.

Everything felt like it was collapsing in on itself. And it had been so perfect. Just minutes before, it had *all* been perfect.

I did this.

Dad's shoulders slumped as he was shoved into the back of the police car, his face a mask of anguish. I caught one final glimpse of his face before Anderson slammed the door.

"… you *bastard*…" Mom was sobbing, crumbling to the floor. "…*you*… *y-you*…"

I saw Hardie's face through the windscreen.

She looked back at me. We stared at each other. Agony streaked my veins, amplified by my mother's excruciating shrieking. It burned through my body like fire.

The car moved down the street, into the distance. Within seconds, they were gone.

A deafening silence followed.

As the world around me fell apart, my thoughts charged to make sense of the destruction.

The letters. The photograph. The note.

Whoever this was—Donnie, Brooke, someone else—*this* had been their intent all along. They wanted to break the family. They wanted to tear it apart, ripping it to shreds from the inside out.

And they'd finally done it.

Even if Brooke came back now—even if she came home, and she was safe—it wouldn't matter. It wouldn't fix this. There was no way that anything could ever go back to the way it was; not now. Not ever.

The sun sank behind the houses ahead of us, engulfing us in a slow encroaching darkness. The light faded, leaving behind a cold, oppressive dusk. Shadows stretched across the street, swallowing the remnants of all that had been left of my family.

I stared into the developing darkness, realizing that the world as I knew it would be wholly unrecognizable the next time I saw the sun.

HAYDEN | 8:00 PM

She was so beautiful.

I just stood there for a little while, taking it in. After the longest few weeks of my life, all the shit I'd been through to get here—it had all been worth it. It hadn't been for nothing.

I couldn't believe how vividly the color stood out; so vibrant, so striking.

Red.

It was a color that seemed to be meant for her; a bold statement of something special. The streetlamps gleamed against the color, making it radiate in the light. The vibrant gleam was a stark contrast to the dull gray of the town around us.

I could already picture the open road ahead of us, the adventures that awaited. *A fresh start.* It was a comforting thought, one that made everything else fade into the background.

"All mine," I muttered, carefully placing my hand on the hood of my car. My very own Beetle.

She was just six years older than me, and yet she felt like a timeless companion, a perfect match for the journey I was about to embark on. I traced the curve of the fender with my fingers, imagining all the places we would explore together.

And she'd only cost $3,870, leaving me with just over a thousand dollars left over—more than enough to cover gas and hotels.

The plan was finally falling into place, piece by piece.

I carefully jabbed the key into the side of the door, feeling it click firmly into place; there was a surge of satisfaction knowing she was safe and secure.

I didn't want to leave her, not even for a moment. I'd actually thought about grabbing a blanket and a pillow and camping out under the stars, tucked away in the back seats. But I had to leave her for now. I had business to complete. Plans to finish.

I'd already given her a name: Björk.

Björk the Beetle.

The weight of the past few weeks started to lift as I pushed through the front door. The house was filled with the buzzing sound blaring from the TV. My mother was slouched on the couch, her eyes glued to the screen. The room was dim, lit only by the flickering glow of the news broadcast.

"Where've you been?" I heard her muttering as I shut the door behind me. "You're not supposed to be out—"

"Curfew's only just started," I cut her off, tugging my sneakers off.

Harleigh began crying when she saw me, trying to climb out of her crib. I tried to ignore her. Mom did too, as she always did. She barely even lifted her head to look at me as I entered the living room; she looked all disheveled and worn out, a bottle of wine clutched in one hand, nearly empty.

Her gaze was vacant, lost in the endless loop of news reports. "Have you heard about this?!" she grunted, almost lobbing the glass bottle at the screen as she gestured toward it. "Dirty old *bastard…*"

I looked up, watching as they zoomed in on the photograph that I had long become familiar with.

The one of Brooke's dad and the cop.

A sense of pride washed over me as I, once again, took in the details. It was a perfect shot—clear, focused, and striking in its clarity. I'd managed to capture the scene just right, the light filtering through the window casting an almost cinematic glow over their faces. It really was a work of art.

My finest piece to date.

"She's one of the cops working on B-Brooke's case…" Mom continued to slur, half turning toward me. "Can you *believe* it?! I-I always knew there was something… *off* about him…"

I thought about Brooke.

I wondered if she was watching this whole thing unfold in real time, just like the rest of us.

"…not that I *blame* him," Mom went on, starting to laugh. "Imagine being married to that… that stuck-up *bitch*… hey, you know what it is?! Women like that, they *don't know* how to keep a man happy…"

I turned up the stairs, moving away from it all. I wasn't even sure if Mom would notice me leaving. I didn't really care, either.

My bedroom door swung open as I pushed through it, slamming it shut behind me. Everything was where I'd left it; polaroids scattered across the carpet, evidence of my meticulous efforts. I glanced at the mess on the floor; photographs of Brooke's dad and Lucy Hardie in various stages of their secret meetings, their faces filled with emotion that I'd captured with such precision. It'd taken me *so long* to pick the right one.

I'd almost killed myself getting that final shot. Almost fell off the fucking scaffolding. And I'd only gotten $50 for it.

Not that I needed the money anymore.

I wasn't even going to send the final picture. It didn't feel right at first, but in the end, it made sense. I mean, I knew it was what she wanted—she hadn't said it outright, but I knew that was what she meant.

I slumped down on the floor, organizing the leftover photographs into piles. There were hundreds of them; pictures of Frank and the cop, pictures of Allie drinking all over town, pictures from the party. I knew they'd each come in handy, especially once the money began to dry up.

Then I picked up the letter.

The paper was semi-crumpled but still readable. I'd read it so many times at this point that I basically knew every word, but that didn't stop me from going back to it every so often.

This letter was my Bible. It was the reason everything had happened. The reason it was still happening.

Come find me.

Those three words stood out from the page, despite the hundreds of other words that had been underlined, highlighted, scrawled in capital letters.

Despite all the other distractions, those were the three words that jumped out at me every time I picked up that letter.

Come find me.

Even after what happened at the party—even after *everything* that had happened between us—she still wanted *me* to be the one to find her.

She still chose *me*.

Youll need money. I don't have a lot.

My dad's having an affair. Her name is Lucy Hardie and she's a police officer. He was with her the night I left.

Allie got pregnant after she slept with Donnie.

Tell the papers. They'll pay you for it.

Tons.

She'd told me—step by step—what I needed to do to get to her.

She'd told me everything… well, except for where she was. And why she'd left. But it didn't take much reading between the lines to figure it out, based on what she'd told me about her family.

And, *boy*, was it a fucking *shitshow*.

She didn't mention anything about blackmailing her dad—I can't let her take credit for that part. That was a stroke of genius on my behalf. Meant that I didn't have to wait as long to save up the money.

And it wasn't as if he didn't *deserve* it, you know? I mean, how the fuck could he *do* that?! And I wasn't even sure, at this point, that Brooke knew that the cop her dad was fucking was *working on her case*.

I took matters into my own hands.

There was no *way* that bitch could get away with that. Brooke would've wanted me to do it—I knew she would've.

If she'd just given me an address, or some way to write back, I would've asked her. But I couldn't.

So, you know… I just did it.

Keep the walkie-talkie on. I'll talk when its time.

Come find me.

Ill call soon.

I have to admit, I was a little surprised when she wrote that letter to her mom.

Not that she said *much*, but, you know… I guess I thought she would've wrote to *me* again before doing that. She'd saved my skin, though, saying in the letter that *she* had gotten the money from her dad. I just wasn't really sure why she would do that, but I didn't want to waste time questioning it.

I already had enough questions.

I reached over to pick up my walkie-talkie from the piles of polaroids without removing my eyes from the page, wrapping my fingers around the hard plastic. She'd call soon.

I just had to wait.

RING-RING—

The sudden abruptness of the phone made me jump a freaking mile. The letter flew out of my hands, landing on the piles of photographs.

I pulled myself up, grabbing the phone as I flopped onto my bed, rolling onto my back. The cord stretched across, knocking a couple of empty soda cans from my bedside table in the process. I pressed the cool plastic to my ear, staring up at the ceiling. "Yeah?"

"*Is Hayden there?*"

"Speaking," I replied cooly, rolling onto my belly to stretch across the bed, grabbing the letter from the floor. "Who is this?"

"*Uh… it's Rhea.*"

I quickly sat up. "Rhea?"

"*Rhea Darlow, from school—*"

"Yeah, I know," I cut her off, narrowing my eyes a little. "What's up?" There was a short silence. The line began crackling a little, piercing through my ears. "Hello?"

"*…I was just wondering if you'd heard the news.*"

"What—about Brooke's dad?" I rolled back onto my back. My head sunk into the pillow. "What about it?"

"*No, no… I mean, that's awful, but… no, I meant about the hearing. The preliminary hearing.*"

"The hell is that?"

"*It's, like, the first step…*" I heard her pause, hesitating. "*…it's when they, you know… present all the evidence to see if there's enough there to take Donnie to trial…*"

The patterns on the ceiling began to swirl around as my brain froze up at the mention of his name.

I felt a jolt of something—fear, anger, I wasn't even sure what. With everything else that had happened, I'd almost forgotten about him. I turned back to the letter, picking out every time that she had written down his name. There were a lot of times. A *lot* of underlining.

"What do you mean?" I asked suddenly, trying to figure it out. "I thought they'd already arrested him. They know he's guilty, right?"

"*That's not…*" She paused again, sighing slightly. "*That's not how it works. They've got to PROVE that he did it.*"

"But he *did* do it."

My eyes locked onto the section of the letter where Brooke had described exactly what had happened—what he did to her on Labor Day. My stomach tightened into knots every time I reread it. "They got it on camera. I *know* they did—"

"*They're trying him for the murders, too. You know that right?*"

I didn't know that.

I mean, I knew a lot of people thought he had done it, but I didn't know it was, you know… a *real thing*. I didn't think they had enough evidence to actually do anything about it.

"Well, *duh*," I lied, pulling a face. "*Obviously* I knew that—"

"*That's why there's a hearing,*" Rhea explained, her tone softening. "*I mean… he's going to prison regardless. He just might go away for longer if they find him guilty of, you know… the OTHER stuff…*"

"Right."

"*Are you okay?*"

"What?" The question caught me off guard. There was a pause, the silence on the other end of the line feeling heavier than it should.

Rhea's voice wavered when she spoke again, softer this time. "...*it's just... I mean, we were both Brooke's friends*," I heard her saying, and I resisted the urge to laugh. My eyes wandered back to the letter; the very confirmation that she was *not* as close to Brooke as she thought she was. "*I'm... well, I've been struggling with it. I miss her. I thought, maybe, we could maybe meet up sometime—*"

"Why? It's not like *we're* friends."

Another silence.

I felt a small twinge of regret, something in the pit of my stomach twisting uncomfortably. For the first time in my life, I actually felt kinda bad for her. I mean, she actually thought that we were in the same boat here... but, the reality was, we weren't. She didn't know what was really going on. And she never would.

But I still felt kinda bad.

I was almost about to apologize when she spoke up again: "*You're right. Forget it.*"

"Are *you* okay?"

Ugh.

It just felt so incredibly lame, even hearing those words out loud. Why the hell was I asking Rhea Darlow if she was okay? It wasn't as if I actually cared. Not really.

"*I'll be okay*," she replied. "*I just... I wanted to let you know. About the hearing.*"

"Word..." I rubbed my neck, looking back up at the ceiling. "Thanks, I guess."

"*Are you coming to school tomorrow?*"

If she'd had any idea what I had to do next—all the plans that had to be put into action—she wouldn't have asked me that. School was the last thing on my mind.

For a second, I actually thought about telling her everything. I mean, it was just *Rhea*. She hadn't told anyone about me hitting her with the car. Maybe she could keep another secret.

But then I remembered her reaction when Allie got attacked in the street, when she was in my car.

That was what solidified it for me, really—there was absolutely no way in hell that she would be able to handle *this*. She just didn't have it in her.

"Maybe," I said finally. "I don't know yet." The phone

crackled as I waited for her reply.

"*...okay... see you tomorrow, maybe.*"

"See you tomorrow," I replied. "Maybe."

The line went dead.

My wrist fell limp, dropping the phone at my side. I kept staring at the ceiling, thinking it all over. Trying to figure out what I was supposed to do next.

I turned on my side, taking another look at the letter.

When its safe, I'll tell you where I am.

When I do, come find me.

The final line—signed with the letter '*B*'—stared back at me, its finality ringing in my head. A single letter, followed by a tiny sketch of an apple. My finger traced over the outline.

All I could do was wait.

ADJACENT

*To be continued in **ADRIFT**.*

ABOUT THE AUTHOR

Kay Embee was born in 1998 and raised in the historic town of Merthyr Tydfil, South Wales. She later moved to Cardiff, where she pursued a degree in English and Creative Writing at Cardiff Metropolitan University. Though she has previously authored a handful of children's books, *Adjacent* marks her fourth publication and her first full-length novel.

Kay began writing the *Adjacent* series at just 16 years old, working on the project as a creative outlet during her time in education. Now, a decade later, the first novel is complete. Drawing inspiration from her Welsh roots and a love for psychological mysteries, her writing captures the intricacies of small-town life under immense pressure.

When she's not writing, Kay enjoys exploring the Welsh coastlines, binge-watching true crime documentaries, and drinking copious amounts of decaf cappuccinos... but, mostly, she just writes.

Printed in Great Britain
by Amazon

56392249R00245